Logan rounded the hedge and nearly ran straight into Rowan.

Logan scrambled backward. "How—" she started before breaking off, lips pinching closed because of course he knew his way about the maze. It was his maze.

His castle.

His world.

Her eyes burned. Her throat ached. She'd struggled for so many years, struggled to provide and be a strong mother, and now it was all being taken from her. Her independence. Her control. Her future.

She didn't want anything to do with him and yet here he was, blocking her path, filling the space between the hedges, tall and broad, so very strong...

"What are you doing?" he asked.

"You've trapped me," she whispered, eyes bright with tears she wouldn't let spill because God help her, she had to have an ounce of pride. "You've trapped me and you know it, so don't taunt me...don't. It's not fair."

And with a rough oath, he reached for her, pulling her against him, his body impossibly hard and impossibly warm as he shaped her to him. She shivered in protest. Or at least that's what she told herself when dizzying heat raced through her and the blood hummed in her veins, making her skin prickle and tingle, and setting her nerves on fire, every one dancing in anticipation.

Her head tipped back and
his eyes, searching the gr
weakness, a hint of softne

D0645900

The Disgraced Copelands

A family in the headlines—for all the wrong reasons!

For the Copeland family each day brings another tabloid scandal. Their world was one of unrivaled luxury and glittering social events. Now this privileged life is nothing but a distant memory...

Staring the taunting paparazzi straight in the eye, the Copeland heirs seek to start new lives— with no one to rely on but themselves. At least that's what they think!

It seems fame and riches can't buy happiness— but they make it more fun trying!

Read Morgan Copeland's story in:

The Fallen Greek Bride

Read Jemma Copeland's story in:

His Defiant Desert Queen

Read Logan Copeland's story in:

Her Sinful Secret

Jane Porter

HER SINFUL SECRET

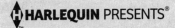

HARLEQUIN PRESENTS®

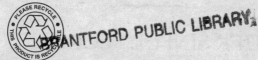

ISBN-13: 978-0-373-06073-3

Her Sinful Secret

First North American Publication 2017

Copyright © 2017 by Jane Porter

This is a work of fiction. Names, characters, places and incidents are either the product of the author's imagination or are used fictitiously, and any resemblance to actual persons, living or dead, business establishments, events or locales is entirely coincidental.

This edition published by arrangement with Harlequin Books S.A.

For questions and comments about the quality of this book, please contact us at CustomerService@Harlequin.com.

® and TM are trademarks of Harlequin Enterprises Limited or its corporate affiliates. Trademarks indicated with ® are registered in the United States Patent and Trademark Office, the Canadian Intellectual Property Office and in other countries.

HARLEQUIN®
www.Harlequin.com

Printed in U.S.A.

New York Times and *USA TODAY* bestselling author **Jane Porter** has written forty romances and eleven women's fiction novels since her first sale to Harlequin in 2000. A five-time RITA® Award finalist, Jane is known for her passionate, emotional and sensual novels, and loves nothing more than alpha heroes, exotic locations and happy-ever-afters. Today Jane lives in sunny San Clemente, California, with her surfer husband and three sons. Visit janeporter.com.

Books by Jane Porter

Harlequin Presents

Bought to Carry His Heir
At the Greek Boss's Bidding
A Dark Sicilian Secret
Duty, Desire and the Desert King

The Disgraced Copelands

The Fallen Greek Bride
His Defiant Desert Queen

A Royal Scandal

Not Fit for a King?
His Majesty's Mistake

The Desert Kings

The Sheikh's Chosen Queen
King of the Desert, Captive Bride

Greek Tycoons

At the Greek Boss's Bidding

Ruthless

Hollywood Husband, Contract Wife

Surrender to the Sheikh

The Sheikh's Disobedient Bride
The Sheikh's Virgin

Visit the Author Profile page at Harlequin.com for more titles.

CHAPTER ONE

"LOGAN, WE'VE GOT a crowd outside. *Logan.* Are you listening?"

Frustrated by yet another interruption, Logan Copeland tore her gaze from her script, yanked off her headset and glared up at her usually very capable assistant, Joe Lopez. She'd come to think of him as a genius and a blessing, but he wasn't much of either at the moment. *"Joe."*

"We've got a problem."

"Another one?" she asked incredulously. They were down to less than twenty-four hours now before tomorrow night's huge gala fund-raiser, the biggest of Logan's career, and nothing was going right in the tech rehearsal for the fashion show that would happen during the gala, and nothing would go right if Logan continued to be interrupted.

"We honestly don't have time for this. *I* don't have time for this. And if you want to run the show tomorrow on your own, that's fine—"

"I don't," he interrupted, expression grim. "But this is big, and I can't manage this one without you."

"Why not? And why does everything have to be a big problem right now?" she retorted, aware that every interruption was costing more time with the crew, which cost more money, which meant less money for the charity. "If this isn't life or death, you need to deal with it, and let me get one good run-through in before—"

"The media has descended. Full-on, out of control paparazzi stakeout. Here."

Logan's expression brightened. "But, Joe, that's great news. The PR team is succeeding. I heard they were the best. How is that a problem?"

"Logan, they're not here because of tomorrow's Hollywood Ball. They're not interested in the Gala or doing good. They're here for *you*."

Logan suddenly found it hard to breathe. She pressed the clipboard to her chest, headset dangling from her fingers. "For the press conference about the Ball," she said firmly, but then at the end her voice quavered, and the fear and doubt was there.

"No." Joe shoved his hands into his jeans pockets. He was a smart, young, artistic twentysomething just a couple years out of college, and he'd been invaluable to Logan since coming to work for her two years ago, a little over a year after her whole world had imploded due to the scandal surrounding her father, Daniel Copeland. Lots of people had wanted nothing to do with Logan after news broke that her father was the worst of the worst, a world-class swindler and thief preying on not just the wealthy, but the work-

ing class, too, leaving all of his clients nearly bank-
rupt, or worse.

Joe had grown up in a tough Los Angeles neigh-
borhood marked with gang violence, so the Copeland
scandal hadn't been an issue for him. He wanted a job.
Logan needed an assistant. The relationship worked.

He, like everyone, knew what her father had done,
but unlike most people, he knew the terrible price
Logan had paid. In most business and social circles
she was still persona non grata. The only place she
could work was in the nonprofit sector. "They are
here to see *you*," he repeated. "It's to do with your
dad."

She stilled. Her gaze met Joe's.

His dark brown gaze revealed worry, and sympathy. His voice dropped lower. "Logan, something's
happened."

The tightness was back in her chest, the weight so
heavy she couldn't think or breathe.

"Have you checked messages on your phone?" he
added. "I am sure you'll have gotten calls and texts.
Check your phone."

But Logan, normally fierce and focused, couldn't
move. She stood rooted to the spot, her body icy cold.
"Was he freed?" she whispered. "Did the kidnappers—"

"Check your phone," a deep, rough, impatient male
voice echoed, this one most definitely not Joe's.

Logan turned swiftly, eyes widening as her gaze
locked with Rowan Argyros's. His green gaze was
icy and contemptuous and so very dismissive.

She lifted her chin, her press of lips hiding her

anger and rush of panic. If Rowan Argyros—her biggest regret, and worst mistake—was here, it could only mean one thing, because he wouldn't be here by choice. He'd made it brutally clear three years ago what he thought of her.

But she didn't want to think about that night, or the day after, or the weeks and months after that…

Better to keep from thinking at all, because Rowan would use it against her. More ammunition. And the last thing a former military commander needs is more ammunition.

He didn't look military standing before her. Nor had he looked remotely authoritative the night she met him at the bachelor auction fund-raiser to benefit children in war-torn countries in need of prosthetics. He'd been a bachelor. She'd helped organize the event. Women were bidding like mad. He would go for a fortune. She didn't have a fortune, but when he looked at her where she stood off to the side, watching, she felt everything in her shift and heat. Her face burned. She burned and his light green gaze remained on her, as the bidding went up and up and up.

She bought him. Correction: she bought *one night* with him.

And it only costs thousands and thousands of dollars.

The remorse had hit her the moment the auctioneer had shouted victoriously, "Sold to Logan Lane!"

The intense remorse made her nauseous. She couldn't believe what she'd done. She'd filled an entire credit card, maxing it out in a flash for one night with a stranger.

She didn't even know then what Dunamas Maritime was. Insurance for yachts? Ship builder? Cargo exporter?

He knew that, too, from his faint mocking smile. He knew why she'd bought him.

She'd bought him for his intense male energy. She'd bought his confidence and the fact that of all the attractive men being auctioned, he was by far the most primal. The most sexual.

She'd bought him because he was tall and broad shouldered and had a face that rivaled the most beautiful male models in the world.

She'd bought him because she couldn't resist him. But she hadn't been the only one. The bidding had been fierce and competitive, and no wonder. He was gorgeous with his deep tan, and long, dark hair—*sunstreaked* hair—and his light arresting eyes framed by black lashes. There was something so very compelling about him that you couldn't look away. And so she didn't. She watched him…and wanted him. Like every other woman at the charity event.

They'd all looked and wanted. And many had bid, but she was the one who'd bid the longest, and bid the highest, and when the heart-pounding bidding frenzy was over, she came out the victor.

The winner.

And so, from across the room that night, he looked at her, his mysterious light hazel eyes holding hers, the corner of his mouth lifting, acknowledging her victory. Looking back she recognized the smile for what it was—mockery.

He'd dared her to bid, and she had, proving how weak she was. Proving to him how easily manipulated.

By morning he would hate her, scorning her weakness. Scorning her name.

But that hadn't happened yet. That wouldn't happen until he'd taken her again and again, making her scream his name as she climaxed once, twice and then, after a short sleep, two more times before he walked out the door the next morning.

The sex had been hot, so hot and so intense and so deeply satisfying. With anyone else it might have felt dirty, but it hadn't been with him. It'd just felt real. And right.

But she did feel dirty, later, once he'd discovered she wasn't Logan Lane, but Logan Lane Copeland, and the shaming began.

It was bad enough being hated by all of America, but to be branded a slut by your very first lover? A man that wasn't just any man, but one of the best friends of your twin sister's new husband?

Of all the people to sleep with…of all the men to fall for…why did it have to be Rowan Argyros with his passionate Irish Greek heritage and ruthless nature? There was a reason he'd risen through the military. He was a risk taker with nerves of steel. A man who seized opportunities and smashed resistance.

She knew, because he'd seized her and smashed her.

Logan exhaled now, blocking the past with its

soul-crushing memories. She hated the past. It was only in the last year she'd come to terms with the present and accepted that there could be a future. A good one. If she could forgive herself…and him.

Not Rowan—she'd never forgive Rowan. It was her father she needed to forgive. And she was trying, she was.

"My father," she said now, her gaze sliding across Rowan—still so tall and intimidating, still so sinfully good-looking—and then away, but not before she realized his long hair was gone. Shorn. He looked even harder now than before. "Is…he…?"

Rowan hesitated for just a fraction of a second, and yet his expression didn't soften. "Yes."

She willed herself not to move, or tremble. She firmed her voice so it wouldn't quaver. "How?"

He hesitated yet again, and she knew that he knew every detail. He was a maritime antipiracy specialist, based out of Naples, with offices in Athens and London as well as a large country estate in Ireland. He hadn't told her any of that. Her sister Morgan and her husband Drakon Xanthis had, after their wedding.

"Does it matter?" he asked quietly, coolly.

"Of course it matters," she retorted, hating him even more. Hating him for taking her virginity and mocking her afterward for enjoying his body and touch and for leaving her to deal with the aftermath on her own, as if he hadn't been the one in that big bed with her…

His silence made her fear the worst. Her heart

hammered. Her stomach fell. She wished she was hearing this from Morgan or Jemma, or her older brother, Bronson. They would all have broken the news differently. "Did they...did they...?"

And then she couldn't wait for the words, the confirmation that her father, kidnapped and held hostage off the coast of Africa, had been killed, possibly executed. It was all too sickening and her legs wobbled and her head spun, her body hot, then cold and then very cold.

She tried to look for Joe, the very best assistant one could ever hope for, but all she saw was Rowan and he was staring her down with those pale hazel-green eyes.

"Don't," he growled, his deep, rough voice now sounding far away, as if he was standing at the far end of a tunnel.

Maybe he was.

She couldn't see him well. Things were cloudy at the edges. He was cloudy, and she blinked, almost amused that Rowan could think he could still dictate to her, once again telling her body what to do...

"You're not doing this now," he snapped.

But she did. Her world went dark.

Swearing, Rowan dove to catch Logan before she crashed to the ballroom floor, but he was too far away and couldn't break her fall. Her head slammed on the edge on the stage as she went down.

He was there to scoop her up and he swore again, this time at himself, for not reaching her more quickly, and then at useless Joe, for not catching her, either.

She was still out cold as he settled her into his arms, her slender body ridiculously light. He shifted her so that her head fell back against his biceps, and his narrowed gaze raked her pale face, noting the blood pooling at the cut on her temple, and beginning to trickle into her thick honey-colored hair. She was going to have a nasty bruise, and probably one hell of a headache, later.

She was also still impossibly beautiful. High cheekbones, full lips, the elegant brow and nose of a Greek goddess.

But beauty had never been her issue. If she'd just been a pretty face, he could forgive himself for their night together, but she wasn't just a beautiful girl, she was Logan *Copeland*, one of the scandalous Copelands, and as amoral as they came.

It was bad enough being bought at a charity auction but to be paid for with embezzled funds?

"Grab her things," he told the man hovering at Logan's side. He wouldn't be surprised if Joe was Logan's lover. A boy toy—

He broke off, unable to continue the thought. He didn't like the thought. But then, he didn't like anything about being here today.

He didn't have to be the one doing this. He could have sent one of his men. Every one of his special ops team at Dunamas Intelligence had come from an elite military background: US Navy SEALs, British Special Forces, Russia's Alpha Group, France's National

Gendarmerie Intervention Group, Spain's Naval Special Warfare Force. Rowan hadn't just interviewed and hired each, he'd then trained them personally for intelligence work and rescue operations.

Any one of his men could do what he was doing. He should have sent anyone but himself.

But Rowan wasn't about to let anyone else near her. He told himself it was to protect them—she was a siren after all—but with her in his arms, he knew it was far more personal and far more primal than that.

He didn't want any man near her because even three years later, her body belonged to him.

Logan struggled to open her eyes. Her head hurt. Her thoughts kept scattering. She was being carried up and up. They were moving, climbing, but climbing what? She could hear breathing as well as the sound of heavy, even thudding close to her ear. She was warm. The arms holding her were warm. She battled to open her eyes, needing to focus, wanting to remember.

She stared hard at the face above her, noting the jaw, a very strong, angular jaw with a hint of dark beard. He had a slash of cheekbone and a firm mouth. And then he looked down at her, and the sardonic hazel-green depths sent a shiver through her.

Rowan.

And then it started to come back. Joe saying there was a problem. Something with her father and then Rowan appearing…

She stiffened. "Put me down."

He ignored her, and just kept climbing stairs.

Panic shot through her. "What's happening? Why are you carrying me?"

She wiggled to free herself.

His grip grew tighter. "Because you fainted, and you're bleeding."

"I didn't."

"You did. You smacked your head on the edge of the stage when you fainted, probably have a concussion."

"I'm fine now," she said, struggling once again. "You can put me down. Now. Thank you."

"You won't be able to make it up the stairs, and we've got to get out of here, so don't fight me, because I'm not putting you down," he said shortly, kicking the door to the roof open. "And if you don't like being carried, then next time don't be clumsy. Faint somewhere soft."

"Where's Joe? I need Joe!"

"I'm sure you do," Rowan gritted as they stepped into the dazzling California sunshine. "Don't worry, he's following with your things."

"My things? But why?"

"I'll fill you in once we're in the air. But enough chatter for now." His cool gaze dropped and swept from her face down her neck to the swell of her breasts. "You're not as light as you like to think you are."

But before she could react, they were at the helicopter and the pilot was jumping out and opening the door. Rowan was putting her in the helicopter in one of the passenger seats but she turned in his arms, leaning past to find Joe.

"Logan," Joe said, trying to reach her.

Rowan kept his arm up, blocking Joe from getting too close. "Put her things down," Rowan directed, "and step back."

But Logan grabbed Joe's sleeve. "Handle things at home, Joe. Please?"

Joe's dark eyes met hers and held. "Where are you going? When will you be back?"

"She'll call you," Rowan said drily. "Now say good-bye."

"Tomorrow's event," Logan said.

Joe nodded. "We'll make it work. I'll make it work. Don't worry."

And then Rowan was climbing into the helicopter and the pilot began lifting off, forcing Joe to run backward to escape the intense wind from the churning blades.

"Nice boy," Rowan said, shutting the door as Joe scrambled to safety. "Definitely on the young side, but so much more trainable before twenty-five."

Logan shot him a furious glance. "He's not my boyfriend."

"Your lover, whatever." He shrugged. "It's not for me to judge what you do with your father's money—"

"I don't have a penny of my father's money."

"I'm sorry. It wasn't his money. His embezzled billions."

She ground her jaw tight and looked away, chest

aching, eyes burning, mouth tasting like acid. She hated him...she hated him so much...

And then he leaned over and checked her seat belt, giving it a tug, making the harness shoulder straps pull tight on her chest.

She inhaled sharply, and his fingers slid beneath the wide harness strap, knuckles against the swell of her breasts.

"Too tight?" he asked, his gaze meeting hers, even as her nipples tightened.

"With your fingers in there, yes," she choked, flushing, her body now hot all over. The linen and cotton fabric of her cream dress thin enough to let her feel everything.

He eased his hand out, but not before he managed to rub up against a pebbled peak.

And just like that memory exploded within her—his mouth on her breast, alternately sucking and tonguing the taut tip until he made her come just from working her nipple.

Her response had whetted his appetite. Not content with just the one orgasm, he devoted himself to exploring her body and teaching her all the different ways she could climax. It had been shocking but exciting. She'd been overwhelmed by the pleasure but also just by being with him. He'd felt so good to her. She'd felt so safe with him. Nothing he did seemed wrong because she'd trusted him—

Logan bit into her bottom lip hard to stop the train of thought. Couldn't go there, wouldn't go there, not now, not when her head ached and the helicopter soared straight up, leaving the top of the old Park Plaza Hotel building so quickly that her stomach fell, a nauseating reminder that she still wasn't feeling 100 percent.

She put a hand up to her temple and felt a sticky patch of blood. She glanced down at the damp crimson streaking her fingers, rubbed them, trying not to throw up. "I know you specialize in rescue and intelligence, but isn't the helicopter getaway a bit much?"

Rowan thrust a white handkerchief into her hands.

She took it, wiping the blood from her fingers, hoping she hadn't gotten any on her dress. This was a new dress, a rare splurge for her these days. As she rubbed her knuckles clean she could feel him watching her. He wasn't amused. She wasn't surprised. He didn't have a sense of humor three years ago. Why should he have one now?

"I just meant, it's a little Hollywood even for you," she added, continuing to scrub at her skin, feeling a perverse pleasure in poking at him, knowing he'd hate anything to do with Hollywood. Rowan Argyros might look like a high-fashion model, but she'd come to learn after their—*encounter*—that he was hardcore military, with the unique distinction of having served once in both the US Navy and the Royal Navy before retiring to form his own private maritime protection agency, a company her brother-in-law had invested heavily in, wanting the very best protection for his Greek shipping company, Xanthis Shipping.

Even more bruising was the knowledge that Morgan and Drakon were such good friends with Rowan. They both spoke of him in such glowing terms. It didn't seem fair that Rowan could forgive Morgan for being a Copeland, but not her.

"Look down," Rowan said tersely, gesturing to the streets below. The huge hotel, built in 1925 in a neo-Gothic style, filled the corners of Wilshire, Park View, and West Sixth Street. "That mob scene is for you."

Still gripping the handkerchief, she leaned toward the window which made her head throb. A large crowd pressed up against the entrance to the building, swarming the front steps, completely surrounding the front, with more bodies covering the back.

It *was* a mob scene. They were lying in wait for her. "Why didn't they go in?" she asked.

"I chained the front door. Hopefully your Joe will find the key, or he'll be in there a while."

Logan reached for her purse and slipped the handkerchief inside and then removed her phone. "Where did you put the key? Joe can't stay in there—"

"That's right. You've left him with instructions to manage things at home." He watched her from beneath heavy lids. "What a good boy."

She ignored him to shoot a quick text to Joe.

Rowan swiped the phone from her hands before she could hit Send.

She nearly kicked him. "Why are you so hateful?"

"Come on, babe, a little late now to play the victim."

Logan turned her head away to stare out the window, emotions so chaotic and hot she could barely see straight. "So where are you taking me?"

"To a safe spot. Away from the media."

"Good. If it's a safe spot, you won't be there." She swallowed hard, and crossed her arms over her chest. "And my father. He's really dead?"

"Yes."

She turned her head to look at him. Rowan's cool green gaze locked with hers, expression mocking. "If it makes you feel better," he added, lip curling, "it was natural causes."

Blood rushed to her cheeks and her face burned. Good God, he was even worse than she remembered. How could that be possible? "Of course it makes me feel better."

"Because you are such a dutiful daughter."

"Don't pretend you cared for him," she snapped.

"I didn't. He deserved everything he got, and more."

She hated Rowan. Hated, hated, hated him. Almost as much as she wanted to hate her father, who'd betrayed them all—and she didn't just mean the Copeland family, but his hundreds of clients. They'd trusted him and he'd robbed them blind. And then instead of facing prosecution, instead of accepting responsibility for his crimes, he'd fled the country, setting sail in a private yacht, a yacht which was later stormed off the coast of Africa—he was taken prisoner. Her father was held captive for months, and as time dragged on, the kidnappers' demands increased, the ransom increased. Only Morgan was willing to come up with money for the ransom…but that was another story.

And yet, even as much as she struggled with her father's crimes and how he'd shamed them and broken their hearts, she still didn't want him suffering. She didn't want him in pain. Maybe she didn't hate him as much as she thought she did. "So he wasn't murdered. There was no torture," she said, her mouth dry.

"Not at the end."

"But he was tortured."

His eyes met hers. "Shall we just say it wasn't a picnic?"

For a long moment she held her breath, heart thumping hard as she looked into his eyes and saw far more than she wanted to see.

And then she closed her eyes because she could see something else.

The future.

Her father was now dead and so he would never be prosecuted for his crimes, but the world still seethed. They demanded blood. With Daniel Copeland gone, they'd go after his five children. And while she could handle the scrutiny and hate—it was all she'd been dealing with since his Ponzi scheme had been exposed—her daughter was little more than a baby. Just two and a quarter years old, she had no defenses against the cruelty of strangers.

"I need to go home," she choked. "I need to go home now."

* * *

Rowan had been watching the emotions flit across her face—it was a stunning face, too. He'd never met any woman as beautiful. But it wasn't just her bone structure that made her so attractive, it was the whole package. The long, thick honey hair, the wide-set blue eyes, the sweep of her brows, the dark pink lips above a resolute chin.

And then the body...

She had such a body.

He'd worshipped those curves and planes, and had imagined, that night three years ago, that maybe, just maybe, he'd found the one.

It's why he became so angry later, when he discovered who she was, because he'd felt things he'd never felt. He'd felt a tenderness and a connection that was so far out of his normal realm of emotions. What had started out as sex had become personal. Emotional. By morning he wasn't doing things to her, he was making love with her.

And then it all changed when he discovered the pile of mail on her kitchen counter. The bills. The magazine subscriptions.

Logan Copeland.

Logan Copeland.

Logan Lane Copeland.

It had blindsided him. That rarely happened. Stunned and then furious, he turned on her.

Many times he'd regretted the way he'd handled the discovery of her true identity. He regretted virtually everything about that night and the next morning, from the intense lovemaking to the harsh words he'd spoken. But over the years the thing he found himself regretting the most was the intimacy.

She'd been more than tits and ass.

She'd meant something to him. He'd wanted more with her. He imagined—albeit briefly—that there could be more, and it had been a tantalizing glimpse at a future he hadn't thought he would ever have. But then he saw it and realized that he wanted it. He wanted a home and a wife and children. He wanted the normalcy he'd never had.

And then it was morning and he was trying to figure out the coffee situation, and instead he was dealing with a liar-deceiver situation.

He wasn't in love. He wasn't falling in love. He'd been played.

And he'd gone ballistic. No, he didn't touch her—he'd never touch a woman in anger—but he'd said things to her that were vile and hurtful, things about how she was no better than her lying, crooked, greedy father and how it disgusted him that she'd bought him with money that her father had embezzled.

He didn't like remembering that morning, and he didn't like being responsible for her now, but he could protect her during the media frenzy, and he'd promised his friend and her brother-in-law, Drakon, that he would.

"There's no going home," he said tersely. "Your place must be a zoo. You'll be staying with me until the funeral."

Her blue eyes flashed as they met his. "I'm not staying with you."

"Things should calm down after the funeral. There will be another big story, another world crisis, people will tire of the Copelands," he said as if she'd never spoken.

"I have a job. I have clients. I have commitments—"

"Joe can handle them. Right?"

"Those clients hired me, not a twenty-four-year-old."

"I did think he looked young."

She lifted her chin, and her long hair tumbled over her shoulder, and her jaw firmed. "He's my assistant, Rowan. Not my lover."

"You don't live together?"

"No."

"Then why would you tell him to manage things at home?"

Her mouth opened, closed. "I work from home. I don't have an outside office."

"Yet he was genuinely worried about you."

She gave him a pitying look before turning to look out the window. "Most people are good people, Rowan. Most people have hearts."

Implying he didn't have one.

She wasn't far off.

His lips curved faintly, somewhat amused. Maybe if he was a teacher or a minister his lack of emotions would be a problem. But in his line of work, emotions just got in the way.

"The tin woodsman was always my favorite character," he said, referencing L. Frank Baum's *The Wonderful Wizard of Oz*.

"Of course he was," she retorted, keeping her gaze averted. "Except he had the decency and wisdom to want one."

CHAPTER TWO

"So where are we going?" she asked as the minutes slid by and they continued east over the city. Los Angeles was an enormous sprawl, but she recognized key landmarks and saw that they were approaching the Ontario airport.

He was slouching in his seat, legs outstretched, looking at her from beneath his lashes, not at all interested in the scenery. "One of my places."

He acted as if he was so casual. There was nothing careless or casual about Rowan Argyros. The man was lethal. She'd heard some of the stories from Morgan after her night with Rowan, and he was considered one of the most dangerous men on the planet.

And she had to pick him to be her first lover.

Genius move on her part.

Although to be fair, he'd never touched her with anything but sensitivity and expertise. His hands had made her feel more beautiful than she'd ever felt in her entire life. His caress had stirred her to the core. It would have been easy to imagine that he cared for her when he'd loved her so completely...

But he hadn't loved her. He'd pleasured her because she'd *paid* him to, giving her a twenty-thousand-dollar lay.

She swallowed around the lump filling her throat. Her eyes felt hot and gritty as she focused on the distant flight tower. She didn't want to remember. She hated remembering, and she might have been able to forget if it hadn't been for the one complication…

Not a small complication, either.

So she regretted the sex but not the mistake. Jax wasn't a mistake. Jax was her world and her heart and the reason Logan could battle through the constant public scrutiny and shame. Twice she'd had to close her Twitter account due to Twitter trolls. She'd refused to shut down her Instagram, forcing herself to ignore the daily onslaught of scorn and hate.

She'd get through this. Eventually. The haters of the world didn't matter. Jax mattered, and only Jax.

"So which home are we going to?" she asked, trying to match his careless, casual tone, trying to hide her concern and growing panic. Jax's sitter left between five and six every day. Even if Joe went to the house to relieve the sitter, he was merely buying Logan a couple of hours. Joe had never babysat Jax for more than an hour or two before. Joe was a good guy, but he couldn't care for the two-year-old overnight. Knowing Joe, he'd try, too, but Logan was a mama bear. No one came between her and her little girl.

"Does it matter?" he asked, pulling sunglasses from the pocket of his jacket.

So very James Bond. Her lip curled. He noticed.

"What's wrong now?" he asked.

She glanced away from him and crossed her legs, aware that she could feel the weight of his inspection even from behind his sunglasses. "Morgan told me how much you love your little games." She looked back at him, eyebrow arching. "You must be feeling very powerful now, what with the daring helicopter rescue and clandestine moves."

"I do like your sister," he answered. "She's good for Drakon. And he for her."

Logan couldn't argue with that. Her sister had nearly lost her mind when separated from her husband. Thank God they'd worked it out.

"Hard to believe you and Morgan are twins," he added. "You're nothing alike."

"Morgan chose to live with Dad. I didn't."

"And your baby sister, Jemma, she just chose to move out, even though she was still a teenager."

Logan swung her leg, the gold buckle on her strappy wedge sandal catching the light. "You're not a fan of my family, so I'm not entirely sure why we're having this conversation."

"Fine. Let's not talk about your family." His voice dropped, deepening, going almost velvet soft. "Let's talk about us."

Let's talk about us.

Her entire body went weak. She stopped swinging her leg, her limbs suddenly weighted even as her pulse did a crazy double beat.

Us. Right.

She couldn't see his eyes, but she could tell from the lift of his lips that he was enjoying himself. He was having fun, the same way a cat played with its prey before killing it.

She could be nervous, show fear, try to resist him—it was what he wanted. Or, she could just play along and not give him the satisfaction he craved.

Which, to her way of thinking, was infinitely better.

She smiled at him. He had no idea who he was dealing with. She wasn't the Logan Lane he'd bedded three years ago. He'd made sure of that. "Oh, that would be fun. I love talking about old times." She stared boldly into the dark sunglasses, letting him get a taste of who she'd become. "Good times. Right, babe?"

For a moment he gave her no response and then the corners of his mouth lifted even higher. A real smile. Maybe even a laugh, with the easy smile showing off very white, very straight teeth. The smile changed his face, making him younger and freer and sexy. Unforgivably sexy. Unforgivably since everything inside her was responding.

Not fair.

She hated him.

And yet she'd never met anyone with his control and heat and ability to own a room...and not just any room, but a massive ballroom...as if he were the only man in the entire place. As if he were the only man on the face of the earth. As if he'd been made just to light her up and turn her inside out.

Her heart raced and her pulse felt like sin in her veins. She was growing hot, flushing, needing…and she pressed her thighs tighter.

No, no, no.

"We were good," he said, still smiling at her, and yet his lazy drawl hinted at something so much more dangerous than anger.

Lethal man.

She'd wanted him that night and the fascination was back, slamming into her with the same force of a two-ton truck.

Something in her just wanted him.

Something in her recognized something in him and it shouldn't happen. There was no reason for someone like Rowan to be her type…

"It was you," she said, feeling generous. And what harm could there be in the truth? Because he was good—very, very good—and he was making her feel the same hot bright need that she'd felt during the bachelor auction. And it'd been forever since she'd felt anything sexual, her hunger smashed beneath layers of motherhood and maternal devotion. "You have quite the skill set."

"Years of practice, love."

"I commend your dedication to your craft."

His dark head inclined. "I tried to give you value for your twenty grand."

She didn't like that jab. But she could keep up. He and the rest of the haters had taught her how to wrap herself in a Teflon armor and just deflect, deflect, deflect. "Rest assured, you did. Now, if I knew then what I know now, I might have given you a few pointers, but I was so green. Talk about inexperienced. Talk about *embarrassing*. A twenty-four-year-old virgin." She shuddered and gently pushed back a long tendril of hair that had fallen forward. "Thankfully you handled the old hymen like the champ you are."

He wasn't smiling anymore.

Everything felt different. The very air was charged, seething…pulsing…

She gave him an innocent look. "Did I say something wrong?"

Rowan drew off his sunglasses and leaned toward her. "Say that again."

"The part about the hymen? Or the part where I wished I'd given you a few pointers?"

His green eyes were no longer cool. They burned and they were fixed intently on her, laser beams of loathing.

She'd finally gotten a rise out of him. She had to work very hard to hide her victorious smile. "But surely you knew I was a virgin," she added gently. "The blood on white sheets…?"

"It wasn't blood. It was spotting."

She shrugged carelessly. "You probably assumed it was just from…vigorous…thrusting."

His eyes glowed and his square jaw turned to granite. "You weren't a virgin."

"I was. And don't you feel honored that I picked you to be my first?" She glanced down at her hands, checking her nails. She must have chipped one earlier, when she fainted and fell. She rubbed a finger across the jagged edge and continued conversationally. "You set the bar very high, you know. Not just for what happened in the bedroom, but after."

He said nothing and so she looked up from her nails and stared into his eyes. "I can't help but wonder, if I hadn't climaxed during each of the…sessions… would you still have called me a whore?" She let the question float between them for a moment before adding, "Was it the fact that I enjoyed myself…that I took pleasure…that made me a whore? Because it was a very fast transition from virgin to whore—"

"Virgins don't spend twenty grand to get laid," he said curtly, cutting her short.

"No? Not even if they want to get laid by the best?"

He'd stopped smiling a long time ago. He had a reputation for being able to handle any situation but Logan was giving him a run for his money.

If it were any woman but Logan Copeland, he'd be impressed and maybe amused. Hell, he'd been amused at the start, intrigued by the way she'd thrown it down, and given it right back at him, but then it had all taken a rapid shift, right around the time she'd mentioned her virginity, and he didn't know how to fight back.

She'd been a virgin?

He didn't do virgins. He didn't take a woman's virginity. And yet he'd done her…quite thoroughly.

Dammit.

"You're taking my words out of context," he said

tightly, trying to contain his frustration. "I didn't call you a whore—"

"Oh, you did. You called me a *Copeland* whore."

He winced inwardly, still able to hear the words ringing too loud in the kitchen of her Santa Monica bungalow. He could still see how she'd gone white and the way her blue eyes had revealed shock and then anguish.

She'd turned away and walked out, but he'd followed, hurling more insults, each a deliberate hit.

He despised the Copelands even before the father's Ponzi scheme was exposed. The Copelands were one of the most entitled families in America. The daughters were fixtures on the social scene, ridiculously famous simply because they were wealthy and beautiful.

Rowan grew up poor and everything he had, he personally had worked for.

He had no time for spoiled rich girls.

How could shallow, entitled women like that respect themselves?

Worse, how could America adore them? How could America reward them by filling their tabloids with their pictures and antics? Who cared where they shopped or which designer they wore?

Who cared where they vacationed?

Who cared who they screwed?

He didn't. Not until he'd realized he'd screwed one of them senseless.

But it hadn't been a screw. That was the thing. It had been so much more.

Rowan's jaw worked. His fingers curled into fists. "I regret those words," he said stiffly. "I would take them back, if I could."

"Is that your version of an apology?"

It had been, yes, but her mocking tone made it clear it wasn't good enough. That he wasn't good enough.

Rowan wasn't sure whether to be offended or amused.

And then he questioned why he'd even be offended. He'd never cared before what a woman thought of him.

He'd be a fool to care what a Copeland thought of him.

"It is what it is," he said, the helicopter dipping, dropping. They'd reached the Ontario airport. His private jet waited at the terminal.

Her head turned. She was looking down at the airport, too. "Why here? Do you have a place in Palm Springs?"

"If I did, we'd be flying into Palm Springs."

"I find it hard to believe you have a place in Ontario."

"I don't." He left it at that, and then they were touching down, lowering onto the tarmac.

Rowan popped the door open and stepped out. He reached for Logan but she drew back and climbed out without his assistance.

She started for the terminal but he caught her elbow and steered her in the other direction, away from the building and toward the sleek white-and-green pin-striped jet.

She froze when she realized what was happening. *"No."*

He couldn't do this again, not now. "We don't have time. I refuse to refile the flight plan."

"I'm not leaving Los Angeles. I *can't.*"

"Don't make me carry you."

She broke free and ran back a step. "I'll scream."

He gestured to the empty tarmac. "And what good will that do you? Who will hear you? This is the executive terminal. The only people around are my people."

She reached up to capture her hair in one hand, keeping it from blowing in her face. "You don't understand. I can't go. I can't leave her."

"What are you talking about?"

"Jax." Her voice broke. "I've never been away from her before, not overnight. I can't leave her now."

"Jax?" he repeated impatiently. "What is that? Your cat?"

"No. My baby. My daughter."

"Your *daughter*?" he ground out.

She nodded, heart hammering. She felt sick to her stomach and so very scared. She'd forced herself to reach out to Rowan when she'd discovered she was pregnant, but he'd been even more hateful when she called him.

"How did you get my number?" he demanded.

"Drakon."

"He shouldn't have given it to you."

"*I told him it was important.*"

He laughed—a cold, scornful sound that cut all the way to her soul.

"*Babe, in case you didn't get the message, it's over. I've nothing more for you. Now, pull yourself together and get on with your life.*"

And so she had.

She didn't tell him about the baby. She didn't tell him he was having a daughter, and whatever qualms she had about keeping the information to herself were eventually erased by the memory of his coldness and hatefulness.

Her father had broken her heart, shaming her with his greed and selfishness, but Rowan was a close second. He was despicable. Like her father, the worst of the worst.

Thank goodness he wasn't in Jax's life. Logan couldn't even imagine the kind of father he'd be. Far better to raise Jax on her own than have Jax growing up with a father who couldn't, wouldn't, love her.

And now, facing Rowan on the tarmac, Logan knew she'd made the right decision. Rowan might be a military hero—deadly in battle, formidable in a combat zone—but he was insensitive to the point of abusive and she'd never allow him near her daughter.

"You're a *mother*?" he said.

She heard the bewildered note in his voice and liked it. She'd shocked him. Good. "Yes."

His brow furrowed. "Where is she now?"

"At home." Logan glanced at her watch. "Her sitter will leave at five. I need to be back by then."

"You won't be. You're not going back."

"And what about Jax? We'll just leave her in a crib until you decide you'll return me?"

His jaw worked, the small muscle near his ear pulling tight. "Drakon never mentioned a baby."

Her heart did a double beat and her stomach heaved. "They don't know."

"What?"

"No one knows."

"How can that be?"

"It might surprise you, but we don't do big family reunions anymore."

He folded his arms across his chest. "Who is her father?"

She laughed coolly. "I don't think that's any of your business, do you?"

He sighed. "What I meant is, can't her father take her while you're gone?"

"No."

"I think you need to ask—"

"No."

"Not a good relationship?"

She felt her lip curl. This would be funny if one enjoyed dark comedy. "An understatement if I ever heard one."

"Can her sitter keep her?"

"No." The very idea of anyone *keeping* Jax made Logan's heart constrict. "I've never been away from her for a night. She's a toddler…a baby…" Her voice faded and she dug her nails into her palms, waiting for Rowan to say something.

He didn't. He stared at her hard.

She couldn't read what he was thinking, but there was definitely something going on in that head, she could see it in his eyes, feel it in his tension. "I need to get home to her." Her voice sounded rough. She battled to maintain control. "Especially if there are paparazzi at the house. I don't want them doing anything—trying anything. I don't want her scared."

"Logan, I can't let you anywhere near the house. I'm sorry." He held up his hand when she started to protest. "I'll get her. But you must promise to stay here. No taking off. No running away. No frantic phone calls to anyone. Stay put on my plane and wait."

She glanced toward the white jet and spotted his staff waiting by the base of the stairs.

He followed her gaze. "My staff will make sure you're comfortable. As long as you stay here with them you won't be in any danger."

Stiffening, Logan turned back to face him. "Why would I be in danger? It's just the paparazzi."

"Bronson was shot late last night in London." Rowan's voice was clipped. "He's in ICU now, but the specialists believe he should make a full recovery—"

"Wait. What? Why didn't you say something earlier?" Bronson was the oldest of the five Copelands and the only son. "What happened?"

"Authorities are investigating now, but the prevailing theory is that Bronson was targeted because of your father. The deputy chief constable recommended that all members of your family be provided with additional security. My team has already located Victoria and is taking her to a safe location. Your mother is with Jemma already. And now we have you."

Logan felt the blood drain from her head. Fear made her legs shake. "Please go get Jax. Hurry."

"Give me your phone."

"I won't call anyone—"

"That's not why I want your phone. I'm taking it so I can be you and make sure Joe understands what I need him to do."

"You're involving Joe?" she asked, handing him the phone.

"You trust him, don't you?"

She nodded. "The password is zero, three, three, one."

Rowan started for the helicopter and then turned around. "Didn't we meet March 31?"

She went hot all over. "That's not why it's my password." She heard her defensive tone and hated it.

"Never said it was. But it does make it easy for me to remember your code." And then he signaled the pilot to start up the chopper and the blades began whirling and he was climbing in and the helicopter was lifting off even before Rowan had shut the door.

CHAPTER THREE

ROWAN WAS GONE for two hours and twenty-odd minutes, and during those long two plus hours, Logan couldn't let herself think about anything…

Not Bronson, who'd been hurt. Or her family who were all being guarded zealously to protect them from a nut job.

She couldn't think about her daughter or how frightened she must be.

She couldn't think about her huge event taking place tomorrow and how she now wouldn't be there to see it through.

She couldn't think about anything because once she started thinking, her imagination went wild and every scenario made her heartsick.

Every fear pummeled her, making her increasingly nauseous.

But of all her fears, Jax was the most consuming. She loved her brother and sisters but they were adults, and it sounded as if they now had a security team protecting them. But Jax…her baby…?

Logan exhaled slowly, struggling to keep it together. Rowan *had* to be successful. And there was no reason he wouldn't be. He was the world's leading expert in hostage and crisis situations and removing a toddler from a Santa Monica bungalow was not a crisis situation. But that didn't mean her heart didn't race and her stomach didn't heave and she didn't feel frantic, aware that all kinds of things could go wrong.

But Rowan being successful meant that he would be with Jax, and this terrified her. The haters and shamers had hardened her to the nonstop barbs and insults, but Jax was her weakness. Jax made her vulnerable. And maybe that's because Jax herself was so vulnerable.

A light from the cockpit drew her attention and she glanced up, noting the three men up front—two pilots and the male flight attendant.

They were an interesting-looking flight crew bearing very little resemblance to the pleasant, professional, middle-aged crew you'd find on a commercial plane. These three were lean, muscular and weathered. They looked so fit and so tan that it made her think they'd only recently retired from active duty with the military. As they spoke to each other in low voices, she tried to listen in, but it was impossible to eavesdrop from where she sat.

Abruptly the three men turned and looked at her and then the male flight attendant was heading her way.

"Did you need something, Miss Copeland?" he asked crisply. He didn't look American, but he didn't have an accent. He was an enigma, like the rest of the crew.

"Is there any water?"

"I'll bring you a bottle. Would you like a meal? Are you hungry?"

She shook her head. "I don't think I could eat. Just water."

But once she had the bottle of water, she just held it between her hands, too nervous to drink more than a mouthful.

The minutes dragged by, slowly turning into hours. She wished someone would give her an update. She wished she knew *something*.

But just when she didn't think she could handle another minute of silence and worry, the distinctive sound of a helicopter could be heard.

She prayed it was Rowan returning—

The thought stopped her short. Just hours ago such a prayer would have struck her as ludicrous. But he'd gone after her baby and she was grateful for that.

Who would have ever thought she'd pray to see him again?

As the helicopter touched down the flight crew stood at the entrance of the jet as if prepared for battle.

Logan arched her brows. Rowan was serious about personal safety, wasn't he?

But then the helicopter was down and the door was opening. Rowan was the first to step out and he was holding Jax, and as he crossed the tarmac, Joe Lopez was close behind carrying two suitcases.

What was Joe doing? Had he insisted on accompanying Jax to be sure she was safe? Or had Rowan wanted Joe along in case Jax got scared?

Either way Logan was delighted when the men stepped onto the plane with the baby.

Jax squealed when she saw Logan. "Momma!"

Logan opened her arms and Rowan handed the child over. "Hello, sweet girl," Logan whispered, kissing her daughter's soft cheek again and again. "How's my baby girl?"

Jax turned her head to kiss Logan back. "I love Momma."

"And Momma loves you. What did you think of the helicopter?" Logan asked her, giving her a little squeeze. "Was it noisy?"

Jax nodded and clapped her hands to her head. "Don't like ear things. Bad."

Rowan met Logan's gaze over Jax's head. "Not a fan of the headset."

"Not surprised. She has a mind of her own," Logan said.

"She does like Joe, though. She insisted on sitting on his lap during the flight. He's good with her, too," Rowan said.

Logan glanced back toward the galley where the flight attendant was taking the two suitcases from her assistant. "It was nice of him to come. Or did you make him?"

"I didn't make Joe do anything. He is apparently very devoted to you—"

"Don't start again."

"Just saying, he's here because he insisted."

"I appreciate it. He's been awesome with her since the beginning." Logan frowned at the size of the two suitcases. "How long are we going to be gone?"

"Your buddy Joe did the packing. Apparently you girls need a lot when you travel."

Logan's eyes met Rowan's. She gave her head a slight shake, her expression mocking. "You sound a little jealous of him, you know."

"Me, *jealous*, of that…kid? Right." Rowan made a scornful sound and turned away as Joe approached Logan.

"You all right?" Joe asked Logan even as he handed Jax a sippy cup with water.

Logan nodded and shot Rowan's retreating back a disapproving look. "I hope he wasn't rude to you," she said to Joe. "If he was, don't take it personally. He's that way with everyone."

Joe smiled and shrugged. "I've met worse."

Logan gave him a look.

His smile broadened. "He doesn't bother me. And he was actually pretty sweet with Jax—"

"Don't say it. Don't want to hear it." Logan cut him short. "So is he going to send you back in the helicopter or are you having to grab a cab back? If you need a cab, just put it on my account. I won't have you paying for something like that. It'll be ridiculously expensive."

"I'll grab a rental car and drop it off at LAX." Joe hesitated a moment. "Are you going to be okay?"

Logan kissed the top of Jax's head and nodded. "Need tomorrow's event to go off without a hitch—"

"It will. The fund-raiser will be huge, and the fashion show will be wonderful. But you're the one I'm worried about."

"Don't. I'm fine. And my company…it's everything. It's my reputation. My livelihood. It's how I provide for Jax—" She broke off, overwhelmed by stress and the weight of her reality. Her reality was harsh. People didn't give her the same benefit of the doubt they gave others. She didn't get second chances or opportunities…no, she had to fight tooth and nail for every job, forced to prove herself over and over again.

"I'll handle it," Joe said quietly, his deep voice firm.

"Thank you."

And then he kissed Jax on the top of her head and he left.

Rowan didn't seem to even notice that Joe had gone and it burned Logan up, how arrogant and callous Rowan was. Joe had been a huge help and Rowan didn't thank him or care.

Why couldn't Logan fall for someone like Joe… someone smart and kind and caring? Someone with *emotions*?

And then as if able to read Logan's mind, Rowan was returning. "We need to go." He nodded at the toddler. "Are you going to hold her for takeoff, or do you want me to buckle her car seat into a chair next to you?"

"Which is safer?" Logan asked.

"Car seat," he answered promptly.

"Then let's do that."

"Has she ever been on a plane before?"

Logan shook her head. "We don't…go out…much." And seeing his expression she added, "We don't need the attention."

"Have things been that difficult?"

"You've no idea." And then she laughed because it was all she could do. The haters and shamers would not win. They wouldn't. She'd make sure of that, just as she'd make sure her daughter would grow up with a spine and become a woman with courage and strength.

Rowan glanced at his watch. They'd been flying four hours but still had a good four to five hours to go. He was glad that the toddler finally slept, though. Earlier she'd cried for nearly an hour when she couldn't have her blanket. Joe had brought the blanket when they met up at the Santa Monica airport. The blanket was either in a seat or on the floor of the helicopter or perhaps it got dropped on the tarmac during the transfer to the plane. Either way, the baby was inconsolable and Logan walked with Jax, up and down the short aisle, patting her little girl's back until Jax had finally cried herself to sleep on Logan's shoulder.

Now Logan herself was asleep in one of the leather chairs in a reclined position, the little girl still on her chest, the child's two miniature ponytails brushing Logan's chin.

Seeing Logan with the child made him uncomfortable.

He didn't like the ambivalence, either. He didn't like *any* ambivalence, preferring life tidy, organized, categorized into boxes that could be graded and stacked.

He'd put Logan into a box. He'd graded the box and labeled it, stacking it in the corner of his mind with other bad and difficult memories. After he'd left her, after their night together, he'd been troubled for weeks…months. It had angered him that he couldn't forget her, angered him that he didn't have more control over his emotions. He shouldn't care about her. He shouldn't worry about her. And yet he did.

He worried constantly.

He worried that someone, somewhere would hurt her.

He worried about her physical safety. He worried about her emotional well-being. He'd been so hard on her. He'd been ruthless, just the way he was with his men, and in his world. But she wasn't a man, and she wasn't conditioned to handle what he'd dished out.

He'd come so close, so many times to apologizing.

He'd come so close to saying he was wrong.

But he didn't. He feared opening a door that couldn't be shut. There was no point bonding with a woman who wasn't to be trusted. Trust was everything in his world, and she'd lied to him once—Logan Lane, indeed—so why wouldn't she lie again?

Maybe the trust issue would be less crucial if he had a different job. Maybe if his work wasn't so sensitive he could be less vigilant…but his work was sensitive, and countless people depended on him to keep them safe, and alive.

Just as Jax depended on her mother to keep her safe.

He wanted to hate Logan. Wanted to despise her. But watching her sleep with Jax stirred his protective instinct.

At two years old, Jax was still more baby than girl, her wispy blond hair a shade lighter than her mother's. They both had long dark eyelashes and the same mouth, full and pink with a rosebud for an upper lip.

Sleeping, Jax was a vision of innocence.

Sleeping, Logan was a picture of maternal devotion.

Together they made his chest ache.

Rowan didn't want his chest to ache. He didn't want to care in any way, but it was difficult to separate himself when he kept running numbers in his head.

March 31 plus forty weeks meant a December birthday. Jax had a December birthday. December 22 to be precise. He knew because Joe had located Jax's birth certificate at the house and put it in a file for Rowan. You couldn't just whisk a baby out of a country without any legal documentation. If they were flying on a commercial plane, he'd have to go through government channels, which would have required a passport.

But since they weren't flying on a private plane,

his pilot had submitted a manifest—which had included Logan Copeland. The manifest had not included the baby as he hadn't known there was a baby until just hours ago.

The baby could potentially be an issue, but as Rowan had diplomatic immunity, he wasn't too worried for himself.

Logan was another matter. She could definitely find herself in hot water should various governments discover she'd smuggled a baby out of one country and into another.

Fortunately they would be landing on Rowan's private airstrip on his private property, so there shouldn't be guards or officers inspecting his jet, or interrogating his guests.

But if they did…what would he say about Jax?

The child born exactly forty weeks after March 31.

Aware that she was being studied, Logan opened her eyes. Rowan sat watching her in a leather chair opposite hers.

He wasn't smiling.

She just held his cool green gaze, her heart sinking. She didn't want to panic and yet there was something very quiet, and very thoughtful, in his expression and it made her imagine that he could see things he couldn't see and know things he couldn't possibly know.

He couldn't possibly know that Jax was his.

He couldn't possibly imagine that she would have slept only with him. Her one and only lover in twenty-seven years. That didn't happen anymore. Women didn't wait for true love...

And so she arched a brow, matching his cool expression, doing what she did best—*deflect, deflect, deflect.* "Was I snoring?"

"No."

"Was my mouth open, catching flies?"

"I want a DNA test."

The words were so quietly spoken that it took Logan a moment to process them. He wanted a DNA test. He did suspect...

Deflect, deflect, deflect. "That's awfully presumptuous, don't you think?"

"You said you were a virgin. You made a big fuss earlier about how I manhandled your hymen—"

"I did not say that."

"—which makes me doubt you were out getting laid by someone else in the following five to seven days."

"Your math is excellent. I commend you. Not just a skilled lover, but also a true statistician, except for the fact that Jax wasn't due for another month. She arrived early."

"Your sweet girl was almost nine pounds, my love. She wasn't early."

Logan's stomach heaved. He knew how much Jax weighed. He knew her birth date. What else did he know? "She's not yours," she repeated stubbornly.

"No, she hasn't been, but she should be, shouldn't she?"

Logan held her breath.

"We'll test tomorrow, after we land."

"You're not going to poke her with a needle—"

"We'll do a saliva swab. Painless."

"Rowan."

"Yes, Logan?"

Logan's heart was beating so fast she was afraid it'd wake Jax. "You don't even like children. You don't want them. And you despise girls—"

"Is this what you've been telling yourself the past three years? Is this your justification for keeping Jax from me?"

You called me a whore. You said the worst, most despicable things to me.

And yes, those words hurt, but that wasn't why she didn't tell him. "I tried," she said, her voice quiet but thankfully steady.

"And when was that?"

"When I called you. Remember that? I phoned to tell you, and instead of a 'How are you? Everything okay?' you demanded to know how I got your number." She stared Rowan down, her gaze unwavering. "Even when I told you that Drakon had given it to me because it was important, you were hateful. You mocked me, saying you'd given me all you could."

Her voice was no longer quiet and calm. It vibrated with emotion, coloring the air between them. "After you hung up, I cried myself sick, and then eventually I pulled myself together and was glad. *Glad* you wanted nothing to do with me, glad you wanted nothing to do with us, glad that my daughter wouldn't have to grow up as I did, with a selfish, uncaring father."

For a long moment Rowan said nothing. He just studied her from his seat, his big, lean, powerful body relaxed, his expression thoughtful. He seemed as if he didn't have a care in the world, which put her on high alert. This was Rowan at his most dangerous, and she suspected what made him so dangerous was that he cared.

He cared a great deal.

Finally he shifted and sighed. "There are so many things I could say."

Logan's heart raced and her stomach rolled and heaved. "Why don't you say them?"

"Because we are still hours away from Galway—"

"Galway?" she interrupted.

"—and I don't feel like arguing all the way to Ireland."

She blinked at him, taken aback. "We can't leave the US. I don't have a passport with me, and Jax doesn't even have one yet."

Rowan shrugged, unconcerned. "We're landing on a private airstrip. There won't be any customs or immigration officers on our arrival."

"And what about when we return? Don't you think it will be problematic then?"

"Could be. But Joe packed your passport when he packed for you, and he sent along Jax's birth certificate, so we do have that."

That's how Rowan knew Jax's birth date. That's how he knew what he knew. But how did Joe know where to find her legal documents? She'd never told him...

Logan watched the slow drumming of Rowan's fingers on his hard thigh, mesmerized by the bronze of his skin and the tantalizing movement of strong fingers, the drumming steady, rhythmic.

The man had good hands. They'd felt so good on her. His touch had a sensitivity and expertise that was so different from his reputation as an elite fighter... warrior...

He'd made her feel things she didn't think she could feel, but no more. Hope and beauty—

No. Couldn't go there again, couldn't remember, couldn't let herself fantasize that what had been was anything but sex. He'd made it clear she was just a lay. Sweat and release...exercise.

Her eyes burned and she swallowed hard, disgusted with herself for still letting his callous words upset her, hurt her. She shouldn't care. She shouldn't.

And yet she did.

Maybe if the sex hadn't been so good she could play this game. Maybe if she hadn't felt hope and joy, and maybe if he hadn't made her feel beautiful... Things she hadn't felt in so long. So many people had been hateful about her father. The world had become ugly and hostile, and then Rowan had been the opposite. He'd been light and heat and emotion and she couldn't help feeling connected to him. Bonded.

And then he discovered the Copeland part of her name, having missed that the night before...

Logan exhaled slowly, head light and spinning, dizzy from holding her breath too long. "I can't do this with you," she said lowly, her hand reaching up to adjust Jax on her chest. "Not with her here."

"What do you think we're going to do?"

"Fight. Be hateful." Her voice sounded strained to her own ears. "But Jax shouldn't be part of that. It's not fair to her, or good for her—"

"I've no desire to hurt my daughter," he interrupted. "And I don't need a damn DNA test to confirm it. We'll have it done so we can correct her birth certificate, but I don't need it to prove anything. She's obviously mine."

"Ours," she whispered, and it killed her to do it, killed her to say it but Jax had to be protected, no matter the cost. "Obviously ours."

The corner of Rowan's mouth lifted and his expression turned rueful. "I suppose it's a good thing that your father died. In time we will even view his passing as a blessing because it brought us all together. You, me and our daughter."

There was nothing frightening in his tone. If anything he sounded…amused. But Rowan's sense of humor was nothing like hers, and her heart lurched.

"So what is the next step?" he asked, smiling faintly, green eyes gleaming. "A wedding at the castle? And do we do it before or after your father's funeral?"

Thank God she was sitting. Thank God for armrests. Thank God Jax stirred then and let out a whimper, saving Logan from having to answer.

Jax whimpered once more and stretched, flinging out small arms in an attempt to get more comfortable.

Logan wanted to whimper, too.

This was crazy, so crazy.

Rowan was crazy.

"I think we do it before," he added reflectively. "It will give everyone something to celebrate. Yes, there will be sadness over your father's life being cut short—he was such a good man, so devoted to his family and community—but then everyone will be able to rejoice over our happy and surprising news. We're not just newlyweds, but proud parents of a two-year-old girl."

"You hate my father, and you hate me—"

"That's the past," he said gently, cutting her short. "It's time to leave the past in the past and concentrate on the future. And you're going to be my wife and we'll have more children—"

"You're having a really good time with this, aren't you?"

His broad shoulders shifted. "I'm trying to be positive, yes."

"I don't think you're trying to be positive as much as sadistic," she retorted, fighting panic because she didn't think Rowan was teasing. He seemed quite serious, which was terrifying as Rowan's entire career was based on his ability to play dirty. "We're not marrying. There won't be more children. There is no relationship. There has never been a relationship. So don't start throwing your weight around because I won't put up with it."

He had the audacity to laugh. "No? What will you do? Call Joe?"

Her cheeks burned. "You have such a problem with him. If I didn't know you better, I'd say you were jealous."

"I don't even know where to begin with that statement...so many ways I could run with it." He smiled at her, a charming smile that made her want to leap from her chair and run.

"Joe," he said politely, "works for *me*."

When her lips parted he held up a hand to stop her.

"He's worked for me since the day you hired him. He didn't attend USC. He never studied art, communications or design. And he's not twenty-four. He's thirty-one, and before he came to work for Dunamas, he was a member of Delta Force."

Logan couldn't wrap her head around what Rowan was telling her. Joe was not a military guy. Joe was young and sweet and hardworking...

But Rowan misunderstood her baffled expression. "First Special Forces Operational Detachment Delta," he said.

"I don't need an explanation for the abbreviation Delta Force. I need to understand how someone I hired from a pool of candidates worked for you."

"They all worked for me."

"No."

"How many résumés and cover letters did you get?"

"Six. No, five. One withdrew hers."

"How many did you interview?"

"Four."

"How many in person?"

"The top three."

"Trish Stevens, Jimmy Gagnier and Joe Lopez. Trish wanted too much money. Jimmy made you uncomfortable because he knew about your family. And Joe was just so dang grateful to have a job." The corner of his mouth quirked but he wasn't smiling. "And you believed him because you wanted—needed—to believe him."

"But I called his references…" Her voice faded as she heard herself and realized how foolish she sounded. She stared hard at a point just past Rowan's shoulder, willing her eyes to stop stinging, willing the awful lump in her throat to stop aching.

She'd trusted Joe.

She'd trusted him with her work and her family and her life…

"I thought he was a good person," she whispered, feeling impossibly betrayed.

"He is. He would have died for you. No questions asked."

"I'm sure that must have cost you a pretty penny."

"Joe did protect you," Rowan said. "And he wasn't a spy—"

"I don't believe that for a minute."

"If he was a spy, he would have told me about the baby. He never did." Rowan's voice deepened, hardened. "His job was to protect you, and he did. He was so devoted to you that he also protected you, and Jax, from me."

Logan had nothing to say to that. She stared at

Rowan, stunned, because theoretically, if Joe was employed by Rowan, he probably should have told Rowan he was protecting a woman and a baby...

"Yes," Rowan said. "He took his job as your security detail very, very seriously. He never once mentioned anything about a pregnancy or a baby or that he spent lots of time working from your home."

She almost laughed, feeling slightly hysterical. "Do you have any idea the things I had him do? The errands after work? The trips to the dry cleaner? He even helped feed Jax dinners when I was working away at my computer..." Logan swallowed hard. "I thought he loved her. And maybe it wasn't love, but I thought he really did care about us."

For several minutes there was just silence and then Rowan made a low, rough sound. "He did," Rowan said shortly. "For two years Joe protected you and your secret. He shouldn't have, though. That was a critical error on his part. I've fired him. He'll find it difficult getting another high-level security job." And then Rowan walked away, heading to the galley.

Logan watched his back, the sting of tears prickling her eyes. She didn't think it was possible, but her very bad day had just gotten worse.

CHAPTER FOUR

ROWAN WAS POURING HIMSELF a neat shot of whiskey when Logan appeared in the narrow kitchen galley.

She stood in the doorway, arms crossed over her chest. She was so much thinner than she'd been three years ago. He'd known she worked hard, but he hadn't expected her to look quite so stressed. If he'd known she was pregnant...if he'd known there was a child...

He threw back the shot and looked at her. "Yes, love?"

"I'm not your love."

His fingers itched to pour another drink but he never had more than one. At least, never more than one in a twelve-hour span. He couldn't afford to lose his head. Ever.

But he had lost it once. He'd lost it March 31 three years ago to *her*. The evidence of that was curled up in a chair, hair in two tiny ponytails. They'd used protection the night of the bachelor auction. He knew he'd used protection. Clearly it hadn't been the right protection, or enough.

"Have you heard anything about Bronson? Is he stable or still in critical condition?"

"Bronson will remain in ICU for another few days, but he's been stabilized. The decision to keep him in ICU is for his protection. It's easier to secure the ICU unit than another floor."

"And Victoria? Where is she is right now? Who exactly has her?"

"By now your sister should be with Drakon and Morgan—"

"Oh, that's going to go over beautifully."

"Why?"

"They don't get along. At all."

"Drakon and Victoria?"

"Morgan and Victoria." She frowned. "I wouldn't leave Victoria there. She should go to Jemma. They're close. Victoria will be far happier there."

"It's too late for that. What's done is done and hopefully your sisters will realize that this isn't the time to bicker."

Her eyebrows rose. "They don't bicker. They've had a massive falling out, over my father. It's painful for everyone."

"Then I wish Drakon well because it's his problem now." Rowan leaned back against the narrow galley counter, the stainless steel cool against his back. He allowed his gaze to slide over Logan's slender frame, studying her intently. "Why didn't you get an abortion?"

If his question shocked her, she gave no indication. "It wasn't the right choice for me," she answered, her voice firm and clear.

She was good, he thought. She sounded so grounded

and smart and reasonable, which just provoked him even more.

He gripped the counter's edge tightly. It was that or grab her by the shoulder and drag her into his arms. His kiss wouldn't be kind.

He was not feeling kind.

It was difficult to feel kind when his cock throbbed in his trousers and his body felt hard and hungry.

He remembered the smell of her and the taste of her and how soft and warm and wet she'd been as he'd kissed her there, between her legs, and made her body tighten and break with pleasure. And then he'd thrust in, burying himself hard, and she'd groaned and stiffened and he'd thought that had been pleasure, too.

Now he knew he'd taken her virginity ruthlessly. Not knowing…

Not knowing the first damn thing about her.

A Copeland. A virgin. A society princess dethroned.

"Don't fire Joe," she said, breaking the tense silence. Her voice was husky. He heard the pleading note, and it made him even angrier. Why did it bother him that she was pleading for Joe? Was it because he worried that she cared for him? Or was it because he wanted her to plead for him…

She'd begged him three years ago, begged for his hands and his mouth, begged to be touched and taken, and he'd obliged.

Now look at them. Parents of a tiny girl.

He wouldn't ignore his responsibilities. He wouldn't

punish the girl the way he'd been punished when his father knocked his mother up.

His father who drank too much and let his fists fly. His mother who drank too much and forgot to come home.

Not that he blamed her. Home was not a nice place to be.

"Please," Logan started again. "Please don't—"

"Joe doesn't need you begging for his job," Rowan said curtly, unable to bear hearing her plead any longer. It was far too reminiscent of a childhood he hated. It was far too reminiscent of a person he didn't want to be. "He knew what he was doing. He made his own choices—"

"For Jax."

"For you," he corrected. "I know he cared for you. I know he developed...feelings...for you. I know when his attachment became more than just a strong sense of duty."

"And yet you left him on the job."

Rowan really wanted another drink, craving the burn and the heat in his veins because maybe then he wouldn't want to push her up against the galley wall and put his hands into her hair and take her soft mouth and make her whimper for him.

He felt like an animal.

He didn't want to be an animal.

His work usually kept him focused but right now he had none. Just her and her wide, searching blue eyes and that dark pink mouth that demanded to be kissed.

"No," he ground out, knuckles tight as he gripped the stainless counter harder. "I didn't *leave* him on the job. I relieved him months ago. Back before the Christmas holidays. He refused to step down. He refused to abandon you."

Her lips curved, tremulous. "Unlike you?"

If she'd been icy and mocking he could have ignored the jab. If she'd shown her veneer, he would have let her be. But her unsteady words coupled with the tremble of her lip made his chest squeeze, the air bottled within.

He'd hurt her, because he'd meant to hurt her.

He was very good at what he did.

Rowan reached for her wrist, his fingers circling her slender bones and he pulled her toward him. She stiffened but didn't fight him. If anything she'd gone very still.

"Let me see your head," he said gruffly, bringing her hips almost to his. He lifted a heavy wave of honey-colored hair from her forehead to inspect her temple.

With one hand still in her hair, he tipped her head, tilting this way and that to get a proper look. It didn't look too bad. She must have cleaned the wound while he'd gone to pick up Jax. The cut was scabbing, and he saw the start of a dark bruise. The bruise would be uglier tomorrow, but all in all, she was healing.

"I'm sorry I didn't catch you," he said, his deep voice still rough. They might not be on good terms but he didn't like that all he did was bring her pain. "You went down hard."

"I've survived far worse," she answered, her smile full of bravado, but the bold smile didn't reach her blue eyes, and in those blue eyes fringed by thick black lashes there was a world of hurt and shadows. Far too many shadows.

He tipped her head farther back to look into her eyes, trying to see where she'd been and all that had happened in the past three years and then he felt a stab of regret, and blame.

He'd left her out there, hanging.

He'd left her, just as she'd said.

He, who protected strangers, hadn't protected *her*.

His head dropped, his mouth covering hers. It was a kiss to comfort her, a kiss to apologize for being such an ass, and yet the moment his mouth touched hers he forgot everything but how warm she was and how good she felt against him. Her mouth was so very soft and warm, too, and her chest rose and fell with her quick gasp, the swell of her breasts pressing against his chest.

He had not been celibate for the past three years. He liked women and enjoyed sex, and he'd found pleasure with a number of women but Logan didn't feel like just any woman—she was different. She felt like his. But he didn't want to explore that thought, not when he wanted to explore her, and he slid a hand down the length of her back, soothing her even as he coaxed her closer, heat in his veins, hunger making him hard.

He wasn't going to force her, though. She could push him away at any moment. He'd let her go the moment she said no, the moment she put a hand to his chest and pressed him back.

And then her hand moved to his chest, and her fingers grabbed at his shirt, and she tugged on the shirt, tugging him toward her.

The heat in his veins became a fire.

He deepened the kiss, his tongue tracing the seam of her lips until she opened her mouth. His tongue flicked over her lower lip and then found the tip of hers and teased that, and then the inside of her upper lip, teasing the delicate swollen skin until he felt her nails dig into his chest, her slender frame shuddering. He captured her hip, holding her close, wanting nothing more than to bury himself in her and make her cry his name again...

She wasn't like any other woman. He'd never met another woman he wanted this much.

The kiss became electric, so hot he felt as if he was going to explode. He didn't want to want her like this. He didn't want to want anyone like this. He didn't want his control tested, didn't want to feel as if he couldn't get enough, that he'd never have enough, that what he missed, needed, wanted was right here in this woman—

He broke off the kiss and stepped back. He was breathing hard, his shaft throbbing but that was nothing compared to what was happening in his chest, within his heart.

She was not the right one for him.

She couldn't be.

He didn't like spoiled, entitled society girls, and

he didn't respect women who'd never had to work for anything…

"One of us should be with Jax," he said curtly. "Make sure she's safe in case there's turbulence."

"I was just on my way back to her," Logan replied turning around and walking away, but not before he saw the flush in her cheeks and the ripe plumpness of her pink lips.

He nearly grabbed her again, wanting to finish what he'd started.

Instead he let her go, body aching, mind conflicted.

There was no love lost between them. They couldn't even carry on a civil conversation but that didn't matter if he took her to bed. They didn't have to like each other. In fact, it might even be better if they didn't like each other. It didn't matter with them. The sex would still be hot.

Logan returned to her seat and carefully scooped Jax back into her arms and sat down with her daughter, not because Jax needed to be held but because Logan needed Jax for safety. Security.

Rowan's kiss had shaken her to the core.

Her heart still pounded, her body flooded with wants and needs that could destroy her. Rowan was not good for her. Rowan was danger…

She swallowed hard and closed her eyes, determined to clamp down on her emotions, determined to slow her pulse.

She didn't want him. She couldn't want him. She couldn't forget what happened last time, and she wasn't even talking about the blisteringly hot sex, but the emptiness afterward. The sex hadn't just been sex. It hadn't felt like sweat and exercise...release... it'd felt transformative.

It'd been...bliss.

And then he'd walked out of her Santa Monica house, door slamming behind him, and her heart had shattered into a thousand pieces. Never mind what he'd done to her self-respect.

She couldn't be turned on now. She couldn't be so stupid as to imagine that he'd be different, that the lovemaking would be safer or that the aftermath would be less destructive.

He was fire. And when he touched her, she blistered and living with burns wasn't her idea of a calm, centered, happy life.

She needed a calm, centered, happy life. It was the only way to provide for Jax. The only way to raise Jax in a healthy home.

Rowan Argyros might be seduction on two legs, but he wasn't the daddy she wanted for Jax, or the partner she needed—and then suddenly he was back, dropping into the leather seat across from hers and extending his legs, his dark head tipping back, his eyes closing, hiding his intense green eyes.

But even with his eyes closed the air felt charged. Magnetic.

She glared at him, hating how her pulse jumped and raced and her body grew hot all over again just because he was close.

Without even opening his eyes he said, "We still

have a good four plus hours to go. I'd sleep if I were you. You'll feel better—"

"This is not my first international trip," she said curtly, cutting him off. Of course he'd think she was staring at him. And yes, she was, but that was beside the point.

The edge of his mouth lifted. "Suit yourself."

"Yes, I will."

The corner lifted higher.

Her stomach tightened. Her pulse raced. She pressed her lips into a thin, hard line, trying to hold back all the angry words she wanted to hurl at him.

He brought out the worst in her. He did. She needed to get away from him, and the sooner the better. But how?

She wasn't dealing with an ordinary man. If she set aside her personal feelings for a moment, she'd admit that he was extraordinary in every way, but that was the problem. With Rowan she couldn't set aside her personal feelings. With Rowan it was nothing but personal.

The night he'd spent with her had changed her forever. His touch was so profound that he might as well have taken a hammer and chisel to her heart, carving his name into the very marrow of her being.

Even now she could feel him as if his hand was on hers.

As if his chest was pressed to hers.

She could feel him because just the smell, touch, taste of him made her burn. She wanted him still. She wanted more.

But more would break her. More would crack her all the way open, draining her until there was nothing left of Logan Copeland.

But maybe that's what he wanted. Maybe he wanted to destroy her.

If so, he was off to a good start.

Logan woke to the sound of murmured voices. Opening her eyes she spotted Rowan standing across the aisle with Jax in his arms. They were facing a big screen and watching a Disney movie featuring fish, and Rowan was discussing the cartoon with her. Jax had her finger in her mouth and seemed more fascinated by Rowan than the huge blue tang searching for her parents.

Jax was already a petite little girl and tucked against Rowan's chest, in his muscular arms, she looked impossibly small.

Logan swallowed around the lump filling her throat. Jax was her world. Her center. Her sunshine. And Logan didn't want to share her, and she most definitely didn't want to share her with someone who didn't deserve her.

Just like that, she heard another voice in her head.

It was her mother's voice, raised, emotional. *He doesn't deserve us…he doesn't deserve any of us…*

She must have shifted, or maybe she made a sound, because suddenly Rowan was turning and looking at her. "You were out," he said.

"How long?"

"Long enough for us to watch a movie." And right on cue the film's credits rolled.

"Dory," Jax said to Logan, pointing to the enormous flat screen.

Logan smiled at her daughter. "You love Dory, don't you?"

Jax nodded and, popping her finger back into her mouth, looked at Rowan. "Dory can't 'member."

Rowan nodded. "But she still found a way to be successful. That's what's important. Never give up." And then his gaze met Logan's over Jax's head. "A good lesson for all of us, I think."

Logan left her seat and reached for her daughter. "I'll take her. See if we can find a snack—"

"She ate while you were sleeping," he answered, handing her back. "She likes chicken. And she couldn't get enough cantaloupe."

And then he was walking away, and Logan gave Jax a little cuddle and kiss, even as her heart pounded, aware that everything in her life had changed. There were men you could escape. There were men you could forget. But Rowan Argyros was neither.

They landed just before noon on a long, narrow runway that sliced an emerald green field in two. The touchdown was so smooth it felt like they'd landed on glass. Logan kissed the top of Jax's head. Her daughter had been awake for the past several hours and she was relaxed and content at the moment, quietly sucking on her thumb. Logan had worked hard to discourage the habit but she let it go now as it probably helped Jax's ears adjust to the change in pressure.

The jet slowed steadily and then did a smooth turn on the landing strip, and began a long taxi back the way they'd just come.

Logan returned her attention to the emerald expanse beyond. It was misty outside, the windows covered with fine water droplets. Now that they were on the ground she could see that the fields were actually a vast lawn, and the green lawns gradually rolled up to a hill dominated by a large gray castle with a tall square stone tower and smaller towers at different corners.

As they taxied, they headed closer to the castle, and different features came into view. The big square tower's parapet. The tall Gothic windows. The arches above the narrow windows. There were no trees or shrubs to soften the starkness of the castle. Instead it just rose up from a sea of green, and it didn't strike Logan as a particularly friendly castle. Maybe it was the dark sky and drizzly rain, but the forbidding exterior made her think it was a fortress, not a home, and the last thing she wanted was to be locked up. Trapped.

"Who lives there?" she asked uneasily, hoping against hope that this was not the Irish estate Morgan had talked about. Morgan and Drakon had visited Rowan's Irish estate a year or so ago and she'd made it sound palatial. This was not palatial.

"I do." Rowan shifted in his chair, legs extended, hands folded on his lean flat stomach. "When here."

She glanced out the rain-splattered window and sucked on the inside of her lip, trying to maintain her calm because as impressive as the castle was, it lacked warmth. She couldn't find anything inviting about such a massive building. "I can see why you don't spend that much time in Ireland."

"I'm here quite often, and I am very fond of the place. I gather you don't like it?"

"It's stark." She hesitated, before adding, "And very gray."

"There's a lot of stone," he agreed. "But it's sturdy. The oldest towers are over six hundred years old. The newer sections are two hundred years. But when I bought it, I refurbished the interior and you'll find it quite comfortable." His smile was crooked. "I love my mother's country but I must have a little too much of my father's Greek blood, or maybe I'm just getting older, but I don't like being cold."

Her gaze met his and there was something mocking in his eyes, but it wasn't unkind as much as challenging. He seemed to be daring her to say something, daring her to disagree, but looking at him there was nothing old or weak about him. He was powerful from the top of his head to the intense gold of his eyes, to the tips of his toes.

"I somehow don't think the cold bothers you all that much," she answered. "At least, I remember your saying three years ago that you trunk it when you surf in California. Even in winter."

He shrugged carelessly and yet there was a flicker of heat in his eyes, as if surprised that she'd remem-

bered. But of course she remembered. That was the
problem. She remembered *everything*.

"I don't like wetsuits." Rowan's deep voice rum-
bled in his chest and his head was turned, his gaze
fixed on the drizzly landscape beyond the window.
"Not even here, when I'm surfing in Wales or Scotland."

The jet had rolled to a stop. The flight attendant
was at the door. Logan glanced at him and then at
Rowan who'd also unfastened his seat belt and was
rising.

"Are there good waves in the UK?" she asked.

"One of my favorite breaks is in Scotland. Thurso
East. I like Fresh in Pembrokeshire, too." He gazed
down at her for a moment, a faint smile playing at
his lips and yet the smile didn't touch his eyes. Those
were a cool green, a much cooler green than the emerald lawns outside, and then he extended a hand to
her. "Fresh can be dangerous, though. The reef break
is heavy and significant, and then there is the army
firing range above. It's not for beginners."

"And you like that it's frightening."

"I'd call it exhilarating." His lips curved ever so
slightly, his expression almost mocking. "Just as I am
finding you exhilarating. I had no idea I had a family. Everything is changing. *Fáilte abhaile*," he said
in Gaelic. "Welcome home."

She'd had three plus years to get over him. Three
years to grow a thick skin…an armor…and yet he'd
dismantled her defenses with just a few words, a careless smile, a hot, searing kiss…

Logan held her own cool smile, even as she drew a slow breath to hide the frantic beating of her heart. "It shall be fascinating to see your home," she said, unbuckling her seat belt and rising, shifting Jax to her hip. "I consider it an adventure. I have always enjoyed a good adventure. And then it will be time for me to return home. As fun as it is to have a little getaway, I've a business in Los Angeles, and obligations there—"

"Your obligations are to your family first, and as the mother of my child, you and I will want to make the necessary adjustments to ensure that you and she are safe." His gaze never wavered. "Castle Ros is safe. If you do not wish to live here year-round we can discuss other options, but there is no place in the United States where you'd be safe right now."

"I don't wish to argue in front of Jax—"

"Then let's not."

She ground her teeth together, determined to keep her composure as an emotional outburst would only alienate Rowan and frighten her daughter. "You don't want me," she said softly, urgently. "And I don't want you—"

"You wanted me very much three years ago. You'll want me again."

Her gaze swiftly dropped to her daughter. Her voice dropped even lower. "Everything I cherished was stripped away by my father. Love is all I have left, and you are not going to take that from me. I deserve the chance to be loved, and we both know that is not something you're offering. And love is the only reason I'd ever marry. The only one," she repeated.

And then, desperate for air and space, she walked past him and headed for the plane door, too agitated to return for her purse and Jax's diaper bag. Purses and diaper bags could be retrieved...replaced. Her sanity was another matter.

Rowan followed Logan off the jet and took a seat next to her in the armored car. He was sure she didn't know the luxury sedan had bulletproof glass and extra paneling in the sides. She didn't need to know that. She didn't need to know that the perimeter of his estate was walled and patrolled and every security measure had been taken to make Castle Ros one of the safest places in Europe—whether for a head of state needing protection or his own woman and daughter.

His gaze rested on Logan's profile.

His woman.

She was.

She'd been his from the moment he laid eyes on her at the auction. She hadn't even known that he'd seen her long before she'd noticed him. He'd picked her from the others, chosen her from every woman there as the one he'd wanted, and he'd willed it, made it happen, focusing on her so that she couldn't help but know who he was...couldn't help but feel his interest and desire.

She, who was working that night at the auction, had scrambled to bid, and he'd kept his attention locked on her throughout the bidding, and she'd done what he'd demanded...

She'd won him.

And he'd rewarded her. All night long.

And as the night turned to morning, he'd lain in bed next to her, watching her sleep and listening to her breathe, and wondering how to keep her and incorporate her into a life where he was rarely in one place long.

He was a bachelor. He needed to be a bachelor. And yet with her he felt settled, committed. He felt as if he'd come home, which was impossible as he'd never had a true home. He'd never belonged anywhere—he'd shifted between continents and countries, languages and cultures. Rowan had been raised as a nomad and outsider, caught between his fierce, moody, ambitious Greek father and his kind but unstable Irish mother. After the initial love-lust wore off, his parents couldn't get along. He still remembered the arguing when he was very young. They fought because there was never enough money, and never enough success. His father was full of schemes and plans, always looking for that one big break that would make him rich, while his mother just wanted peace. She didn't need a big windfall, she just wanted his father home. And then his father hit the jackpot, or so he thought, until he was arrested and sent to prison for white-collar crime.

The time away broke the family.

It broke what was left of the marriage and his mother.

Or maybe what broke the marriage, and his mother, was losing Devlin, Rowan's little brother. Devlin drowned while Father was in prison.

Rowan tensed, remembering. Devlin's death at two and three quarters had been the beginning of the end.

Rowan's father blamed Rowan's mother. Rowan's mother blamed Rowan's father. And then Rowan's father was out of jail, and the fighting just started over again. Rowan was glad to be sent to boarding school in England, and he told himself he was glad when his parents finally separated, because maybe, finally, the fighting would end. But the divorce dragged on for years, and school holidays became increasingly chaotic and painful. Sometimes he'd visit one parent in one country, while other times neither parent wanted him and if there was no classmate to invite him home, he'd remain at school, which was in many ways preferable to visits with strangers, including his parents who became little more than strangers as the years went by.

After finishing school, he went to university in America, and then returned to Britain to serve in the Royal Navy and never again returned home. Because there was no home. He'd never felt at home, which is why the attachment to Logan had been unsettling.

How could she feel like home when he didn't know what home was? How could he care for her when he didn't know her?

It had been almost a relief to discover she was a Copeland. She had been too good to be true. His rage had been swift and focused, and he'd let her feel the full impact of his disappointment. But it wasn't Logan he was truly angry with. He was angry with himself for dropping his guard and allowing himself to feel.

Emotions were dangerous. Emotions were destructive. He couldn't let himself make that mistake again.

And now she was back in his life, and she wasn't merely a beautiful but problematic woman, she was also the mother of his child.

And that changed everything. That changed him. It had to change him. There was no way he'd allow his child to be caught between two adults battling for control. Nor would he let Logan disappear with his daughter the way his mother, Maire, had disappeared with him after Devlin's death.

So there would be a wedding, yes, but beyond that?

Rowan didn't have all the answers yet. He wasn't sure how he'd keep Logan and Jax in Ireland. He wasn't sure how he'd ensure that they couldn't disappear from his life. He only knew that it couldn't happen. And it wouldn't happen. He'd keep Logan close, he'd make her want to stay, and if he couldn't do it through love, he'd do it through touch…sex. Love wasn't the only way to bond with a woman. Touch and pleasure would melt her, weaken her, creating bonds that would be difficult, if not impossible, to break.

Was it fair? No. But life wasn't fair. Life was about survival, and Rowan was an expert survivalist.

Fáilte abhaile mo bride, he repeated silently, glancing once more at Logan's elegant profile, appreciating anew her stunning gold-and-honey beauty. *Welcome home, my bride.*

CHAPTER FIVE

THE LUXURIOUS INTERIOR of Castle Ros hid its technology well. At first glance one didn't see the modern amenities, just the sumptuous appointments. The scattered rugs and plush carpets. The rich paneling and decoratively papered walls. The glow of lights in intricate fixtures. The oil portraits and massive landscapes in ornate gold frames. But then as Logan settled into her suite of rooms, a suite that adjoined Rowan's, she noticed the electrical outlets and USB ports tucked into every surface and corner.

There was a remote on the bedside table that controlled the temperature, and the blackout blinds at the windows, and an enormous painting over the fireplace that turned into a flat-screen TV. A refrigerator, sink and marble-topped counter had been tucked into one of the adjoining closets. On the white marble counter stood an espresso machine, and next to that was a lacquered box lined with pods of coffee. Milks and snacks filled the refrigerator. A small wine rack was stocked with bottles of red and white wine.

Apparently Rowan—or his estate manager—had

thought of everything. There was no reason Logan couldn't be comfortable in the lavish suite.

Now Jax was another matter.

The castle wasn't child-friendly. There wasn't a small bed or even a chair suitable for a two-year-old anywhere, never mind the massive fireplaces—with fires—missing screens, and the steep stone staircases without a gate or barrier to slow a curious toddler's exploration.

But before Logan could voice her concerns, Rowan was already aware of the problem. "I recognize that the house poses a danger for Jax. While it's impossible to make the entire castle child-safe, I can certainly ensure that she has rooms—or an entire floor—that have been made secure, free of hazards, giving her plenty of space to play and move about."

And then he was gone, and Logan was alone with Jax in her huge suite with the high ceilings, crackling fire and tall, narrow windows.

Logan frowned at the fire. At least this one had a grate and screen, but the fire worried her.

But then, everything worried her. She'd lost control. Her carefully constructed world was in pieces, shattered by the appearance of Rowan Argyros.

He wasn't supposed to be in her life. She didn't want him in her life. She didn't want him near Jax. And yet here they all were, locked down in his high-tech, high-security castle.

She needed to get away. She needed to get Jax away from here as soon as possible. Logan didn't know how. She just knew it had to be done, and

quickly. And while time was of the essence, strat-
egy would be important as it wasn't going to be easy
leaving Rowan's fortified home, nor would it be simple sneaking a two-year-old away.

After a bath and a light meal, Logan and Jax
napped and then before Logan was ready to be awake,
Jax was up and eager to play.

Logan's head throbbed. She needed sleep. Her
body seemed to think it was the middle of the night—
and back in California it was—but Jax was adjusting
to the time change far better and Logan allowed the
busy toddler to take all the shimmering silk pillows
to the huge empty walk-in closet to play.

Logan made coffee and sat down with a notebook
to figure out the next steps to take, and she was still
sitting with the notebook—pages perfectly blank—
when a knock sounded at the door.

Opening the bedroom door, she discovered a fresh-
faced young woman in the hall.

"I'm Orla." The young woman introduced herself
with a firm handshake and quick smile. "I've been a
nanny for five years, but I'm not just a child minder,
I'm a certified teacher, specializing in early education. So where is my lovely girl? I'm looking forward
to meeting her."

Logan drew a short, rough breath, as Orla stepped
past, entering the bedroom suite. "I'm sorry," she
said awkwardly. "There must be a mistake. I haven't
hired anyone."

"Your husband—"

"I don't have a husband."

Orla turned around and faced Logan. "Mr. Argyros—"

"Not my husband."

"Your fiancé—"

"He's not my fiancé."

The young woman didn't blink or flush or stammer. Her steady blue gaze met Logan's and held. "Your daughter's father."

Logan bit down on her tongue. She had no reply for that.

"He hired my services," Orla continued in the same calm, unflappable tone, her dark hair drawn back in a sleek, professional ponytail. Orla appeared to be a good five to ten years younger than Logan, and yet she was managing to making Logan feel as if she was a difficult child. "He said there'd been a recent death in the family," she added, "and you had matters to attend to. I'm here to help make everything easier for you."

Again, Logan couldn't think of an appropriate response. Somehow Rowan was getting the best of her, and he wasn't even here. "But I'm not working. I don't need any *help* with my daughter." She tensed as she heard her voice rise. She was sounding plaintive and that wouldn't do. "I enjoy my daughter's company very much, and right now I need her. She's such a comfort."

"But the wedding preparations will only tire her out. I can promise you she'll have great fun with me. I've brought toys and games and dolls. Does Jax like playing with dolls? I have a set of little fairies—

they're a family and absolutely adorable—and most girls—"

"Fairies?" The connecting door to the massive walk-in closet flew open and Jax came running out, dragging one of the embroidered silk pillows behind her. She'd been happy in the closet, but apparently playing with fairies was far more appealing than tasseled silk pillows. "I love fairies!"

Orla was already on one knee, putting herself at eye level with Jax. "I have a whole family of fairies in my bag. Would you like to see?"

Jax nodded vigorously, and Logan held her breath, counted to five, and then ten, aware that her immediate presence was not needed here. "If you don't mind, I'll go have a word with Rowan."

Jax ignored her and Orla just flashed a cheerful smile. "Of course, Ms. Copeland. We'll be here, having a healthy snack and creating our fairy garden. We'll show you our garden when you're back."

Rowan wasn't surprised to see Logan at the door of his office. He rolled back from his desk where he'd been reading updates on situations he was monitoring and answering brief emails with even briefer replies.

He casually propped one foot on top of the other as she entered. "Everything all right?"

"No," she said curtly, crossing the floor. She'd changed since they'd arrived, and was dressed now in black trousers and a black knit sweater that clung to her high full breasts and hugged her narrow waist.

Her thick, honey hair was parted in the middle, and the long, straight silk strands framed her face, drawing attention to the arched brows and haunting blue of her eyes.

He'd remembered she was pretty, but had forgotten how her beauty was such a physical thing. She crackled with energy, and just looking at her made his blood heat. "What's happened?" he asked, tamping down the desire. "Maybe I can help."

"You're the problem, and you know it." She stood before him, a hand on one hip, drawing attention to her lean figure, made even longer by her black leather boots. The heels on her leather boots were high. And incredibly sexy.

"Me?" he drawled.

Her arched eyebrow lifted higher, her expression incredulous, and Rowan didn't think she'd ever looked so fierce, or so desirable.

The fierceness was new, as was the crackling energy. She hadn't been fierce three years ago. She hadn't burned with this intensity, either. Becoming a mother had changed her.

He liked it. He liked her on fire. But then, he'd always loved a good fight, and she was itching for a fight now.

"Would you like to sit down?" He gestured to a chair not far from the desk. "We can talk—"

"You're not my partner or spouse," she said, cutting him short. "You will never be my partner or spouse, and you've no right to hire a nanny for my daughter without my permission." Temper flashed in her eyes. "Are you listening, Rowan? You need to understand what I'm saying."

His upper lip ached to curl. He wanted to smile but fought to hide his amusement, aware that she wouldn't appreciate it. "I'm listening, Logan."

"Good. Because you have an agenda—that's clear enough—but it's not my agenda, and I'm not going to be bulldozed into going along with your plan."

He'd found her impossibly lovely three years ago, the night he'd spotted her at the auction. She had an intent gaze, focused and watchful, and in her delicate silver and periwinkle gown, she'd shimmered, her beauty mysterious...that of a remote, untouchable princess. The untouchable quality drew him in. He saw it as a challenge. He couldn't resist a challenge.

Now there was an entirely different challenge before him. A different woman. And he understood why she'd changed. She'd had to be everything for Jax—mother and father, protector and nurturer—and she'd done it truly alone, cut off from family, mocked by society, and the pressure and pain had stripped Logan down and reshaped her, giving her an edge, giving her strength. This woman standing before him was no doormat. This new woman exuded power and resolve. This new woman was sexual, too, dressed head to toe in black, the light of battle blazing in her eyes, illuminating her stunning features.

"I don't want to bulldoze you. That wouldn't be fair to you or our daughter."

He saw her tense when he said *our daughter*. "She is *our* daughter."

"She's not a bargaining chip."

"I would never make her one."

She rolled her eyes. "I don't believe that for a second and neither should you. You are the most ruthless man I have ever met, Rowan, and that is saying a great deal considering my father is Daniel Copeland."

"I spent ten years in the military as an officer. I have nothing in common with your father."

"Don't kid yourself. Nothing stopped him from taking what he wanted. And nothing will stop you, either. You take what you want, when you want, and discard—"

"I didn't discard you."

Her eyes burned overbright. She swallowed once, and then again, struggling to hold back words.

He sighed inwardly. "I treated you badly, yes. But it won't be like that with Jax."

"You're right, it won't be, because she is not part of this…she is not part of us. She is herself, and lovely and everything that is best in the world, and I will protect her from those who'd hurt her, and that includes you, Rowan Argyros."

"You don't need to protect her from me."

"I wish I could believe that."

"I'm not a monster."

Logan looked away, lips compressing, a sheen of tears in her eyes.

His chest tightened and it felt as if somewhere along the way he'd swallowed rocks. They made his stomach hurt. He'd hurt her badly because he'd intended to hurt her, and the unfairness of it made him sick. But it wouldn't change the outcome of this conversation. He wasn't going to lose Jax.

And he wasn't going to lose Logan.

They'd be a family because it was the right thing. Because it was the best thing. Because it would keep both of them safe, and that was the world he knew best.

Safety. Security.

No one would get to them, no one could hurt them. He knew it, and in her heart, she had to know it, too.

Rowan rose and moved past her to drag the tapestry-covered armchair forward. "Sit, *mo chroí*. You'll be more comfortable, I promise you."

She shot him a derisive look. "You want me to sit because it will make me more passive. But I'm not interested in being passive or docile. I'm not interested in being managed or accommodating you in any way."

She wouldn't like it if she knew he found her so appealing right now.

She wouldn't like it if she knew how much he wanted to touch her. How much he wanted to cover her mouth and drink her in, tasting her, taking her, making her melt.

He could make her melt.

He could.

He could do it now, too. Even when she crackled and burned. It'd be easier now, when she was on fire, her temper stirred, because anger and passion were so very close, anger flamed passion, anger made passion explode…

Logan straightened and stepped away from the club chair, closing the gap between them. It only took that one step and he saw the flicker in her eyes and the bite of teeth into her soft lower lip.

She was not so indifferent, this fierce woman of his.

She was not unaware of the crackle and fire in the room and the tension pulsing between them.

He gazed down into her upturned face, her eyes wide and blue, her breathing ragged. He could even see the erratic pulse beating at the base of her throat. They were so very close. If he drew a deep enough breath his chest would touch hers.

If he shifted, his knee would find her thighs. He'd be there between her thighs. He very much wanted to be between her thighs, too.

One touch and he'd have her.

One touch and she'd be his.

"I want you to sit," he said quietly, gently, his blood humming in his veins, his body taut, hard. "Because I'm very, very close to stretching you across my desk and having my way with you." He stared into her eyes, the faintest of smiles creasing the corners of his eyes, even as he let her see the challenge in his eyes, and allowed her to feel his leashed tension. She needed to know that things were getting serious. This wasn't a game. "But somehow I think you're not yet ready for us to pick up where we left off—"

"That's not even a possibility."

And then he did what he knew he shouldn't do, not because she'd resist him, but because it wouldn't help his position—that he was good for her and Jax, and that he was the right one to take care of them.

But there was something about Logan that made him throw caution to the wind and he was done with restraint. Clasping her face in his hands, he captured her mouth and kissed her deeply, kissing her with that heat and hunger he knew she responded to, and she did.

Her lips trembled beneath his and her mouth opened to him. His tongue stroked the inside of her lip and then in, finding her tongue and teasing her until he felt her hands on his arms, her grip tight. She leaned in, leaning against him, and she was so warm and soft and…his.

His, but not his. Because he still didn't understand why he felt so possessive about this woman. He didn't understand the attraction and wasn't even sure he wanted to be attracted. The fact that she could even test his control, provoked him.

"I could make you come right now," he murmured against her mouth, as aware of his erection straining against the fabric of his trousers as he was of the hot, honey taste of her on his tongue, "and you'd love it."

She stiffened but didn't pull away, her chest rising and falling against his own.

He'd offended her, and it'd been deliberate. Just like before, he lashed out at her when truthfully he was frustrated with himself.

So really, he was no different from three plus years ago.

God almighty.

Rowan let her go and stepped away. He hated himself just then.

What was he doing?

This wasn't like him. His career had been built on defending and rescuing others. He was a protector.

Except when it came to Logan.

Rowan went to his desk, rifling through papers, pushing aside a stack of folders, needing time to calm down and clear his head.

He needed to be able to think. He needed her to think. They both needed to make the right decisions. Decisions about marriage and the future. Decisions about where they'd raise Jax together, protecting Jax.

This wasn't about love, but responsibility.

And yet he'd fulfill his duty as a husband. He'd make sure Logan's needs were met. He'd be sure she was satisfied.

"You can't have me," she whispered, drawing a rough breath and taking an unsteady step back. "And you can't have Jax, either." She retreated another couple of steps, arms folded tightly over her chest. "Just because you swept us out of the country and deposited us here in your Irish estate, doesn't mean we're yours. We're not."

"*She* is."

"You didn't want her. You didn't want anything to do with us—"

"You never told me I was a father."

"I phoned. You mocked me. Scorned me."

"You keep talking about you. You never told me about her. What about *her*?"

A shadow crossed her face and Logan's expression shuttered. He'd scored a direct hit. She knew he was right.

He shrugged impatiently. "In your heart you know you gave up too easily. If you truly love her as much as you say you do, you should have fought for her rights. Fought to do what was best for her."

"You think you're best?" Her chin notched up and yet her full lips quivered, the soft full lower lip swollen from the hard, hot kiss. "You think you're father material?"

His jaw tightened. "It doesn't matter what you think. What matters is the law. As her biological father, I have rights, and I intend to exert those rights, and you can be part of our family, or—"

"There is no *or*, Rowan. I am her family."

"Just as I am her family, too."

"You said you wouldn't use her as a bargaining tool."

"Correct. I will not bargain for her. I will not bargain with her. I am claiming my rights, and my right to parent my daughter, and we can either do this together, making these decisions together, or we can take it to the courts and let them decide."

"You wouldn't win custody."

He gave her a long look. "Your late father is a crook…one of the greatest of this century. You've hidden my daughter from me—"

"You're twisting everything."

"But can't you see how this will play out in court? Can't you see that you've been duplicitous? Every bit as deceitful as your father?"

"No."

"But yes, love, you have. Legally you have." He fell silent, and the silence stretched, heavy, weighted, pointed. She needed to face the truth, and in this case, she was wrong. The court would take issue with her choices. The court would penalize her for those choices.

Silence stretched and Logan's heart beat fast as she watched Rowan reach for another sheaf of papers, carelessly flipping through them.

She continued to hold her breath as he leaned over and scrawled a few words—his signature maybe?—at the bottom of one page, and then flipped to another page and scrawled something again.

She hated this so much.

She hated bickering and fighting, especially when it was about a child. Her child.

And yes, Rowan was her biological father but it was impossible to wrap her head around the fact that he wanted to be in Jax's life. That he wanted to be a true father.

Or maybe she was misunderstanding. Maybe he didn't want to be hands-on. Maybe this was about power...control.

"My father rarely spent time with his children," Logan said flatly, trying to hide the thudding of her heart and the anxiety rippling through her. "He spent his life at the office. And then after the divorce, he saw Morgan, but not the rest of us. But that was because Morgan went to live with him, feeling sorry for him."

Rowan lifted his head, his gaze locking with hers. "But you didn't."

"It was his choice not to see us. Mother never kept us from him. He didn't care enough about us to maintain a relationship."

"But you view him as your father."

She struggled with the next words. "He paid our bills."

"So you really couldn't care less about him."

"I didn't say that."

"You want to attend his funeral."

"He was my father."

"Ah." Rowan dropped into his chair, and studied her from across the office. "And you don't think our daughter will care about her father? You assume she doesn't need one?"

"I never said that."

"But you've blocked me from her life. Kept her from knowing she has a father."

Logan closed her eyes and drew a slow breath. "There's a difference between paying for a child's expenses, and being engaged…and loving."

"And you assume I can only pay bills?"

Tension knotted her shoulders. Balls of ice filled her stomach. Logan flexed her fingers trying to ease the anxiety ricocheting inside her. After an endless moment she touched her tongue to her upper lip, dampening it. "You have assumed only the worst of me. You have judged me based on my name. You have treated me incredibly harshly, and it's difficult, if not impossible, to believe that you would want to be a father, much less a loving one."

"You were introduced to me as Logan Lane."

"Lane is my mother's name, and my preferred name. It is my name."

"Are you telling me you dropped the Copeland from your name?"

"I was in the process of legally changing my name. Yes. *Copeland* is a distraction."

He continued to study her, his expression impossible to read. He had such hard, chiseled features and his light eyes were shuttered. And then his mouth eased and his fierce expression softened. "No need to look so stricken. The good news is that we have the chance to fix things. You and I can sort this out without a judge…without the courts. It will be far less messy and painful if we manage our affairs privately. Surely you don't want your *distracting* name bandied about in the press? I would imagine that by now you've had enough media attention to last a lifetime."

Her stomach heaved. The very idea of being in the papers made her want to throw up. She couldn't bear to be chased again. It had been awful when the reporters and photographers shadowed her every move several years ago. She'd felt hunted. Haunted. And that was before Jax. No, Jax's picture could not be splashed about the tabloids. The reporters and photographers were merciless. They'd harass them, and terrify Jax by shouting at them, by pulling up in their cars, honking horns, creating chaos just to get a photo.

Logan exhaled slowly, clinging to her composure. "I have lived very quietly these past few years to stay out of the media."

"A custody battle will just put you right back in the headlines."

She stared at him, furious, frustrated, defiant.

His broad shoulders shifted. His gaze dropped to the papers in his hand. "The funeral has been set for a week from today. It will be held in Greenwich, Connecticut. Your sister Morgan is making the arrangements. Your mother and sisters will be there. It is hoped that you will be there, too." He looked at her once more. For a long moment he was silent before adding, "I hope we will be, but that is up to you."

"This is absurd."

"The grand service for your father…or that we'd attend together?"

"We're not a couple."

"Yet. But we will be."

"Many parents raise children in different homes—"

"Like mine," he interrupted. "And it was hell. I won't have my daughter—"

"Your daughter?" she interrupted bitterly.

"My daughter," he continued as if she hadn't spoken, "being dragged back and forth. It's unsettling for a young child. It's upsetting for an older child. We need to do better than that for her."

She hated that he was saying the very things that she believed to be true.

She hated that he was being the one who sounded responsible and mature.

Having grown up in a divorced family it wasn't what she wanted for Jax, but at the same time, she couldn't imagine a peaceful home, not if she and Rowan were living together in it. "It is better for a child to have two homes than one that is fraught with tension," she said tightly.

"That's why we need to put aside our differences and focus on Jax."

Logan looked away, a lump filling her throat. He made it sound so easy. He made it sound like a trip to an amusement park…but living with Rowan would be anything but fun. He'd hurt her so badly…he'd nearly broken her with his harsh rejection…

"I don't trust you," she whispered.

"Then I must win your trust back."

"That will take forever."

"We don't have that much time. The funeral is in a week."

She shot him a baffled glance. "I'm not sure I follow."

He dropped the papers and sat down in his chair. "We need to marry before the funeral because, if we're to go, we go united. You and me. A family."

"What?"

"We go united," he repeated firmly.

"There is no way…how could we possibly marry this week?"

"Not just this week, but tomorrow. That way we can slip away for a brief honeymoon before flying to Connecticut with Jax for the service."

"And if I refuse?"

"We stay here."

CHAPTER SIX

THEY'D STAY HERE?

Logan's legs went weak. Boneless, she sank into the chair behind her. Her voice was nearly inaudible. "You'd keep me from his service?"

His gaze was cool, almost mocking. "I could say so many things right now… I could say you never told me you were pregnant. I could say you kept me from my daughter—"

"Yes. This is true. But two wrongs don't make a right."

"So, Logan *Lane*, make this right."

Her eyes stung. She blinked hard and bit hard into her lip to keep from saying something she'd regret.

The only thing that had kept her going these past three years when it had been so hard was the belief that one day her life would be different. That one day she and Jax would have everything they needed, that their future would be filled with hope and love and peace…

But there would be no peace with Rowan.

It wasn't the future she'd prayed for. It wasn't the future they wanted or needed.

It wasn't a future at all.

Rowan leaned forward, picked up a thick stack of glossy colored pages and held them out to her. "Pick one or two that appeal and they will be here later tonight."

She took the pages before she realized they were all photographs of couture wedding gowns. Fitted white satin gowns that looked like mermaids and slinky white satin gowns with narrow spaghetti straps, and princess ballgowns with full skirts and gorgeous beading of pearls and precious stones...

The virginal wedding gowns were a punch in the gut and she nearly dropped the stack of designs before letting them tumble onto a nearby end table.

"We'll marry tomorrow night," he added, not sounding in the least bit perturbed by her reaction. "And steal away for a brief honeymoon, and then join your family in Greenwich."

"I'm not getting married like this. I'm not being forced into a marriage against my will."

"I don't want an unwilling wife, either. I want you to want this, too—"

"That's not going to happen."

"Not even for Jax?"

She took a step toward him and her gaze fell on the stack of bridal designs, the top one so outrageously fancy and fussy that it made her stomach cramp. "You don't know me. You know nothing about the real me. You and I would not be compatible. We weren't even compatible for one night—"

"That isn't true. We had an amazing night."

"It was sex."

"Yes, it was. Very, very good sex."

"But four hours or six hours of good sex isn't enough to justify a life together."

"Correct. But Jax is."

His reasonable tone coupled with his reasonable words put a lump in her throat. He was the bad guy. He was the one who'd broken her heart. How dare he act like the hero now?

She blinked away the tears and shook her head and headed for the door.

"We don't have a lot of time," he called after her. "If you won't pick a dress, then I'll have to select it for you."

She stood in the doorway, her back to him. "Your desire to protect Jax means crushing me," she said quietly. "And I know I don't matter to you, that I mean nothing to you, but you should be aware that I wanted more in life, and once I was a little girl, just like Jax, and on the inside, I am still that little girl, and that little girl within me deserves better."

Leaving his paneled study, she walked quickly down the long high-ceilinged hall and, spying an open door before her, went through that, stepping outside into the late afternoon light.

It was no longer raining but the sky was still gray, and the overcast sky turned the vast lawn and banked shrubbery into a landscape of shimmering emerald.

Logan descended the stone steps into the garden, feet crunching damp gravel. She began to walk faster down the path before her, and then she went faster, and then she broke into a run, not because she could escape, but because there was nothing else she could do with the terrible, frantic emotions clawing at her.

She dashed toward a stone fountain and then past that, focusing on the tall neatly pruned green hedges beyond. It wasn't until she was running through the hedges, making turn after turn, confusion mounting, that she realized it was a maze, and then abruptly her confusion gave way to relief.

It felt good to be lost.

There was freedom in being lost…hidden.

She slowed, but still moved, feet virtually soundless on the thick packed soil, so happy to be free of the dark castle with the thick walls and small windows…so happy to be far from Rowan's intense, penetrating gaze.

He didn't know her and yet he seemed to know too much about her, including the worst things about her…such as her weakness for him.

It was true that she couldn't seem to resist his touch, and it shamed her that she'd want someone who despised her. It shamed her that she despised him in return and yet she still somehow craved him.

This wasn't how it was supposed to be.

The physical attraction…the baffling chemistry… was wrong at so many levels.

She rounded a corner and nearly ran straight into Rowan. Logan scrambled backward. "How—" she started before breaking off, lips pinching closed because of course he knew his way about the maze. It was his maze.

His castle.

His world.

Her eyes burned. Her throat ached. She'd struggled for so many years, struggled to provide and be a strong mother, and now it was all being taken from her. Her independence. Her control. Her future.

She didn't want to share a future with him.

She didn't want to share Jax with him.

She didn't want anything to do with him and yet here he was, blocking her path, filling the space between the hedges, tall and broad, so very strong...

"What are you doing?" he asked, his brow furrowing, his expression bemused. "It's damp out. You don't have a coat."

"You've trapped me," she whispered, eyes bright with tears she wouldn't let spill because, God help her, she had to have an ounce of pride. "You've trapped me and you know it, so don't taunt me...don't. It's not fair."

And with a rough oath, he reached for her, pulling her against him, his body impossibly hard and impossibly warm as he shaped her to him. She shivered in protest. Or at least that's what she told herself when dizzying heat raced through her and the blood hummed in her veins, making her skin prickle and tingle and setting her nerves on fire, every one of them dancing in anticipation.

Her head tipped back and she stared up into his eyes, searching the green-gold for a hint of weakness, a hint of softness. There was none.

"I do not know what *fair* means," he said, his voice pitched low as his head dropped and his mouth brushed her temple and then the curve of her ear. "It's not a word that makes sense to me, but you, *mo gra*, you make sense to me when you shouldn't. You make me think that there is something bigger at work here."

"It's sex."

"Good. I like sex."

"It's lust."

"Even better." His lips brushed her cheek and then kissed the corner of her mouth. "I know what to do with that."

"But I want love, not lust." She put her hands on his chest, feeling the hard carved plane of the pectoral muscle and the lean muscular torso below. "I want selfless, not selfish. I want something other than what I've known."

"People are flawed. We are human and mortal and there is no perfection here. Just life." His mouth was on hers and he kissed her lightly and then again, this time the kiss lingered, growing deeper and fiercer, making her pulse jump and her body melt and her thighs press together because he was turning her on… again.

Again.

Just a touch and she ached. A kiss and she went hot and wet and everything in her shivered for him.

And when he bit at the softness of her lower lip, she knew that *he* knew. She knew that he understood her hunger and desire, and the worst part of all was that their history, that one torrid night, meant that she knew he could assuage it, too. But it burned within her, this physical weakness. It burned because she despised any weakness that would give Rowan the upper hand.

"I hate you," she whispered hoarsely.

"You don't." His hands twisted in her hair, tilting her head back, exposing her throat. His lips were on her neck and the frantic pulse beating beneath her ear. He kissed that pulse and then down, setting fire to her neck and the tender collarbone. "You don't hate me. You want me."

She gasped as his hand slid between them, fingers between her thighs, the heel of his palm against her mound.

And he was right. She did want him. But that only intensified her anger and shame.

She should be better than this. Stronger. Smarter.

Or at the very least, more disciplined.

Instead she let her eyes close and her body hum, blood dancing in her veins, making her skin warm and everything within her heat and soften.

She couldn't remember now why she'd found making love to him so incredible and so deeply satisfying, but her memory had clung to the pleasure, and his mouth on her skin was lighting fire after fire, making her legs tremble, dispatching what was left of her resistance.

"We can make this work without love," he said, his hand slowly sliding from her waist up her rib cage to just graze her breast.

She heard his words but they didn't compute, not when she was arching into his hand, longing to feel more, wanting the pressure of his fingers against her sensitive skin, wanting more friction everywhere to answer the wild heat inside of her.

"We don't have to be best friends to find pleasure with each other, either," he added. "We just have to agree that Jax comes first. And I think we can do that."

Then he kissed her so deeply that her brain shut up and her heart raced, silencing reason. She shouldn't want this, but she did. She shouldn't crave the intensity, and yet it ached and burned, demanding satisfaction. With their history, she should know that nothing good would come of this…sex would just be sex… and afterward she'd feel used and hollow, but that was the future and this was the present.

"So is that a yes?" he murmured against her mouth.

"No," she whispered, wanting the pleasure but not the pain.

"You want to be mine."

"No."

"You're mine already. You just need to admit it."

Her lips parted to protest but just then his hand brushed the swell of her breast and the words died unspoken. She shuddered, and the ripple of pleasure made her acutely aware of him. He was tall and muscular and hard. She could feel his erection straining against her. He wanted her. This…chemistry… wasn't one sided.

He brushed the underside of her breast again and she sighed, even as her nipple tightened, thrusting tautly against the delicate satin of her bra.

"Rowan," she choked, trying to cling to whatever was left of her sanity, and yet the word came out husky and so filled with yearning that she cringed inwardly.

"Yes, *a ghra*?"

"This is madness. We can't do this—"

"But we already have. Now we just have to do right by our daughter." He released her, and drew back, his hard handsome features inexplicably grim. "So the only real question is, do you intend to select your bridal gown or am I to do it?"

With the distance came a breath of clarity. "I refuse to be rushed into marriage."

"We're short on time, Logan."

"We're not short on time. We have our entire lives ahead of us. Jax is so young she doesn't know the difference—"

"But *I* do. I want her to have what I didn't have, which is a family."

"No, you had a family. They were just dysfunctional…as most families are." Logan's voice sounded thin and faint to her own ears. She was struggling to stay calm, but deep down had begun to feel as if she was embroiled in a losing battle. Rowan was strong. He thrived on conflict. Just look at his career.

High risk, high stakes all the way.

"You are so focused on the end goal—getting Jax, being with Jax—that you don't realize you're crushing me!"

"I'm not crushing you. I'm doing my best to protect you. But you have to trust me—"

"I don't." Her voice sounded strangled. "At all."

"Then maybe that's what you need to work on."

"Me?"

He shrugged, as if compromising. "Okay, *we*. We need to work on it. Better?"

Back in her suite of rooms, Logan paced back and forth, unable to sit still. It was late, and Jax was asleep in the modified bed that had been assembled earlier against one wall of the huge walk-in closet, which had been turned into a bedroom for the toddler with the addition of a small painted chest, large enough to hold toddler-sized clothes, and provided a place for a lamp. It was a small, brass lamp topped with a dark pink shade that cast a rosy glow on the cream ceiling chasing away shadows and gloom. A framed picture of woodland fairies hung on the wall over the chest, giving Jax something to look at while in her snug bed. Rowan had even made sure Jax would be safe from falling out by adding a padded railing that ran the length of the bed.

But with Jax in bed for the night, Logan had far too much time to think and worry.

And she was worried.

She was also scared.

She was caught up in a sea of change and she couldn't get her bearings. She'd lost control and felt caught, trapped, pushed, dragged about as if she were nothing more than a rag doll.

But she wasn't a doll and she needed control. And

if she had to share power, she'd share with someone she liked and admired and, yes, trusted.

Someone with values she respected.

Someone with integrity.

Rowan had no integrity. Rowan was little more than a soldier. A warrior. Great for battle but not at all her idea of a life partner...

Logan swallowed hard, trying to imagine herself wedded to Rowan. Trying to imagine dinners and breakfasts and holidays, never mind attending future school functions with him...

She couldn't see it.

Couldn't imagine him driving Jax to school or returning to pick her up or sitting in the little chairs for parent-teacher conferences. She couldn't see him being that father who was there. Present.

And then a lump filled her throat because maybe, just maybe, she didn't trust Rowan to love Jax because her father hadn't loved her. Maybe this wasn't about Jax at all—history was full of men who were good parents.

Logan had grown up surrounded by men who knew how to put their families first. Men who were committed and involved. She'd envied her classmates for having devoted fathers...fathers who routinely made it to their daughters' soccer games and dance recitals. Men who zipped up puffy jackets before they took their little girls outside into the cold. Men who'd put out an arm protectively when crossing a busy street. Men who didn't just show up in body but were there emotionally. Men who taught their daughters to ride bikes and drive cars and navigate life.

Logan's eyes stung. She held her breath, holding the pain in.

She'd wanted one of those fathers. She'd wanted someone to teach her about life and love and boys and men.

She'd wanted someone to tell her she was important and valuable. She'd wanted someone to say she deserved to be treated like a princess…like a queen…

Logan blinked, clearing her eyes.

But just because she didn't have a loving, attentive father, it didn't mean that Jax couldn't. Maybe Rowan could be a proper father. Maybe Rowan could teach Jax about life and love and boys…

And men.

Exhaling slowly, Logan glanced from the door of the closet—open several inches so she could keep an ear open in case Jax needed her—to the bedroom door that opened onto the castle hall.

She needed to speak to Rowan.

She didn't know what she'd say, only that she needed to speak to him about the whole marriage thing and family thing and understand what it meant to him. Was he going to be a father in name only or did he really intend to be part of Jax's life?

Because being a father had to be more than carrying on one's family name. Being a father meant *being* there. Being present. Being interested. Being patient. Being loving.

Logan peeked in on Jax and in the rosy pink glow she could see her daughter was fast asleep, her small plump hand relaxed, curving close to her cheek.

Jax's steady breathing reassured her. She was sleeping deeply. She shouldn't wake for hours—not that Logan would be gone hours. Logan planned to find Rowan and speak to him and then return.

She'd be gone fifteen minutes, if that. It'd be a short, calm conversation, and she'd try to see if they couldn't both discuss their vision for this proposed... marriage...and find some common ground, create some rules, so that when she returned to the bedroom she'd feel settled, and perhaps even optimistic, about the future.

At the foot of the staircase Logan encountered an unsmiling man in a dark suit, wearing a white shirt and dark tie.

"May I help you?" he asked crisply, revealing an accent she couldn't quite place.

"I was just going to see Rowan," she answered faintly, brow knitting, surprised to see someone so formally dressed at the foot of the stairs, and then understanding seconds later that he wasn't just anyone in a suit and tie, but a bodyguard...probably one of Rowan's own men. Which also meant he was probably armed and dangerous. Not that he'd pose a threat to her.

"Is he in his study?" she asked, nodding toward the corridor on the opposite side of the stairwell.

"He's retired for the night."

She didn't know how to respond to that, unable to imagine Rowan *retiring* from anything.

"His room is upstairs, just down from yours," the man added.

She knew where Rowan's room was. It was just on the other side of Jax's closet. The suite of rooms all had interior connecting doors, with the closet being shared by both bedrooms, but the door to Rowan's room had been locked and the chest of drawers had been placed in front of it, making the closet more secure.

It had been Rowan's suggestion.

He'd thought Logan would sleep better if she knew that no one could enter the room without her permission.

He was right. She did feel better knowing that the only way in and out of her suite was through the door to the hall, a door she could lock, a door she could control.

She'd been grateful for Rowan's understanding.

"Did he turn in a long time ago?" she asked.

"Quarter past the hour maybe. I can ring him for you, if you'd like."

"Not necessary," she answered lightly. "I can just stop in on my way back to my room."

She hesitated, glancing to the heavy front door across the entry hall.

She wondered just how far she'd get, if she ran for the door. Would she be allowed out? Somehow she suspected not. She sensed that this bodyguard wasn't just there to keep the bad guys out of Castle Ros, but to keep her and Jax *in*.

Rowan wasn't taking any chances.

And just like that she thought of Joe, and how Joe once upon a time must have been a bodyguard very much like this, a tall, silent man in a dark suit. That is, back before Rowan sent Joe to her, and Joe dropped the suit and intense demeanor to become her Joe, the recent college grad grateful to have a job…

Even though he was already employed, and apparently drawing two salaries. Her mouth quirked. She ought to speak to Joe about that.

"I'll head back upstairs," she said. "Good night."

His head inclined. "Good night."

And then she retraced her steps, footsteps muffled on the thick carpeting on the stone steps. The same carpet ran the length of the second-floor gallery with the corridor stretching east and west, marking the two wings of the castle.

Rowan opened his bedroom door just moments after she knocked, dressed in gray joggers and a white T-shirt that stretched tight across his chest and then hung loose over his flat, toned torso.

She couldn't help wondering if he'd been expecting her.

"Can we talk?" she asked.

He nodded and opened the door wider, inviting her in.

As she crossed the threshold, she flushed hot and then cold, her skin prickling with unease. She wasn't sure this was a good decision. She wasn't sure how she'd remain cool and calm if their conversation took place here.

As he closed the door, her eyes went to his oversize

four-poster bed and then to the heavy velvet curtains drawn against the night. The room was close to the same size as hers and had the same high ceiling, but it felt far more intimate. Maybe it was the big antique bed. Or maybe it was the thick drapes blocking the moon. Or maybe it was the man standing just behind her, sucking all of the oxygen out of the room, making her head dizzy and her body too warm.

She drew an unsteady breath and turned to face him, thinking she'd made a mistake. She shouldn't have ever come here, to him.

A tactical error, she thought. And worse, she'd voluntarily entered dangerous territory.

Swallowing her nervousness, she glanced to the chairs flanking the impressive stone hearth. "Can we sit?"

"Of course."

"It's not too late?"

"Not at all. I was just reading. I don't usually sleep for another hour or two."

Her gaze slid over the bed with its luxurious coverlet folded back, revealing white sheets.

She wanted to leave. She wanted to return to her room. It was all too quiet in here, too private. "Maybe it's better if we talk tomorrow. I'm sure you're as tired as I am—"

"Not tired yet. But I will be, later."

"I'm tired, though. Probably too tired to do this tonight. I just thought since Jax was asleep it might be convenient, but I'm worried now she'll wake and be scared…" Her voice drifted off and she swallowed, her mouth too dry.

He said nothing.

Her heart hammered harder. She felt increasingly anxious. He was so intense, so overwhelming. Everything about him made her nervous, but she couldn't tell him that. She couldn't let him know how powerless she felt when with him, and how that was bad, really bad, because she needed control. She needed to be able to protect herself. And Jax.

Logan grasped at Jax now, using her as an excuse to leave Rowan's room. "Let's schedule a chat for the morning. It would be best then. I wasn't thinking when I came here. I really don't want Jax to wake up and be frightened."

"I have security cameras. We'll know if she stirs. You'll be able to be at her side before she even wakes up."

Logan straightened, shocked. He had cameras? *Where?* "You're watching our rooms?"

"I monitor the entire castle. There are cameras everywhere."

"You've been spying on us in our room?"

He sighed and crossed to a wall with dark wood paneling. Shifting a small oil landscape, he pushed a button, and suddenly the wall split, opening, revealing a massive bank of stacked TV screens. There had to be five screens across, and five down, and some of the screens were blanks, while others showed interior castle rooms and corridors, and others revealed exterior shots: entrances, garden paths and distant iron gates.

She walked to the wall of monitors and searched for her room with the pretty canopied bed, but the only thing she could see was the closet door, slightly ajar, just as she'd left it. And then she found another monitor showing the hall outside her room.

No bed shots.

Nothing that indicated he was watching her. At least, not until she'd exited her room and approached his.

So he could have known she was coming to see him. He could have watched her leave her room and walk toward his.

She turned to face him. "You knew I was looking for you. You saw me downstairs talking to the bodyguard."

"I knew you'd left your room. But I don't have the sound on. I never do. It'd be too distracting."

"So you didn't know I was asking for you?"

"I thought maybe you wanted a snack."

She just stared at him, trying to decide if she believed him or not. She wanted to believe him, but there was no trust, and that was a huge problem. "So you closed the door on the cameras when I knocked on your door?"

"Yes."

"You didn't want me to see them."

"I don't want anyone to see them. Security is my business."

"But you showed me."

"I thought you should know they are there. I thought you'd be reassured that Jax isn't alone or in danger."

"But if the door is closed on the screens, how do you monitor movement in the castle?"

"The cameras also alert me to movement, and I get those alerts on my computer, my phone and my watch."

"Can you turn those off?"

"I can disable them or mute them. Usually I just glance at the screen, note the alert and then ignore. I never disable them. It defeats the purpose of being secure."

She turned to pace before the fire.

Rowan said nothing for several minutes, content to just watch her. Finally he broke the silence. "What's on your mind, Logan?"

He didn't sound impatient. There was nothing hard in his tone and yet she felt as if she was going to jump out of her skin any moment now. "I thought maybe we could discuss your proposal," she said, unable to stop moving. Walking didn't just distract her, it helped her process, and it minimized her fear and tension. She didn't want to be afraid. She didn't want to make decisions because she was panicked. Those were never good decisions. "I thought we could see if we couldn't come to some agreement on the terms." She paused by the hearth, glanced at him. "Clarity would be helpful."

"The terms?" he repeated mildly. "It's not a business contract. It's a marriage."

She stiffened at the word *marriage*. She couldn't

help it. It was one thing to imagine Rowan as a father to Jax, but another to consider him as her husband. "Relationships have rules," she said cautiously.

"Rules?"

She ignored his ironic tone and the lifting of his brow. The fact that he sounded so relaxed put her on edge. "Most relationships evolve over time, and those roles, and rules, develop naturally, gradually. But apparently we don't have time to do that, and so I think we should discuss expectations, so we can both be clear on how things would...work."

He just looked at her, green gaze glinting, apparently amused by every word that came from her mouth. His inability to take her seriously, or this conversation seriously, did not bode well for the future. "This isn't a game," she said irritably, "and I'm trying to have an adult conversation, but if you'd rather make a joke of this—"

"I'm not making a joke of anything. But at the same time, I don't think we have to be antagonistic the night before our wedding."

She shot him a fierce look. "We're not marrying tomorrow. There is absolutely no way that is going to happen tomorrow, and should we one day marry, we will not need a honeymoon. That is the most ludicrous suggestion I've heard yet."

"I thought all brides wanted honeymoons."

"If they're in love!" Her arms folded tightly across her chest. "But we're not in love, and we don't need alone time together. We need time with Jax. She ought to be our focus."

"An excellent point. Now please sit. All the marching back and forth reminds me of cadets on parade."

"I'll sit, but only if you do," she said, gaze locking with his. She wasn't about to let him score any points on her. She hadn't survived this long to be beaten by him now. Her father's betrayal and abandonment had been one thing, but to be betrayed and abandoned by her first lover? That had opened her eyes and toughened her up considerably.

"Happy to sit," he replied. "I imagine we will have many future evenings in here, in our respective chairs, you knitting, me smoking my pipe—"

"You don't smoke and I don't knit."

He shrugged. "Then we'll find another way to enjoy each other's company."

She was fairly certain she knew what he meant by *another way to enjoy each other's company*. He'd always been about the sex. Maybe that's because that was the only way he could relate to women. "You're being deliberately provocative."

"I'm trying to get you excited about the future."

"Mmm." She arched a brow. "Are you also going to sell me beachfront property in Oklahoma?"

"No. That's the kind of thing your father did. I'm honest."

Her jaw tightened, hands balling into fists. "You don't have to like him, but I ask you to refrain from speaking of him like that in front of Jax. She doesn't need to be shamed."

"I'm not shaming her. And I'm not shaming you, either—"

"Bullshit."

"I'm just not going to be fake. If I'm upset, I'll tell you. If I'm content, you'll know. And since we're going to raise Jax together, it's better if we're both forthright so there is no confusion about where things stand." He gave her a faint, ironic smile. "Or sit, since that was the whole point."

She shot him a look of loathing before crossing to the hearth and sitting down in one of the large leather chairs, watching as he followed and then took his time sitting down in the chair across from hers.

He smoothed his T-shirt over his lean, flat stomach before extending his legs and crossing them at the ankle, and then he looked up into her eyes and smiled.

"Better?" he asked.

She ground her teeth together. Rowan Argyros was enjoying himself immensely.

"My father was the breadwinner," she said flatly. "My mother was a homemaker. It meant that when they divorced, she still had to depend on him to provide. I will never do that. If we marry, I'm not giving up my career."

"When we marry, we won't end up divorced."

"I'm not giving up my career."

"You barely scrape by. I make millions every year—"

"It's your money. I want my own."

"I'll open a personal bank account for you, deposit whatever you want, up front, and it'll be yours. I won't be able to touch it."

"It will still be your money. I don't want your money. I'm determined to be self-sufficient."

"Why?"

She gave him a long look. "Surely you don't really have to ask that."

"You're the mother of my child. You've struggled these past few years to provide for her. Let me help."

"You can help with Jax's expenses. We will split them. Fifty-fifty."

"What if I provide for Jax and the family, and then you can use your own…money…for your personal expenses?"

She leaned forward. "Why do you say *money* like that?"

"Because you have virtually nothing in your bank account." He rolled his eyes, apparently as exasperated with her as she was with him. "I'm not hurting financially. According to the *Times*, I'm one of the wealthiest men in the UK. I can afford to make sure you're comfortable."

"My work gives me an identity. It gives me purpose."

"Being a mother doesn't do that?"

"This isn't about being a mother. It's about being a woman, and I don't want to be a woman who depends on a man. My mother spent her life living in my father's shadow, and as we both know, he cast a pretty big shadow. I don't want to be defined by a man, and I like being able to contribute to the world."

He said nothing and she added more quietly, a hint of desperation in her voice. "Work makes me feel valuable. It tells me I matter." She looked away, throat working, emotion threatening to swamp her. "I need to matter. I must matter." Her eyes found his again. "Otherwise, what's the point?"

"But you do matter. You're the sun and moon for Jax. You're her everything."

"And what if something happens to Jax? What if—God forbid—there was a tragedy, and I lost her? I'd be lost, too. I'd be finished. There would be nothing left of me." Her voice cracked but she struggled to smile. She failed. "She's everything."

"Nothing is going to happen to her," he said gruffly. "Why would you think that?"

She couldn't answer. She bit down into her lip, her heart on fire, because bad things did happen. Her parents had divorced when she was young and her father had virtually forgotten her and then later it turned out that he was a criminal…he'd stolen hundreds of millions of dollars from his clients…

"Nothing is going to happen," Rowan repeated more forcefully.

She nodded, but tears were filling her eyes and she was pretty sure that she hadn't convinced either of them of anything.

For a long minute it was quiet. Logan knit her fingers together in her lap, knuckles white. Rowan didn't say anything, deep in thought. She glanced at him several times, thinking he'd lost the glint in his eyes, aware that his hard features had tightened, his mouth now flattened into a grim line.

She couldn't handle the silence any longer. "Maybe I shouldn't feel that way. Maybe it seems irrational—"

"It doesn't." His voice, pitched deep, cut her short.

She looked at him, surprised.

His broad shoulders shifted. "My little brother's death destroyed my mother, and it ended my parents marriage."

"You lost a brother?"

He nodded. "I was seven. Devlin was two, nearly three."

Jax's age.

He knew what she was thinking. She could see it in his eyes.

"But that won't happen to Jax," he added roughly, his voice as sharp as ground glass. "I will make sure nothing happens to her. And that's a promise."

She couldn't look at him anymore, couldn't stomach more of the same conversation. Jax was so valuable. Jax was perfect and innocent, not yet hurt by life or other people. She didn't yet know that people—even those who claimed to care about you—would fail you. Hurt you. Maybe even deliberately hurt you.

Logan hadn't remained a virgin so long because she didn't have options. Her virginity wasn't kept because there weren't men available but because she wanted to hold part of herself back. She wanted to save herself for the right person. She'd wanted to give that one thing—that bit of innocence—to a man who'd value her.

How she'd gotten that wrong!

Being disappointed was a fact of life. Learning to

deal with that disappointment, another critical life lesson. And it was fine to learn about life, and have to accept loss and change, but far better if those lessons came later. If the individual self was shaped and formed. Strong.

"You and I can make sure Jax is safe," Rowan said quietly, drawing her attention to him. "With vigilance we can give her the life I know you want for her."

Logan blinked tears away. "What life do I want for her?"

His gaze held hers for an extra long moment. "You don't want her crushed. You don't want her broken. You want her to remain a child as long as possible— safe, loved, cherished." He hesitated, and the silence hung there between them, weighted. "You want to give her the childhood you never had."

His words cut, pricking her when she didn't have the proper defenses. Startled, uncomfortable, she left her chair, crossing the floor a ways to stand before the bank of monitors. Jax's door remained ajar, just as she'd left it. She suddenly wished she could see Jax, though. She wanted to be sure the little girl was still soundly sleeping.

"Do you have sound, if you wanted it?" she asked thickly, keeping her back to him even as the threat of tears deepened her voice.

"Yes."

"Can you turn it on in her room? Or in my room? So we can check to see if it's quiet or if she's crying?"

"I could turn the camera in her room on. If you'd like?"

She glanced at him now. "So there is a camera in the closet?"

"I disabled it earlier, but I can turn it on."

"I didn't see one in the closet. Where is it?"

"It's positioned in the crown molding, hidden in the shadows of the woodwork."

"It's very small then?"

"No bigger than the head of a writing pen."

"Are cameras truly manufactured that small?"

"Mine are."

"You make cameras?"

He shrugged. "One of my companies manufactures cameras and security equipment. These small cameras are now used all over the world, in every big hotel, casino, government building." He crossed to her side, tapped several buttons on a panel and suddenly one of the dark screens came to life, and then he tapped another key on the panel and she could see Jax in her little bed, still sound asleep, although she now lay on her back, arms up by her head.

Logan shot him a troubled look. "I hate that you can spy on us."

"I don't spy on you. I haven't spied on you ever."

"Joe…?"

"Protection. And the cameras that remain are for protection.

"I deactivated all of the cameras in the closet, the bathroom, the bedroom, but the one positioned on the closet door. I thought it was important to know if Jax wandered out."

Logan shot him another assessing look. "Or if someone wandered in."

"Yes."

"Does that include me?"

"You're her mother."

"Which is why you're afraid I might try to run away with her."

He made a soft, tough mocking sound. "It's crossed my mind," he agreed. "More than once."

The smiling curve of his firm mouth just barely reached his eyes. His green gaze wasn't as warm as it was challenging. She didn't understand what she saw, didn't understand the tension or emotion…if it was emotion. But then he was an enigma, and he had been from the start.

That night at the auction he'd given her the same look—long, searching, challenging.

He'd looked at her with such focus that he didn't seem to be standing across the room, not part of the auction, but all by himself, and it was just the two of them in the room.

Everyone fell away that night in March.

The music, the sound, the master of ceremonies at the microphone.

There was just Rowan standing on the side of the stage looking at her, making her go hot and cold and feel things she didn't know a stranger could make her feel.

"And why would I run from you?" she asked, her chin lifting, her voice husky. She wasn't going to be the one to break eye contact. She wasn't going to back down. Not from him, not from anyone.

"Because you know when I take you to bed, it'll change everything. Again."

Her stomach flipped and her head suddenly seemed unbearably light, as if all the blood had drained away. "That's not happening." Thank God her voice was relatively firm because her legs were definitely unsteady.

"You sound so sure of yourself."

"Because I know myself. And I know you now, and I know how devastating it would be to go to bed with you—and not because you're good in bed, but because you're cruel out of bed, and I don't need more cruelty in my life."

"That was three years ago."

"Perhaps, but standing here with you, it seems like yesterday."

He shrugged. "I can't change the past."

"No, you certainly cannot."

And then he was reaching out to lift a heavy wave of hair off her face, his palm brushing her cheek as he pushed the hair back, slipping it behind her ear. "But I can assure you the future will be different."

His touch sent a shiver coursing through her. "I don't want—" she started to say before breaking off, because he was still touching her, his fingers sweeping her cheekbones, his fingertip skimming her mouth, making it tingle.

"Mmm?" he murmured, eyebrow lifting. "I'm listening, love."

She stared up into his eyes, her heart racing even faster, beating in a hard, jagged rhythm that made it difficult to catch her breath, much less speak. But how could she speak when her thoughts were scattered, coherent thought deserting her at the slightest touch?

"You know," he said thoughtfully, combing her hair back from her face to create a loose ponytail in one hand, "I never asked you about relationships you might have left behind…is there someone significant…?"

He was seducing her with his touch. She couldn't resist the warmth, couldn't resist the tenderness in his touch. She hated that she responded to his caress this way, hated that she felt starved for affection. He wasn't the right man for her. He'd never be the right man. "No."

"Why not? You're young and stunning—"

"And a mother with a young child dependent on me."

"You didn't want to meet someone…someone who could help you, make things easier for you?"

"*No.*"

"Why not?"

"Surely it doesn't surprise you that I don't have a lot of confidence in men? That the men I've known—" she gave him a significant look "—cared only for themselves, too preoccupied by their own needs and their own agendas to take care of anyone else."

"You're not describing me."

"Oh, I most certainly am."

"Then you don't know me, and it's time to change that. Starting now. Tonight."

CHAPTER SEVEN

HE CAPTURED HER MOUTH with his, shaping her to him. The kiss had fire and an edge that revealed far more of his emotional state than he preferred her to know, but right now he was damned if he cared about anything but taking what he wanted. And he wanted her.

He would bed her tonight.

He would claim her as his.

He wondered if she even realized that she didn't stand a chance because, now that she was here at Castle Ros, he wasn't about to lose her.

He'd made the mistake once. He wouldn't make the same once twice. And, no, his feelings weren't tender or loving, but passion and possession didn't require love. Passion and possession needed heat, and there was plenty of that.

"Mine," he murmured against her mouth, making her heart race.

She heard him but couldn't decipher it, not when heat flooded her, making her weak.

His kiss did this to her. His kiss turned her inside out, confusing her, making her forget who she was and why they didn't work…

Because right now they did work. Right now he tasted like life and hunger and passion, and she wanted more, not less. And no, it wasn't safe, but she hadn't lost control in years…not since she was last with him…and suddenly she was desperate to be his…desperate to feel him and know him and remember why she'd given herself to him.

What had made him the one?

He shaped her to him, his powerful body hard against her and his mouth firm, nipping at her lip, parting her lips, tasting her. He wanted more from her, too. More response. More heat. The insistent hunger of his kiss made her head dizzy and legs tremble.

She clung to him, feeling one of his hands at the swell of her breasts. She shuddered and then shuddered again as he cupped her breast, sending sensation rushing through her. She made a hoarse sound of pleasure and he practically growled with satisfaction.

She felt his hands on the hem of her sweater, lifting the hem and tugging it up over her head, and then he was at the waistband of her trousers, tugging the zipper down before glancing at her feet and noticing the boots. He pushed her back onto the bed so that he could remove one boot and then the other, and then the trousers were gone, leaving her in just her bra and matching pantie.

She reached for his coverlet, wanting to hide, but he leaned over her, pinning her hands to the mattress.

"I want to look," he growled, his voice deepening, his Irish accent becoming pronounced.

She felt shy and she closed her eyes, but even with

her eyes closed she could feel his burning gaze, which drank her in the way a parched man drinks a tall, cool glass of water.

His head dipped, and his lips brushed her jaw and then the column of her throat.

Air bottled in her lungs and her toes curled as he kissed down her throat to the hollow between her collarbones.

She shouldn't like this so much. She shouldn't want his mouth and his tongue and his skin…but she did.

She loved his firm grip on her wrists and the way he pinned her to the bed, his body angled over hers, his knees on the outside of her thighs.

His mouth trailed lower, his lips between her breasts and then light on the silky fabric of her bra, his breath warm through the delicate fabric, teasing the pebbled nipple with the lightest scraping of teeth, making her arch up, and her hips shift restlessly.

He worked his way to the other breast, teeth catching at the edge of the bra, and then sliding his tongue along the now-damp fabric, his tongue tracing the line of her bra against her skin.

She could feel the rasp of his beard and the heat of his mouth and as erotic as it was, it wasn't enough.

Her hips rocked up. She felt hot and wet and empty.

He could fill her. He should fill her. Hard. Fast. Slow and fast.

Anything, everything.

"You know what I want," she whispered, licking her upper lip because her mouth had gone so dry.

His head lifted, and he gazed down at her. "And you know what I want," he answered.

"I want sex and you want a wife." She'd meant it bitterly but her voice was so husky the words came out breathless. "Something seems wrong here."

"It's easy to have sex. It's harder to find the right wife."

"I'm not the right wife."

"You are now."

"Because of Jax."

"Because of Jax," he agreed, head lowering, his mouth capturing one taut nipple and sucking hard on the sensitive tip.

He worked the nipple until she was writhing and panting beneath him.

"Rowan, Rowan—"

"Yes, *mo chroi*?"

"You're torturing me."

"Just as I will torture you every night in my bed." He blew on the damp silk of the bra, warm air across the pebbled nipple. "I'm going to do this to your pussy, until you come."

"Rowan. I want you in me."

"I know you do, but I'm not ready to give you what you want. I think you need to be punished—"

"For what?"

"Where do I start?" He bit down on the nipple making her cry out. "You should have told me who you were...you should have told me you were a virgin...you should have told me you were pregnant..." He looked down at her, green-gold eyes blazing. "Should I go on?"

"But that's it. That's all. There's nothing else I've done wrong."

"So you admit you were wrong."

Her eyes closed as she felt his hand on her hip, caressing the hipbone. "I could have been better at communicating," she whispered, pulse racing, thinking she should tell him to stop even though she didn't want him to stop.

And then his hand was between her thighs, cupping her mound, the heel of his palm pressing against her, filling her with hot sharp darts of sensation, and his mouth was taking hers again, all heat and honey and mind-drugging pleasure.

She'd wanted him that first night they'd met, and oh, she wanted him again now. Maybe even more because she knew how good he felt, his body buried deep in hers, making her body come to life with each maddening thrust, the slow deep strokes making her hope and want and feel, and she'd cling to him just as she had then, and for those moments they were joined, there was nothing else she needed...

And then his head lifted and his heavy-lidded green-gold gaze searched hers. "You want me."

It was impossible to deny when her arms were now wrapped tightly around his neck. "Yes."

"You need me."

Her body was on fire. "Yes."

"But you don't like me, you don't trust me and you won't marry me."

"We don't know each other. We're just...good in bed."

The corner of his mouth lifted. "But it's a start."

"We can't base a marriage on sex!"

His broad shoulders shifted and yet his eyes bored into hers. "There are plenty of couples who don't even have that."

A lump filled her throat. She loved the feel of him against her, the weight of his muscular body and the heat of his chest where it rested on hers and she dug her fingers into the short, crisp strands of hair at his nape and tugged. "I'm tired of being grateful for small mercies."

"Sometimes all we get are small blessings."

Her heart did a painful thump. "I want more." It hurt to speak but she forced herself to add, "I refuse to settle for less."

And then after a long moment where she felt as if he was staring deep into her soul, his head dropped and he was kissing her again, his hand sliding around to unfasten the hook on her bra and peeling it away. His lips captured an exposed nipple, and her breath caught in her throat as he licked the tip, making it wet and then moving to the other nipple. The combination of warm wet mouth and then cool air made her belly clench and her thighs press tight. She tugged on his hair, holding him to her breast, as he began to suckle harder.

It was impossible to silence her husky groan of pleasure, impossible to not lift her hips to find his. She needed more from him. She needed all of him.

She'd gone years—three years—without his touch… without any touch from any man…and yet now, together like this, she felt as if she'd shatter if she didn't have him tonight.

He was peeling off her panties, dragging the scrap of satin down her bare legs and then tugging off his own T-shirt and joggers.

His erection sprang free and her gaze went to his torso with the sculpted muscle, the hard taut abdomen, the corded thighs and of course, the thick, long shaft at full attention.

The air caught in her throat as she took him in.

He was beautiful.

Her first. Maybe her last.

It didn't make sense and yet in some ways, it was exactly as it should be. She'd lost her head over him, giving him not just her virginity but her heart.

And she had given him her heart.

She'd fallen for him hard, so hard, and she'd imagined that he'd cared for her, thinking it was impossible to make love the way they had without feelings being involved...

She'd been sure there were feelings, the lovemaking so intense it'd felt somehow as if they were soul mates. Perfect and perfectly made for each other.

And now, here they were, three years older and wiser and yet she still craved the feel of his mouth and the taste of him and the feel of him...

"Look at you, such a bold thing," he drawled, shifting over her, his knees pushing between hers, making room for him between her thighs. "Getting an eyeful, are you?"

Her lips curved faintly. "There's a lot to look at."

"Disappointed?"

"You know you've got the…goods."

"Small blessings, *mo chroi*."

"I wouldn't say small in this case." She reached out and touched his rigid length. He was warm and silken and hard all at the same time. She heard his sharp inhale as she stroked the length of him so she did it again. He pulsed in her palm, straining against her. Just the feel of him made her ache on the inside. "Definitely not small."

His eyes gleamed as he lowered himself to kiss the valley between her breasts and then down her rib cage to her belly. He'd slipped a hand between her thighs, parting them wider and giving him access to her delicate skin and tender pink folds.

Logan sucked in a breath as he found her, gently exploring her sex, and she was ready for him, already so wet. Her eyes closed as she felt his hands moving, touching, stirring her up, making her shiver.

She was ready for him, so wet, and she could feel him slipping a teasing finger over her dampness and then tracing the softness, lightly dragging the moisture up over silken skin to her sensitive nub. He knew just how to touch her and the pressure of his finger against her clit made her heart pound. Sparks of light filled her head while honey poured through her veins…

He kissed her taut, tense belly as he stroked her, and then he kissed down her abdomen, until he was parting her inner lips to lick the tender clit. She gasped as his tongue flicked across her, making her go hot and cold. The pleasure of his mouth on her was so intense it was almost painful. Her toes curled and she buried her hand in his hair, her breath coming faster, shorter as he pressed fingers into her core, finding that invisible spot that heightened sensation. He thrust deeper into her, stroking that spot as he sucked on her nub and did it again and again so that she couldn't hang on to a single rational thought, her body no longer her body but his to play with and control.

Logan dragged in great gulps of air as he brought her closer and closer to orgasm. She dug one heel into the bed, trying to resist, doing her best to hold off from climaxing, in part because she wasn't ready for something so intense, but also because it felt so amazing she wasn't ready for it to end. But Rowan wasn't about to let her escape. He was far too clever with his fingers, and he knew how to control her with his mouth and teeth and tongue, and then the tip of his tongue flicked over her so slowly that she broke, the orgasm so intense that she almost screamed, but caught herself in time. Tears filled her eyes instead.

Hell.

He took her to heaven and then dropped her into hell.

It wasn't supposed to be this way. It wasn't supposed to feel this way. She shouldn't want him when he'd wounded her so deeply.

And then he was stretching next to her, his large powerful body pulling her close, and he kissed her, deeply, and even though he'd yet to bury his body inside her, she knew he was staking claim. His hands cupped her face, his mouth drank her in.

Mine, his fierce carnal kiss seemed to say. *You belong to me.*

But then he was drawing back, and he studied the tears slipping from her eyes. "What hurts?" he asked.

She looked up into his eyes. It was hard to breathe when it felt as if a concrete block rested on her chest. It took her forever to answer. "My heart."

He held her gaze for another long moment and then his head dropped and his lips brushed hers. "Hearts heal." And then, kissing her, he shifted his weight, his hips wedged between her thighs.

She felt the thick smooth head of his shaft against her, pressing at her entrance and it felt good. He felt good.

She hated that.

She wished she could tell him to get lost, to go screw himself, to leave her alone but she didn't want that. She didn't want him anywhere but here, against her, with her.

"You make me want to hate you," she choked even as his thick rounded tip just pressed inside her body. She was wet and he was so warm and smooth and even though the tip was just barely inside her, intense pleasure rippled through her. It was the most exquisite sensation, him with her.

"You hate me because you like it so much," he answered, nipping at her neck, finding more nerves, creating more pleasure.

He was right. She shouldn't welcome his touch

when she didn't like him, but separating sensation and reason was impossible when he was close to her. Something happened when he was near…something so intense it was like a chemical reaction.

He was a drug.

Potent. Dangerous.

Like now.

He was there at her entrance, the tip just barely inside her. He didn't thrust deeper. He didn't even move his body. And yet her body was going wild, squeezing him, holding him, desperate to keep him with her, in her.

"So hate me," he murmured, slipping in just another inch, if that. "I don't mind."

Her body pulsed. She struggled to get air into her lungs. Her skin felt so hot that she wanted to rip it off.

"You love this," she gritted, her nails raking his shoulders.

"I love that I can make you feel so good."

"If you really wanted me to feel good, you'd do something."

"I think you're feeling really good right now."

She didn't know about that. Her body felt wild. Her inner muscles were convulsing, squeezing the thick rounded tip of his shaft, again and again. She'd never felt anything like this and she couldn't figure out if she loved it or hated it, so hard to know what she wanted when everything within her was so turned on.

"It's not enough," she said breathlessly.

"What would you like then?"

"You know."

And he did know, because he did it just then, thrusting hard into her body, seating himself deeply.

She nearly groaned out loud. *This*...this was what she wanted. Her arms wrapped around his shoulders and she held him tightly to her, her eyes burning and her throat aching because she felt overwhelming emotion...

She'd missed him somehow.

She had.

Even though he'd broken her heart, she'd missed him and this...

And the tears seeped from beneath her lashes, as she struggled to contain the emotion and the pain.

"Don't cry, *mo chroi*," he said, shifting his weight to his forearms to pull out and then thrust in again, slowly, deeply. "It's not bad to feel good. Let me make you feel good."

Her head knew everything about this was dangerous. Everything would just fall apart later but right now she couldn't think clearly. She had no defenses against this...against him. He made her come alive. He made her feel. Her spine tingled. Her skin prickled.

"Make me feel good then," she whispered, giving in.

He began to move, burying himself deeply just to draw back out, his length so warm inside of her. Each thrust brushed against that sensitive spot within her, and each thrust put pressure on her clit, so that he stroked nerve endings inside and outside and there was no way to resist the tension coiling within her. It was just a matter of time before she'd come again.

It was just a matter of time before he'd make her shatter again.

His tempo increased, and his body thrust harder, faster, and she clung tighter, answering each thrust with a lift of her hips, pressing up against him to create the most tension and friction.

He growled his pleasure, and from his quickening tempo, she knew he was close to coming but he held back for her, determined to give to her, and she wanted to hold back just to defy him…it seemed so important to defy him…but his hand moved between them and he was stroking her clit and there was no resisting him. She climaxed just seconds before he did and he bore down on her, driving into her, filling her with his seed.

It was only then that her little voice whispered, *This is how one gets pregnant…*

Of course.

A great way to trap her was to put another baby into her womb. Give them another life to protect.

She didn't want to cry now. She wanted to hit him. Fight him.

"You may have made me pregnant," she said hoarsely as he shifted his weight, settling onto his side on the mattress next to her.

"Yes," he answered, pulled her onto her side so that he could hold her close to his chest, his long legs tangling with hers.

She stiffened. "That's not a good thing."

"Jax would like a brother or a sister."

"How can you say that?" She struggled to sit up but he didn't let her escape. "You don't even know her!"

He shrugged, his arms like iron bands. "All kids benefit from a sibling."

And then when he said no more, she glanced back at him and his eyes were closed, his long lashes resting on his high cheekbones. His even breathing told her he was already asleep.

She told herself she'd never be able to sleep like this. She told herself it would be impossible to relax. How could she doze off when her mind was racing? And yet somehow, minutes later, she was asleep, still captive in Rowan's muscular arms.

CHAPTER EIGHT

ROWAN LAY AWAKE, Logan sleeping at his side. He'd been awake for the past hour, listening to her breathe and thinking about the night.

It'd been years since he'd felt so much hunger and need, years since he'd wanted a woman the way he wanted Logan tonight.

Just remembering the lovemaking made him hard all over again. He'd found such erotic satisfaction in the shape of her, the softness of her skin, the scent of her body, the intensity of her orgasms.

He loved the taste of her and the urgency of her cries as she climaxed.

He hadn't felt this way about a woman since...

The March 31 when he'd first bedded Logan Lane.

The corner of his mouth pulled and he lightly stroked her hair where it spilled across his chest.

She wanted things he couldn't give her—romance, love—but he could give her other things, important things...stability, security, permanence.

He wasn't going anywhere. He wouldn't abandon her. He'd never betray their daughter, either.

And just because he couldn't give love, that didn't mean their relationship had to be empty or cold. This physical connection was hot. There was no reason they couldn't enjoy the heat and pleasure. They should take pleasure in each other. There would be no other.

Marriage was a commitment. He would be committed. Love wasn't necessary. In fact, love was a negative. It added pain and unnecessary complications. They didn't need the emotion. He didn't need it, and she'd be fine without it, too.

Logan woke and for a moment she didn't know where she was.

The bed was strange. Huge and imposing with its monster antique four-poster frame—and yet the white sheets were so soft and smooth they felt delicious against her skin.

Stretching, her body felt tender. Between her thighs it felt very tender.

And then she remembered it all. Rowan's mouth on her. His cock filling her. His expertise that made her come once, and then again.

And in the next moment she remembered Jax and she glanced at the wall of monitors to check the camera in Jax's room, but the screens were dark. The monitors were turned off.

Logan flung herself from bed, panicked. She grabbed the nearest piece of clothing—Rowan's T-shirt—pulled it over her head and raced back to her room. The curtains were open, sunlight poured through the tall, narrow windows, the sky beyond a hopeful blue.

Jax's bed in her closet bedroom was empty.

Logan tried to calm herself, knowing that in this place nothing bad would happen to Jax. The Irish nanny, Orla, probably had her. They were undoubtedly playing fairy-something somewhere, but until Logan saw Jax, and knew without a doubt that Jax was safe, Logan couldn't relax.

She stepped into shorts and dashed from her room, running down the stairs by two.

There were no bodyguards at the foot of the stairs today. The huge stone entry was empty. She went to Rowan's study. That was empty, too.

Where was he? Where was everyone? Had Rowan taken Jax and gone? Leaving her here?

She retraced her steps, returning to the impressive staircase but turning left instead of right and kept going until she reached the castle's kitchen. It was a cavernous vaulted space made of stone and dramatic arches. The huge commercial oven was tucked into what once must have been a medieval hearth, and a bank of tall, sleek stainless-steel refrigerators took up another wall. The kitchen was warm and smelled of yeast and warm bread. A woman had been bent over in front of the wood-topped island and now straightened. Startled by the appearance of Logan, she plunked her mixing bowl of rising dough on the island and wiped her hands clean on a nearby dish towel. "Hello. Can I help you with something?"

"My daughter," Logan said urgently. "I can't find her."

"Your little one is with Mr. Argyros." She turned to the stove, and pulled out a tray of golden scones and then another and placed them on top of the stove. "You'll find them outside in the garden." The cook nodded toward the garden beyond the kitchen door. "You can go that way. It's quickest."

"Thank you."

The air was cool and the gravel path hurt her feet. She should have worn shoes but Logan wasn't going back until she found Jax. She hurried down the path, trying not to shiver, telling herself there was no need to be afraid, but what if Jax was scared and Rowan wasn't patient? What if Jax was in one of her toddler moods—

She stopped short as she rounded the corner.

There between the hedges and the castle's kitchen herb garden was a little round table with matching painted chairs. A delicate lace cloth covered the pale blue wooden table and in one chair sat Jax, a tiny crown on top of her head, and in the other sat Rowan, looking beastly big in his pixie-sized chair. He was holding a miniature china cup and Jax was reaching for her cup and beaming up at him as if she was a real princess and Rowan her prince.

Logan couldn't breathe. She'd never seen Jax look at anyone like that. Not even Joe, whom she adored.

Logan's pulse still raced but her heart felt unhinged, flip-flopping around inside of her, hot emotions washing through her, one after another.

They were having a tea party in the garden. A father-daughter tea party.

And not just a casual affair, but this one had an arrangement of purple pansies in a little milk pitcher, and a silver tiered tray of sweets filled with little iced cakes and fragrant golden scones.

Someone had gone to a great deal of effort. Had Orla planned this? It seemed to be the sort of thing a professional nanny would think of, and yet there was something about the way the pansies spilled out of the pitcher that made Logan think this wasn't Orla, but someone else…

Her gaze settled on Rowan. He was smiling at Jax, his expression infinitely warm and protective. Doting, even.

Logan's eyes burned and she struggled to get air into her lungs but she couldn't see and she couldn't think, not when she was feeling so much.

Rowan looked like a giant in the small blue chair, his shoulders immense, drawing his shirt tight across his broad back, while the fine wool of his black trousers outlined his muscular thighs.

But Jax wasn't the least bit intimidated by the size of Rowan. If anything, she was delighted with her company, beaming up at Rowan as she sipped her tea, her chubby fingers clutching the little cup before she set it back down to ask if he needed more tea.

He nodded and Jax reached for the pot to top off his cup. As she started to pour the tea, she noticed her mother, set the pot down with a bang, and waved to Logan. "Mommy!"

"Hello, sweet girl," Logan said, blinking away tears before Jax could see them.

"We're having a party!" Jax cried, reaching up to adjust her tiara. "I'm a princess."

"Yes, you are." Logan walked toward their little table, but avoided Rowan's gaze. He was too much of everything.

Jax frowned at her mother's bare legs. "Where are your clothes, Mommy?"

"I need some, don't I?"

"Yes. You look naked." Jax sounded scandalized.

"I know, and it's a princess party. I'm terribly underdressed. I'm sorry."

Logan leaned over and dropped a kiss on her daughter's forehead. "Is that real tea you're drinking?"

Jax nodded vigorously. "Yes."

"If apple cider is tea," Rowan replied, his voice pitched low, but even pitched low she heard the amusement in it.

She darted a glance in his direction, not sure what to expect, but thinking he'd be smug this morning, after last night.

Instead his expression was guarded. He seemed to be gauging her mood.

Logan wished she knew how she felt. Everything was changing and she felt off balance and unable to find her center. "Is this her breakfast?" she asked, noting the little cakes and miniature scones on the tiered plate taking center stage on the table.

"It's *tea*, Mommy," Jax said sounding a bit exasperated. "Breakfast was at breakfast." She then looked at Rowan, and her expression softened, her tone almost tender as she asked him, "More tea?"

"I haven't drunk my last cup," he answered Jax regretfully.

"Then drink it." Jax turned back to her mother, earnestly adding, "We only have two cups. Sorry, Mommy."

Logan couldn't help thinking that Jax didn't seem the least bit sorry that her mother couldn't join them. The little girl was soaking up the attention. "That's okay. I should probably go dress." But Logan found it hard to walk away. The party was so charming and Jax had never not wanted her company before. It was new, and rather painful, being excluded.

Rowan glanced at her, looking almost sympathetic. "You don't have to leave. We can find you a chair, if you'd like."

The fact that he seemed to understand her feelings made it even worse. He wasn't supposed to be the good guy. He was the bad guy. And yet here he was, dressed up in black trousers and a white dress shirt, balancing himself in a pint-size chair, and drinking apple cider in a cup about the size of a shot glass.

"How nice of Orla to arrange this," she said, injecting a brisk cheerful note into her voice. "I'll have to thank her when I see her."

"Orla won't be here for another half hour," Rowan answered.

Logan frowned, confused. "But she made arrangements for the tea, yes?"

"No," he said.

"My daddy did," Jax said, casting another loving look on Rowan.

Her daddy.

Daddy.

He'd told her.

Logan shot Rowan a disbelieving look, and he was prepared. He didn't shy away—instead he met her gaze squarely, apparently utterly unrepentant.

She felt completely blindsided and her lips parted to protest, but she swallowed each of the rebukes because this wasn't the time, not in front of Jax.

"We'll talk when Orla arrives," he said casually, as if he hadn't just pulled the ultimate power play, rocking her world again.

How dare he? How dare he?

She was so shocked. So upset. Anger washed over her in hot, unrelenting waves. "Is that what this party was for?"

"Orla will be here in thirty minutes." His voice was calm and quiet but she heard the warning underneath. *Don't do this now. Don't upset Jax.*

She bit back the hot sharp words that filled her head and mouth, battling the sense of betrayal.

He played dirty. He'd always played dirty. He would never change.

Her eyes stung and her throat sealed closed and it was all she could do to hold her emotions in. No wonder he'd been so successful in his career. He was extremely strategic. And he had no conscience. He didn't care who he hurt, not as long as he won.

"You've time for a hot bath and a light bite," he added conversationally. "I'm sure you'd feel better with some coffee and food in you. It's already past lunch. You must be hungry."

"It's past lunch?"

"Yes. It's already after two."

"Two?"

"You had a good sleep-in, and a well-deserved one." He briefly turned his attention to Jax as she'd just offered him a little iced cake from her own plate. The cake was now looking a tad sticky but he accepted it with a smile of pleasure.

He held his smile as he focused back on Logan. "I'm glad you slept. I think you were...spent."

She heard his deliberate hesitation and knew exactly what he was implying. She was spent because he'd worn her out with his amazing performance last night.

"It was a grueling day," she agreed shortly, turning away because there was nothing else she could do. She wasn't wanted at the garden party and she was cold in just the T-shirt.

Shivering, Logan returned to the kitchen to see about coffee and one of those scones she'd spotted coming out of the oven.

"Do you think I could get some coffee and one or two of those scones?" she asked the cook.

"I'll send up a tray immediately," the cook promised.

The tray with coffee and scones, and a bowl of fresh berries, was delivered just minutes later to Logan's bedroom, and Logan sat cross-legged on the large bed, enjoying several cups of coffee and the warm flakey scones slathered with sweet Irish butter and an equally thick layer of jam, before bathing and dressing.

By the time Jax returned to the room, Logan was very much ready to shift into mommy mode, but Jax had other ideas. After giving her mother a big hug and kiss she announced that she and Orla were going to watch a movie in the castle theater.

"But wait, how was tea?" Logan asked.

"Lovely."

Lovely. Now that wasn't a word American toddlers used often. "Did Orla teach you that word?"

"No, my daddy did."

Once again, *her daddy.*

She ground her teeth together, struggling with another wave of resentment. For the past two plus years she'd been the center of Jax's world, fiercely vigilant, determined to be both mother and father, and yet overnight her role had been changed. She'd been nudged over—no, make that shoved—and she was supposed to be good with it. She was supposed to just accept that Rowan was now in their lives, making changes, shifting power, redefining everything.

"What do you think of him?" she asked carefully.

"My daddy?"

"Yes."

"He's nice."

Logan smiled grimly. "He is, isn't he?"

"Orla says he's lovely."

So that's where she learned the word. Wonderful. "And where is Orla?" Logan asked, determined to hide her anger from Jax, even as she made a mental note of yet one more thing to discuss with Rowan. It was unprofessional for nannies—even cheerful Irish ones—to refer to their male bosses as lovely.

"Outside, in the hall."

Logan went to the door and opened it, and yes, there stood Orla with her ready smile. "Good afternoon," Orla greeted Logan with a lilt in her voice. "Did Jax tell you we're going to go see *Cinderella* in the theater?"

"No." Logan was finding it very difficult to keep up with all the twists and turns in the day. "There's a theater here?"

"Yes, ma'am. Downstairs in the basement."

"Castles have basements?"

"Well, it was the dungeon but we don't want to scare the little girl." And then she winked at Logan. "Or the big girls, either."

And then Orla and Jax were off, walking hand in hand as they headed for the stairs, both apparently very excited about the movie. The movie, undoubtedly, being Rowan's idea.

Which meant it was time to deal with Rowan.

Logan stepped into shoes, grabbed a sweater, and went to find him. It wasn't a simple thing in a castle the size of Ros. She checked the study and then outside, walking through one garden and then another, before returning to the house and climbing the stairs back to the second floor where she opened the door of his bedroom to see if by chance he was there.

He was. And he was in the middle of stripping off his clothes and he turned toward her, completely naked.

Her gaze swept over him, lingering on the thick planes of his chest, the narrow hips, the tight, honed abs and then below. He was gorgeous.

He knew it, too.

"Come back for more, have you?" he asked, his smile cocky.

Logan flushed but didn't run away. She closed the door behind her. "You had no business telling her you were her father—"

"Oh, I absolutely did." His smile was gone. "You were in no hurry to tell her."

"I had a plan."

"I'm sure you did. One that didn't include me." His dark hair was damp. His body still gleamed with perspiration. He made no attempt to cover himself. "But I'm not interested in being shut out or being relegated to the background as if I'm on your staff. I'm her father, not a babysitter or hired help."

She wished he'd put his clothes back on. How could she argue with Rowan when he was naked? "I've never said you were hired help," she snapped.

"You certainly haven't treated me as an equal, have you? But you're a Copeland. Why should I expect otherwise?"

"Not that again!"

He walked toward her, muscles taut, jaw tight.

"Not that again? I'm not allowed to be troubled by your family? By your sordid history? I'm not supposed to care that your father destroyed my family?" He made a rough low sound, correctly reading her surprise. "Yes. Your father quite handily dismantled my family. It's embarrassing how quickly he ruined us. I blame my father, too. He was the one who chose to work for your father."

He paused to search her face. "Yes, my father once worked for your father. Did you know that?" He laughed shortly, mockingly. "And your father was underhanded even then, already an expert in white-collar crime."

Her heart raced and she held her breath, shoulders squared, bracing herself for the rest.

"Your father has been a sleazy con artist forever. But he was able to get away with it for years, hiding behind his big Greenwich house, with his big Greenwich lifestyle."

Logan swallowed, pulse thudding hard, and yet she refused to say a word, aware that he wasn't done, aware that anything she said would just infuriate him more. The fact that he couldn't accept that she and her father were two different people was his problem, not hers, and it had been his problem from the very beginning. She also understood now that it would never change.

He would never change.

"He was able to hide, your dad, by creating a veneer of sophistication with money. Other people's money. Taking their incomes and their nest eggs and draining them dry so he could pose and preen, a con-sciencless peacock—" He broke off, and looked away, toward the window with the view of the rolling green lawn and the dark hedges beyond.

"There is power in money," he added flatly, harshly after a moment. "It provides an extra layer or two of protection, allowing your father to continue his charade for decades, whereas others, those who worked under him, or for him, were caught up in the schemes and exposed. And those men paid the price early. They went to jail. They served time."

His voice roughened, deepened, and Logan's skin prickled as she suddenly began to understand where Rowan was going with this.

His dad had worked for her father years ago.

Her father had been a con artist even then.

Her father had gotten away with the…schemes… while his father hadn't.

Finally she forced herself to speak. "Your father," she said huskily, "he served time?"

"Yes."

"How long?"

"Long enough." He faced her, expression hard. "It destroyed his reputation, while your father escaped unscathed."

"I don't remember any of this."

"It happened before you were born. I was just a boy, and my brother was a toddler."

She balled her hands into fists, her fingernails digging into her palms. "Why would my father be able to escape unscathed? Why did just your father take the fall?"

"Because my father was paid to take the fall." Rowan's voice was as sharp as glass. "And it wasn't a lot, not even by a poor man's standards, but your father didn't care. It wasn't his problem how the Argyros family survived. It wasn't his problem that a young Irish wife with two young children wouldn't be able to get by when Mr. Argyros went to prison, taking away income. Depriving the family of a father, a husband, a breadwinner."

For a moment there was just silence.

"If your father had been exposed then, if my father had refused to take the fall alone, your father wouldn't have been able to defraud thousands of people billions of dollars. Your father's career as a con artist would have ended. Instead, my father caved and took the blame and served the time, destroying all of us, but leaving you Copelands privileged, spoiled, glamorous and untouched."

And this is why he hated her father so much.

This is why he'd scorned her when he'd discovered who she was.

She was a privileged, spoiled, glamorous, untouched Copeland girl, while he was the son of a man who served time for her father's machinations. "I'm sorry," she whispered, and she really, truly was. She felt the shame of her father's actions so strongly. She'd been deeply ashamed for years, and the weight of the shame had almost suffocated her years ago. It's why she'd moved from the East Coast to the West.

It's why she'd pushed her family away. It's why she'd dropped the *Copeland* from her name. Not to hide. She wasn't an ostrich. She'd never buried her head in the sand. She knew how selfish her father was. But it was impossible to survive mired in guilt. The move to California was a desperate, last-ditch effort to shift the pieces in her heart and head so that she could have something of a life. So that she could be someone other than Daniel's daughter.

But Rowan would never see her as anyone but Daniel's daughter.

For Rowan she would always be the enemy.

He shrugged carelessly, callously and turned around, heading for his en suite bathroom. As he walked away from her, she didn't know where to look or what to think or how to feel.

From the back he looked like a Greek god—the very broad shoulders, the long, lean waist, his small tight glutes.

But he also had the cruelty of the Greek gods.

He would punish her forever. He'd never forgive her. She'd spend the rest of her life punished and broken.

Hot tears stung the back of her eyes. "I'm not my father," she shouted after him. "I have never been him, and you are not your father!"

He disappeared into the bathroom. He didn't close the door, but he didn't answer her, either.

"And you have been punishing me from that very first morning in Los Angeles for being a Copeland,

and you're still punishing me, and I'm tired of it. I'm tired of this. Your motives aren't pure—"

"No, they're not." He reappeared in the doorway, still stark naked, the hard, carved planes of his body reminding her of the large marble statue of Hercules she'd seen in Rome years ago. "But I take being a parent seriously, as I know how important parents are for young children, and you had no right to cut me out of my daughter's life. I just thank God that your father did die, and I was the one to come for you because otherwise I'd still be oblivious that she even exists."

Fine, he could be livid, but she was seething, too. "I should have been part of that conversation today, Rowan."

"Theoretically, yes, but you weren't there."

"So wait until I am there."

"I'm done waiting," he ground out.

"I should have been there when you told her," she shot back, walking toward the bathroom. "I should have been part of that conversation."

"Theoretically, yes," he answered, leaning against the door frame, all taut, toned muscle and leashed power. "But there was a moment during our tea when she told me she didn't have a daddy and I was right there, and what was I to do? Pretend I hadn't heard her—"

"She did not say any such thing!"

"She did, *mo ghra*, and so I told her that I was her daddy." He shrugged, straightened. "I didn't make a big deal out of it. I didn't want to overwhelm her. I

simply told her I was her father, and I was very sorry
to have been away so long, but I wouldn't leave her in
the future. I explained that we will all live together
now, and we'll be a happy family, the three of us,
and hopefully with time, she'd have a baby brother
or sister, or both."

Her gaze had been sliding down his body but she
jerked it back up, taking in his chiseled jaw, faintly
smiling lips, and that impossibly smug expression.
"You did not!"

"Oh, I did. And she was excited. She said she'd
love a baby brother or sister. Or both. Maybe twins.
Twin boys. Twin girls. The more the merrier." He
gave her a searching look. "You do want a big family, too, don't you?"

"That's not funny."

"Jax and I are quite serious."

"Don't include Jax in this. She's just a baby herself, which is why you shouldn't lead her on. You'll
just disappoint her—"

"But, love, think about it. We didn't use protection
last night. You could very well be pregnant already."

She didn't know what to respond to first, his continued use of the word *love* or the suggestion that she
could be pregnant. She focused on the second one
since they'd both already established that he didn't
love. "It takes longer than that for the sperm to travel
to the egg," she retorted frostily.

"Maybe I have super sperm." And then flashing
her a maddening smile, he turned around, displaying
more of his assets, and disappeared into the bathroom.

Logan stood there, fuming, clenching and un-clenching her hands. He was so satisfied with himself and so infuriating. And yet, to be fair, she couldn't blame him for feeling victorious. Rowan was proving to be an expert at getting things done, *his way.*

"By the way," Rowan suddenly called to her, even as she heard the shower turn on. "I heard from Drakon earlier today. There seems to be some drama in your family at the moment, and he hoped you could call Morgan after dinner, and I hope so, too, since you've no reason to fight with me———"

"You're trying to pick a fight with me right now."

"I'm trying to get you to focus on the big picture. Your family is in turmoil. You don't need to quarrel with me."

"So just marry you and be done with it. Not want anything for myself. Not need love or kindness."

"I'm very kind to you."

"Rowan!"

"I am. I made you feel so good last night."

"That's not kindness. That's sexual expertise. You're experienced. Technically sound. Big deal."

"It was last night." His voice was somewhat muffled but she still heard the hint of laughter.

"And this is today," she snapped, walking closer to the bathroom. "So what is happening with my family?"

"Your sisters are fighting."

She rolled her eyes. She wasn't surprised. She didn't even need to ask him which sisters. "I warned you that Morgan and Victoria don't get along."

"They seem to have done all right for a day, but then they began discussing the memorial for your father and things fell apart."

"I'm sure I know what happened there. Morgan wants a service and Jemma and Victoria don't, and Morgan's hoping she can convince me to take her side."

"Yes. How did you know?"

She grimaced and rubbed her knuckles over her chin. "It's the story of our family. Even when we try, we can't get along."

"But the news always depicts you four sisters as being very close."

"Lies, all lies," she sang and then her mocking smile slipped. "We've spent our lives being painted as those scandalous Copelands, but we're a family much like anyone else. We have problems. We struggle to agree on things. We have different goals and dreams. But that is far less interesting to the media. I'm afraid we'll always be tabloid fodder."

"Explain the family dynamics to me."

"That would take all day."

"Give me the short version."

"The judge allowed us as children to choose which parent we would live with. We all initially chose to live with Mom, but then Morgan—the most tender-hearted of us—felt sorry for Dad and decided to go live with him, even though he had zero interest in being a father or being there for her. But once she made her decision, she stuck with it, and to this day, she's tried to side with him, which actually just means taking care of him."

"Even though your father stole millions from Drakon?"

She grimaced. "It certainly complicated their marriage, didn't it?"

"So why are Morgan and Victoria so antagonistic? That doesn't make sense to me."

"Morgan wants everyone to forgive Dad, but Victoria isn't sure she can forgive Morgan for siding with Dad. It's endless and exhausting, and between us, I'm tired of it. That's why I moved to California, to get away from the family and the drama."

"Hmm." His deep voice was a rumble from inside the bathroom. "So if Morgan was Team Daniel, and Victoria was his archenemy, where are you on the spectrum?"

She tipped her head, rested it on the door frame. "Probably closer to Victoria, but not as extreme. It's hard because there was Dad and the bitter divorce, and then there was Dad, the investor turned swindler. He made a lot of really bad decisions in his life and now there are five of us trying to move forward, burdened with his…legacy."

Rowan was silent for a bit. "Do you have any good memories of him?"

"Not that I can remember."

"So the memorial service isn't important to you."

"I don't think we need one, but you can't tell Morgan that. She had such a different relationship with him than the rest of us did."

"She's your twin."

"Fraternal. We're nothing alike."

"But weren't you close growing up?"

"Yes. Until she left to go live with Dad." She fell silent a moment, thinking about the complex dynamics. "I do love her, though. She and I have a good relationship. I don't like her being upset."

"According to Drakon she's very upset, but then, so is Victoria."

"And they're still together, under one roof?"

"No, as a matter of fact. Victoria is now on her way to Jemma's, and based on what I heard from Drakon, you're not going to get your sisters together anytime soon, whether for a memorial service or anything else."

Jemma was married to the powerful King of Saidia, Sheikh Mikael Karim, who'd married her against her will. He was seeking revenge on Daniel Copeland, but by the end of their honeymoon, Jemma and Mikael had fallen in love. He still was not a fan of her father but Mikael was fiercely protective of Jemma. "So they won't be attending our wedding?" Logan said.

The water turned off.

The bathroom was silent except for the drip, drip of water.

Logan grimaced and shook her head. Why did she just say that? What was she thinking? "I was making a joke," she called to him. "Trying to lighten the mood."

He said nothing.

She squirmed, giving herself a mental kick. "That was a joke," she repeated. "We're not getting married. I was trying to be funny."

"I'm sure Drakon and Morgan would come for the wedding," he answered, turning the water back on. "Mikael and Jemma would, too. And probably your mother—"

"Rowan, stop. It was a joke. A bad joke." She peered into the bathroom, unable to see all the way in, but she got a glimpse of the large mirror, clouded with steam. "But speaking of family members. How is Bronson? You haven't said much about him."

"I've been waiting for an update from his doctors." His voice was muffled. The shower sounded louder than before. "There was a setback early this morning."

"A setback?" She waited for him to add more, but he didn't. She took another step into the bathroom. "And? What happened? What's going on?"

"Come all the way in so I don't have to keep shouting."

"I don't want to come in. You're showering."

"I'm sure you've seen a man shower before."

She hesitated. "Actually, I haven't."

For a moment there was just silence and then she heard his low laugh. "Then you *definitely* must come in. Consider it remedial education."

"Not necessary. My education was excellent, thank you. I attended some of the best schools in the world."

He laughed softly again.

CHAPTER NINE

ROWAN'S WARM, HUSKY LAUGH sent a ripple of pleasure through her, unleashing butterflies in her middle and a rush of warmth in her chest. Why did she respond like that to him? Why did she have to find him so appealing?

He'd simply laughed. That was all. And yet his laugh made her feel good. His laugh didn't just turn her on, it warmed her from the inside out. Damn him.

Logan hovered inside the bathroom doorway and tried to force herself to focus. "How serious is Bronson's setback?" Rowan didn't reply immediately, and she took another tentative step into the warm, humid bathroom. "Is Bronson okay?"

"He's getting the best medical care possible but he's not responding as well as the team hoped." He paused, before asking, "When was the last time you saw him?"

She had to think. "It's been a while. A couple years, maybe. I was pregnant, and then I had Jax, so I wasn't traveling and Bronson is always working. He's spent the past three years working tirelessly to pay back as many of Dad's clients as possible. It's a thankless job, though. Most of the clients are so angry—and yes, they have a right to be, I know—but Bronson didn't steal from them. Bronson had nothing to do with Dad's company, and they don't realize, or maybe they just don't care, that he's sacrificing everything to pay them back."

Water just sluiced down. There was no reply. Not sure if he'd heard her or if he was done talking, she cleared her throat "Why did you ask? Is there something I should know, something you haven't told me?"

Again silence stretched before Rowan said, "He's almost destitute…just one step up from living on the streets."

"No."

"He's been ill, too. He's not in good shape."

"I had no idea. Poor Bronson. So who is with him? Mom?" She found it difficult to reconcile her tall, handsome, successful brother with the one in the hospital. "Are there any leads on who attacked him?"

"Your mother isn't there. She's been fighting something and isn't strong enough to travel."

"So he's alone?"

"Yes, but there is good news. The London police have taken someone in for questioning. It looks like the attack was an isolated incident. Victoria should be able to return home soon."

"That *is* good news."

"So Jax and I could return home soon, too."

"You're free to travel wherever you like."

"Seriously? So I could go to my room and pack right now?"

"Yes."

"You're not worried about losing me?"

"No, because you'd return frequently to see Jax—"

"I'm not leaving Jax here."

"I'm her dad. She needs to be with me."

"I'm her mother, Rowan. She belongs with me."

"Then I guess you might not want to travel for long periods, because this is her home now. And it's your home, too, Logan. That's why we're getting married. We both want Jax to have a family, and stability. There shouldn't be confusion on that." He was silent a moment before adding, "Do you want to come in and give me a hand?"

"A hand doing what?" she asked suspiciously.

"Well, you could wash my back…or something."

She went warm all over, picturing the *something*, and picturing the something growing larger, heavier.

She definitely was curious, and she squirmed a bit, listening to the water stream down, but she didn't like him and didn't trust him, and she hated how he used sex and temptation against her.

"You don't play fair," she called to him, trying not to wonder if he used a lot of soap or body wash, and if he'd lathered himself everywhere. Would he stroke himself as he lathered? Was he stroking himself now? But going down that road…exploring any of those questions would just lead to trouble. He was trouble. Hot, sexy, serious trouble. The trouble that made her drop her guard and lose her reason and she

had adorable little Jax as proof. "So, no. Not interested in washing your back. Or anything *else*."

"Should we talk about the wedding then?"

"Rowan."

"Jax *is* expecting brothers and sisters."

"Then Jax is going to be disappointed," she answered firmly.

"And what if you are pregnant?"

She really didn't want to think about that. She
wasn't pregnant. She couldn't be pregnant.

But he had gotten her pregnant the first time they
were together. It could happen again.

"We have to use protection from now on," she said
firmly. "We can't take these risks."

"I was thinking we'd get married tomorrow. Jax
should be there, of course—"

"No!"

"It's her dream."

"It's also her dream to be a fairy and fly, but that
isn't going to happen, either."

"You have no sense of adventure."

He was such a jerk.

Taking a breath for courage, she entered the
steamy bathroom. It was a modern bathroom with
stylish finishes—marble everywhere, even up to the
high ceiling, a huge mirror running the length of a
double vanity, and a shower the size of a walk-in
closet, the spacious marble shower outfitted with multiple heads to give him an overhead soak as well as
a full body spray.

Rowan was standing directly under one of the faucets, dark head tipped back, muscular arm lifted as he ran fingers through his hair, rinsing the shampoo out. His thick biceps was bunched and his flat, hard abdomen was a perfect six pack.

The man was too attractive.

He opened his eyes and looked at her. "You're sure you don't want to wash my…something?" His green eyes glimmered.

"No."

"Fine. But do you mind if I do?" he asked pouring body wash into his hand.

Her eyes widened.

Laughing softly he spread the liquid across his chest and then streaked it down his stomach, and then lower to his cock, which was coming to life.

"I did not come in here for a peep show," she said sternly.

"Just trying to get clean, love."

She grimaced, and looked away, not wanting him to know that it was fascinating watching his shaft spring to life and even more fascinating to see how he held it, fisting the length, paying special attention to the thick knob at the end.

And she knew how he was gripping his erection by the reflection in the clear glass shower doors as those hadn't fogged up.

"What's going on with my sister?" she asked, trying to focus on what was important.

"Why didn't you see her for a couple years?" he asked.

From her position she could see his reflection

continue to work the soap over his erection. He was slowly, firmly stroking down, working his hand up over the head. Her breath caught in her throat. She squirmed on the inside. "Um," she said, unable to think clearly. "Because I was pregnant…"

"Right." He was stroking down again, the muscles in his forearm cording.

God, he was sexy.

Awful. And sexy. Awfully sexy. Damn him. She dragged in a breath. "So…what's your point?"

"Think about what I'm saying."

"I can't. Not when you're doing…that."

"I knew you were watching." His deep voice was even huskier now than it had been a few moments ago. "Do you want to watch me finish?"

"No!" And then she turned around quickly to look at him. "Are you really going to come?"

His gaze met hers, and one dark eyebrow lifted. "Is that a problem?"

"It just seems…rude…since I'm standing right here."

"You're in my bathroom."

"You invited me in."

"Because you wanted to come in. You were curious. Admit it."

"I wasn't," she protested and then realized he'd stopped handling himself. He still had a huge erection, but he was rinsing off the suds and lather, and then turning off the water.

She glanced uneasily at his erection. "You're just going to leave that, that way?"

"Yes." He leaned out of the shower and grabbed a plush towel from the rack.

"But doesn't it hurt?"

"Not that much."

She couldn't stop looking at him, watching as Rowan dragged the towel over his face, mopping his dark hair and then down his body.

He stopped toweling as he reached his cock. "Sorry. Maybe I'm being dense. Did you want to finish me off?"

"No!" she cried, pretending to be horrified, but then ruined the effect by grinning. "But you should know that that *thing* is very distracting."

He held his arms open, as if giving himself to her.

Logan backed up a step. "I wouldn't even begin to know what to do with it."

"I think you did just fine last night."

"That's because you took the lead on everything."

"I just touched you, love."

That was true. And it had felt wonderful.

She eyed the long, smooth, thick length of him, capped by that equally thick head. She wondered what he'd feel like in her mouth. She wondered what that rounded cap of his would feel like against her lips. She wondered what he'd do if she put her mouth on him.

Pulse quickening, she took a step back toward him. "Can I touch you?"

He nodded, his lashes lowering, hiding his intense green gaze. She was glad. His eyes had a way of seeing too much.

She took another step toward him and, having closed the distance, she put her hands on his chest, his skin so warm beneath her hands, and slid her palms down from his pecs over his ribs to his pelvis with that impressive V-shape.

And then after stealing a peek up into his face—his expression was shuttered and impossible to read—she knelt down in front of him, and dragged her hands down over his hips, along the front of his thighs, his quadriceps rock hard.

His cock bobbed in front of her mouth. She looked at it a little bit warily even as her pulse jumped, adrenaline getting the best of her.

And Rowan, to his credit, just stood there, waiting.

Leaning toward him, she kissed the tip lightly, curious. He was firm, but the skin was soft, warm. She kissed him again, leaving her mouth against him, drinking in his heat and the silky softness as she opened her mouth to touch him with her tongue.

She thought he made a hoarse sound, and she looked up at him, but his expression was blank and so she opened her mouth wider and covered just the tip, and then sucked gently.

He grew even harder as she gently sucked, pulling on him, creating warm wet friction around the head, and then using her tongue to taste and tease the underside of the head.

He made another hoarse sound, and this time she smiled to herself. He didn't hate it. That was something.

Emboldened, she swallowed him even deeper and

wrapped what she couldn't take into her mouth with a hand, holding him tightly, and stroking him with her mouth and hand the way she'd seen him touch himself in the shower.

She continued to work him, struggling to get a rhythm going, but feeling awkward as she ran out of air more than once and needed to pull away so she could get another breath.

He groaned as she broke the rhythm a third time, and she froze, looking up at him apologetically. "I'm sorry. I'm not good at this and you're so big—"

"Don't apologize," he ground out, drawing her to her feet before lifting her up onto the bathroom counter.

He flipped her skirt up and spread her knees wide and then put his mouth on her, over the satin of her panties, and then, pushing the fabric aside, his tongue found her between the slippery folds. She gasped and arched as he flicked her sensitive nib.

"You're already so wet," he said, thrusting a finger into her.

She rocked against his hand, helplessly grinding against him as his sucked on her clit, already close to climaxing. "Sucking on you turned me on," she panted.

"It turned me on, too." His voice was rough, hoarse. "But don't come yet. You have to wait until I tell you."

"I don't think I can—"

He abruptly pulled away and she gasped as he left her. She struggled to pull down her skirt but instead he was taking her off the counter, peeling off her panties and turning her around, bending her over the slab of marble covering the vanity so that her bare butt was exposed.

"Watch me take you," he said. "Watch me fill you. Watch how good we are together."

And then he was parting her legs and running fingers over her, finding her where she was wet. She felt the moment his arousal replaced his fingertips, his thick insistent shaft pressing at her hot core. Her senses spun as he took the thick head and rubbed it up and down her, taking her creamy heat and spreading it over the tip, making them both slick.

"Watch," he commanded, putting a hand into her hair and tugging her head back to see her face in the mirror. "Watch as I fill you."

And then he was there, entering her, pressing the thick tip in, stretching her, slowly pushing deeper and deeper.

Her lips parted in a silent gasp of pleasure. He felt so big, and so hot inside her. It was hard to feel anything but him buried deep inside her, her body still trying to accommodate his size.

But then Rowan's hands were on her hips, stroking the outside of her hips and then over the round curve of her backside, kneading her ass until she wiggled, ready for more, wanting more.

His hands were under her now, cupping her breasts, rubbing the nipples, making her gasp.

"Look at you," he growled. "You're so beautiful."

"No."

"You are, and you're mine. We belong together, *mo ghra*. Can't you see that?"

She didn't know where to look. She was pressed close to the mirror, and she felt so much that it was hard to take in what she was seeing. Instead she got impressions—her pink cheeks, her bright eyes, her lips parted and swollen, while behind her Rowan was all hard, taut muscle. He looked powerful and primal and…happy.

It crossed her mind that he might just like her.

That he might truly want her.

She exhaled in a rush as he rubbed her sensitive nipples, kneading them, making her hotter, wetter, making her tighten convulsively around him.

"Keep watching." His deep voice was practically purring. "Watch us."

Her breath hitched as he slid a hand from her breasts, down over her belly, to settle between her thighs, and then hitched again as he parted her curls and the soft inner lips to stroke her swollen clit.

He played her clit without moving his hips and it wasn't fair—to feel so much fullness within her while he teased all those nerve endings—she wouldn't be able to resist him long.

"I'm going to come," she said breathlessly. "I can't stop it this time."

"Yes, you can."

"No, I can't."

And just like that his hand fell away, and he pulled out of her, and she nearly screamed with frustration at the deep intense ache within her that was part emptiness and part pain. Tears started to her eyes and turning around she beat him on his chest. "I hate you for doing that. Why do that?"

"Because when you delay an orgasm, it makes it even stronger when you do finally come—"

"I don't *want* it to be even stronger. I just want you." She beat one more time on his chest, this time for emphasis. "So stop messing around. Give me you." Her hands reached for his neck and she pulled his head down to her and she kissed him desperately. "I want you, you awful horrible addictive man." And then she was kissing him again, kissing him as if her life depended on it.

The kiss felt different.

Rowan had kissed Logan before. He'd kissed countless women before. But there had never been a kiss quite like this one.

It was hot and fierce and edged with a hunger that stirred his blood, but there was something else in it, too. Something…open. Something vulnerable.

Not that she was giving herself to him, but instead asking for something of him. And it wasn't a sexual commitment. It was bigger than that. Deeper.

She wanted *him*.

As his hands rose to clasp her face, his palms cradling her jaw so that he could kiss her more deeply, it struck him that she was looking for truth. She was looking for safety. She was looking for someone who would accept her, offering herself in return.

She'd been like this that first night together, the night of the auction…fierce, intense, warm, open.

He hadn't known her then. He hadn't realized she was a virgin. Hadn't understood that she hadn't merely been offering her body, but she'd been giving him her heart.

He understood it now. He understood her.

And this time, he wasn't throwing her gift away.

Rowan scooped her up in his arms and carried her through the bathroom to the bedroom where he placed her on the bed.

He stretched out over her, and she parted her knees for him, making room for him.

"I won't stop this time," he murmured. "And I'm not going away. I'm going to make you feel good, and I'm going to keep making you feel good until you and I are finally on the same page."

"That's going to take a lot of sex."

"Good thing we both like it."

He positioned himself between her thighs, finding her where she was so soft and wet and ready for him. He heard her sigh as he slid in, felt her hips tilt to welcome him. He nearly growled with pleasure as she accepted him, taking him deep. She was tight and hot and her body clenched him, holding him.

He loved being buried within her. Everything felt right when he was with her like this, and everything would be perfect if he knew he hadn't hurt her.

But he had.

And he couldn't go back, and he couldn't change his reaction that morning in her kitchen, and he couldn't change the fact that he'd scorned her when she phoned weeks later, but he could give himself to her now. He could be real with her now.

He pressed up, resting his weight on his forearms, then he slowly drew out of her before burying himself deep again. He kissed her as his hips thrust, his tongue probing her mouth, stroking to match the friction of his shaft.

It felt so good being with her. He felt so good with her. He didn't want the pleasure to end. This was sex, but not merely sex, it was more. He couldn't explain it, and didn't want to try. He just knew that he'd taken so many women to bed, and no one had ever felt like Logan. No one had ever made him feel the way Logan did. With her, he felt settled. Calm. Whole.

Logan was trembling. She was so close…so close to coming but she couldn't come. The two almost times in the bathroom had made it impossible to go over the edge. Instead she was restless and aching, everything inside her wound so tight that she couldn't stop her legs and body from trembling.

Rowan's mouth covered hers and his large, powerful body rode hers, but she felt almost frantic as the orgasm remained out of reach.

Her hands slid down his back to cling to his hips. She flexed her fingers against his firm butt, his skin so warm, his body creating friction everywhere— his chest against her breasts, his cock inside of her. And yet the friction was just that, delicious sensation, but she couldn't reach the point that would give her relief.

She whimpered, muscles tight, need flooding her. She closed her eyes, trying to concentrate to see if she could find relief, but his hard heat inside of her wouldn't push her to that pinnacle.

"Rowan," she pleaded, gripping his hips. "Rowan… I can't…"

"You can." And then he slipped his hand between them, finding her sensitive nub and one, two and the sensation focused and narrowed, tension building, tightening, until there was no turning back.

She shattered, and kept shattering, the orgasm going on and on as if it would never end.

In a distant part of her brain she registered Rowan's deep groan, and his hard thrust, reaching release, before holding still, and just holding her.

She didn't know how long they lay there, warm and spent. She was truly spent, too. Her eyes closed. She exhaled and was soon fast asleep.

Logan didn't know how much time had passed when she finally opened her eyes because the room was swathed in shadows but it wasn't completely dark outside. She must have slept a good couple of hours though because she'd been dreaming until just a few moments ago, and the dream was good. She woke up feeling happy.

Stretching slightly she shifted, and became aware of Rowan's arm wrapped around her waist. She turned to look at him. He was awake and watching her. "Do you know what time it is?" she asked, her voice rough with sleep.

"Almost time to get up," he answered, kissing her forehead. "We're having dinner with Jax soon."

"We are?"

"Yes."

"You make it all sound so normal. As if we're a real family."

"We are a real family, and it is our new normal," he answered quietly, but there was no smile in his voice or eyes. His expression was somber. Even his green eyes looked dark.

We are a real family... And this is our new normal.

"We don't feel like a family," she said carefully, after a moment.

"Not yet maybe. But we will, with time."

She stared into his eyes, wishing she could see past the beautiful dark green color, wishing she could see him. "I know nothing about you, you know. We've only had sex."

"And a child."

"But it's really just been sex—"

"We did talk about your family earlier. It could almost be considered a real and meaningful conversation."

She felt like punching him in the chest again. "So tell me about your family. Open up about your world. Have a *meaningful* conversation with me."

"To be honest, I'd prefer to make you come again."

"Yes, I'm sure you would."

"Sex isn't a bad thing," he answered mildly, reach-

ing out to stroke the swell of her breast and the firming nipple. "Sex creates life, and intimacy—"

"So does conversation, and sharing. And it's your
turn to share. Tell me more about your family. Where
are your parents now? What happened to your father after he served time? Do you see either of them
often? And why did you go into the military? What
was its appeal?"

He rolled onto his back and drew her with him so
that she lay on top of his chest. "I'd rather not talk
about boring things when we can talk about us. Did
you like seeing us together in the mirror? How did it
make you feel to watch me take you?"

"We're not discussing sex!" She shoved up, pushing away from his chest. "And you have to tell me
something about you. I can't keep sleeping with a
complete enigma!"

"You can if you like him."

"I don't particularly like him." She glared down
at him, frustrated and yet aware that he was really
handsome, and really appealing, and she could maybe
see a future with him, but not as a married couple...
rather, as lovers. Lovers that coparented. Or something of that nature. "And you have to share relevant
things that I want to know. Otherwise, we can't keep
doing this."

"Now you're just punishing yourself. We both
know you like doing what we do."

She gave him a thump on his chest. "What were
your parents' names?"

He sighed. "Darius and Maire. He was Greek

American and she was Irish American, but neither lived long in the US. My mother was from this area, and my father from Rhodes, Greece, and they both had strong accents, hers Irish, his Greek. They drank hard, they loved hard, they fought hard, and they seemed determined to make it work, even when Dad went to prison, but when my little brother died, the love died, leaving just hard drinking and lots of fighting."

She closed her eyes and rested her head on his chest. "Do you remember Devlin?"

"Yes."

"What was he like?"

"Sweet. Happy." He paused, drew a breath. "Devlin was a truly happy little boy. He was always smiling. He had a huge laugh." His voice deepened, roughened. "I remember I used to love to carry him because he smelled good. He still had that baby smell."

Logan blinked back tears. "You must have taken his death so hard."

Rowan didn't answer but she felt the tension within him.

After a moment he said quietly, "Jax looks a lot like him. It's a bit disconcerting. If I could find a picture of Devlin I'd show you."

"I believe you."

He smoothed her hair. "What else?" he asked after a moment. "What are you aching to know?"

She smiled at his choice of words. "Do you like having dual citizenship?"

"I had three passports at one point—Greek, Irish

and American, but I tried not to travel with three. It's confusing for border agents."

The corner of her mouth curled higher. "And your parents? Are either of them still alive?"

He hesitated. "Dad died of lung cancer a couple years ago, and she has dementia but I go see her every week or so when I'm here."

"She still lives near here?"

"Yes, she's in a care facility just down the road."

"You didn't want her here?"

"She was here until six months ago when she escaped her minder and tumbled down the stairs." He was no longer smiling. He looked tense and grim. "Her new home is top-notch and provides excellent care."

"I'm not judging."

He exhaled slowly. "No one wants to put their mother in a home. It doesn't feel natural."

Logan said nothing, sensing that he wasn't done, and she didn't want to stop him from saying more.

After a moment he shrugged. "I'd like to take Jax to meet her. You can come, too. But Mother rarely recognizes me these days. She thinks I'm that nice man who plays the piano for dancing."

"Do you play the piano?"

"No. But she and my father met at a party and there was dancing, so maybe she thinks I'm my father." His brow furrowed. "Or the piano player."

Logan leaned up and kissed him. "They both sound like nice people," she whispered, kissing him again. "And I think it's a lovely idea to take Jax to see your mother."

They ended up making love again and it was different than it had been so far, sweeter and calmer but emotionally more intense.

Logan felt connected to Rowan in a way she hadn't felt before.

Maybe it's because she'd had a glimpse behind the mask. She was grateful he'd shared with her, even though it was clear he didn't like sharing. She was also touched that he'd tried to keep his mother with him, at Castle Ros, and that it had been a struggle putting her in a care facility.

Clearly he wasn't all bad.

Clearly he was rather good…maybe even very good…

She held her breath, scared to admit to everything she was feeling. It was confusing and overwhelming. So much was happening but she wasn't sure if any of this was right. She didn't want to go through life on her own, a single mother forever, but at the same time, sharing Jax would mean relinquishing control.

It would mean trusting Rówan to do the right thing.

It would mean trusting that she would do the right thing.

It would mean compromising and yielding and sacrificing independence, too.

Could she do that? Did she even want to do that?

Which brought her back around to the issue of control. Control was such a huge thing for her because the loss of control always resulted in loss. As soon as she lost control, bad things happened. Without control she wouldn't be able to protect herself, never mind Jax.

Panic building, Logan rolled away from Rowan. "Time to get dressed," she said, rolling off the bed and heading for the bathroom.

She was quickly gathering her clothes when Rowan followed her in. "I feel like you're running away," he said, blocking the doorway. "Why?"

"Not running away. It's just getting late, and I need to shower and dress for dinner," she answered, unable to look at him.

"Everything was fine and now you're shutting down again—"

"I'm not shutting down!" she snapped, shooting him a fierce look. "And I'm certainly not running away, either. How can I run when you've brought me to your high-tech castle with bodyguards and security cameras and massive hedges everywhere?" Her voice cracked. "Look at me, Rowan! I'm naked in your bathroom with you blocking the doorway. I'm trapped."

"You're not trapped," he retorted impatiently, moving toward her.

She retreated, moving away until she bumped into the thick glass shower enclosure. "No? Then what do you call this..." she gestured wildly at the shrinking space between them because he was coming toward her again, rapidly closing the distance. "You're everywhere and you're overwhelming and overpowering, and I can't breathe or think or feel when you're with me—" She broke off as he pressed himself against her, his knee between her legs, his hands capturing hers, pinning them to the glass above her head. "See?" she choked as his fingers entwined hers and his head dipped, his mouth on her neck, setting her skin on fire. "You're doing it again... confusing me...overpowering me...making it impossible to think."

"What do you need to think about, *mo chroí*?" he murmured, kissing higher, just beneath her earlobe. "And why do you need to fight me? We work, you and I. We fit."

She shuddered against him, her breasts firming, nipples tightening as heat flooded her. She ached on the inside again, ached for him again. She loved the feel of him, loved it when he was in her, making her body feel so good, but he had the opposite effect on her head and heart.

He wasn't good for her. He wasn't right for her. He wasn't what she wanted—

No, not true.

She wanted him, but that didn't make it right. She needed a man who allowed her to be calm. She needed a man who made her feel safe—not safe in terms of keeping the bad guys of the world away, but safe emotionally. Safe as in loved.

He touched her and created energy and passion and excitement, but it was all so wild and dangerous.

And then he was kissing her, his lips on hers and there was so much heat and hunger that all the wild, chaotic emotion rushing through her slowed, thickened, turning to honey and wine in her veins.

He made her feel so much...

He made her want so much...

He made her want everything…and that included love. The more he touched her, the more pleasure he gave her, the more she wanted love.

His love.

Tears burned the back of her eyes, and her chest squeezed tight, her heart turning over. Making love made her want his love, and he was the first to admit he didn't love. No, he just offered sex. Lots and lots of hot sex, but sex without love was empty, and it would hollow her out, leaving her empty.

"Your idea of a happy relationship is sex," she answered, her voice faint. "But my idea of a happy relationship is love. Do you love me? Can you love me? Can you answer that?"

"When I touch you, do I make you feel good? When I hold you, do you feel desirable?"

"I want love and you want sex!"

"I want you, and I feel close to you through sex." He swore, and he rarely swore. "Hell, I am close to you during sex. I'm in you, love. We're as close as two people can be."

She didn't know how to respond to that.

"Sex can be a lot of things," he added. "Tender, rough, sweet, aggressive. It changes, just as we change, but sex creates a bond, creating something we only have together."

"But that's the problem. I don't want to bond through sex. I want love because love is the ultimate bond. It is the thing that keeps people committed when desire fades or someone is ill. If all we have is sex, what happens when sex isn't available? Does the relationship end? Are we done? What will keep us together?"

"Jax," he said promptly. "She'll keep us together."

She made a rough sound. "And what if something happens to her?" He said nothing and she searched his eyes, and she had the answer there.

Nothing would keep them together. Their relationship would end and the time they spent together would have meant nothing.

Logan shook her head. "This is why I keep repeating myself—I'm not settling. I'm not getting married for sex. If I marry, it will be because I've made a commitment for life to a man. That's the only reason to marry. Because I want to be with him. Forever."

His hands fell away. He stepped back.

She swallowed the lump in her throat. "Can I please dress now?"

He let her dress and go.

CHAPTER TEN

THEY HAD DINNER with Jax in the castle's "small" dining room, a room that still featured massive wooden beams and a huge iron chandelier and tapestries on two walls depicting a violent medieval battle, not to mention two suits of armor.

Jax was fascinated by the armor and the stone fireplace and the tapestry with the violent battles. She was the one to point out that even the intricate carvings worked into the mantel were of "fighting."

"Ireland is a very old country," Rowan explained to her. "It has a long history, and fortunately, or unfortunately, there have been many battles fought here."

Jax turned her wide blue eyes on him, studying him now with intense interest. "Fighting is bad."

"Fighting isn't good, no," he answered, "but sometimes you fight to protect things…your country, your family, your home."

She digested this in silence and then just moments later, slid out of her chair again to go study the fireplace once more.

In the end, there was very little real eating done,

and mostly explanations and exploration, but Logan didn't mind. She'd found it difficult to eat tonight, her emotions still raw, her thoughts painfully convoluted.

And Jax was even doing her a favor, providing a diversion, keeping Rowan occupied with all her questions about war and Ireland and the coats of armor at both sides of the room, keeping Logan and Rowan from speaking to each other very much.

But finally, after dessert had been served, Orla appeared and offered to give Jax a bath and read her a story, promising Logan and Rowan that she'd let them know when Jax was ready to sleep, so they could come up and kiss her good-night.

Rowan glanced at Logan as if to let her decide.

Logan looked at her daughter who was already talking animatedly to Orla and seemed more than happy to leave the dining room and return upstairs.

Logan nodded consent, unable to argue with the plan, while at the same time aware that once Jax was gone, she and Rowan would be left alone together and they'd have to address the uncomfortable tension that had hummed in the dining room since the beginning of the meal.

"What do you want?" he asked her, breaking the silence. "What will make this better? What else can I tell you about my family, or my past, to show you who I am and help you believe that I'm committed to you—to us—and that I think we can be happy without all the hearts and fuss and romance."

"I'm not asking for hearts and fuss," she answered.

"And you mock me when you imply that my needs are so trivial."

"I'm not trying to mock you, or trivialize what you feel. If anything I'm frustrated that you don't understand that what we do have is good. What we have physically is explosive and intense and deeply satisfying, and it's not often like this. To be honest, I've never known this with any other woman. I've only ever found this with you."

She froze, not certain what to do with that. She searched his face, scrutinizing his hard, masculine features, wishing she could believe him.

Would he lie to her?

Her brow creased, as she struggled to remember if he'd ever lied to her. He'd been harsh…cruel…but she didn't think he'd ever lied before, which was key. She hated liars. Hated to be played…

Her father had played them. Her father had turned them all into fools.

"But maybe I'm wrong," he added after a moment. "Maybe you've found this…connection…with someone else. Maybe there was someone who made you feel better."

"I've never been with anyone but you, so I wouldn't know," she answered flatly.

She saw the moment her words registered.

"You've only *ever* been with me?" he asked.

Her shoulders twisted. She kept her voice cool. "The night in California and then here."

He exhaled slowly, his forehead furrowed, expression troubled. "So you really don't know about… You have nothing to measure this—us—by."

She didn't know what he meant by that or how to answer something like that, and so she didn't.

Thank God he didn't ask why, because that would mean he truly didn't understand how difficult the past few years had been. That would mean he still believed she was that spoiled, pampered, selfish Copeland girl…

But he didn't ask why and she didn't have to defend herself. She didn't have to throw in his face that society continued to ostracize her and her siblings, making it almost impossible for them to make a living.

No, life had not been easy, and especially for her, once pregnant, it became downright brutal. There had been no time for men. There had been no time for herself.

And even if there had been time to date…she wouldn't have. She didn't want another man. She'd wanted him. She'd fallen for *him*. Which, in many ways, was the greatest shame of all.

"We can make this work," Rowan said abruptly, leaving his chair, and walking toward her. "We can give Jax something better than what I knew and better than what I had. I want her to have stability and laughter and fun and adventure, and that can happen, but you and I, we have to get along."

"Isn't that what we're doing now? Trying to figure out how we can make this work?"

"I'm not sure anymore. I worry that you've already

decided that it won't work, and you're just placating me until you can leave." He stopped in front of her, expression brooding. "But if you leave, it means Jax won't ever have one home. She'll end up like me, bouncing back and forth between homes and countries…different cultures, different customs, different schools. It's a lonely life for a child—"

"As well as a lonely life for me. Do you think I want my daughter living halfway around the world without me? Do you think I want to miss Christmas with her or a birthday celebration?" She was on her feet, too, her dinner chair between them, because God help her, he couldn't touch her again. She couldn't let him close because every time he reached for her, she melted, but giving in to him only made things worse. It made her hate him despite herself. "I don't want to live without my daughter. But I won't be forced into living with you, either!"

"I'm not forcing you. I want you to want to be here—"

"But I don't want to be here. I didn't choose to be here. And I didn't choose *you*."

"You did once."

She flushed, remembering the auction and how she'd put herself into a terrible financial situation just to be with him.

Even then, she was weak.

Even then, she was a fool.

"Yes, you're right," she whispered, heartsick all over again. "I did choose you and then you crushed me. Like a bug under the heel of your shoe." She gulped air, arms folding tightly across her chest to keep from throwing up. "And I'm just supposed to forget about what you did, right? I'm just supposed to act like it didn't happen. Well, it did happen! And it *hurt*. You almost broke me, Rowan. You made me question my own sanity and I'm not interested in ever feeling that way again."

She drew deep rough breaths as she backed away from him. "For one night I was yours, Rowan. All yours. And then I discovered what it means to be yours. And I have no desire, ever, to be yours again."

She started for the door, walking quickly to escape the room as fast as possible, but his voice stopped her midway.

"Forgive me, Logan," he said quietly. "Please."

For a long moment there was just silence. She couldn't bring herself to answer, and she wouldn't let herself look at him, either.

Finally when the silence had become suffocating and her body quivered with tension, she shook her head, and without a glance back, walked out.

But once at the stairs, Logan choked on a smothered cry, and dashed up the steep steps, taking them two at a time, trying to escape the hot, livid pain streaking through her heart.

Jax was asleep when Logan reached the room, and after saying good-night to Orla, Logan changed into her pajamas, but she couldn't get into bed—she was too wound up.

She paced until she couldn't take another step, and then she finally sank onto the plush rose-and-ruby carpet in front of the fireplace, and closed her eyes, trying to clear her head and get some much needed calm and perspective.

But every time she drew a deep breath, she felt a sharp ache in her chest and it hurt so much that she couldn't focus.

He'd asked her to forgive him, and she'd refused. *Refused.*

That was horrible. She felt horrible, but if she forgave him, truly forgave him, then she'd have no way to resist him, because she already cared too much for him. She was already far too invested.

Her anger was all she had left to try to protect herself. Without her anger she'd have no armor, and without armor, he could break her all over again.

But hanging on to the anger would destroy her, too. Anger was so toxic. It was poison for the soul.

She didn't want to be angry with him, but she also didn't want to stay here and give up the last of her dreams. She wanted a family for Jax, but she also wanted love for herself and it wasn't enough to be Rowan's sex kitten.

As much as she enjoyed being in his bed, she wanted his heart more than his body.

It was time to leave.

She'd pack tonight and leave tomorrow. Rowan would have to let her go. She rose and went to pull her suitcase out from beneath her large canopy bed but was stopped by a knock on her bedroom door.

It was Rowan, she was sure of it. She could feel his very real, very physical energy on the other side of the door and her pulse quickened in response, her heart beating faster.

She retrieved the suitcase, placing it at the foot of the bed, and then went to open the door.

Rowan was not a masochist, and he was not looking forward to another conversation with Logan tonight. The last one had been more than sufficient for a single evening. But he'd promised to let her know if there was news regarding her brother, and there was news. And it wasn't good.

Logan opened the door. She was wearing red and pink plaid pajama pants and a pink knit top that hugged her breasts, making it clear she wasn't wearing a bra. But there was no smile as she looked at him, her jaw set, her eyes shadowed.

"Hope you weren't asleep," he said gruffly.

"No." Her lips compressed and her chin lifted. "I don't want to do this with you, Rowan. I don't want to keep fighting—"

"Bronson's not doing well," he interrupted quietly. He gave her a moment to let his words sink in. "His body seems to be shutting down."

She blinked, and looked at him, clearly confused.

He hated this next part and drew a swift breath. "They suggested it might soon be time to think about saying goodbye."

"What?"

"Are you comfortable leaving Jax with Orla? We could fly to London first thing tomorrow and be at the hospital by nine?"

"No. *No.* He's only in his midthirties. How can his body be shutting down?"

"He wasn't strong before he was shot and he's not responding well to treatment."

Logan struggled to speak but the words wouldn't come. She looked away, eyes gritty, throat sealing closed. "Why isn't he responding to treatment?"

"He'd been ill for weeks before he was shot. His body just can't keep fighting."

"I want to go to him now."

"They have him sedated. You won't be able to see him until tomorrow."

"I want to be there when he wakes up."

"You will be. We'll go in the morning—"

"I'll go in the morning," she corrected. "Jax and I will go. This is a Copeland family matter, and you hate the Copelands."

"You can't take Jax to the hospital."

"We're going, Rowan." She stepped aside and gestured to the suitcase by the bed. "I'd already planned on leaving. You just need to put us on a plane and get us to London so I can see my brother. He needs me."

He heard the words she didn't say. Bronson needed her, whereas he, Rowan Argyros, didn't. "And what about Jax?" he said gruffly.

Her eyes suddenly shone with tears. "You'll miss her, but not me," she said with a rough, raw laugh before shaking her head. "Don't worry. I won't keep her from you. I promise to sort out custody and visitation rights, but surely we can do it later, when my brother isn't dying?"

Rowan's chest squeezed. He felt an odd ache in his chest. And looking at her in the doorway, in her pink-and-red pajamas, wearing no makeup, her long hair in a loose ponytail, she looked young and impossibly pretty, and it crossed his mind that one day Jax would look just like this: fresh, sweet, pretty. Little girls did grow up. Little girls became grown-up girls and grown-up girls should never be crushed. Not by anyone.

"We can make this work, Logan. You just have to give us a chance."

She made a soft, rough sound and blinked away tears. "I did. And the sex was great. It was fantastic. But I don't want your body, Rowan, not without your heart."

CHAPTER ELEVEN

THE FLIGHT TO LONDON was short, just an hour and
fifteen minutes long. Rowan had let them go, putting them on his plane first thing in the morning.
But he hadn't sent them off alone. He'd sent Orla
with them as well as passports, including a brand-
new Irish passport for Jax.

She had no idea how he'd managed that feat. But
then, he had incredible connections, having worked
for several governments.

Logan looked from Jax's new passport to Jax
where the little girl sat quietly in Orla's arms across
from her, and then to Orla herself and suddenly something about the Irish nanny made Logan stare harder.

Orla looked less like an Irish nanny this morning
and more like…

Protection.

Logan frowned slightly, brows pulling.

Orla must have read Logan's expression because
she suddenly asked Logan, "Are you okay, Miss Copeland?"

Logan nodded once, but she wasn't really okay.

Her heart hurt. And she was worried about Bronson. And she couldn't see the future. And she wasn't even sure the nanny was a real nanny anymore...

"Orla, are you really a professional nanny?" Logan asked, feeling foolish for voicing the question but unable to stop herself.

"I did go to nanny college, and I have worked for quite a few years now as a nanny. Why do you ask?"

"Because you remind me a little bit of Joe."

Orla's eyebrows arched.

"Joe was my assistant in Los Angeles," Logan added. "Or I thought he was my assistant. It turned out he was a former member of an elite military group and an employee of Dunamas. And I just wondered if maybe you were also Dunamas."

Orla just looked at her.

"Because I don't see Rowan letting us leave Ireland without security. I can't help thinking that maybe you're...security."

Orla's lips curved, her expression amused. "You know Mr. Argyros well."

Castle Ros felt empty without Logan and Jax. Rowan felt empty without Logan and Jax. He missed them already and they'd only been gone four hours.

He paced his study and then the library and then the length of the castle and finally the gardens, ignoring the drizzly rain.

He shouldn't have let them go. It was a mistake to let them go. And he'd been the one to put them on the jet this morning. He'd personally escorted them onto the plane, checking seat belts, trying to do whatever he could to keep his family safe.

He'd come so close to telling Logan that he'd changed his mind, that they couldn't go. Or at least, they couldn't go without him. But she'd refused to look at him, refused to speak, other than to murmur a quiet, taut thanks.

And then he'd walked off the plane and the crew shut the door and the jet raced down the runway, before lifting off.

He felt as if his heart had gone with them, which was so odd as he didn't have a heart. He was, as Logan mocked, worse than the Tin Man...

But she was wrong. He had a heart and he did care. He just didn't know how to prove it to her since he didn't trust words. He'd never liked them. Actions always spoke louder.

Actions, not words.

Once on the ground, they transferred into a waiting car. It was raining and the city streets were crowded but the driver navigated the traffic with ease, getting them to the private hospital in less time than the driver had anticipated.

Logan, who had been calm until now, was nervous, her stomach doing uncomfortable flips. She leaned down to kiss the top of Jax's head, trying not to let her anxiety get the best of her. Bronson had to be okay. Bronson was the most ethical, moral man she knew. He'd spent the last three years trying to pay every investor back, working tirelessly to make amends.

She looked up and her gaze met Orla's. Orla's expression was sympathetic.

"I'm scared," Logan confessed.

"It'll be all right, now that you're here," Orla answered firmly.

"You think so?"

"Everyone needs family. He'll do better now that you're at his side."

Logan nodded and exhaled, forcing a smile. "So what are you and Jax going to do while I'm with Bronson? Go straight to the hotel or...?"

"I think we will go check in and maybe have a snack and perhaps a nap. Don't worry about us. Focus on your brother."

She nodded again, hands clenched as she glanced out the window at the streets of London, but she couldn't focus on the city, not when she kept thinking about Bronson, and then Rowan.

Rowan who'd let them go.

Rowan who'd stopped fighting her and given in.

Funny how he finally gave her what she wanted, but she felt no relief. She felt just pain.

Just waves of sorrow, of deep aching grief.

The driver slowed before the hospital and then parked beneath the covered entrance and came round the side of the car to open the passenger door.

Logan kissed Jax goodbye and then stepped from the car, squaring her shoulders as she faced the hospital's front door.

There were several rounds of desks and locked doors to pass through, some of the locked doors security to protect Bronson from outsiders, while the last was the hospital's intensive care unit, where they were fighting to keep Bronson alive.

After checking in at the desk in ICU, she went to Bronson's room. She stopped in the doorway and struggled to process everything. The hospital equipment. The monitors. The patient in the bed.

Tears filled her eyes. She drew a quick fierce breath, and then entered, going straight to the side of the bed, where she leaned over Bronson and carefully, tenderly kissed his cheek.

For the next four hours Logan sat next to Bronson's bed. He slept the entire time she was there. The doctors and nurses came and went, checking the monitors, changing IV bags to keep him hydrated, shifting the bed a little to raise his head to ease his breathing.

She felt so guilty as she sat there next to him. He'd spent the past three years fighting to repay debts that were not even his. He'd battled alone, determined to clear the Copeland name.

It was an unbearable burden.

A thankless job.

And he'd never once complained.

Blinking away tears, she reached for his hand again. He needed to be okay. He needed to recover and have a life that mattered, because he mattered. But it wasn't easy keeping vigil. He wasn't the brother she remembered.

Bronson was handsome, heartbreakingly handsome, and yet he'd never paid the slightest bit of attention to his looks. He wasn't shallow or superficial.

He had heart. And integrity. So much integrity. He was nothing like their father...

"Hey, Lo," a rough voice rasped.

She sat up quickly and moved closer to him. *"Bronson."*

His blue gaze met hers. He struggled to smile. "What brings you to London?"

"You." She leaned down, kissed his forehead and then murmured, "Oh, Bronson, what's happened to you?"

"Doesn't matter. I'm just glad to see you. I've missed you."

Tears filled her eyes and she couldn't stop them. "I've missed you, too, and I'm so sorry I wasn't here before."

"You're here now," he rasped, before closing his eyes again.

Bronson slept for another three hours and Logan just sat next to him, unable to imagine leaving him here alone.

She was grateful she didn't need to worry about Jax. Grateful that Orla was there. Grateful that Rowan had sent Orla. Grateful that Rowan wouldn't let anything happen to Jax...or her.

Bronson woke up again just before dinner. He seemed pleased, even relieved, to see that Logan was still there. "Still here, Lo?"

She smiled at him. "Where else would I be?"

"Home, taking care of your baby."

"She's not much of a baby anymore. Jax is two, and she's here in London right now, not California."

"I'd love to meet her. I'm sorry I haven't been out your way—"

"We've all been busy. It's not been easy. I know." She reached for his hand and gave it a squeeze. "Bronson, I need you to get better. And I'm going to do whatever I have to do to make sure you have the right care…the best care—"

"I am getting it," he rasped, gesturing up toward the equipment. "I couldn't get better care than this, and it's because of you."

"Not me."

"Yes, you. Your friend Rowan did this. Arranged this. I'm alive because of him."

Her friend Rowan.

Her eyes burned and her throat sealed closed. She gripped his hand tighter. "He's not my friend." Her voice was hoarse and unsteady. "But he is the father of my daughter."

Bronson's gaze met hers. "Why isn't he your friend?"

"He's not. He's never been my friend."

"Then why would he do all this? Get me this help? Fly you here?"

"How did you know he flew me here?"

"Well, you're here, and he's here, so…" His voice faded as his gaze lifted, his attention focused on the door.

Logan turned around, glancing toward the door, and yes, there was Rowan, on the other side of the observation glass.

Her heart thudded extra hard. She had to blink to clear her eyes.

"Jax's father," Bronson said even more faintly, clearly tired.

"Yes." She turned back to her brother. His eyes were closed. "Sleep," she murmured, giving his hand a squeeze. "I'll be here when you wake."

Logan left Bronson's side and stepped out of his room into the hall. Rowan was no longer outside Bronson's room but heading for the elevator.

She raced after him, catching him before he could take the elevator down. "What are you doing? Where are you going?" she demanded breathlessly.

"I left some things for you. Some snacks, a toothbrush, a change of clothes. Knowing you, you're not going to want to leave him tonight."

Her chest squeezed, making her heart ache. She searched his face, trying to see what he was thinking or feeling but Rowan was so damn hard to read, never mind reach. "But why were you leaving without speaking to me?"

His powerful shoulders shifted. "I think everything has been said already."

Her eyes burned and frustration washed through her, hot and fierce. Not true, she thought. He hadn't yet said the things she needed to hear.

She saw him look past her, down toward her brother's room. "How is he?" Rowan asked.

"Weak, but mentally clear." She swallowed. "He said you arranged for his care. That he's here in this hospital because of you."

Rowan shrugged carelessly.

Logan struggled to find the right words. "He

thinks you're my friend. I had to correct him. Because we're not friends. We've never been friends."

He just looked at her, eyes bright but hard. Just like the rest of him.

She pressed on, emotion thickening her voice. "We were lovers and then enemies. And now parents."

"What do you want me to say?" he demanded tautly.

She was silent a moment, thinking. "I just want to understand."

"Understand what?"

"What would have happened that morning if we'd had coffee and breakfast in my kitchen, and you'd glanced at the magazine and my name had simply been Logan Lane...what would have happened with us if I hadn't been Logan Lane Copeland?"

He didn't take long to answer. "I would have married you," he said flatly.

She went hot then cold. It was the last thing she'd expected him to say.

His green gaze darkened. "You weren't just sex. You were never just sex. You were home."

She couldn't breathe. She couldn't think. She just stared at him, numb.

"I'd never felt that way with anyone before," he added curtly. "And I doubt I'll ever feel that way again." His strong jaw tightened. "I've only ever wanted you. And I still only want you."

I still only want you.

"Because the sex was so good?" she whispered.

"Because you were so good. You were…are…the other half of me."

Her eyes burned and she didn't know where to look or what to say. If that wasn't a declaration of love, she didn't know what was, and yet she'd told him so many times that she wanted love. She wanted to be loved. And it suddenly crossed her mind that maybe they were just using different words for the same thing. *"Rowan."*

But he took a step back, putting space between them, and pushed the elevator button again. "Go back to Bronson. Know that I'm with Jax and everything is fine."

But everything wasn't fine.

Nothing was fine.

They weren't ever going to figure this out, were they?

They were just going to keep getting it wrong.

"Why did you come?" she whispered. "Why bring me a snack and clothes and a toothbrush?"

"Because you needed them." He stepped into the elevator, the doors closed and he was gone.

Logan spent the night in a recliner in Bronson's room. She dozed off and on, wanting to be available should Bronson wake up, but he didn't wake again until morning, and she stepped out as the doctors and nurses made their rounds and did what they needed to do.

Her hair had come down and she felt tired and disheveled but grateful Bronson was getting such excellent care.

He would be all right. He would be.

She used the visitor restroom to wash her face and brush her teeth and try to wake up. She craved coffee but didn't want to go all the way to the hospital cafeteria. Eventually she'd need to leave to see Jax and shower but she'd return. Hopefully her sisters could come soon, too, so Bronson would know he was loved and supported. It was time for the family to come together and be a proper family again. She loved them. All of them. Her mother. Bronson. Her sisters. Jax.

Rowan.

A lump filled her throat.

Lovers to adversaries—but maybe they could be friends. Maybe they could find a way to get along for Jax's sake. There was no reason they couldn't figure this out.

She stepped out of the ladies' room to discover Rowan standing guard outside Bronson's door. The nurses were still with Bronson, changing bandages and linens.

Her pulse jumped when she spotted Rowan and kept pounding as she walked toward him.

"Thought you might like this," he said, handing her a tall paper cup. "With milk and just enough sugar."

She'd thought she'd wanted coffee, but now that he was here, she only wanted him. Gorgeous, horrible, awful, wonderful Rowan Argyros. "Thank you," she said, accepting the cup while wishing he'd hug her instead.

She felt so sad. All night she'd been so sad. Why couldn't they make it work?

"How is everything?" he asked.

She glanced through the observation window to her brother. "He slept all night," she said. "The doctors seemed pleased earlier."

"That's good news."

She nodded. She struggled to find the words that would move them forward. Or back. Or to whatever place they needed to be so she could be close to Rowan again. She loved being close to Rowan. She'd never felt safer than when in his arms.

But Bronson had seen them and was struggling to sit up.

Logan shot Rowan an intense, searching look before turning away to enter Bronson's room.

"Don't do that," Logan said, moving to the side of her brother's bed and gently pressing him back. "Save your energy for getting better, not for entertaining us."

"But I do feel better already," he answered, his voice still raspy but significantly steadier than yesterday.

"You sound better," Rowan agreed, standing next to Logan. "And I know the police want to ask you more questions, but they're waiting until you're stronger. I've told them they need to give you time. They have a suspect in custody and he's confessed to shooting you, even though you were in the process of writing him a check."

"He really confessed?" Logan asked.

Rowan nodded. "He blames Daniel and Bronson for the collapse of his marriage and other problems."

"He didn't understand that Bronson was trying to pay Dad's clients back?"

Rowan shrugged. "Over 63 percent of your father's clients have been reimbursed, not from Bronson, but from money the government was able to seize from offshore accounts your father established. Bronson has been working on paying the remaining clients back, but it's taking him a while and many of those clients need money now, not in the future."

"It's true," Bronson said unsteadily. "I get letters daily from clients who have nothing—they lost everything. They're hurting. They've lost their retirement money, and the seniors have nothing else. They're old and vulnerable, and because of Father they're losing their homes." His voice was rough. "I've been getting these letters for years and every time I get one, I wire money and try to cover the bills. But no matter how much I send, there are still hundreds of people who need help."

"Dad embezzled the money, Bronson, not you."

"But I'm a Copeland. I couldn't live with myself if I didn't try to make amends."

"But you've worn yourself out."

"I'm not a victim. I won't play the victim."

She took his hand and held it tightly. "Bronson, you weren't the one who hurt those people—"

"It doesn't matter. I accept responsibility—"

"And so do I," Rowan said, interrupting. "It's my turn to help. You've done enough. I've spoken with Drakon and Mikael, too. We are taking over, and we will make sure the rest of your father's clients receive restitution."

Logan's jaw dropped. "Are you serious?"

Again Bronson struggled to rise. "That's not necessary—"

"But it is." Rowan's deep voice was flat and unemotional. "We have the ability to do this for the family, and we want to."

Bronson sagged back against the pillows. Logan just stared at Rowan. "Why would you do this?" she whispered.

He shrugged. "Because I can, and I want to."

"That doesn't make sense." She was truly baffled. "You hate my father. You hate him so much—"

"But I love you so much more."

Logan's lips parted but no sound came out. She stared up at Rowan, not just bewildered but overwhelmed.

"I grew up without money," he added, "and I've discovered that money can make life easier. It buys things and gives one the ability to do things, but it doesn't buy happiness, and it doesn't buy love. I would rather give away what I have, and help the people I love, than sit on a fortune and let you and your family suffer."

She blinked back tears. "You love us."

"Yes."

She rose and moved into his arms. "You really love us?" she repeated, even more urgently than before.

"Yes, *mo chroi*, I've been trying to tell you that for days."

"But you never used those words!"

"I told you that you were home."

"But *home* doesn't mean love—" She broke off, hearing herself, and made a soft, hoarse sound. "But it should, shouldn't it?"

"Yes." And then he was kissing her, and they forgot about Bronson until he made a rough sound and they broke apart, embarrassed but also laughing.

"So, you are friends," Bronson said with a faint smile.

Rowan looked at Logan, a brow arched.

Blushing, smiling, she nodded. "Yes." And then she moved back into Rowan's arms and whispered. "I love you. You know that, don't you? I've loved you from the moment I first laid eyes on you."

He grinned. "And you thought it was just great sex," he said huskily, voice pitched so low that only she could hear him.

And then he was pulling her out into the hallway to kiss her again. And again. And again.

"Marry me, *mo chroi*," he murmured against her mouth. "Marry me, please. I need you with me. I want you with me. Tell me you'll come home with me, please."

"Yes." She smiled up into his eyes. "Yes, yes, yes!"

EPILOGUE

THEY WAITED THREE MONTHS to marry because Logan insisted that Bronson be the one to walk her down the aisle, and he needed time to recover.

The three months also gave them a chance to plan the wedding so that it wasn't a rushed affair, but the wedding of a lifetime.

After receiving her invitation, Victoria had at first sent her regrets, citing an unfortunate work commitment, but in the end every Copeland was there, flying to Ireland to attend the intimate ceremony at Castle Ros.

They were married at twilight in the castle's chapel with dozens of tall, ivory candles glowing at the front of the church, with more candles on each of the stone windowsills. The flickering candlelight illuminated the stained glass and the dramatic Gothic arches that formed the ceiling.

Logan wore an off-white silk gown that Jax picked out because Jax was the expert on princess gowns. The bridal gown's bodice was fitted through the waist and then turned into a huge bustled skirt.

The gown had needed last-minute alterations because the snug bodice became too snug. Logan was indeed pregnant, with twins.

She and Rowan had elected not to find out the sex, and they were waiting until after the wedding to share the news with the rest of the family.

They'd tell Jax first, of course, because this had been her wish after all.

Logan's wish was that the babies would be healthy.

Rowan said he had no wishes because they'd all come true already. He had his wife—his *m'fhiorghra* or true love—his babies and his family, and he was referring to the Copelands as his family, too.

And so the beautiful candlelight wedding ceremony marked the end of the scandalous Copelands and the beginning of the happily-ever-after Copelands, as each of them moved forward with hope and love.

* * * * *

If you enjoyed the final part of Jane Porter's
THE DISGRACED COPELANDS,
why not explore the first two installments?

THE FALLEN GREEK BRIDE
HIS DEFIANT DESERT QUEEN

Available now!

#3541 THE SECRET KEPT FROM THE GREEK
Secret Heirs of Billionaires
by Susan Stephens
Damon Gavros and Lizzie Montgomery's searing desire sweeps her back to their exquisite night eleven years ago! But Lizzie's hiding something, and Damon's determination to discover it is relentless. Until he finds out Lizzie's secret is his daughter!

#3542 THE BILLIONAIRE'S SECRET PRINCESS
Scandalous Royal Brides
by Caitlin Crews
Princess Valentina swaps places with her identical twin, but she quickly realizes that fooling her "boss" Achilles Casilieris is going to be difficult when he makes her burn with longing. Their powerful attraction will push Valentina's façade to the limit...

#3543 WEDDING NIGHT WITH HER ENEMY
Wedlocked!
by Melanie Milburne
Allegra Kallas both *detests* and longs for Draco Papandreou, so she's horrified when he's the only man who can save her family's business. Draco has a sinful plan: he'll make Allegra his wife and seduce her into his bed...

#3544 CLAIMING HIS CONVENIENT FIANCÉE
by Natalie Anderson
When Catriona breaks into her old family mansion to retrieve an heirloom, she doesn't expect to get caught by Alejandro Martinez! Kitty's recklessness ignites Alejandro's animal urges. So when Kitty is mistaken for his fiancée, he'll take full advantage—and unleash their hunger!

YOU CAN FIND MORE INFORMATION ON UPCOMING HARLEQUIN® TITLES, FREE EXCERPTS AND MORE AT WWW.HARLEQUIN.COM.

HPCNM0617RB

"You're offering to buy my baby? Are you out of your
mind?"

"I'm giving you the opportunity to make a fresh start."

"Without my baby?"

"A baby will tie you down. I can give this child everything
it needs," Ariston said, deliberately allowing his gaze to drift
around the dingy little room. "You cannot."

"Oh, but that's where you're wrong, Ariston," Keeley
said, her hands clenching. "You might have all the houses
and yachts and servants in the world, but you have a great
big hole where your heart should be—and therefore you're
incapable of giving this child the thing it needs more than
anything else!"

"Which is?"

"Love!"

Ariston felt his body stiffen. He loved his brother
and once he'd loved his mother, but he was aware of his
limitations. No, he didn't do the big showy emotion he

suspected she was talking about, and why should he, when he knew the brutal heartache it could cause? Yet something told him that trying to defend his own position was pointless. She would fight for this child, he realized. She would fight with all the strength she possessed, and that was going to complicate things. Did she imagine he was going to accept what she'd just told him and play no part in it? Politely dole out payments and have sporadic weekend meetings with his own flesh and blood? Or worse, no meetings at all? He met the green blaze of her eyes.

"So you won't give this baby up and neither will I," he said softly. "Which means that the only solution is for me to marry you."

He saw the shock and horror on her face.

"But I don't want to marry you! It wouldn't work, Ariston—on so many levels. You must realize that. Me, as the wife of an autocratic control freak who doesn't even like me? I don't think so."

"It wasn't a question," he said silkily. "It was a statement. It's not a case of if you will marry me, Keeley—just when."

"You're mad," she breathed.

He shook his head. "Just determined to get what is rightfully mine. So why not consider what I've said, and sleep on it and I'll return tomorrow at noon for your answer—when you've calmed down. But I'm warning you now, Keeley—that if you are willful enough to try to refuse me, or if you make some foolish attempt to run away and escape—" he paused and looked straight into her eyes "—I will find you and drag you through every court in the land to get what is rightfully mine."

Don't miss
THE PREGNANT KAVAKOS BRIDE
available July 2017 wherever
Harlequin Presents® books and ebooks are sold.

HARLEQUIN Presents.

Next month, look out for the final installment of the thrilling
The Secret Billionaires trilogy! Three extraordinary men
accept the challenge of leaving their billionaire lifestyles
behind. But in *Salazar's One-Night Heir* by
Jennifer Hayward, Alejandro must also seek
revenge for a decades-old injustice...

Tycoon Alejandro Salazar will take any opportunity to expose the
Hargrove family's crime against his—including accepting a challenge
to pose as their stable groom! His goal in sight, Alejandro cannot
allow himself to be distracted by the gorgeous Hargrove heiress...

Her family must pay, yet Alejandro can't resist innocent Cecily's fiery
passion. And when their one night of bliss results in an unexpected
pregnancy Alejandro will legitimize his heir and restore his family's
honor...by binding Cecily to him with a diamond ring!

The Secret Billionaires

Challenged to go undercover—but tempted to blow it all!

Di Marcello's Secret Son
by Rachael Thomas

Xenakis's Convenient Bride
by Dani Collins
Available now!

Salazar's One-Night Heir
by Jennifer Hayward
Available July 2017!

Stay Connected:

www.Harlequin.com

 /HarlequinBooks

 @HarlequinBooks

 /HarlequinBooks

Get 2 Free Books,
Plus 2 Free Gifts—
just for trying the Reader Service!

The Rough Guide to

Kids' Movies

written by

Paul Simpson

ROUGH GUIDES

Contents

A note on ratings

The boffins responsible for certifying whether a movie is suitable for a certain age – 12, 15 or 18 – don't apply the same standards across the world. In the **US**, films weren't rated at all until 1968 and not all have been rated when reissued on video or DVD. So if a movie has no US rating listed it simply means it was approved under the Production Code film-makers used to adhere to. In the **UK**, some films/programmes aren't rated at all because they're regarded as essentially harmless. In general, the British Board of Film Classification is slightly more laid back than its American counter-part. Movies that earn a PG certificate (for parental guidance) in the US are often declared suitable for all (certificate U) in the UK.

Here is how the US and UK film boards define their relevant ratings.

US
G General audience. All ages admitted.
PG Parental guidance. Some scenes may not be suitable for children.
PG-13 Parents strongly cautioned, some material may be inappropriate for children under 13.
R Restricted. Children under 17 not admitted unless accompanied by a parent or adult guardian.
NC-17 No children under 17 admitted.

UK
U Universal. Suitable for all.
PG All ages admitted, but parental guidance is recommended. It is the board's policy that movies rated "PG" should not disturb a child of about 8 years of age or older.
12A/12 No one under 12 years of age may see a "12A" film in a cinema (unless accompanied by an adult) or rent or buy a "12" video.
15 No one under 15 years of age may see a "15" film or rent or buy a "15" video.
18 Suitable only for adults. No one under 18 years of age may see an "18" film or rent or buy an "18" video.

Unrated
NR in our listings means "Not Rated" – usually an old film, or a TV and especially cartoon series that has been reissued on video or DVD.

Introduction

"Never judge anything by its appearance – even carpetbags."
Mary Poppins

Children watching movies is often seen as a slightly negative activity: most parents, it seems, would rather their kids spent the time reading books or playing sport. Yet a good kids' film can be just as liberating for the imagination as a classic novel. Every child deserves the chance to meet Totoro, the benevolent forest sprite in Miyazaki's magical animation *My Neighbour Totoro*, bounce along to "Chitty bang bang oooh chitty chitty bang bang", or laugh out loud as Will Ferrell's vertically unchallenged elf jumps on a Christmas tree in *Elf*. Not that it's always so simple. If, for example, you and your kids watch Eddie Murphy's *The Nutty Professor*, you'll need to be ready to answer questions about sexual practices not covered in the standard manual. But, then, if you've checked the reviews in this book, you will be prepared...

The main purpose of this guide, however, is not so much about fears and moral panic, as to give simple direction – to help you steer a path through the DVD store to find the kind of movies that entertain, stimulate and delight kids. In creating the book, I've had in mind a target age of up to 11 – as, after that, to be honest, kids are about as likely to take your advice on what movies to watch as to seek your opinion on their choice of streetwear. But 11 is by no means a cut-off for enjoyment of the films reviewed in these pages. As movie critic Pauline Kael pointed out, "I can't think of a single good children's movie that adults can't enjoy." A good movie is a good movie.

For ease of use, and an aid to browsing and coming up with ideas, the guide is arranged by **genre**. Most of these are self-explanatory: Action, Animals, Animation, Cartoons, Christmas, Classics (films of classic novels), Comedy, Dinosaurs, Documentaries, Drama, Fairytales,

Fantasy, Musicals, Romance, Schools, Sci-fi, Sports, Superheroes, Under-5s, and Westerns. Most of the films reviewed in these sections are categorisable as being made primarily for kids. But we've included – for most genres – short reviews of **"more grown-up" movies** that kids might equally enjoy. That's one of the pleasures of watching movies with kids: not just your having an excuse to watch *Finding Nemo*, but introducing kids to the pleasures of a real car chase in James Bond, or the slapstick of *Singin' in the Rain*, or the mad farce of *Some Like It Hot*, or even an adult western like *Shane*.

In each movie review we have tried to give a flavour of the **plot**, an opinion on the film's **merits**, an idea of the **age range** it might appeal to, a note on its availability, and a **warning** if the movie contains any sex, bad language, violence or seriously scary scenes. The very best movies, in our reviewers' opinions, have been given **Must See!** icons and extended reviews.

Scariness is obviously a subjective concept. Children who can sit quite happily through all *The Lord Of The Rings* movies may, for example, have nightmares after watching Robert Helpmann's devastating turn as the child catcher in *Chitty Chitty Bang Bang*, while novelist J.G. Ballard recalled a similar reaction to *Snow White*: "That vicious queen took up residence in my brain for months afterwards." If the review doesn't mention sex, violence, swearing or scariness, assume that none of these appears in the film.

On the whole, films included are rated as suitable for **all ages, PG or 12/PG-13** (see previous page). However, we have included a few **15/R** rated films which in our reviewers' opinion are no more violent, offensive or scary than others certificated as PG or 12. Sometimes this is about how old they are: the ratings boards used to be a lot stricter, and a movie such as *Blazing Saddles*, for example, rated 15 (UK) and R (US) on release, would probably merit only a PG these days. We have detailed the ratings for each film for the UK and US (where they exist) at the end of each review, along with listing of each film's availability on video ▭ and DVD ◉ in the UK and US.

If you disagree strongly with any of the views expressed – or want to nominate a movie for inclusion in a future edition – please do email me: *paul.simpson@haynet.com*

Paul Simpson

A very brief history of kids' movies

Children's movies have been with us for as long as Hollywood. The first **cartoons** appeared in 1906 as J. Stuart Blackton's *Humorous Phases Of Funny Faces* – a three-minute epic which kicked off with genuine animated drawings before using cardboard cutouts to create most of the illusions. The **cartoon series** was born in 1909, invented by Emile Cohl, and four years later, a formally dressed billy goat in striped pants called Old Doc Yak starred in the first animated cartoon series. **Walt Disney** began making his first comedies, the Alice series, about a girl who ventures into an animated world, in 1923, more than sixty years before Bob Hoskins rubbed shoulders with Roger Rabbit.

Meantime, the first bona fide **child star**, Jackie Coogan, made his screen debut, in a Charlie Chaplin film called *A Day's Pleasure*, in 1919. Coogan was just 5 years old then and though he made a fortune he would discover, 19 years later, that his parents had spent all but $250,000 of it, the kind of simple, but bitter, twist of fate that plagued many of his child-star successors. Children were certainly an essential part of cinema audiences, from the outset. **Nickelodeons** – makeshift movie theatres which cost a nickel to enter – sprang up across America in the 1900s, and the first **Saturday children's matinees** took place in London as early as 1906.

To fill cinemas on Saturday mornings, you have to have movies and the production line was soon in full swing on both sides of the Atlantic. "Grown-up" movies which children could enjoy, such as Douglas Fairbanks Jr's swashbuckling masterpiece **The Thief Of Baghdad**, were the crossover hits of their day. And in 1920, **Felix The Cat**, a character inspired by Rudyard Kipling's story *The Cat That Walked By Himself*, heralded children's cartoon characters on the big screen, with **Mickey Mouse** – who made his big-screen debut in **Steamboat Willie** in 1928 – close on his heels.

Progress was not always smooth. MGM boss Louis B. Mayer decided against putting Mickey Mouse under contract because he feared a ten-foot-high rodent on screen might frighten pregnant women. In the 1930s, characters like **Betty Boop**, **Pluto** and the dynamic duck duo **Donald and Daffy** took a bow, while MGM's long-running wholesome-as-apple-pie series of **Andy Hardy** movies for slightly older kids kicked off in 1937. The definitive child star **Shirley Temple** made her uncredited screen debut in 1932.

In 1940, the release of Walt Disney's **Fantasia** showed that the children's movie – and animation – had come of age. **Disney**'s grip on children's imagination would be strengthened, from the mid-1950s to the early 1970s, by the astonishing regularity with which it turned out such classics as **Snow White And The Seven Dwarfs**, **One Hundred And One Dalmatians**, **Mary Poppins** and **The Jungle Book**. In Britain, meanwhile, the Children's Film Foundation was founded in 1951 to create home-grown movies whose very titles (*The Battle Of Billy's Pond*, *The Boy Who Turned Yellow*, *The Monster Of Highgate Ponds*) seem nostalgically evocative of a different era.

In the 1960s, children's movies, like **Pollyanna** or **Mary Poppins** or **Chitty Chitty Bang Bang**, were still clearly demarcated from "grown-up" films. But the distinction soon began to lose much of its meaning as movies filled TV schedules across the world, and in the 1970s, a decade where film directors were worshipped as gods, children's movies rather fell into the void. Somewhere between **Bedknobs And Broomsticks** (1971) and **Robin Hood** (1973), Disney mislaid its magic – and its grip on children's imaginations.

Its place was taken by fantasy productions, such as **Star Wars** (1977), George Lucas's record-breaking sci-fi smash, or Steven Spielberg's **Raiders Of The Lost Ark** (1981), an adventure romp that proved well-made, fast-moving movies that could be enjoyed both by older kids and adults could make a mint. And then Disney returned gloriously to form with **The Little Mermaid** in 1989, a triumph that ushered in something of a new golden age for animation, with **Pixar**'s run of hits – **Toy Story**, **A Bug's Life**, **Monsters, Inc**, **Finding Nemo** – DreamWorks' **Shrek**, and the wonderful creations of Japanese anime master **Hayao Miyazaki**.

Today, almost every top-grossing movie is tailor-made to appeal to parents and kids. And with the re-emergence of classics on DVD, the range of movies on offer to kids has never been broader.

1

Action & Adventure

the fast and the furious

I f the action's fast, furious and well-staged, moviemakers know we'll forgive a few holes in the plot – and the simple narrative drive of an action or adventure film is often enough to hook younger viewers, especially when these tales of derring-do have been served with a chaser of humour. And as **Pirates Of The Caribbean** so memorably proved, a well-crafted action and adventure yarn isn't just for the boys...

CLASSIC ACTION

You'll find more action and adventure movies in the 'Classics' chapter, devoted to great films made from great books. Films reviewed there are:

Armageddon 1998

Shot like a trailer – "something for the MTV generation" was director Michael Bay's brief – this stirring hoopla boils down to Bruce Willis saving the world from an asteroid. The result is 150 minutes of almost undiluted adrenaline, with comic moments supplied by Steve Buscemi and his fellow oil drillers/astronauts. The story is so implausible it won't disturb kids (anyone over 8 could thrill to this), while adult critics might reflect on its self-referential wit: as Anthony Lane wrote in the *New Yorker*, this is a film about the danger of a large pointy lump of rock landing on your head which affects you as if someone had dropped a large pointy rock on your head.

UK, US ◉UK, US │ 12 (UK) PG-13 (US)

Around The World in 80 Days
1956 & 2004

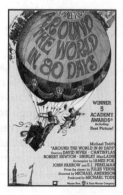

Or, around the world in 100 locations - or 69,000 extras - as the **1956 original** might also be called: a deserved family classic, with David Niven perfectly cast as the Victorian gent, Phineas Fogg, who bets he can circumnavigate the world in the requisite time available, with Mexican heart-throb Cantinflas as Passepartout his faithful valet. Niven holds the film together, delivering lines such as "It's not often you need elephants in a hurry"

with his own unique insouciance. There are enough stunts to keep kids amused, and splendid theme music. For grown-up movie buffs, there's added fun in spotting the cameo roles: producer Mike Todd, then married to Liz Taylor, managed to persuade a stellar cast to offer support.

The **2004 version**, with Steve Coogan as Fogg, is good, goofy fun, and once again packed with cameos (Arnold Schwarzenegger's Turkish prince is a highlight). As might be expected, the movie is stolen by Jackie Chan as Passepartout, with his agility and willingness to mug for the camera. All in all, one of Hollywood's less pointless remakes. The PG rating is for fairly mild violence and language.

ORIGINAL VERSION ▣ UK, US ◉ UK, US | NR
2004 VERSION ▣ ◉ FORTHCOMING | PG (UK) PG (US)

Ben-Hur 1959

This Charlton Heston classic is not short – 212 minutes – so you may have to take it in stages. But there's much to admire in William Wyler's story of a Jewish prince sold into slavery and the Roman who betrayed him. The chariot race, above all, is a masterpiece, filmed and staged with almost insane intensity by Wyler, Heston (who took chariot driving lessons) and ace stuntman Yak Canutt – the man who taught John Wayne to ride a horse.

▣ UK, US ◉ UK, US | PG (UK) G (US)

Captain Horatio Hornblower 1951

C.S. Forester's modest, slightly pot-bellied, hero with a gently receding hairline gets a Hollywood makeover in this swashbuckling Raoul Walsh epic, with Gregory Peck as Hornblower and the lovely Virginia Mayo as his love interest. Walsh knows how to create a great action scene and the crew includes some of Britain's finest supporting thespians, such as James Robertson Justice. Forester conceived of his hero as an ordinary man, with physical flaws and doubts about his own worth, and Peck's awkwardness suits his concept very well.

▣ UK, US | U (UK)

The Castle Of Cagliostro 1979

MUST SEE!

This is one of the greatest movies by Japanese anime director Hayao Miyazaki: an animated James Bond/Raffles style adventure featuring the sympathetic master-thief Lupin III and his sidekicks, who must rescue the beautiful Princess Clarisse from the impregnable castle of the evil Count Cagliostro, whilst avoiding the clutches of the goofy Inspector Zenigata of Interpol. A feast of action, fantastical staging, and creative animation, the film also fizzes away with humour (including the odd bit of dodgy language). Needless to say, it is an absolute must-see for kids aged 7 and above – and their fortunate parents. Much below 7, kids may find the count's robotic guards just a little too scary.

The *Cagliostro* adventure – like other Japanese films based on the Lupin III character – is inspired by a turn-of-the-century French novel *The Memoirs Of Arsene Lupin* by Maurice Le Blanc. But Miyazaki's Lupin character is a very modern hero, funny, inventive and manic, chain-smoking his way through the movie with his weapons expert mate, Jigin, as they find a way into the castle. As in a Bond movie or Tintin film – to both of which *Cagliostro* is distantly related – the tone is light and the violence is most often comic-book in style. Momentum is never lost for a moment, though, and the detailing, throughout, is wonderfully drawn and authentic – whether it's Clarisse's Citroën 2CV, or the count's tur-

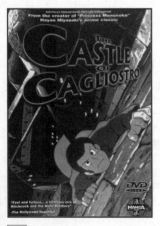

bine-powered boat, or the underwater entrances to the castle. Miyazaki's obsession with flight gets a brief outing. too, as Lupin escapes from the castle by piloting the count's autogyro.

In Japan, the Lupin III character has run through three TV series, spanning more than 200 episodes, as well as a dozen made-for-TV movies. Save for two TV episodes, none was directed by Miyazaki, and none of them, frankly, is a patch on *Cagliostro*. Most of the TV movies (which are available in English dubs on DVD) are crudely drawn by comparison, and several feature quite overt sex scenes. If you are hooked on Lupin, however, **Voyage to Danger** (1993) has its moments amid a lot of weaponry (including some neat exploding chewing gum), and minimal sex. And Miyazaki aficionados may want to try and track down an old US video, **Lupin III's Greatest Capers**, which combines his (diverting but not movie-quality) TV episodes, *Albatross: Wings Of Death* and *Aloha, Lupin*.

See p.52 for more on the matchless **Miyazaki**.

▭ UK, US ◉UK, US | PG (US, UK)

Clash Of The Titans 1981

After filming *Clash Of The Titans*, special-effects genius Ray Harryhausen said he wanted to make *Sinbad Goes To Mars*. Sadly, this never materialised, and *Titans* turned out to be his swansong. As celluloid farewells go, it's a fine one. True, mythological Greece does seem to have an inordinate number of medieval warriors and what seem to be extras from the latest Jesus biopic wandering the streets. But for Harryhausen, historical accuracy always came a very poor second to spectacle. In essence, though, this is a retelling/fudging of the Perseus and Andromeda myth, and the Greek gods and heroes are portrayed by a suitably starry cast (Burgess Meredith, Maggie Smith, Claire Bloom, Laurence Olivier – as Zeus, naturally) which just about compensates for Harry Hamlin's lack of charisma as Perseus. Harryhausen's stop-motion animation works surprisingly well, given that this was released four years after *Star Wars*. Very young kids might get scared occasionally but there's not much to trouble any boy or girl of 6 and over.

▭ UK, US; ◉UK, US | PG (UK, US)

Dick Tracy 1990

If you take *Dick Tracy* as a movie for kids of all ages, Warren Beatty's turn as the incorruptible cop (and sporting a watch boys would die for) works pretty well. The villains' make-up – and the occasional grisly end – may seriously scare younger kids but for ages 7 and over, it is all something of a treat, and teenagers will be intrigued to find Madonna showing up. There are enough gags and in-jokes, too, notably

Al Pacino's OTT turn as a bad guy and Dustin Hoffman's cameo as a mumbling nonentity, to keep older movie buffs amused.

📼 UK, US ◎UK, US | PG (UK, US)

The Flashing Blade 1969

This fondly remembered British-aired TV series featured swashbuckling action set in a long-forgotten war between France and Spain in which the Flashing Blade (Robert Etcheverry in a very tight perm) and his loyal aide Guillet wreak havoc on the Spanish. The horses set a frenetic pace, the theme tune is instantly catchy ("As long as we have done our best, then no one can do more") and there's enough action to intrigue most kids under the age of 9.

📼 UK | NR

Gilligan's Island 1964

Unpretentious slapstick, stereotypical characters and endless reruns on American TV hold the key to this show's position at the very heart of American popular culture. In each episode, seven castaways from the *SS Minnow* are allowed to discover some means of getting off their island but Gilligan always seems to mess things up. The original 1964 series – which was directed by, among others, Richard Donner (*Superman*) and Jack Arnold (*Creature from the Black Lagoon*) – has been lovingly reissued on DVD.

📼 US ◎UK, US | NR

The Goonies 1985

You'd hope for a bit more from this Steven Spielberg production. After all, the premise is terrific: what child wouldn't want to be a goony? You head head off with friends to unknown turf, meet villains, hunt for treasure, and find a pirate ship – and you don't get told off when you return home, because you've saved the day. But nothing quite lives up to the promise. The acting is cheesy (with gratuitous bad language), the effects seem awfully dated, the comic-villains aren't funny, and the scares (too many for kids under nine) come in a remorseless roll-call of skeletons. Nevertheless, some kids rate it.

📼 UK, US ◎ UK, US | PG (UK, US)

The Great Waldo Pepper 1975

Action-minded boys will identify immediately with Robert Redford as a gifted pilot so depressed by missing the opportunity to be a World War I ace that he spins Walter Mitty fantasies in which he really did fight a Red Baron-style pilot... and at the end gets to fight the German ace for real in Hollywood. There are a couple of shocking death scenes (one involving a young Susan Sarandon), and director George Roy Hill's assumption that Redford and co have a God-given right to fly is questionable, but this is, for the most part, thrilling stuff, and the wing-walking scenes will give the whole family goosebumps.

📼 UK, US ◎ UK, US | PG (US, UK)

Hercules: The Legendary Journeys 1996

This American made-for-TV retelling of the story of the son of Zeus is now more famous for giving the world a warrior princess – **Xena** (see p.18) – than for anything Kevin Sorbo did in the title role. But this shouldn't be overlooked. It's not as strange as *Xena* but it's still entertaining with, at times, some very scary monsters trying to defeat the hero. One of its many merits is that the stories don't often stray too far from the original Greek myths.

📼 UK, US ◎ UK, US | 12 (UK)

Indiana Jones Trilogy (1981, 1984 & 1989)

 For many of us, this is the greatest ever action adventure series: a triumph for directors Spielberg and Lucas, and emerging star Harrison Ford. For years (well, ever since the third movie was released in 1989), people have been talking about whether the team could pull it off once more, in a much-touted Episode Four. But there is enough magic in this trilogy to satisfy movie buffs of any age and the ingredients are a classic recipe for adventure films: take an intrepid archeologist, set him a series of near-impossible tasks, stir in a variety of global villains and locations, and watch him ride a rollercoaster of thrills from snakes and spiders to *Great Escape*-style chase sequences and gory dinner parties.

By general agreement, **Raiders Of The Lost Ark**, the first film, is the best, Indiana Jones swaggering through a sequence of adventures that have your hand-in-mouth every ten minutes. Episode Two, **The Temple Of Doom**, is more violent fare, gratuitously so at times, with ritual sacrifice, monkey brains to eat, a screechy female sidekick (Kate Capshaw, the future Mrs Spielberg) and a rather patronising presentation of the Indian characters. But the moviemakers returned strongly to form with **The Last Crusade**, thanks in large part to the rapport between Ford and Sean Connery. These first and third films in the trilogy are simply a must-see for kids of 7 and over.

Oddly, despite all the action, the Indiana Jones movies are as much laconic as gung ho, possibly because that was the attitude on set. After being dragged behind a truck a few times, Ford was asked if he was worried he would get badly injured. "No," he said, "it can't be danger-

Indiana Jones – looks like he's on to something

ous or they'd have filmed more of the movie first."

UK, US ◉UK, US | PG (UK) U (US)

Ivanhoe 1952

Spangler Arlington Brugh as Ivanhoe doesn't quite have a ring to it, so the 1950s answer to Harrison Ford changed his name to Robert Taylor to play the title role in Walter Scott's classic novel, opposite love interests Liz Taylor and Joan Fontaine. Ivanhoe and Robin Hood join forces to defeat King Richard's evil brother, John, and rescue the girl. In essence the plot is the same as many swashbuckling adventures, but the Taylors look good and George Sanders as the villain is cynical as ever.

UK, US | U (UK)

Jason And The Argonauts 1963

The movie which brought the talents of special-effects genius Ray Harryhausen to the masses. The final fight sequence between three actors and seven stop-motion skeletons was, in its time, as celebrated as the effects in Peter Jackson's *Lord Of The Rings* trilogy. Jason, sent to find the Golden Fleece with the aid of the legendary Hercules and a crew of the finest men in Greece, must battle ancient beasts including harpies, a hydra and a skeleton army. The bony soldiers took Harryhausen four months to produce for a three-minute scene. It was worth it – even today the stop-motion action is a joy to watch. Forget the accuracy of the mythology here; just enjoy the adventure.

UK, US ◉UK, US | U (UK) G (US)

Jumanji 1995

 Inexplicably panned on release, this Spielberg adventure is one of those films that, as the final credits roll, seems to prompt a child to say, "When can I watch that again?" The hook is so simple it could have come from an Enid Blyton book: a couple of kids find an old board game called Jumanji and start playing it – and out leaps the game's previous owner, Alan Parrish

(Robin Williams), pursued by a jungle hunter and a prowling lion. By the time it's game over and matters are resolved, bats, giant mosquitoes, a stampede, a monsoon and quicksand have to be braved.

The film's power comes from the fact that the rollercoaster ride is as much about emotions as actions. The tone of the movie changes quite significantly as it progresses: the beginning is slow, then quite dark – almost a kids' horror flick (and a bit much for anyone under 7, or so). But as the game sets in motion, the tale gets more and more fantastic, and Indiana Jones-ish – with a bit of humour, too, to lighten proceedings. All in all, an unfairly neglected gem – and as game-films go, an awful lot more diverting than *Pokémon*.

📼 UK, US 💿 UK, US | PG (UK, US)

The Last Flight Of Noah's Ark 1980

A pilot (Elliott Gould), a missionary (Genevieve Bujold), and some kids crash land on a remote island where, together with two Japanese soldiers who didn't realise World War II was over, they plot their escape. A Disney live-action adventure with some of the sentimentality that implies but still an effective time-killer, derived from the story by Ernest K. Gann, who also wrote the John Wayne classic *The High And The Mighty*. On release, the movie crashed faster than Gould's plane.

📼 UK, US 💿 UK, US | U (UK) G (US)

The Mask Of Zorro 1940 & 1998

Inspiring Clark Kent, Bruce Wayne and many others, Zorro was the first popular hero with a secret identity, by day weak and ineffectual, but by night a masked avenger fighting for truth and justice. Tyrone Power took on the role in 1940 and coped brilliantly, although it helped to have Basil Rathbone as his refined, menacing adversary. The more recent adaptation saw Antonio Banderas play Zorro (the first Spanish man to play the Spanish hero), the elder, retired Zorro (Anthony Hopkins) coming out of retirement to drill the new Zorro in swordplay, with Catherine Zeta-Jones as the heaving-bosomed heroine. Both are a bit heavy on the romance (which younger kids will find boring), but suitable for ages as young as 7. The Hopkins/Banderas combo might tempt your kids more.

🔲 UK, US ◉UK, US | U (UK) & PG (UK) PG-13 (US)

Mission Impossible 1996

Is this a kids' movie? Probably. Although even kids might spot that the high-octane action plot doesn't make any sense whatsoever. Heck, even Tom Cruise did. But then the film *was* directed by Brian de Palma. It's glossy, fast-moving, empty in parts and daft in others, and irresistible. Cruise is the American agent who must act alone to save his name. And acting muscles are supplied by Vanessa Redgrave, Kristin Scott Thomas and Jean Reno. There's some mild obscenity, even milder love scenes and enough box-office appeal to inspire a more comprehensible sequel, **m:i-2**, while a third instalment is due in 2005.

For dads of a certain age, of course, nothing can top the original **1966 TV series**, complete with tape that self-destructs in five seconds, Martin Landau, Leonard Nimoy, and Barbara Bach – who was then semi-officially known as the "most beautiful woman in the world".

MOVIES 🔲 UK, US ◉UK, US | PG (UK) PG-13 (US)
TV SERIES 🔲 UK, US (12 vols) | PG (UK) NR (US)

October Sky 1999

There are tons of movies which promise children that if they have the imagination and determination they can be whatever they want to be. This is one of the more convincing takes on that hoary old theme, as it's based on the autobiography of former NASA worker Homer Hickam. Current hot property Jake Gyllenhaal plays Homer, a young kid from a 1950s mining town, inspired by the launch of Sputnik to change his destiny and shun the mines for the space race. As *Rolling Stone* magazine observed, "The real drama in the film is watching them blow shit up as they experiment and learn." A great feel-good movie for kids of all ages. A corny classic.

🔲 UK, US ◉UK, US | PG (UK, US)

Pirates Of The Caribbean 2003

Making a movie based on the name of a Disneyland ride sounded a very naff idea. But never underestimate Disney. This swashbuckling extravaganza turned out a genuine thrill and with a tongue-in-cheek knowingness that appealed to both kids and grown-ups.

The plot is oddly complicated (not that this matters a jot), but in essence Will (Orlando Bloom) is a poor blacksmith who loves Elizabeth (Keira Knightley), daughter of the governor (Jonathan Pryce), who, so her dad thinks, should marry rapidly rising naval officer Geoffrey Rush. When she is kidnapped by ghostly pirates, Bloom rescues her, aided by loveable rogue and pirate Jack Sparrow (Johnny Depp), with Rush and Pryce in pursuit.

This is wall-to-wall action – the opening duel between Bloom and Depp is a corker – with only a hint of romance, although Knightley is fetching and feisty. Depp steals the movie as easily as his character steals boats. He says he based his character loosely on Keith Richards, an inspired role model for what Roger Ebert applauded as "a drunken drag queen ... minc(ing) ashore". In truth, the picture loses a percentage – maybe as much as ten – of its oomph whenever Depp isn't on screen, and at 143 minutes, it is probably at least 15 minutes longer than it need be. But that's really nit-picking. So long as kids aren't alarmed by the sight of a load of skeletons in hand-to-hand combat with British sailors, they should have almost as much fun as Depp.

📼 UK, US ⊚ UK, US | 12A (UK) PG-13 (US)

The Prisoner Of Zenda 1937

Errol Flynn is usually regarded as the swashbuckler king, but Ronald Colman very nearly takes the crown in this charming romantic adventure based on the novel by Anthony Hope. Colman plays both King Rudolph and his lookalike cousin who is asked to impersonate the king in order to foil a assassination attempt. When Rudolph is kidnapped, he must keep the ruse going until the real king is rescued. In the meantime, the king's betrothed notices a change in her intended and falls in love with the wrong man. All clear, then? Aiding Colman is an all-star cast including David Niven, Mary Astor and Douglas Fairbanks Jr. The action is harmless yet exciting, making this a lovely slice of old-fashioned escapism, perfect for any age. The movie was remade in 1952, shot for shot, with Stewart Granger in the dual role, but didn't work half as well.

UK, US | NR

The Road To El Dorado 2000

An animated version of the Bob Hope-Bing Crosby "Road" movies, this is slapstick animation from the DreamWorks team, perfect for younger children. Tulio and Miguel (nicely voiced by Kevin Kline and Kenneth Branagh) are two bumbling 16th-century Spanish con men who win a treasure map in a poker game thanks to loaded dice. The pair spend the next 90 minutes getting themselves out of one scrape after another, more often by sheer luck than ingenuity. Later developments are taken straight from Kipling's *The Man Who Would Be King*, as the pair are mistaken for gods. The big disappointment is the music: Tim Rice and Elton John's songs are poor. Still, the scene where basketball is invented, with a living creature for a ball, is a real treat.

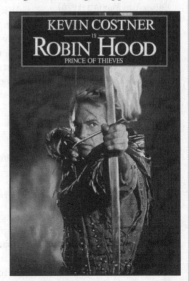

UK, US ⊚ UK, US | U (UK) PG (US)

Robin Hood, Prince of Thieves 1991

Kevin Costner plays himself, as Robin, which wasn't such a bad idea, and appears in England with his Moorish mate Azeem (Morgan Freeman), which introduces a more sophisticated take on the Crusades than you'd get from, say, George W. Bush. But as

More men in tights

Kevin Costner's Robin Hood was only the latest Hollywood appearance for the outlaw, who has featured in twenty or so movies – none of them, oddly, a classic. These have their merits:

Adventures Of Robin Hood (1938) Well, this is almost a classic, with Errol Flynn in the title role and Basil Rathbone just as effective as the villain.

Rabbit Hood (1949) Bugs Bunny takes the lead in this highly enjoyable Chuck Jones spoof.

Robin Hood (1973) Peter Ustinov and Terry-Thomas offer sublime comic moments as Prince John and Sir Hiss in this Disney animated version of the classic tale.

Robin And Marian (1976) Sean Connery and Audrey Hepburn in a poignant tale of Robin and Marian in their elder years. More romance than adventure.

they and the Merry Men leap through the jungle and do battle with the evil Sheriff of Nottingham (nice casting for Alan Rickman) you can't help feeling this could be any adventure film. Good entertainment, nonetheless, and suitable for age 7 and up.

📼 UK, US ⊚UK, US | U (UK) PG (US)

Romancing The Stone 1984

Michael Douglas – an adventurer, capable of rivalling Indiana Jones – agrees to help mousy romantic novelist Joan Wilder (Kathleen Turner) find her kidnapped sister. The pair fall in love, save the sister and nab a huge precious stone in the process. With mud-slides, car chases and jungle perils to contend with, adventure abounds, whilst the chemistry and repartee between Turner and Douglas propels the film along, and Danny DeVito offers light relief. There's some swearing but this rip-roaring tale of derring-do should intrigue most kids of 7 and over.

The trio reassembled for the sequel, **A Jewel Of The Nile**, but, as usual, it isn't a patch on the original.

📼 UK, US ⊚UK, US | PG/12 (UK, cut/uncut) PG (US)

The Seventh Voyage Of Sinbad 1958

The voyages of Sinbad have provided much fodder for the movie business but Ray Harryhausen's stop-motion brilliance brings something extra to the party here. Sinbad and his crew are saved from a homicidal cyclops by a magician and his magic lamp. The lamp is lost in battle and when Sinbad refuses to retrieve it, the magician casts a spell on his fiancé which can be reversed only if Sinbad retrieves the lamp. Harryhausen's skill in creating cyclops, dragons and skeleton warriors makes this work. The first of his many collaborations with composer Bernard Hermann, this movie now has one of the most sought-after soundtrack albums of all time. The DreamWorks animation, **Sinbad: Legend Of The Seven Seas** (2003), with Brad Pitt voicing the title role, isn't bad if your kids don't take to Harryhausen.

▭ UK, US ◉ UK, US | G (US)

Shanghai Noon 2000

Jackie Chan movies can look desperate in their efforts to be funny, but this works surprisingly well, possibly because Chan cleverly shares the movie with Owen Wilson. The plot is just an excuse for Jackie's stunts. There are some drug references and, inevitably, violence but this is a decent, amusing, martial arts western with Chan in action showing the grace of Buster Keaton.

▭ UK, US ◉ UK, US | 12 (UK) PG-13 (US)

Sons Of The Musketeers (At Sword's Point) 1952

In this "sequel" to *The Three Musketeers* (see p.108), the siblings of the original musketeers are recruited by Queen Anne to sort out some pesky rebels. Cornel Wilde and the ever sublime Maureen O'Hara ("I am no lady when I fight") play two of the offspring, alongside Alan Hale Jr whose father played Porthos in the 1939 *The Man In The Iron Mask*. With sword fights and chases aplenty, this is a good old-fashioned gem of a swashbuckler and a nice, gentle spoof of the genre.

▭ UK, US | U (UK)

The Storyteller: Greek Myths 1987

In the mid-1980s, Jim Henson (*Muppets*, *Labyrinth*) and Anthony Minghella (*The English Patient*) filmed a series of Greek myths and fairytale stories (see p.167) for HBO. A new DVD collection features all four of the myths (the videos have two apiece). Each of them is introduced by Michael Gambon as the Storyteller, who gives way to dramas scripted and directed by Minghella, with a top-name British cast (Derek Jacobi, Art Malik, David Morrisey, Frances Barber), and creatures created by Henson. All in all, a pretty winning combination. The stories are Theseus and the Minotaur, Orpheus and Eurydice, Perseus and the Gorgon, and Daedalus and Icarus.

US ◉ UK, US | NR

Tarzan 1999

Tarzan was one of Disney's most exhilarating releases of the 1990s – a film so successful that it has spawned an extended run as a (comparatively lame) TV series. But forget those TV episodes, *Tarzan* the motion picture is the business: a compelling, imaginative, well-animated and exciting tale, replete with nicely villainous villains, superbly voiced by Tom Goldwyn (Tarzan) and Minnie Driver (Jane), and marred only by the Phil Collins songs.

UK, US ◉ UK, US | U (UK) G (US)

Those Magnificent Men in Their Flying Machines 1965

Low-cost airlines didn't exist when this was made – otherwise the subtitle (*How I Flew From London to Paris in 25 Hours 11 Minutes*) might have been received rather differently by audiences. A labour of love for director Ken Annikin, *Those*

Tarzan in the movies

For some reason the story of a human brought up in the jungle has become a 20th century classic, adapted for the silver screen in seven decades. As well as the Disney classic, kids might enjoy seeing these earlier treatments:

Tarzan, The Ape Man (1932) Clark Gable was deemed too flabby for the Tarzan role, but when writer Cyril Hume saw former Olympic champion Johnny Weissmuller he knew he had his ape man. Filming this, the first of his twelve outings as Tarzan, he let the chimps know who was boss at their first meeting: when one of the eight chimpanzees looked set to attack him, Johnny took a knife, let the chimp smell it, then hit him on the head with the handle. This and its follow-up *Tarzan and His Mate* (1934) were the best outings.

Greystoke: The Legend Of Tarzan (1984) This family blockbuster kicks off with the origins of Tarzan, stranded in the wilds of Africa following the death of his parents, and brought up by a female ape, but its core story takes place twenty years later when he is discovered by an Englishman who believes him to be an earl. An oddly serious movie, but with exciting moments.

Magnificent Men is a memorable, in parts, piece of Hollywood fluff devoted to an aeronautical race across the English Channel in the days of biplanes, stiff upper lips, and national stereotypes (pompous Germans, lecherous Frenchmen, hysterical Italians). The cast is over the top (with Terry-Thomas, Sarah Miles, Eric Sykes, Red Skelton, Benny Hill, James Fox and Robert Morley just a few of the stars) and clichés abound, but none of this really matters because they do crash a lot of planes and they crash them very well indeed. And the theme tune is pretty catchy, too.

UK, US ◉ US | U (UK) G (US)

Troy 2004

Troy took quite a panning from the critics on release: the Wooden Horse being the least wooden performance was a memorable jibe. Yet if you take this as kids' action movie, a Hollywood treatment of one

Beware of Greeks bearing gifts – not a cliché, back then

of the great epic stories, well, it's pretty damn good, and even manages to carry a message of the weariness and futility of war. That said, the fight scenes – in particular Achilles (Brad Pitt) v Hector (well played by Eric Bana) and Paris (Orlando Bloom) v Menelaus (Brendan Gleeson) – are the highlights; the battles are not far short of *The Lord Of The Rings* quality; and there's a terrific skirmish as Achilles takes the Trojan beaches with his crack squad of Myrmidons. The love interest, frankly, is rubbish, but presumably it was the few brief, inoffensive sex scenes (rather than the not too horrendous violence) that led the censors to deem this unsuitable for anyone under 15. Don't let that bother you for – a nipple or two and a spot of panting aside – this is great entertainment for any kids with a passion for Greek myth and/or action movies.

📼 UK, US ◎ UK, US | 15 (UK) R (US)

Xena The Warrior Princess 1995–98

"Another day, another defilement"… yes *Xena The Warrior Princess* has always been a bit different. Lucy Lawless became a lesbian icon as the heroine in this odd, yet riveting, series which was originally a spin-off from **Hercules: The Legendary Journeys** (see p.7), but by the late 1990s had become a bigger pop cultural phenomenon than the *X Files*.

The plot has Xena set aside her bad old bloodthirsty ways to roam the world with a fast-talking village girl and have a rollicking good time. Her high-kicking, horse-riding, chakram-throwing adventures are many and varied – in one episode she tells a doctor she cannot be "up the duff" as she so charmingly puts it because she is a "love-free zone". While the show is not consistently brilliant – and it ran for four lengthy series – even the weaker episodes have some redeeming features. As you might have guessed from the name, there's quite a lot of fighting, hence the UK rating for the video, but most kids of 9 and older aren't going to be spooked, nor see anything they ought not to.

Series One is, by popular consent, the best of *Xena*, though its DVD reissue is poor quality, and you may prefer to buy it on VHS.

📼 UK, US ◎ UK, US | 12 (UK) NR (US)

Young Sherlock Holmes 1985

Dubbed "Indiana Holmes" on its release, this is Spielberg's (as executive producer) take on Sherlock Holmes. John Watson joins a new boarding school and befriends Holmes, an exceptionally intelligent adolescent. When several murders occur, the pair investigate, uncovering an Egyptian cult and hallucinogenic drugs. The plot is easy to follow; kids as young as 7 shouldn't have problems. Holmes comes across as a bit of a nerd, too smart for his own good, but he's not so annoying as to put you off this stirring murder mystery.

▭ UK, US ◉ UK, US | PG (UK) PG-13 (US)

Zulu 1964

As if the heroic tale of Rorke's Drift – a hundred British soldiers keep thousands of Zulus at bay until the attackers get fed up and go home - wasn't spectacular enough, the posters screamed "Dwarfing the mightiest! Towering over the greatest!" But beneath all the hype, this was a stirring, well-told tale, with Michael Caine, as the lieutenant, in the role that would make him a star (and – not many people know this – but one of Caine's co-stars was Mangosuthu Buthelezi, the future leader of the Zulu nation). There are some odd battle scenes where soldiers obviously don't bayonet their opponents, Jack Hawkins is below par as the vicar, and, in some shots, you can see that the Zulu soldiers mysteriously have no legs (the budget stretched to only 500 native attackers) but for all that this is remarkably compelling, especially as it lasts for 138 minutes.

Zulu Dawn, the prequel, isn't bad but doesn't offer quite the same thrills. If your kids like this you could try them on **The Alamo** (the John Wayne version); and they can do their homework in the slow bits.

▭ UK, US ◉ UK, US | PG (UK) NR (US)

• •

MORE GROWN-UP ACTION MOVIES

Kids don't have a monopoly on action and adventure movies – many of those reviewed in the pages preceding were intended almost as much for adults. The movies detailed below, by contrast, are not kids' films, and most contain "adult" themes of some kind. However, they are all worth considering watching with kids aged 8 or over.

James Bond movies 1962–2003

The man every boy (and quite a few men) wanta to be, James Bond has it all. Here is a selection of his most accessible and suitable adventures. All are available on video and DVD in the US and UK.

Dr No (1962) The original and best Bond film. Connery is dark but not brooding, the girl (Ursula Andress as Honey Ryder) is sweet and innocent and the action is fast. Bond survives electrocution, burning and near drowning. **PG (UK, US)**

From Russia With Love (1963) SPECTRE, speed boat and helicopter chases and Russian spies: the second Bond film errs on the side of action. **PG (UK, US)**

The Man With The Golden Gun (1974) Now better known as Saruman thanks to the hobbit adventures, Christopher Lee is no less appealing here as the greatest assassin in the world, with Bond his next victim in line. **PG (UK, US)**

GoldenEye (1995) Pierce Brosnan is a far better Bond than his predecessor Timothy Dalton, the girls are feisty, the baddies evil and Brosnan makes 007 charismatic again. **12 (UK) PG-13 (US)**

The Great Escape 1963

You remember the thrills – Steve McQueen on a motorbike, the booze made from potatoes, the tunnelling – but don't be too surprised if the kids get a bit restive – this is, after all, two hours and 52 minutes long. Still, it's a cracking mix of humour and tragedy and the nasty bits – the mass machine-gunning – are often implied rather than shown. Older boys, maybe 7 or over, will want to stay with this.

📼UK, US ⊚UK, US | PG (UK) NR (US)

The Man Who Would Be King 1975

Sean Connery and Michael Caine are two British soldiers who persuade a remote tribe that Connery is a god, a conceit which works until he betrays his humanity by bleeding. Connery's character also falls for a local beauty, played by Caine's off-screen wife, Shakira. One of the finest movies John Huston ever made – and one of the greatest Rudyard Kipling adaptations.

📼 US ⊚UK, US | PG (UK) PG (US)

Master And Commander: The Far Side Of The World 2003

Peter Weir excelled in directing this first instalment of Patrick O'Brian's series of naval novels. It's the atmosphere and detail of Captain Aubrey's *HMS Surprise* that is so convincing: you believe entirely in the ship and its crew, as they pursue the *Acheron* – a superior French warship (it was American in the original book). Russell Crowe as Aubrey and Paul Bettany as the ship's surgeon put in top performances, as does the sea, in a tremendous storm scene. There is a brutal fight scene, and sad losses at sea, but the 12/13 ratings seem a bit over the top.

📼UK, US ⊚UK, US | 12 (UK) PG-13 (US)

North By Northwest 1959

Alfred Hitchcock and Ernest Lehmann created the dream role for the only actor Hitch ever loved: Cary Grant. The former Archibald Leach is sublime as advertising executive Roger O. Thornton (the O stands for nothing, just as in David O. Selznick), who is hunted by criminals who have mistaken his identity. Thrilling, rather than scary, the movie abounds in the kind of set pieces which youngsters found in *Indiana Jones* and is very nearly perfect.

📼UK, US ⊙UK, US | PG (UK)

Small Soldiers 1998

After being fitted with computer chips capable of learning commands, a group of toy soldiers called the Commando Elite, and led by Major Chip Hazard, try to take over an Ohio suburb from another group of toys, the Gorgonites. Some parents may not appreciate the violence – even if only toys are involved – and the scenes where the kids are genuinely surrounded by aggressive toys are genuinely scary. But *Small Soldiers* rattles along furiously, and there's an amusing touch in the voicing of the Commando Elite by members of *The Dirty Dozen*, and the zany Gorgonites by Spinal Tap. It's on the dark side, but suitable for 10 or up.

📼UK, US ⊙UK, US | PG (UK) PG-13 (US)

Walkabout

Nudity, violence, animals getting killed, a father who shoots at his kids and then sets himself and his car on fire... this isn't a kids' movie, by a long chalk. Yet director Nicolas Roeg's first film beautifully evokes the wonder experienced by Jenny Agutter and Lauren John, Roeg's son, as, left alone in the wilderness, they discover nature and an aborigine boy (David Gulipil). Agutter later said the cast had no idea what Roeg wanted them to do no next and, watching it, the viewer is almost as baffled. But this is a genuinely magical experience for older kids.

📼UK, US ⊙UK, US | 12 (UK) PG (US)

Where Eagles Dare 1968

"Major, you've got me just as confused as I'll ever be," Clint Eastwood tells Richard Burton at one point. After a few turns in this far-fetched, yet fun, adaptation of the Alastair MacLean novel, you'll probably be as confused as Clint. Not that it matters – the parachute jumps, bomb rigging and motorbike rides keep the momentum going as our heroes try to rescue an American general, imprisoned in one of the world's most impenetrable fortresses, right from under the Nazis' noses.

📼UK, US ⊙UK, US | PG (UK) PG (US)

Animals

talking dogs, bugs, pigs...

There's nothing like an animal to sell a kids' movie. Doesn't matter if it's a lion (*Born Free*, *The Lion King*), a dog (too many to mention), a pig (*Babe*), a bug (*Antz*, *A Bug's Life*) or a flock of geese (*Fly Away Home*), moviemakers have realised that animals make perfect bait with which to hook families at the local cinema. The movies reviewed below all have animals – real or animated – centre stage and at the core of the story. Stories which are basically about humans, but played by animals (*The Aristocats*, *The Rescuers*, etc), are reviewed in the **Animation** chapter, following.

One Hundred And One Dalmatians 1961 & 1996

"Cruella de Vil! Cruella de Vil! If she doesn't scare you, no evil thing will". De Vil has all the best tunes in Disney's classic animated movie. Cruella sees 101 Dalmatians as fashion statements. Silly, really, because she'd make more of a splash in sable or ermine. This is, as Roger Ebert observed, an uneven movie with flashes of inspiration illuminating a conventional kidnap and rescue tale. Cruella, voiced by Betty Lou Garson, steals the movie. In the 1996 live-action remake, Glenn Close, gifted as she is, didn't quite work the same trick, and the live dogs, gifted though *they* are, were no longer quite top dogs. Try both, but you'll find kids replaying the animation, every time.

📼 UK, US ◎ UK, US | U (UK) G (US)

Alakazam The Great 1961

Alakazam was once listed among the fifty worst movies of all time, but don't let that put you off. In the English-language version of this Japanese anime, 1950s teen idol Frankie Avalon is the singing voice of Alakazam, a mischievous monkey, who becomes king, learns magic and uses his gifts to steal from the gods. For its time, this was a sympathetic repackaging of a Japanese anime movie with a decent vocal cast, and there's a neat moral in the way Alakazam is forced to learn humility.

📼 US | U (UK) NR (US)

An American Tail 1986

Fievel is a Russian mouse who, in this animated tale from Don Bluth, has to find his family, fleeing from feline oppression, and, in so doing, discovers America – not in a Christopher Columbus fashion, just for himself. This is an essentially Jewish parable, the kind of story you find in *Fiddler On The Roof*, but in this instance, the Jews have become mice. There's a heartwarming ending but a lot of heartache on the way, and a lot of threatened feline violence which may trouble really young kids. The 1991 sequel **Fievel Goes West** is more upbeat.

📼 UK, US ◎ US | U (UK) G (US)

Andre 1994

Andre the orphaned seal pulp does wonders for the popularity of Toni (Tina Majorino) at her New England school and her dad (Keith Carradine) handily builds him an indoor bath... then the Maritime Mammals Agency move in. But don't worry, there's a happy ending. Based on a true story, this was rejected by many studios but the charms of a sea lion called Tory (no seal pup could be found) got this movie made. Affecting stuff – good for kids of 6 and over.

▭▭ UK, US ◉UK, US | U (UK) PG (US)

Antz 1998

Antz was the victim of very bad timing – an animated comedy about insects released at almost exactly the same time as *A Bug's Life*. With its Woody Allen-voiced hero, Z, it may well offer subtler, slightly darker, pleasures than its rival from Disney, but the animation wasn't quite so engaging, nor the story so dramatic. That said, it is actually a very good Woody Allen movie – better than anything he's done in years. The plot, as Z puts it, is "your basic boy-meets-girl, boy-likes-girl, boy-changes-the-underlying-social-order story". Allen's unhappy worker ant foils a sinister plot, becomes a hero, and raises quite a few laughs. Allen is joined by a fantastic vocal cast which also includes Sharon Stone, Sylvester Stallone, Jennifer Lopez, Gene Hackman and Dan Aykroyd. Good for kids aged 4 and over. And most grown-ups.

▭▭ UK, US ◉UK, US | PG (UK, US)

Babe 1995

Babe really is the *Citizen Kane* of talking animal pictures. Officially a kids' film, it is full of characters – both people and animals – who behave more intelligently than characters in most "adult" movies. On one level, this is a charming comic allegory about daring to be different. On another, it's a buddy movie in which one of the buddies is porcine. For younger kids, it's just an amusing, enthralling, yarn where the title character, a pig raised as a pup by a female collie, proves to be to herding sheep what Michael Jordan

Babe and Ma giving cute a good name

was to basketball. Movies like this are in danger of giving cuteness a good name. The talking pig, in case you were wondering, is a combination of 48 talking pigs and an animatronic double. The wonder is the sheer difficulty of making this story work on celluloid didn't exhaust everyone concerned but the script works as hard as the animation. Another pig movie, *Gordy*, released at the same time, offers none of the grown-up delights *Babe* offers. But it is good-hearted and may entertain younger kids.

The film's sequel, **Babe: Pig In The City** (1998) is a much darker movie, verging at times on the surreal as Babe finds himself in a nightmarish big city hotel for animal outcasts. For younger kids it's all too weird, and downright scary.

UK, US ◎UK, US | U (UK) G (US)

Balto 1995

This is a real-life story, about a half-wolf, half-husky dog, who in 1925 led a sled team 600 miles across Alaska: their mission, a race against time, was to bring vital medicines to protect kids in the town of Nome endangered by a diphtheria outbreak. The animated canines get a somewhat bigger billing in this retelling than their masters, and acquire some surprising knot-tying skills. However, this is an exciting and engaging movie, good for the youngest of kids, and well voiced, with Kevin Bacon as top dog. Enthusiasts may want to move on to the more fanciful follow-up, **Balto 2: Wolf Quest** (2001), in which our doggy heroine sets out to track down and rescue an errant pup.

📼 UK, US ⊚UK, US | U (UK) G (US)

Bambi 1942

Was there ever a bigger animal weepie than *Bambi*, the Disney classic about an orphaned deer who has to find his way in the world? Amazingly, it made a loss at the box office on initial release, but after being rerun and redubbed into various languages (among them, Russian and Arapaho), it nicely recouped the $2million Walt had spent on it – a budget that included lengthy observation of two real deer to give the animators clues as to their behaviour. Don't be fooled by the re-ratings, if by some chance you haven't seen it. Be warned: *Bambi* is strong stuff, and Mrs Bambi's demise must have triggered a million childish tears over the years. The tragedy is, if anything, more heartrending for being offscreen (the original script had Bambi discovering his mother's bloodied corpse), and the pain doesn't stop there as Bambi learns about hunters, killing and forest fires. Today, the movie seems to offer a rather old-fashioned take on domestic roles – mother's death is all the more acutely felt because she looks after Bambi while dad is being a mysterious, remote, authority figure. Still, this is an enduring movie about how hard, and downright cruel, growing up can be. And even though Bambi has his own family at the end, it can be an uncomfortable experience, especially for younger kids.

📼 UK, US | U (UK) G (US)

Beethoven 1992

A slobbering St Bernard befriends Charles Grodin's family and escapes the clutches of sinister Dean Jones, the actor whose good-humoured charm made some of those *Herbie* movies bearable. This monster hit spawned four **sequels** and a TV series. The first is by far the most watchable, with more than a few laughs. And look out for David Duchovny before he became Agent Mulder.

UK, US ◉ UK, US | U (UK) PG (US)

The Black Stallion 1979

If you watch only one movie about a black horse with your kids, make it this one, based on the Walter Farley novel, in which young Alec (Kelly Reno) is stranded on a deserted island with a black stallion. For want of anything better to do, he trains the horse. Horse and boy are then rescued and taken to New York where, after a few melancholic interludes, they race the world's two fastest thoroughbreds with inevitably joyous results. Mickey Rooney won a fourth Oscar nomination as Alec's trainer. Directed by Carroll Ballard (see box on p.28), this is family entertainment at its finest and, for once, that phrase needn't put you off. The sequel, **The Black Stallion Returns** (1983), isn't quite as good but it's still watchable.

Desert island buddies – Kelly Reno and his steed

The man behind The Black Stallion

Never work with children or animals is one of the oldest dictums in Hollywood. Carroll Ballard makes a habit of doing both. With *The Black Stallion*, *Fly Away Home* (a classic heartrending tale about a girl and her father who try to help geese find their way home), and *Never Cry Wolf* (about a researcher and a wolf) under his belt, Ballard is to animal movies what John Ford is to westerns.

LA born and bred, and a former university classmate of Francis Ford Coppola, Ballard has made seven movies in the last 25 years. The epic *Never Cry Wolf* took him three and a half years to make and came in at twice the budget so he doesn't always find it easy to fund a movie, when the Hollywood accountants move in. Most of his movies have a similar premise, examining the relationship between man and nature, and often touching on families disrupted temporarily (*The Black Stallion*) or permanently (*Fly Away Home*).

Ballard's biggest problem is whittling down the footage he shoots. He had such trouble editing the 750,000 feet of film for *Never Cry Wolf* that Disney threatened to take the movie off him. But the critic Pauline Kael says, "The visual imagination Ballard brings to the natural landscape is so intense that his imagery makes you feel like a pagan – as if you were touching when you're only looking." Sometimes, the imagery overwhelms the story. In *Wind* (1992), Ballard's touch is never as sure with the characters or plot as it is with the sailing sequences. But *The Black Stallion* (1978), *Never Cry Wolf* (1983) and *Fly Away Home* (1996) are all essential viewing – for you or your kids.

And if you feel the urge for another black horse movie, there is **Black Beauty** (1994), directed by Caroline Thompson, in which the horse narrates the story, as it did in the classic 1877 novel. It's not perfect but it's more faithful to the source than the 1971 version.

📼 UK, US ◉ UK, US | U (UK) G (US)

Brother Bear 2003

This is a strange tale of an Inuit who, seeking revenge for his brother's death against a bear, actually becomes one and, given the chance to rejoin the human race, decides to stay one. Eco-friendly, mystical, even New Age, this Disney animated feature doesn't outstay its welcome, thanks in part to a comical couple of moose, a strong narrative drive and an emotional resonance which may have something to do with it being a loose reworking of the *King Lear* story – with three siblings but without the mad old king.

📼 UK, US ◉ UK, US | U (UK) G (US)

A Bug's Life 1998

MUST SEE!

You'd have to be awfully curmudgeonly not to fall hook, line and sinker for this cunningly crafted animated insect extravaganza in which

John Lasseter applies the lessons he learned from *Toy Story* and creates a lot of fun — for himself and for us. The pitch? A misfit ant recruits a gang of weird, pretend mercenaries to stop his colony being persecuted by aggressive grasshoppers. The movie is easier to enjoy than *Antz* partly because the makers have gone for a much broader range of visual characterisation. And it is superbly animated — you feel the colony is being water-bombed during a rain storm. There are plenty of sly laughs, too, and some laugh-out-loud outtakes at the end.

[cassette] UK, US [disc] UK, US | U (UK) G (US)

Cats And Dogs 2001

This comedy about the high-tech espionage war between felines and canines over the fate of humankind is good, undemanding, family-friendly entertainment — but it is so well performed (and with such fine lip-synching from the dozens of cats and dogs involved) that you find yourself wishing it could have aimed a little higher. Your kids probably won't share your concerns — they'll be too busy watching those parachuting Ninja cats or laughing at the feline Bond villain Mr Tiddles (on the DVD, one of the better extras is a sequence showing the fiendish feline testing for various classic Hollywood parts).

[cassette] UK, US [disc] UK, US | PG (UK, US)

Cats Don't Dance 1997

Danny is a song-and-dance cat from Kokomo, Indiana, who hops on a bus to find fame and fortune in 1930s Hollywood. He lands a one-line part ("Meow!") in a Darla Dimple musical (promoted with the slogan "Simple! It's Dimple!") but falls foul of her Erich von Stroheim-like butler. The animation is not exactly cutting edge, but the film as a whole is well done, with some witty allusions to Hollywood's golden age, including an obvious homage to *Singin' In The Rain*, and the songs, written by Randy Newman, are very easy to listen to. Not a great movie but a very good one that deserves to be better known.

[cassette] UK, US [disc] UK, US | U (UK) G (US)

Chicken Run 2000

Northern England in the 1950s. Ginger is dedicated to organising a great escape from Tweedy's chicken farm. Take the expertise of Nick Park, a $50 million budget from Steven Spielberg's DreamWorks, and throw in a stellar vocal cast (Mel Gibson, Jane Horrocks, Miranda Richardson, Phil Daniels) and you ought to have something magical. But rather like the film's hero Rocky (voiced by Mel Gibson), the movie never quite soars of its own accord. Still, there are plenty of magnificent moments here, a great deal of whimsical charm and quite a few laughs. Your kids will love it and so, probably, will you for the first couple of viewings – but not, perhaps, as often you would enjoy revisiting the adventures of *Wallace & Gromit*.

▭▭ UK, US ◎UK, US | U (UK) G (US)

Digby: The Biggest Dog in the World 1973

A timely reminder of what can happen to a sheepdog if it eats a bowl of secret liquid growth formula called Project X by mistake. Unfairly panned on release, *Digby* has a definite wayward charm and a cracking ending, even if it doesn't quite live up to the promise of its slogan "The Biggest Howl Ever Unleashed!" But it's entertaining, with Jim Dale and Spike Milligan on form, though the effects aren't great.

▭▭ UK | U (UK) G (US)

Dr Dolittle 1967

OK, this film of the classic Hugh Lofting stories is technically a musical, but with Rex Harrison, in the title role, doing much of the singing, that seems a stretch. Rex doesn't sing, he talks; and Anthony Newley as his sidekick, Stubbins, is no Robbie Williams either. But that's a small concern in this charming period piece, which transports you to the doctor's home in Puddleby-by-the-Marsh, where he is hard at work learning sea-creature languages for his quest to find the giant pink sea snail. Keep the remote to hand – so you can fast forward all the songs except for "Talk to the Animals" – and everyone should be happy enough, following the doctor's travels to the South Seas, and meeting his animal friends such as the Pushme-Pullyou. And if your kids like this, try them on the books, which are witty, exciting and fun.

UK, US ◎ US | U (UK) G (US)

Dunston Checks In 1996

Family farce in which Kyle, the son of the manager of a five-star hotel in New York, discovers that an evil English lord (Rupert Everett, of course) has an orang-utan concealed in his trunk – one that he trains, brutally, to burgle the other guests. The ape escapes and, after avoiding being shot, goes off to live in Bali with Kyle's family. Throw in Faye Dunaway as the nasty hotel owner and you have a slapstick comedy that isn't half bad, although one grumpy critic dismissed it as "a bad episode of *Fawlty Towers* – minus Basil Fawlty". Orang-utan aficionados may prefer **Every Which Way But Loose** (1978), in which Clyde is more charming than Clint Eastwood.

UK, US ◎UK, US | PG (UK, US)

Finding Nemo 2003

The real novelty here may have nothing to do with Pixar's ingenuity – this may be one of a handful of animated kids' movies in which the hero is a dad. A neurotic worrywart (as voiced by Albert Brooks) but still, as he seeks to rescue his missing son Nemo, a clownfish with too little fin muscle and too much curiosity, from a dentist's aquarium, a hero. Who else could have the patience to cope with his sidekick Dory (Ellen DeGeneres) and her recurring short-term memory problems? At times, delightfully improbable – the fish imprisoned in the aquarium have to rely on a friendly pelican to aid their rescue – and at other times, peppered with gags that will sail a full four fathoms over kids' heads, this is a bit of a gem. However, Pixar should take note: in many cinemas, the grown-ups were laughing louder and more often than the kids.

UK, US ◎UK, US | U (UK) G (US)

Flipper 1963

Long before *Free Willy*, Flipper was an aquatic movie star – in fact, so big was this loveable dolphin she even co-starred in an Elvis movie, the forgettable *Clambake*. The dolphin appears almost human in this tale of a boy (fetchingly played by Luke Halpin). It is, as the slogan says, absolutely fin-tastic! The 1996 remake stars Paul Hogan and Elijah Wood but, as Roger Ebert said, after you've watched the dolphin's umpteenth stunt you wonder "why the producers didn't have him revise the screenplay too".

UK, US | G (US)

Fly Away Home 1996

MUST SEE! Director Carroll Ballard – see box on p.28 – kept rewriting the script of *Fly Away Home* to suit the geese, the weather and the microlight aircraft. But the film has a human story to tell. When her mother dies, 13-year-old Amy (Anna Paquin) has to leave New Zealand to live in Canada with the father (Jeff Daniels, who is selfless in support) she hasn't seen for nine years. At first, the only things that rouse her are the geese and, when goslings adopt her as a surrogate mother, her dad tries to lead them on their usual winter migration in a

Goose alert for Amy and Pa

microlight. This is a splendid fantasy, which rises above the genre of
kids-freeing-animals movies typified by *Free Willy*. Daniels is just the right side of insane as the dad whose planes keep crashing and Paquin, playing a reasonably normal teenager for a change, is effective, bar the odd bit of histrionics. The mother's death opens the movie, a silent car crash which occurs during the credits, but otherwise there's nothing here to distress kids of any age.

📼 UK, US ◉ UK, US | U (UK)

Free Willy 1993

Free Willy delivers a whale of a time – as long as Kelko, in the title role, and boy Jason James Richter are on screen. Away from the aqua park, the film can feel grounded by political correctness and hampered by some frankly hammy villains, but for the most part Australian director Simon Wincer knows just what heartstrings to tug and when to tighten his grip. There's a sweetness about this tale of a bid to free a whale which you may well find endearing and the movie mixes models and the real orca almost seamlessly. Sequels were inevitable, almost as inevitable as the fact that they weren't as good, though **Free Willy 2**

Freeing Willy for the very first time

deserves to be treasured if only for its notion of a whale that can hear, and interpret, harmonica noises at some distance.

▦ UK, US ◉ UK, US | U (UK) PG (US)

Lassie Come Home 1943

At one point in the filming of *Lassie*, Liz Taylor was sent back to her dressing room to have her false eyelashes removed – only for director Fred Wilcox to realise they were genuine. And Liz very nearly steals the limelight from her canine co-star who walks the length and breadth of Britain to be reunited with his impoverished family, who (don't ask why) had been forced to sell him to some mean aristocrat up in the Scottish Highlands. This was one of the first and greatest dog movies, and features a flawless performance from Pal, as Lassie, especially given that he was a male dog playing a bitch with a patch over his testicles. Eight dogs were to star in the film's sequels, all of them trained by the remarkable Weatherwax family, whose many other canine credits include Toto in *The Wizard of Oz* (1939), John Wayne's collie in *Hondo* (1953), and Spike the mongrel in *Old Yeller* (1957).

▦ UK, US | NR (UK) GS (US)

The Lion King 1994

The Lion King is as big as a movie gets: it has sold 55 million videos (a record), spawned a monster hit soundtrack, "inspired" two sequels and been spun off into a musical which is doing good business at a theatre near you. But the film itself still stands up – and to repeated viewings. While millions of pre-*Lion King* kids grew up mourning Bambi's mother, Disney has ensured that for their successors their defining emotional experience on film will be the death of Simba's dad, Mufasa, and the fine work of Messrs Elton John and Tim Rice is as good an introduction to musicals as any could hope for.

And there are film-buff diversions even for adults pressing "Play" for the 27th time. Watch Timon perform "Hakuna Matata" again and you notice that one of the bugs he pulls out of a knothole is wearing Mickey Mouse ears. Check the scene of the goose-stepping hyenas and you'll find it modelled pretty closely on Leni Riefenstahl's Nazi propaganda work, *Triumph Of The Will* (1934). Scar's scar is in the same position on his face as the scar on Tony Montana's face in *Scarface*. The plot, as you already knew, is loosely derived from Shakespeare's *Hamlet*. And one more pop cultural gem: Pumbaa the warthog was the first ever Disney character to experience flatulence on screen.

As to the plot and characters – well, you have seen the film, haven't you? Dramatic highlights are many, and the characters as good as anything in Disney, particularly Scar, a memorably sardonic, charismatic, villain voiced by Jeremy Irons, and the comic duo, Timon and Pumbaa, who, with their continual sniping, some critics have suggested are Disney's first openly gay animated couple. It is a mark of the film's quality that it is pondered over for subtexts and hidden meanings.

The Lion King, it should also be said, is quite violent at times, and Muphasa's death is a hammer blow, so kids under 4 may find this upsetting at times.

📼 UK, US ◎UK, US | U (UK) G (US)

Milo and Otis 1986

An awwwww-some story of a cat and a dog accidentally separated who embark on a hazardous trek. Anticipating *Homeward Bound: The Incredible Journey* (1993), this Japanese movie features thirty Otises and Milo's, all of whom were urged by Japanese author Masanori Hata to act instinctively. A paean in praise of loyalty, devotion and tolerance – even among foxes and hens – this live-action movie is one of the most remarkable of its kind. For kids of 4 to 8.

📼 US ◎UK, US | G (US)

My Dog Skip 1999

 You know Will, the lonely child at the heart of this movie, is in trouble when at his birthday party he gets a present of a bow tie. Not getting on with his dad (Kevin Bacon), who lost a leg – and part of his heart – in the Spanish Civil War, not

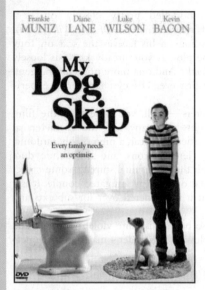

surprisingly Will (Frankie Muniz) is closest to his dog, Fink. But then, after teaching his pet to become a Yankee Doodle Dog, he gets angry with Skip and the dog runs off. Will sets out to find him with his only friend Dink (Luke Wilson) who has just come back from the war, ostensibly a coward. Based on a memoir by American journalist Willie Morris, this overcomes its inherent absurdities (notably the subplot about moonshiners) and will mean something to anyone, child or grown up, who has ever cycled around, shouting their dog's name, in the increasingly forlorn hope that the treasured pet will return.

UK, US ◉UK, US | U (UK) PG (US)

Never Cry Wolf 1983

Wolves finally get to tell their side of the story. Such is director Carroll Ballard's gift (see box on p.28) that he can make the process of discovering complex truths about the relationships between two species – the wolves and the caribou – a moving, entertaining experience. Charles Martin Smith excels as the government researcher, sent to investigate the menace of wolves, who realises that his survival skills are as inadequate as the official line about wolves. It's a low-key performance but a vital one. Although the film is based on the real-life story of a scientist called Farley Mowat, one wrong note and his re-education by two Inuit locals could feel horrendously corny. Ballard's cinematography is always superb but the cast help balance the film – which never feels like a wildlife programme.

US ◉UK

Old Yeller 1957

It's Texas in 1870. A boy brings a yellow dog home – and the two get into the usual scrapes with raccoons, bears... Godzilla. Actually, there are no monsters on the boy's ranch. This isn't that kind of movie, it's the kind of movie where characters say things such as "If that don't beat all, I never saw such a dog". You will, of course, have seen plenty of movies like this but it's still moving, well made and entertaining. Some even claim this is Disney's best live-action movie, and the best dog movie ever made (or as the song at the beginning and end tells it, "The best dog-gone dog in the West"). Be warned, though: the ending, in which Old Yeller dies, is as heartbreaking as *Bambi*, and there is some mild violence, too. So you may not want to introduce this to kids under the age of six. And even grown-ups may need the Kleenex.

⊚ US │ U (UK) G (US)

Paws 1997

A stranded Jack Russell terrier, with a PC disk, is wired up to a computer-controlled vocal unit which serves two purposes. One, it gives Billy Connolly the chance to amuse by voicing the dog, and two, it enables 14-year-old Zac to figure out what kind of predicament he's in now he's got stuck with this dog. Made when moviemakers were still boggled by the profits of *Babe*, this is short on irony but longer on laughs.

▭ UK │ U (UK)

Turner & Hooch 1989

In many fast-moving Hollywood buddy-buddy action comedies of this era, it can be hard to distinguish the principal characters. No such problem here. As the *Washington Post* noted, "One says 'where's my motivation?' and the other says 'Arf!'". Tom Hanks served a long apprenticeship in light comedies before he graduated to Oscar-winning emoting in *Philadelphia*, and he plays the fussy small detective well enough – even so, he's outplayed by Hooch who, as the *Post* again put it so eloquently, is "an ungainly mastiff whose jowls flap in the breeze when he runs, has a serious saliva problem, chews upholstery, smashes stereo speakers, drinks more beer than E.T. and generally drives his reluctant owner Turner insane." The film-makers have no greater ambition than to make you laugh – and you will.

UK, US ⊙UK, US | PG (UK, US)

Watership Down 1978

Don't be misled by the anodyne yearning of Art Garfunkel's chart-topping theme "Bright Eyes", the rabbits in this adaptation of the famous Richard Adams novel are desperate creatures scrapping for a life. Director and scriptwriter Martin Rosen told the animators: "Think of this not as a story about rabbits, but as an adventure full of courage, aggression and loyalty." The result is that some of the fighting is extremely gory, and indeed there's a grim air about the whole film, so it's probably not for kids under 5. The vocal talent on offer varies from Sir Ralph Richardson to Zero Mostel.

UK, US ⊙UK, US | U (UK) PG (US)

White Fang 1990

Young Jack (Ethan Hawke) and a beast which is part dog, part wolf, protect each other in the wildness of the Klondike at the turn of the 19th century. The movie makes no serious claim to be a version of the classic Jack London novel – the makers gave up on the idea that the movie, like the book, could be narrated from White Fang's point of view – but it is magnificently photographed, well acted (especially by Hawke and Klaus Maria Brandauer as a hard-bitten prospector) and it is adventurous, imaginative and genuinely thrilling at times. Good for kids of 7 and over.

UK, US ⊙UK, US | PG (UK, US)

• •

MORE GROWN-UP ANIMAL MOVIES

Born Free 1966

This true-life story was filmed – and took place – in Kenya, where a husband-and-wife team of animal trainers, Joy Adamson (Virginia McKenna) and her husband George, released Elsa, the lion cub they reared from birth, back into the wild. John Barry's score, with a fine title song crooned by Matt Monro, almost steals the movie but the lion action is impressive, and this is good-hearted, entertaining, viewing.

It took more than thirty years for a *Born Free* sequel to emerge, and **To Walk With Lions** (1999) is a grittier and much more adult film (rated 12 in the UK) in which George (Richard Harris) takes on animal hunters trading in rhino horns and ivory; the very hunters who had brutally murdered his wife.

📼UK, US ⊙UK, US | U (UK) PG (US)

Gorillas In The Mist 1988

The true story of primatologist Diane Fossey (Sigourney Weaver) and her struggle to protect gorillas, which led to her murder, is probably stronger in detailing its cast of apes than explaining the motivations of its heroine. The scenes in which she gradually gains the gorillas' confidence are finely observed whereas her romance with *National Geographic* photographer Bryan Brown feels a bit canned. Obviously, given the denouement, this isn't for younger kids but those aged and over may find themselves fascinated by the gorillas who, despite Weaver's towering performance, are the real stars here.

📼UK, US ⊙UK, US | 12 (UK) PG-13 (US)

Kes 1969

Ken Loach's sour variation on the boy-and-pet movie uses the Barry Hines novel *A Kestrel For A Knave* to say a lot about the British class system in the late 1960s. David Bradley gives a remarkable performance as the boy who escapes from the pain and tedium of everyday life with a kestrel and there is some raw humour (Brian Glover's PE teacher scene is still a classic) but the ending is abrupt and painfully sad – so probably for older kids (8 and over) only.

📼UK, US ⊙UK, US | PG (UK, US)

Ring Of Bright Water 1969

What is it about otters? Gavin Maxwell fell in love with the sea otters around his home in the Scottish Highlands, and you are guaranteed to follow suit, watching this film based on his nov-elised account. It's almost entirely a delight for kids to watch, as the Maxwell character (Bill Travers) accidentally adopts Midge in London, gets thrown out of his flat and moves to Scotland, where he romances Virginia McKenna. There is a rather big sting in the tale, though, as Midge is thoughtlessly killed by a worker repairing the ditches, a shock the film's upbeat ending can't transcend.

⊙UK, US | U (UK) G (US)

Tarka The Otter 1978

This heartwarming, tear-jerking tale was derived from Henry Williamson's novel of the same name, based on years of studying river life in Devon. The story of orphaned otter Tarka and how he tri-umphs over adversity and otter-hunters (a practice made illegal in the UK before the film was released) is told without undue sentimentality. Williams, who had resisted attempts to film his novel, was finally won over by a team that included

Gerald Durrell as scriptwriter and Peter Ustinov as narrator, but he died the day the last scene was shot. It is a moving film, with some harrowing scenes, and is probably best for kids of 7 and up.

📼 UK ◉ UK | PG (UK, US)

Turtle Diary 1985

A middle-aged couple (Ben Kingsley and Glenda Jackson) strike up an unlikely camaraderie at London Zoo, where they are both fascinated by the large sea turtles. After Kingsley grills keeper Michael Gambon for his turtle lore, the duo hatch a plan to give the creatures a chance to swim home to the Ascension Island. The movie rolls on, gently and a little predictably, but it's a good story, nonetheless, from a novel by Russell Hoban.

📼 UK, US | PG (UK, US)

3

Animation

from Disney to Miyazaki

A nimation is such a huge genre, ranging through Disney and its newer rivals, Pixar and DreamWorks, through to Japanese anime master Hayao Miyazaki. So, in a bid to make this section manageable, we have taken out **Cartoons** and given them a chapter of their own. And we've also assigned a number of animated films to the **Action & Adventure**, **Animals**, **Christmas**, **Classics**, **Fantasy** and **Under-5s** chapters. There's an index of these at the end of this chapter, if you are wondering where to find the likes of *Tarzan* (Action), *Finding Nemo* (Animals), *Scooby-Doo* (Cartoons), *Castle in the Sky* (Fantasy), or *Dumbo* (Under-5s).

The golden age of animation is usually held to be the 1940s and 1950s when Walt reigned supreme on the Disney lot. But with a succession of stunning recent movies, and the technical revolution pioneered by Pixar (on *Toy Story* and beyond), it's maybe no exaggeration to suggest we're amid a new platinum era, one where animators can create whole new worlds. So impressive has this growth been that it has left some of us – well Homer Simpson, actually – trying to catch up. In one famous episode of *The Simpsons*, Homer is told, rather snottily by a TV executive: "We don't do animation live, Homer, it would place a terrible strain on the animators' wrists."

Aladdin 1992

This movie marked a turning point in Disney's history. Back in 1992, the studio was in the doldrums, having produced a string of saccharine and forgettable pictures. *Aladdin*, in which the frenzied tones of Robin Williams were brought in, was an entirely different show. Williams drove the film along like a real actor, recording his part before a single frame was drawn – indeed, with the animators working to his ideas. Which is how the movie ended up with a genie who can do Robert De Niro impressions, and an Aladdin modelled on Tom Cruise. Aladdin's love, Jasmine, may be doe-eyed but she too knows what she wants. Based on the traditional *The Thief Of Baghdad* (see p.94), Aladdin emerged as a thoroughly modern romantic adventure.

(see p.94)

▭▭▭ UK, US ◉ UK, US | U (UK) G (US)

The Aristocats 1970

The first animated Disney feature to be released after the death of the studio's founding genius, *The Aristocats* isn't as innovative as *Pinocchio* or *Snow White And The Seven Dwarfs*, but it remains one of the funniest films the studio made. Phil Harris brings his warmth, humour and charisma to the voice of J. Thomas O'Malley and Eva Gabor sounds sultry as his love interest, the duchess who should, with her three kittens, be inheriting a fortune. But evil butler Edgar has other ideas. If you've already seen it, the mere mention of the title will probably have you humming "Everybody Wants To Be A Cat", the big production number whose rousing delivery nearly demolishes a house. There's a decent madcap chase. And there's enough going on to obscure the fact that this is, essentially, a feline retread of *Lady And The Tramp* and that the animation isn't always topnotch. All in all, kids and adults should have a seriously good time.

📼 UK, US ◉UK, US | U (UK) G (US)

Asterix 1975–99

For years before Disneyland opened in Paris, the French dismissed the empire of the mouse as a non-starter alongside their own cartoon theme park – Parc Astérix. And why not? The Asterix cartoon books of René Goscinny and Albert Uderzo are wonderfully funny and original creations: Asterix the wily Gaul and his man-mountain side-kick Obelix, fuelled by the potions of their village Druid, Getafix, and creating havoc across the Roman Empire, and even straying occasionally over to Britain, or even America. Of the 32 cartoon books, seven have been made into animated features, and most of these have appeared at one time or another, in English, on video. But alas, none is currently available, so picking an Asterix movie is really down to pot luck on eBay. Good ones to look out for include **Asterix And Cleopatra** (1968) and **The Twelve Tasks Of Asterix** (1976), both of which were co-directed by Goscinny and Uderzo, and have a relative lightness of wit (not that you should expect subtlety from a 20-stone Gaul carrying a rock around). **Asterix In Britain** (1985) is also very funny – not least in the animators' decision to put all the British road signs in French.

More recently, two live-action productions **Asterix & Obelix Take On Caesar** (1999) and **Asterix & Obelix: Mission Cleopatra** (2002), have been made, with Christian Clavier and Gérard Depardieu as Asterix and Obelix respectively. Thankfully, the transition to live action failed to impede Obelix chucking the Romans around at will.

ANIMATIONS 📼 Currently unavailable | U (UK) NR (US)
LIVE ACTION 📼 UK, US ◉UK, US | U (UK) G (US)

Casper 1995

The town may be called Friendship, but the manor is haunted by three malevolent spirits (Stretch, Stinkie and Fatso) and their essentially decent, but lonely, nephew Casper. The boy ghost becomes so friendly with the daughter of the house's new occupant that he gives up his last chance of life to save her father. The makers used 29 trillion bytes of computer memory to create these ghosts, and the effects and the animation are the real stars, although younger kids will identify with the hero. There's some cursing – but of course, kids of 7 to 10 may enjoy this. The **Casper** sequels are only for the insatiable.

▣ UK, US ◉ UK, US | PG (UK, US)

Charlotte's Web 1973

It was rather an inspired idea to animate E.B. White's sublime story in which a pig called Wilbur is prevented from becoming bacon by a spider. Charlotte weaves words into her web, attracts national publicity, and then dies, leaving 514 eggs behind, all of which hatch, and three of which, the runts, stay with Wilbur. The songs, by the Sherman brothers, are solid rather than unforgettable but this is a charming animated movie for the over-5s. The straight-to-video sequel, **Charlotte's Web 2: Wilbur's Great Adventure** is mediocre.

▣ UK, US ◉ UK, US | U (UK) NR (US)

The Emperor's New Groove 2000

This hip Disney cartoon comedy is built around comedian David Spade's persona as surely as *Aladdin* was built around Robin Williams. For once, this being Disney, there's no great message, just more than the usual quota of laughs as Spade plays the arrogant emperor who gets turned into a llama after a spell designed to kill him goes wrong. Before becoming a llama, Spade was planning to build a summer palace on top of a mountain – where there happens to be an inconveniently sited peasants' village. But it is one of these peasants (John Goodman) who saves the llama/emperor. Fast-moving, with Spade more likeable as a voice than he can sometimes be as a face, this fair zips along – despite the fact that Sting has written some of the songs. Good for kids from 5 to 9.

▣ UK, US ◉ UK, US | U (UK) G (US)

Fantasia 1940

When you marvel – and even today this is a work of great imaginative power – at this masterpiece, remember that its creator, Walt Disney, regarded it as a failure, one he said loomed like a shadow over his whole life. This animation marked many firsts, major and minor: the first movie to be released in stereophonic sound; the first to show Mickey Mouse with whites in his eyes, not just black circles; the first Disney feature to rub away the hard edges of old-fashioned animation. And you might add to that, the first Disney film that is not really aimed at kids. The work illustrates eight pieces of music with cartoons, in a cycle which encompasses the evolution of life on Earth and still finds time to dwell on some cute dancing mushrooms. However, kids of 7 and over should still enjoy it, even if they take it one musical interlude at a time. **Fantasia 2000** (1999) is entertaining but not as innovative or as powerful as the original classic.

▭ UK, US ◉ UK, US │ U (UK) G (US)

FernGully: The Last Rainforest 1992

As you might expect from the title, this at times feel like propaganda for Greenpeace but, didactic as it is, it still manages to be, in the words of the *Washington Post* reviewer, a "whopping good time". The artists went to Australia to experience real rainforests and to recapture some off those details in their animation. Foxy young fairy Crysta is at the heart of the story – she teaches the shrunken lumberjack to respect the forest. As you might expect, Robin Williams steals the show – as a bat, his inspirational improvisations provide a nice relief from some of the more formulaic characters. Good for kids of 5 to 8 – any younger and they might be scared by Tim Curry's smug monster.

▭ UK, US ◉ UK, US │ U (UK) G (US)

Freddie As F.R.O.7 1992

Ben Kingsley is the voice of Freddie, a man-sized frog with an eye for the ladies and a French accent thicker than vichyssoise soup, who is sent to save Britain from evildoers who want to destroy tourism. It seems likely that Freddie the Frog didn't go down too well in Paris but the tale of this Croak Monsieur (geddit?) is too surreal for anyone to be offended for long. Who knows what you or your kids will make of it, but you won't be bored.

▭ UK | G (US) NR (US)

Hercules 1997

The wonder is that Disney took so long to grapple with Greek mythology. Here they cheerfully turn cute, strong Hercules into a kind of Superman figure, give him a personal trainer (Danny DeVito) and a diabolical villain, Hades, marvellously voiced by James Woods. Hercules wasn't as original or successful as *The Hunchback of Notre Dame.*, released the summer before, but it is probably an easier film for younger kids to enjoy. The animation is based on the spiky drawings of Gerald Scarfe, and the script is almost as spiky. All in all, a lot of fun.

▭ UK, US ◎ UK, US | U (UK) G (US)

Ice Age 2002

Sweet-natured and smart, *Ice Age* is a kind of prehistoric *Monsters, Inc* for younger kids, in which a woolly mammoth, a sabre-toothed tiger and a sloth team up to reunite a human baby with its parents. Although the animation gives this a beautiful painterly look, it's the characterisation of the animals that makes the movie more effective than its premise might suggest. The end is a bit schlock-filled but the journey, for the characters and for the viewer, has been such fun, you don't really mind.

▭ UK, US ◎ UK, US | U (UK) PG (US)

Jimmy Neutron: Boy Genius 2001

"One day, Carl, an influx of hormones that we can't control will overpower our better judgement and drive us to pursue the female species against our will." With observations like this, it's easy to see why Jimmy Neutron is regarded as a boy genius. So clever is he, that he inadvertently invites aliens to town. The extra-terrestrials kidnap all the kids' parents which is kind of fun for a while but Jimmy (sneered at as

Jimmy says hi to the nice aliens

"Nerdtron" by his classmates) converts a few amusement park rides into spacecraft and they set out on a heroic mission to rescue their folks. This doesn't cross over into adult territory, like *Shrek*, but kids of 7 and under will have plenty of laugh-out-loud moments. And you'll probably secretly enjoy it.

📼 UK, US ⊚UK, US | U (UK) G (US)

The Jungle Book 1967

Not to rain on anyone's parade, but the Beatles didn't do the voices for the vultures in *Jungle Book*. That was the plan but Walt, whose grip on popular culture had loosened somewhat by the mid-1960s, assumed they were a flash in the pan. Not that they are particularly missed. The vultures are just some of the soundalikes on offer here: Phil Harris, as the voice of loveable bear Baloo, sounds so like John Wayne you wouldn't be astonished if he told Mowgli to get up off his horse and drink his milk. And Louis Prima sounds more like Satchmo than Louis Armstrong sometimes did. The voice that captures the movie, though, is the bored, sardonic, sinister drawl of Shere Khan as provided by George Sanders, an actor who, in real life, was so bored he committed suicide. The tale of Mowgli, lost in the jungle, reared by wolves, befriended by bears and panthers, hunted by tigers and snakes, is nicely told, with the Sherman brothers producing some of Disney's finest songs (especially "Bare Necessities" and "I Wanna Be Like You"), and a beautiful water-carrying girl to distract the young man cub at the denouement.

The Jungle Book 2 (2003) isn't a patch on the original but younger kids might still enjoy it. The original, by contrast, is one of those movies that your kid will probably want to watch again as soon as it's finished. And rightly so.

📼 UK, US 💿 UK, US | U (UK) G (US)

Kiki's Delivery Service 1989

Gently paced, not too heavily plotted, Hayao Miyazaki's tale of a young apprentice witch who has to learn her trade in a strange new city is so sweet-natured it's hard not to be won over. As ever, Miyazaki's cast of characters seem somehow more human than many other animators', possibly because they're not created with a cynical eye on box-office demographics. (It's worth noting, for example, how often sympathetic, intelligent, older people who aren't annoyingly cute appear in Miyazaki's movies.) Kiki's broom-flying delivery service gives the director ample excuse to indulge his obsession for flight. And the story, in which Kiki loses and rediscovers her magic powers, stresses the importance of friendship and independence. You'll feel better for watching this and so will children.

📼 UK, US 💿 UK, US | U (UK) G (US)

Kirikou And The Sorceress 1998

The fact that this French-African animation tied with the far more commercial *Chicken Run* as best European feature in the 2002 British animation awards says something about its quality. Based on a West African folk story, this is a tale of innocence triumphing over evil – and then (plot spoiler alert!) curing evil. Kirikou is the remarkable baby who, alone, has the guts and guile to take on the sorceress who has been plaguing his village. He has to undergo a dangerous journey – a cliché to which writer-director Michel Ocelot adds a new twist, as Kirikou's journey is dangerous yet ordinary and he triumphs through wit as much as by courage. The colours are joyous, there are no attempts to Disnefy the story or the animation style, and there's a sublime soundtrack from Senegalese singer Youssou N'Dour. The simplicity of the story may mean that it's a film to watch just once, but it's something of a masterpiece and deserves to be much, much better known.

▣▣▣ UK ◉UK | U (UK) NR (US)

Lady And The Tramp 1955

Lady and the Tramp have more chemistry than most real movie stars – certainly more than Harrison Ford and Kate Capshaw in *Indiana Jones And The Temple of Doom*. The Tramp is a charming chancer, Lady is an uptown bitch with big soulful eyes whose life gets turned upside down by the arrival of a baby in her household and, if you need any further reason to watch this movie, Peggy Lee sings "He's A Tramp But I Love Him" while two Siamese cats croon "We Are Siamese If You Please". You can't beat it.

▣▣▣ UK, US ◉UK, US | U (UK) G (US)

The Miracle Maker 2000

This modest BBC production of the story of Jesus Christ is well paced for youngsters, and the innovative stop-motion techniques, allied with a team of meticulous Russian puppeteers, create an impressively authentic look. A great vocal cast (Ralph Fiennes, Julie Christie, Miranda Richardson and William Hurt) add distinction. And this isn't a reinterpretation, or a re-evaluation, just the story as told in the Gospels told reasonably straight.

▣▣▣ UK, US ◉UK, US | U (UK)

Monsters, Inc 2001

We've all – adults and kids – watched too many movies based on an original idea which turns out, on execution, to feel not very original at all. The seriously clever thing about this Pixar comedy is not the gags, or the animation (brilliant though it is), it's how fully the original vision is realised. We believe, throughout the movie, that the staff of Monsters, Inc are employed to make kids scream so their terror can power the city of Monstropolis.

Director Pete Docter said, "With *Monsters*, I was trying to hook into something we believed as kids. We knew that when we closed the door, the toys came to life." The laughs come so thick and fast in *Monsters, Inc* because the story has its own logic. Demented, probably. Far-fetched – certainly. But a logic all the same, so it's all the funnier when we realise that the inhabitants of Monstropolis fear children because they're toxic. This idea, which critics feared would alienate kids, actually helped make the movie extraordinarily successful – both at the box office and as a comedy.

The voice talent helps. Billy Crystal as the voice of Mikey, a creature with two horns, one eye and an endless stream of gags, probably has his best time in a movie since *City Slickers*. John Goodman, as Sulley, the walking shag carpet who is supposed to be the ultimate scarer but is actually as sweet as a confectioner's, is almost as amusing. John Ratzenberger and Steve Buscemi offer sterling support. And there are lots of small, nice touches – such as the frustrated fire-breather who keeps setting alight the newspaper he's trying to read.

The **bonus short** released with the movie on video and DVD, with Mikey trying to drive a car, could also power a city – if only someone could find a way of turning laughter into energy.

▭ UK, US ◉UK, US | U (UK) G (US)

Mulan 1998

Not as hip or as flip as *Toy Story*, *Mulan* is often undeservedly overlooked. The eponymous heroine pretends to be a boy to spare her old father the trial of defending China against the invading hordes. This being Disney, she must be accompanied by a comic sidekick, a street-smart dragon well voiced by Eddie Murphy, and, this still being Disney, her early feminist inclinations are tempered when she falls for the dishy captain. But the animators have drawn on the depiction of nature in classical Oriental art and there are scenes here, which for scope and grandeur, exceed anything in *Toy Story* or *The Lion King*. The battle sequence is particularly fine – as the enemy troops sweep down a snowy mountainside, you almost feel as if you're watching a Sergei Eisenstein movie. The only real let down are the songs which are time-passing rather than memorable. But kids of seven and under should enjoy this and it makes a pleasant change for girls to have a heroine at the centre of the action.

UK, US ⊚UK, US | U (UK) G (US)

My Neighbour Totoro 1988

Fans of Japanese animator Hayao Miyazaki have been known to argue long and hard over which is his defining master-piece. *My Neighbour Totoro* must surely have a considerable claim – in the US, where it has been available for some years, it is often voted one of the five best family movies of all time, which is amazing for an un-hyped film from a foreign studio.

The Totoros of the story are benevolent, mute, slightly fierce-look-

ing, forest sprites, inspired, apparently, by the Moomins. They can be seen only by children and, together with a Catbus, they act as guardians and chaperones for two sisters – Mei and Satsuki – who have moved out to the country with their dad, while they wait for their mother to recover from an unspecified illness and come home from hospital. This movie has many beauties, not the least of which is the touching relationship between the girls and their dad, who seems entirely open to the possibility that Totoros exist. The hand-crafted animation is simply astonishing – at times it looks like a water colour, at others there are lovely touches of realism (such as a bottle lying, unremarked, at the bottom of the waterfall). Best of all, the story seems to grow. A Disney or a DreamWorks movie would feel obliged to resolve the issues of the mother's illness and the existence of Totoro and his Catbus friend, but Miyazaki doesn't. Instead, like life itself, the movie is inconclusive – occasionally sad, sometimes a bit frightening, often funny – and always entertaining. Even the songs and theme tune are magic, and like many of the scenes, as when little Mei curls up on Totoro's tummy, or when the girls are saved by the timely arrival of a Catbus, will lodge long in your memory.

If you haven't seen *My Neighbour Totoro* yet, or come across any of Miyazaki's films, then you have a series of life-enhancing treats in store. Children's films really do come no better than this.

🎞 UK, US ◉UK, US | U (UK) G (US)

More Miyazaki? The Japanese animator is, simply, a genius, and most of his output is either aimed at kids, or accessible for slightly older kids. Reviews of his movies are spread throughout this book: see **Castle of Cagliostro** (Action & Adventure), **Kiki's Delivery Service** (Animation), **Sherlock Hound** (Cartoons), **Castle in the Sky** (Sci-fi), **Spirited Away** (Fantasy), and **Panda! Go, Panda!** (Under-5s).

Pocahontas 1995

"A Disney musical with the usual first-rate animation and humma-ble tunes but without the big laughs, the cute talking animals, the magic props and the happy ending. It's practically un-American." So said *Rolling Stone*. Modern Disney is – understandably – at its most politically correct when dealing with Native American heroes, but this approach made Pocahontas less of a heroine than a symbol: of some idealized, imagined innocence which, the movie suggests, existed in North America before the big bad settlers arrived from Europe. Even so, when Pocahontas teaches John Smith (the voice of Mel Gibson), you're not sure he listens because he respects her views or because she's exceptionally beautiful. As short on jokes as it is on ambiguity, this movie may tax the patience, especially of boys, as it lacks a decent scoundrel. But it's well drawn, the song "Colors Of The Wind" is a standout, and it is ambitious. There is some violence

(Pocahontas's fiancé is killed), but nothing that kids of 5 and up can't handle.

📼 UK, US ◎ UK, US | U (UK) G (US)

The Prince Of Egypt 1998

An animated movie about Moses in which the lawgiver was voiced not by Charlton Heston but by Val Kilmer might have seemed like a high-risk project. But DreamWorks also called on the vocal talents of some truly stellar co-stars (Michelle Pfeiffer, Helen Mirren, Ralph Fiennes, Steve Martin, Sandra Bullock, Jeff Goldblum, Danny Glover) and the finest computer animators to tell this story. "One imagines [Cecil] deMille had a film like this in mind before he had to reduce it to reality," applauded critic Roger Ebert, while even the professional sceptics at *The Onion* concluded this told the story of Moses "as God intended". The ten plagues of Egypt are especially well realised, and the only low point, as with *Mulan*, is the selection of songs – forgettable, bland, soundtrack fillers with lyrics on the can-do theme of "You can make if you really try" don't quite match the grandeur of the story. Good for kids of 5 and over.

📼 UK, US ◎ UK, US | PG (US, UK)

The Rescuers 1977

The 1970s wasn't a great decade for Disney and the animation in *The Rescuers* looks a little cheap by the standards of what went before and came later. But this is a genuinely engaging story: two mice, Bernard (Bob Newhart) and Bianca (Eva Gabor), from the International Rescue Aid Society, set out to help an orphan girl kidnapped by treasure hunters. They track the girl down to the swamps of Louisiana, flying out, in a very funny sequence, on a chatterbox albatross voiced by Jim Jordan. There they need to outwit the evil Medusa (a Cruella de Vil reborn), her henchmen and crocs.

Although one of the less well-known Disney movies, *The Rescuers* really should be up there in the canon, and it has the bonus of a rather good sequel, **The Rescuers Down Under** (1990). This is far better technically, with a beautifully realised flight scene, and it has an equally engaging story. And down under being Australia, it adds a kangaroo mouse to the team.

▭ UK, US ◉ UK, US │ U (UK) G (US)

The Secret Of NIMH 1982

In 1979, Don Bluth and sixteen other animators left Disney determined to show Walt's heirs where the studio was going wrong and hark back to the old classic Disney formula. He never really quite delivered, but this rather Tolkienish story came close, and was by far their best effort. The story is quite dark – a mother mouse has to enlist the aid of some rats and befriend a crow to save her sick son – but it is carried very well by the traditional animation, which is superb in the depiction of the rats' underground city. Sadly, the movie was a financial failure and, by the 1990s, Disney was back to its best, while Bluth was producing largely the kind of insipid fare he had rebelled against.

▭ UK, US ◉ UK, US │ U (UK) G (US)

Mouse and Crow on a mission of mercy in NIMH

Shrek 2001, 2004

As you probably already knew, Shrek is Yiddish for monster, and this comedy was as big a box-office monster as they come: a film that *everyone* loved, and which left us all clapping and stamping, calling for the sequel.

So where did it all go so right for the DreamWorks team? First off, of course, the film looked fantastic – unlike any film that had preceded it, with its new-style animation constantly jolting you to wonder if you're watching cartoon or live action. That will be repeated many times, for sure, but we saw it first here. And second? Well, it has to be the writers (Ted Elliott, Terry Rossio, Joe Stillman and Roger S.H. Schulman, with additional dialogue by Cody Cameron, Chris Miller and Conrad Vernon). This is simply one of the wittiest kids' movies in years, and an absolute gift for such voice talents as Mike Myers (Shrek the nice ogre – oh come on, you *have* seen this film) and Eddie Murphy (braying supremely as Donkey). And then … you have to put a credit in for whoever chose the soundtrack. It rocks. It's modern but nostalgic, it's irresistibly feel good (with Smash Mouth's reinvention of "I'm A Believer" leading the pack).

The moral lesson – beauty is only skin deep – seems fair enough even if, in real life, the virtuous big green stinking ogre doesn't always get the girl at the school disco. But that's beside the point because this is a film where the characters just worm their way into your affections, without once making you feel even slightly nauseous. Kids of any age could savour this and they'll enjoy it, over and over again. If you buy it on DVD, the American edition is considerably more complete than its European counterpart, but both give you terrific extras, including a hilarious karaoke section featuring Donkey and the band.

Oh yes – and there *was* a sequel, **Shrek 2** (2004) in which our loveable ogre gets to meet the in-laws. While inevitably not such a gust of fresh air as the original, and relying more on big set pieces than plot, it is still very funny indeed, with the honours this time round going to Antonio Banderas as the voice of Puss In Boots, upstaging Myers and Murphy in a role that sends up his own performance *Zorro*. Other cinematic homages abound but some of the biggest laughs come from the rivalry between Puss and Murphy's donkey for the position of "most annoying talking animal".

UK, US ◎UK, US | PG (US, UK)

Thunderbirds Are Go! Supermarionation

Gerry Anderson is the presiding genius of a bizarre TV genre known as **Supermarionation**. The name refers to the technology used to move puppets' lips in synch so they look like they are speaking. With this unlikely, even daft, premise, Anderson became one of the first British TV producers to create shows which made it on to American TV. He also pioneered special-effects techniques which George Lucas and Steven Spielberg would use.

The arrival of the long-awaited, live-action **Thunderbirds** movie will likely rekindle interest in Anderson's work. But for the purists, there's nothing like the real thing – the puppets doing their stuff in series which, for all the gimmicks and catchphrases, were often surprisingly adult in theme. In **Stingray**, there's a hunka hunka unrequited love in the claustrophobic world of the World Aquanaut Security Patrol and the characters aren't afraid to knock back a stiff drink.

Anderson's formula, once perfected, didn't change much: global organisation for good combating nefarious opponents, a catchy theme, male characters often modelled on current movie or TV stars, some eye candy and a boffin. But it worked beautifully until Anderson started working with real actors in shows such as **Space 1999**. Most of the shows have now been reissued on video and DVD – here's a quick memory jogger for those who grew up with supermarionation or, if you've never seen them, a brief introduction to the best of Anderson's work.

Captain Scarlet
Catchphrase: "Spectrum is green."
The pitch: Captain Scarlet is the heroic officer in Spectrum, an organisation trying to save the world from the Martian Mysterons. Somehow, in the opening credits, a squealing cat and broken milk bottles get embroiled in this inter-planetary conflict.
Eye candy: Harmony, Rhapsody and Melody, slinkier than Farrah and co's Charlie's Angels.

Fireball XL5
Catchphrase: "I want to be a fireball, a fireball, a fireball."
The pitch: Hotshot pilot Colonel Steve Zodiac protects earth from alien attacks in his Fireball XL5, possibly the only craft – and TV series – to be named in honour of an oil, Castrol XL.
Eye candy: The lovely Venus.

Joe 90
Catchphrase: "He's only a boy!"
The pitch: A 9-year-old orphaned secret agent defends the world with the aid of his adopted dad who can transfer specialist brain patterns into Joe, enabling him to be a test pilot, a brain surgeon and lots of other clever occupations.
Eye candy: None to speak of.

Stingray
Catchphrase: "Anything can happen in the next half hour."
The pitch: Troy Tempest (modelled on James Garner) and Bones try to foil underwater villains, while Troy, Atlanta and Marina struggle with an unrequited love triangle.
Eye candy: Mute, cute Marina and lovelorn Atlanta.

Supercar
Catchphrase: "Satisfactory. Most satisfactory!"
The pitch: Mike Mercury travels the world looking for adventure which, if you've got a flying prototype car and a 10-year-old orphan on board, proves surprisingly easy to find.
Eye candy: None.

Thunderbirds
Catchphrase: "Thunderbirds are go!"
The pitch: International Rescue do pretty much what the name suggests, but truly to avert peril they need a secret base, a fantastic fleet of Thunderbird flying machines, a submarine and a space station almost as pointless as the real one being built today.
Eye candy: Lady Penelope Parker – posh pin-up whose style has influenced successors such as Liz Hurley.

Tintin 1960s, 1990s

Created by Belgian-born Georges Remi (known professionally as Hergé since 1924), Tintin and his faithful wire-haired fox terrier, Snowy, were born on January 10, 1929, and appeared in print the following year. From that time until Hergé's death in 1983, the dog and the boy detective underwent 22 book-length adventures, ranging through Egypt (*Cigars of the Pharaoh*), China (*The Blue Lotus*), Syldavia (*King Ottokar's Sceptre*), South America (*The Broken Ear; The Seven Crystal Balls; Prisoners of the Sun; Tintin and the Picaros*), the USA (*Tintin in America*), Scotland (*The Black Island*), the Sahara (*The Crab with the Golden Claws*), the Arctic (*The Shooting Star*), the Deep Sea (*The Secret of the Unicorn; Red Rackham's Treasure*), the Middle East (*Land of Black Gold; The Red Sea Sharks*), the Moon (*Destination Moon; Explorers on the Moon*), Borduria (*The Calculus Affair*), the Himalayas (*Tintin in Tibet*), France (*The Castafiore Emerald*), and the Pacific (*Flight 714*).

The books – with their inspired cast of associates (Captain Haddock, professor Calculus, the Thompsons) and villains (notably Rastopopoulos) – were surefire material for films, and the first (black and white) animations appeared in France in 1946. The process got more serious in the 1960s, when a series of cartoons were made, and aired in tantalisingly brief episodes on British TV. These included **Tintin And The Shooting Star**, which was among the films issued on video in the 1990s, along with new films of each of the books (except the two early and politically dodgy ones – *Land of the Soviets* and *In the Congo*). These have recently transferred to DVD (UK format only), with four stories on each disc (and a bargain boxed set with all 21 films). Enthusiasts will want to see them all; they include English and French soundtracks for those who prefer Snowy to be called "Milou".

If you have younger kids, the best ones to start with are the double-bill **Secret Of The Unicorn** and **Red Rackham's Treasure**, with lots of deep sea excitement and pirates, or the gently paced **Tintin In Tibet**; while you may want to avoid the genuinely scary **Seven Crystal Balls** and its sequel, **Prisoners Of The Sun**. But those caveats aside, all the Tintin films are essential viewing, with the possible exception of **Tin Tin And The Lake Of Sharks** – a 1972 movie that was, uniquely, not based on one of Hergé's books.

📼 UK ◉ UK | NR

Toy Story 1995

Forget the talk of how many computers, at how many bytes a seconds, it took to make this completely digitally animated feature work. The simple joy of the film is best captured by the glorious tag line: "The toys are back in town!" Pixar's animation techniques, even today, are something of a triumph but *Toy Story* and its almost equally great sequel work because, as Tom Hanks (the voice of Woody) says, they are classic pieces of American folklore.

For anyone who missed it, the story revolves around two rival toys – Woody the cowboy and Buzz the astronaut ("To infinity and beyond") – who have to become buddies to save themselves, and their other toys, from the psychotic designs of the kid next door. At the heart of the story is something most kids will understand – the fear of rejection. In both *Toy Story 1* and *2*, Woody has to deal with the fear that he's losing his place in the affections of his owner, Andy. You see, even toys need to be loved. Hanks says voicing Woody was "acting full-bore one hundred percent" and the other actors (especially Tim Allen as Buzz and Don Rickles as Mr Potato Head) emulate Hanks's approach. Disney had insisted, to Pixar's chagrin, that there be songs, but these, written and sung by Randy Newman, are woven so beautifully into the action that they enhance the story, bringing out some of the hidden emotions in this fast-moving, amusing, tale.

Toy Story 2 is, inevitably, not quite as fresh as its predecessor and loses something for not having the weird kid and his freakish mutant toys (their place being taken by a toy collector – and grown up). But it has some fantastic sequences, notably the toys crossing the road in traffic cones, and still rates as one of the best children's movies released in the last decade.

▭▭ UK, US ◉UK, US | PG (UK) G (US)

Wallace & Gromit 1990–95

It's amazing what you can achieve by adjusting little clay figures 24 times a second. When Nick Park – who made his name with **Creature Comforts**, a deliciously wry short film in which zoo animals are voiced by disaffected urban dwellers – started out he can hardly have imagined that he would create the most endearing twosome since Laurel and Hardy, make a movie in which Hollywood stars such as George Clooney queued up to lend their vocal talents... and even save the Wensleydale cheese factory.

Cheese-obsessed Wallace, whose intellect is as full of holes as Switzerland's annual output of Emmenthal, mentioned "Wensleydale" in *A Close Shave* and the publicity generated helped save the cheese factory, which had fallen on hard times, from bankruptcy. Gromit, as a Fido Dogstoyevsky-reading canine, would not have been at all astonished at such a twist in the tale.

The *Wallace & Gromit* movies have a lovely ramshackle air, a Heath Robinson quality of inventiveness. The inventions – robotic trousers, automatic sheep-shearing devices – all behave in unexpected ways, adding to the surrealistic complexity which Park manages to generate from some very simple premises (a trip to the moon in *A Grand Day Out*, a venture into window cleaning in *A Close Shave*). But at the heart of their collective appeal is the mysterious comic chemistry between the two unlikely central characters.

All three *Wallace & Gromit* films – **A Grand Day Out** (1990), **The Wrong Trousers** (1993) and **A Close Shave** (1995) – are gathered together on the current DVD and video releases. They are all wonderful, with *A Close Shave* perhaps the best of all, with its hint of film noir romance and arguably the definitive example of the chase scenes which have become a trademark. But *The Wrong Trousers* has its advocates, too, directed as a spoof thriller – and with a slightly darker twist than the other films. It is suitable for any age, though, and will scare only those children – and adults – who are unnerved by Feathers McGraw, an ominously silent, yet sinister, penguin whose nefarious plans for a diamond heist turn crucially on stealing Gromit's "ex-NASA" robotic trousers.

US ⓞUK, US | U (UK) G (US)

Who Framed Roger Rabbit 1988

"A man, a woman, and a rabbit, in a triangle of trouble". For once, the studio tag line captures the zany charm of this ground-breaking movie which mixes animation and live action, comedy and thriller, to splendid effect. Bob Hoskins, as the down-at-heel private eye Eddie Valiant, grew so effective at reacting to imaginary, invisible, characters that he suffered from hallucinations and his son never quite forgave him for not bringing his cartoon co-stars home. This is, as Roger Ebert says, "the kind of movie that gets made once in a blue moon because the film-makers have to make a good movie and invent new technology". It has a storyline and in-jokes to keep grown-ups watching, and is such joyous fun that kids will never get bored. Roger Rabbit is framed for the murder of a gag-gift mogul and Valiant, after some sultry persuasion from Jessica Rabbit (Kathleen Turner, with enough seduction in her voice to make a bishop kick a hole through a stained-glass window), is hired to clear him. Be warned, though, that the spiralling plot, and rat-a-tat-tat gags, eventually lead to a quite scary denouement – you might have to hold younger kids' hands as the villain gets his comeuppance.

▨ UK, US ◉UK, US | PG (UK, US)

Yellow Submarine 1968

Deadpan understatement; free-flowing, inventive animation, great songs; a whimsical intelligently punning script, *Yellow Submarine* may be the most successful blend of animation and music since *Fantasia*. The Beatles did this animated film only to get out of a three-movie contract, had little input into it, but liked the first cut so much they agreed to appear in a live-action sequence singing "All Together Now" to round off the movie. The film was unjustly neglected after its release – withdrawn from cinemas in 1982 and not available in any format for twelve years – because it was regarded as too much of its time. Watch it today, and it looks a masterpiece. It's not just the songs, it's the detail in the humour – the way Ringo picks up a black hole and, to get them out of a scrape, remembers "I've got a hole in my pocket!" There are a few dull patches but, almost all the time, this is the Fab Four's real magical mystery tour.

▨ UK, US ◉UK, US | U (UK) G (US)

FILE UNDER ACTION, ANIMALS, CARTOONS, FANTASY, ETC

The animated movies below are all reviewed in other chapters of this book.

continued overleaf

continued....

Cartoons

shorts on the TV

What's the difference between cartoons and animated films? You could debate that one for ever. We went for a traditional definition: short, animated films, many of which first appeared – or continue to appear – on TV, and for simplicity, cartoon feature film spin-offs of series such as *Rugrats* and *Scooby-Doo* (yes, even live-action Scooby). If your favourites aren't reviewed here, don't give up on us before checking the chapters on **Animation**, **Animals**, or **Under-5s** (where you'll find cartoons that appeal more or less exclusively to this age group).

Animaniacs 1993–97

Animaniacs was an audacious enterprise, Steven Spielberg using old classics as inspiration for a series to rival *Looney Tunes*. In the first episode, the Warner Brothers (and Sisters) were old-time *Looney Tunes* characters locked in the Warner Bros water tank for making no sense. Escaping, they wreak havoc on the world with their zany antics. Playing on the theme of the wildest and wackiest, kids were subsequently introduced to Pinky and The Brain – laboratory mice bent on world domination (Brain based on Orson Welles), the Three Goodfeathers – a mob of New York pigeons, and Chicken Boo – a giant chicken. Voiced by such cartoon luminaries as Rob Paulsen (Raphael Ninja Turtle) and Nancy Cartwright (Bart Simpson), this wacky cartoon – good for almost any age – has become a modern classic, compiled on half a dozen videos, though not yet on DVD.

📼 UK, US | U (UK) NR (US)

Cat In The Hat 1971

Dr Seuss (see box on p.65) has not been well served by film-makers – witness the awful mess that was Mike Myers's *The Cat in the Hat* (2003). Fortunately, you can see just how good the *Cat In The Hat* concept is, and how charming a film it makes, by checking out this 1971 made-for-TV version directed by (it must be his real name) Hawley Pratt. It is filmed absolutely faithfully from the book, with simple but quirky animation, a nice clear narration of the original poem, and some absolutely cracking songs ("Calculatus Eliminatus"and "There's Always Some Fish"). You need to make sure you get the right version, however, for – confusingly – in addition to the Myers debacle, there is another made-for-TV *Cat In The Hat*, dating from 1972, which is a completely static animation.

Pratt also animated **The Lorax** – Dr Seuss's environmental plea, about pollution – and this, too, has recently emerged on DVD, as has the classic **Green Eggs And Ham**, which again is straightforward animation with some good songs.

📼 US, UK ◉ UK, US | NR

Count Duckula
1987–90

A spin-off from *Danger Mouse*, *Count Duckula* emerged in *The Four Tasks Of Danger Mouse* as a baddie, but his appeal as a foppish vegetarian vampire led creators Cosgrove Hall to give him his own series. The result is an unpredictable comedy, best appreciated by kids of 6 up. David Jason voiced the count, while Ruby Wax supplied additional voices and additional laughs. Episodes to seek (there are various videos still available) include *No Sax Please – We're Egyptian* where Duckula goes in search of a mystical Egyptian saxophone, and *The Ghost Of McCastle McDuckula* with the count heading for Loch Ness.

📼 UK | U (UK) NR (US)

Cow And Chicken, Volume 1 2000

Cow is a dainty, feather-brained schoolgirl while her big brother, Chicken, is a sour-faced, cranky… chicken. Chicken's efforts to teach Cow the ways of

The Great Dr Seuss

The trademark of Theodor Seuss Geisel is the rhyming couplets he wrote most of his books in. But the titles are a bit of a giveaway too: *The 5000 Fingers Of Dr T*, *The Cat In The Hat*, *Yertle The Turtle* (his spoof of the Nazis), *Hoober-Bloob Highway*, even *Dr Seuss I Am Not Going To Get Up Today…* they all betray a certain comic sensibility. However, translating that sensibility to the screen has, for most movie makers, proved as cheerily straightforward as alchemy – the obvious recent example being Mike Myers's dismal version of **Cat In The Hat** (see previous page), or the almost equally humourless Jim Carrey version of **How The Grinch Stole Christmas** (see p.83).

Part of the problem is that Seuss (it's pronounced to rhyme with voice, not loose) doesn't call in the seventh cavalry – the strings, the sugary sentiment, the comforting reassurance that all will be well – until very late on in a story, if at all. This makes moviemakers, especially those trained in Hollywood, uneasy. Part of the difficulty may be that what works in cartoon format on the printed page or, as with the cruelty in *Tom And Jerry*, in animated cartoons, can seem mean-spirited, even vicious, as soon as you bring in a human cast. Indeed, the only live-action movie of Seuss's stories that really clicks is **The 5000 Fingers Of Dr T** (reviewed in *Musicals*).

Dr Seuss was an iconoclast who never had any children and, as soon as his books became successful, spent most of his time alone in the studio. Born in 1904, educated at Dartmouth College and Oxford University, he had worked as a commercial artist – and as a major in the US Army in World War II, serving in a propaganda filmmaking unit with Frank Capra. Although he wrote such stirring, one-sided documentaries as *Your Job In Germany* (1945), the experience affected him deeply – judging by his anti-war story the *Butter Battle Book*. He turned to other political themes, warning against the destruction of the environment in *The Lorax*, but was never at his most effective as a polemicist. He died in 1991, at a time when his books were just being rediscovered.

The best of his work on film are the relatively straight animations – the 1971 **Cat In The Hat** version reviewed on the previous page, the Chuck Jones animations of *The Grinch* and **Horton Hears A Who!** (see Christmas, p.83), and **The Best Of Dr Seuss**, which includes the *Looney Tunes* version of *Horton Hatches The Egg* (1942).

the world are plagued by the dastardly villain Red Guy. If you're expecting cute, cuddly animals and merry adventures you're in for a shock, *Cow And Chicken* (on Cartoon Network) is a favourite with students as well as children thanks to its unusual, at times surreal, comedy. Episode to watch – *The Cow Chicken Blues* featuring B.B. King as guest vocalist.

📼 UK | U (UK) NR (US)

Danger Mouse 1981–87

DM to his friends, Danger Mouse is the greatest superhero in the world, or so the song goes. Based on Patrick McGoohan's 1960s hero Danger Man, its creators (Cosgrove Hall) modelled Silas Greenback and his white caterpillar on Bond's nemesis Blofeld and his cat and Colonel K on Q. DM even has a not-so-super sidekick in Penfold. With mysteries to rival Sherlock Holmes and the voices of David Jason and Terry Scott, this is a cartoon for all the family, and is available on numerous video compilations.

📼 UK, US ◎ UK | U (UK) NR (US)

Dexter's Laboratory 1996–present

Dexter is a red-haired, spectacled boy genius with a secret science lab in his bedroom. There he creates all manner of amazing inventions and potions unbeknown to his parents who don't even bat an eyelid when he arrives at the dinner table as a mutant. His sister Dee Dee knows his secret, as does his enemy, the evil genius Mandark. A spin-off like *Cow And Chicken* from *What A Cartoon Show*, this intelligent and loud (visually and in pure volume) cartoon has clever scripts often referencing sci-fi classics such as *Star Wars*. There are various video issues. Purists say the first two seasons were the best. One to avoid is *Dexter's Rude Removal*, never shown on television due to its adult nature.

📼 UK | U (UK) G (US)

Dogtanian And The Three Muskehounds 1981

Based on the adventures of Alexander Dumas's 17th-century musketeers, this Japanese cartoon is one you will either love or hate.

Dogtanian is a fresh-faced young pup under the tutelage of three musketeers and, in each episode, all four battle against the evil Cardinal Richelieu. The action is exciting and there's a catchy theme tune to singalong ("One For All, And All For One"), but Dogtanian is a little too green around the gills and his love for Juliet gives the cartoon a romantic edge, not always appreciated by children. On the DVD, you and your kids can learn the catchy theme song in four languages.

📼 UK ◉UK, US | U (UK) NR (US)

Donald Duck: Everybody Loves Donald
2003

Walt Disney's Donald Duck (see box) is one of the great cartoon pioneers, along with his great rival Mickey Mouse. As you'd imagine, Donald has had a few video releases over his sixty-year career, and this one is probably the best general compilation.

📼 UK, US ◉UK, US | U (UK) NR (US)

The Flintstones 1960s

The Flintstones was such an unparalleled success in the 1960s

Donald Duck

There was always something a bit odd about Donald Duck – a strangeness only partly explained by the revelation that Clarence Nash, whose vocal chords expressed Donald Duck's thoughts and emotions for half a century, based the duck's familiar diction on the "wa-ah-ah-ah" sound his pet ewe made when she fed on her bottle. But that's not all of it. As far back as the 1930s when the insufferably cheery Mickey Mouse was already establishing the kind of irrepressibly good-humoured persona which would persuade millions to chant "M-I-C-K-E-Y M-O-U-S-E", Donald Duck was carving out his own niche as a grumpy, anti-social, icon, the first animated anti-hero. Watch him for a few seconds and it's easy to believe the urban legend that Donald Duck was once banned by the Finnish censors – because he wasn't wearing any trousers.

Donald Fauntleroy Duck, to use his full name, made his screen debut in *The Wise Little Hen* on June 9, 1934. He was redesigned, becoming fuller and rounder, in 1937 and was given his own cartoons, a love interest (Donna, soon to become Daisy) and, soon after, a trio of nephews (Huey, Dewey and Louie). By 1941, war had turned audiences off the Shirley Temple cuteness of Mickey and Donald had become more popular than Disney's first great icon. But some bad career decisions, notably the studio's insistence on him being the victim of those smarmy rodents Chip'n'Dale, meant that his star waned in the 1950s.

But Donald remains a significant part of global culture, resident around the world at Disneyland, and no stranger to politics. In Sweden, apparently, the Donald Duck Party would, if its votes over twenty years of elections were added up, be the country's ninth largest political party. Just as well the law has been changed to stop Swedes voting for fictional ducks and other characters that aren't eligible for office. However, the Finns have taken over, and in most general elections Donald remains their leading "joke" candidate.

that poor old Mel Blanc (the voice of Barney and Dino) was forced, when recovering from a coma, to record episodes from his hospital bed with the entire cast huddled into his room. Recent poor attempts to bring the series to the big screen have tainted the show's brilliance, but revisit the original Bedrock and the prehistoric lives of Fred, Wilma, Barney and Betty (based on characters in *The Honeymooners*) and you'll see why it was the longest running prime-time animated TV show in the US before *The Simpsons*. For the first two years the show was actually in black and white, so kids might prefer to skip those.

▣ US ◉US | NR (UK) G (US)

Hong Kong Phooey 1970s

In the 1970s Hanna-Barbera created a string of cartoons based around trends of the day. Of the batch, their tribute to the martial arts craze was the best, albeit not the most successful with only sixteen episodes made. Penry was a mild-mannered dog working as a police station janitor who, hearing that a crime was going down, would jump into a filing cabinet and emerge as a kung-fu fighting superhero complete with a robe, mask and the Phooeymobile which could turn into any vehicle he wished. Like all good superheroes he had a sidekick: Spot the stripy cat, the brains of the operation. There is nothing startling about the animation or the stories, but Scatman Crowthers's vocal talents as the hero, dishing out one-liners and talking to the audience, lifts this out of the ordinary.

▣ UK | U (UK) NR (US)

Jackie Chan Adventures 2000–present

If you had a karate belt for every time Jackie says "Jade!" with a mixture of anxiety and exasperation in his cartoon series, you'd be one of the world's foremost martial experts. Animated Chan is even more likeable than Chan the actor as he struggles to fight the baddies and keep his uncle and niece Jade out of mischief. Neatly done, with a totally trivial Q&A at the end in which kids ask, "Jackie, have you ever played baseball?" and it's good to see a hero who isn't infallible – he loses quite a few fights and actually looks hurt!

▣ UK, US ◉UK, US | NR

Jamie & The Magic Torch 1978

With plans afoot for a film version of *Jamie*, this 1970s classic is set for a revival. Produced by Cosgrove Hall, who were also making the equally surreal *Charlton And The Wheelies*, this is *Tintin* meets *Yellow Submarine*. Thanks to Jamie's magic torch, when his mum turns the lights out, he and Wordsworth are transported to Cuckooland, full of cuckoo characters such as Bullybuddy, the show-business rabbit with huge feet and an ego to match a unicycling, truncheon-eating cop; and Mr Boo, a roller-skating professor. These eccentric characters have equally startling pop-art appearances, making this an unusual treat. Best for kids of 7 and above.

📼 UK | U (UK) NR (US)

The Jetsons 1962–63, 1990

 Only 24 episodes of the **original 1962–63 series** of this sci-fi/comedy cartoon were made but *The Jetsons* – Joseph Barbera's finest moment without William Hanna – remains one of the most hugely influential cartoons of all time. Indeed, the family name may ring a bell, softly, even with people who haven't seen the original, as it was a prime influence on Matt Groening's *Futurama* and a less obvious, but still powerful, influence on *The Simpsons*. For the uninitiated, the Jetsons live in the world of the future – a world where irate parking meters bang cars whose owners haven't bought parking tickets. George is the patriarch, and employee of Spaceley's Sprockets, whose fortunate wife has gadgets to clean the house for her. Watched today, it's an entertaining insight into how, in 1960s America, the future was supposed to look. But the comedy still stands up – when Judy says, "Daddy, if you dance like that in front of my friends I have to go live in another galaxy", daughters everywhere know exactly what she means. The **1990 cartoon movie remake** is, as the *Washington Post* put it, "colorful and bouncy, at least for kids, and for adults, weird enough to keep you open-mouthed with disbelief".

📼 UK ◉US | U (UK) NR (US)

Johnny Bravo 2000

It's no coincidence that Johnny Bravo lives in Aron, a city named after Elvis's middle name, for Bravo is himself based on "The King". This isn't necessarily a compliment as Bravo is a blonde, quiffed egomaniac with an eye for the ladies and a brain the size of a pea. He's also a mama's boy, most episodes seeing Johnny taught a tough new lesson about life by his mama or his best friend Carl (once voiced by Mickey Dolenz). Still running today, most episodes spoof television shows and movies. Ones to look out for include *Enter The Chipmunk*, a chipmunk helping Johnny become a karate star, and *Some Like It Stupid* with Johnny and Carl in drag. Generally, the earlier episodes are smarter. Best appreciated by kids of 5 and above.

▭ UK | U (UK) NR (US)

Josie And The Pussycats 1970s

A litter tray full of kittenish fun, this 1970s Hanna-Barbera cartoon about singing sleuths, which inspired the 2001 live-action movie, is almost as entertaining as *Scooby-Doo*. There's a decent soundtrack – Josie and co having their own group – and plenty of laughs as banned-from-the-band Alexandra tries to lure hunky Alan away from the microphone and Josie.

▭ UK, US ◎ UK, US | NR

Looney Tunes 1930s–present

In April 1, 1930, Warner Bros, having seen Disney's success with the cartoon-talkie *Steamboat Willie*, launched its own animation house, partly as a way of promoting its huge music library (initial releases always focused around a song owned by Warner). Continuing to use Disney as a model, Warner's first character, Bosko, was based on Mickey Mouse, whilst their first series, *Looney Tunes*, was a blatant imitation of Disney's own *Silly Symphonies*. Initial releases continued in the Disney vein but from 1933, with an influx of new animation directors, Warner slowly began to establish its own innate style (see box p.71).

Seventy-five years on, the series continues to air, and to be re-invented, for TV and cinema – most recently with the cinema release

A Rough Guide to Looney Tune Animators

Here is a whistlestop guide to the likes of Friz Freleng, Chuck Jones and Tex Avery – the classic Looney Tunes animators who helped Warner lead the field in cartoon animation.

Friz Freleng

A former Disney protégé, Freleng got his big break in 1933, when he was promoted to director. Within two years he had created one of Warner's most memorable characters – a stuttering, ineffectual pig by the name of **Porky**. Freleng was also instrumental in the creation of **Yosemite Sam**, **Sylvester**, **Speedy Gonzales** and the **Pink Panther** cartoon.

Tex Avery

Living by the motto "In a cartoon you can do anything", Avery broke boundaries by creating larger-than-life characters and putting them in unusual situations, often drawing on fairytales – one of his favourite genres. He helped make **Porky Pig** a star and laid the foundations for the **Bugs Bunny** character with his 1940 cartoon *A Wild Hare*. However, **Daffy Duck** was his greatest creation. The wisecracking duck first appeared in the Porky Pig short, *Porky's Duck Hunt*, and offered viewers a different kind of lunacy. Unfortunately, a disagreement with bosses over his new super-cool rabbit, led Avery to leave Warner's for MGM where he created **Droopy Dog**.

Chuck Jones

Despite working under Avery's tutelage, Jones was quick to establish his own style at Warner's, providing the studio with the likes of **Road Runner**, **Wile E. Coyote** and **Pepe Le Pew**. His reinvention of established characters such as **Daffy**, **Bugs Bunny** and **Elmer Fudd** cemented his reputation.

Robert McKimson

Often ignored by critics, McKimson drew the definitive **Bugs Bunny** image, the laid-back rabbit lounging against a tree, carrot in hand. Although perhaps the most artistically talented of Warner's stars, his key characters, notably **Foghorn Leghorn**, lacked the staying power of others in the stable.

Bob Clampett

The cartoons by Warner's zaniest animator were frequently described as surreal, violent and irreverent. Clampett's most notable works include **Tweety Pie** and **Beaky Buzzard**.

Looney Tunes Back in Action (2004) featuring Bugs Bunny and Daffy Duck – and has a hugely successful website, with games based around the cartoon characters. But it the classics that are really the most fun, best explored on the **Golden Collection** DVD, currently available only in North American format, which makes up for certain flaws in presentation (poor quality track listing, over-promising on the extras) with 56 classics. The discs in this set have all been released separately outside the US.

📼 UK, US ◎ US | NR

The Pink Panther 1960s

When director Blake Edwards commissioned Friz Freleng to create a three-and-a-half minute cartoon to fill the opening credits of his movie, he could never have imagined it would prove more durable than the film itself. Yet the pink, mute mysterious feline, his appearance heralded by Henry Mancini's unforgettably humalong theme, appealed to audiences across the world. Freleng's creation often spoofed Sixties trends, dwelling on the psychedelic panther in *Psychedelic Pink* and a secret agent panther in *Pinkfinger*. In 1969 the panther got his own television show, with the cartoon capers of *The Inspector* (based on Inspector Clouseau) running between the panther toons. The Inspector, later replaced by Ant and Aardvark and Crazy Legs Crane, remains the Panther's most pleasing companion. If you are getting a video, look for the **1960s cartoons** rather than the **1993 series** in which Mr Pink, regrettably, speaks.

📼 UK, US | U (UK) NR (US)

Pokémon 1999–present

If you missed the craze, it's hard to believe the tales of playgrounds at war over a Pikachu card, when Pokémon was at its height. But Pokémon was, for a year or two, an enormous global phenomenon, and much of its appeal was down to this cartoon series, imported like the cards from Japan. Drawn in the Japanese anime style, the story is basically a quest: Ash, his friends Misty and Brock, and their eternal ally, Pikachu, roam the world to find all 150 Pokémon (just as kids should collect all the cards) and help Ash become the world's greatest ever trainer. The pals invariably fall out during an episode but are reunited by the close, as they stroll off into the sunset, having learnt the value of – and the qualities required for – true friendship. They come into conflict with a long-haired, short-skirted villainess, Jesse, and her hapless errand boy, James, but win almost as often as Jerry beats Tom. The centrepiece of each instalment is a duel in which Ash and his opponent call on all sorts of Pokémon creatures to battle each other. Unlike the dreadful *Digimon* which followed, *Pokémon* offers a coherent narrative, enjoyably repetitive plot themes (Brock always falls for the first girl they meet but never for Misty) and no real violence. Suitable, despite the alarms, for kids of 4 and over, though whether you would want to buy kids a DVD or video, rather than just switching on the odd episode on TV, is a bit more debatable.

📼 UK, US ◉ UK, US | U (UK) NR (US)

Recess 1997–present

Recess is a nicely observed series about fourth graders at Third St Elementary School (named after millionaire philanthropist Thaddeus T. Third III) and stuff that happens to them in their break times. The ensemble cast of characters is believable, and well differentiated, and the gags aren't bad either. Watching their nemesis Mrs Finster, Mikey says, "She looks so happy like that," to which Ashley Spinelli replies: "Yeah, let's go destroy her life." There's stuff about boys kissing girls, and vice versa, but it's suitable for kids aged 5 and up, and in many ways a natural successor to *Rugrats*.

📼 UK, US ◉ UK, US | U (UK)

Rugrats 1991–present

American rhyming slang for babies (Brats), *Rugrats* follows the adventures of four babies, Tommy, Chuckie, Phil and Lil, and Tommy's mean cousin Angelica. A staple of Saturday-morning television for some time, the show has proven appeal to kids and adults alike. Inspired by the creators Arlene Klasky and Gabor Csupo's own children (your heart goes out to them), the Rugrats offer quirky animation and not too slapsticky comedy. The show has attracted – à la *Simpsons* – a host of guest stars including Hollywood actors Kim Cattrell, James Belushi and Stacey Keach. And as indie-music-fan new parents are forever pointing out, the (decidedly oddball) soundtracks are by Mark Mothersbaugh of that strangest of post-punk bands, DEVO.

The golden age of *Rugrats* – when there was almost undiluted wit and weirdness – was 1991-93, and videos of the **TV series** from these years are the most fun, assuming you view an episode or two at a time. The full-length movies are more of a mixed bag. **The Rugrats Movie** (1999) is quite fun, with a certain manic quality to the storyline of a runaway buggy, while **Rugrats Go Wild** (2003), in which the kids get marooned on a Pacific island only to find they are mixing it with the Wild Thornberrys, is a neat idea which they almost carried off. **The Rugrats In Paris** (2000) is, by contrast, witless trash with poo-poo level jokes.

▭ UK, US ◉UK, US │ U (UK) G (US)

Scooby-Doo 1969–present

Debuting in 1969, Hanna–Barbera's Scooby-Doo was a creation close to genius: a talking dog named after a nonsense phrase at the end of Frank Sinatra's "Strangers In The Night", who had slapstick adventures with his pals in Mystery Inc. True, the episodes were formulaic in the extreme. Scooby and his muchacho Shaggy would get separated from the rest of their gang and see the baddies first, sexpot Daphne would be in mortal peril (relying on smug Fred to rescue her), then each episode would conclude with the culprit, stripped of their fiendish disguise, muttering "Those pesky kids" and Scobby burbling "Scooby dooby doo!" But that was how we liked it, and there was enough variety to sustain years of episodes, as Mystery Inc solved mysteries involving abandoned fairgrounds, old mineshafts and the like.

The series' long-running success has tempted over-zealous writers to add new elements to the half-hour cartoon, none of them necessary, and most unnecessary of all a string of Scooby relatives – hillbilly cousin Scooby-Dumb and possibly the most annoying cartoon character in history, Scrappy-Doo. However, Scooby has been surprisingly well served by his feature-length movie writers, with the highest marks, by general consent, going to **Scooby-Doo On Zombie Island**, **Scooby-Doo And The Cyber Chase**, **Scooby-Doo And The Witch's Ghost** and **Scooby-Doo And The Alien Invaders**.

Fans of the cowardly canine cowered when talk of a live-action movie was mooted. But **Scooby-Doo Live-Action Movie** (2002) was surprisingly good, almost living up to its tag line, "Through the ages one hero has cowered above the rest." The plot was the usual, though, with hints of girl-on-girl entanglements between Daphne and Velma and a touch of martial arts action leading to a PG rating in the UK and US. Yet,

for all that, it was good-humoured, reasonably fast-moving, and didn't give the odious Scrappy-Doo too much screen time. If you're watching it for the umpteenth time, you can amuse yourself by spotting the continuity errors (clue: watch Daphne's clothes at the airport). The spooky bits may be a little scary for nervous kids under 5. A US gross of $153 million made a sequel inevitable, and, predictably enough, **Scooby-Doo 2 Monsters Unleashed** (2004), although fast-moving, was not nearly as funny.

CARTOONS 📼 UK, US ◉ UK, US | U (UK) G (US)

LIVE ACTION 📼 UK, US ◉ UK, US | PG (UK, US)

Sherlock Hound 1981

Conan Doyle fans might not be overly impressed by Hayao Miyazaki's rendering of the Sherlock Holmes stories – which he adapts very loosely and sets in an animated cartoon world populated by dogs. But young kids, from 4 years and up, are likely to go for these short and often very funny episodes, originally produced for Japanese TV. There are five DVDs available of the series, each including three episodes; the first six stories (contained on Case Files I and II) were scripted and directed by Miyazaki, the others were not, and are a little less fun. Each has an English soundtrack, but don't miss out on giving the Japanese version a go, too, for some truly funny voice sequences.

◉ US | U (UK) G (US)

The Simpsons 1989–present

One of the really big issues that every parent now has to deal with is: at what age do you allow your innocent offspring to tune in to the subversive, sarcastic, sometimes crude, often violent, and invariably hilarious *The Simpsons*? The crux of the matter is that although *The Simpsons* is basically an adult show, it's animated, and its jokes span the range from slapstick (and a nice line in puerile) through to political satire way above the heads of most child viewers. And, worse than that, it is packed with examples of *stuff kids shouldn't do*. Indeed, its hero Bart Simpson ("Eat my shorts!") is *the* anti-role model for kids.

Which, of course, has meant a decade of frenzied newspaper head-lines, on both sides of the Atlantic, claiming that kids across the world are turning into Bart clones. In the UK, the Independent Television Commission investigated the show's effect on kids after complaints from parents that their primary school kids were mimicking the characters and indulging in the kind of surly truculence normally reserved for 13-year-olds; in their report, they found that parents couldn't actually identify any behaviour that kids had mimicked from the show. (In fairness, *The Simpsons* wasn't the only programme in the dock: *WWF Wrestling* and *South Park* were cited too.)

When the shows were released on video in the UK, they were clas-sified as PG – which, ultimately, seems to sum it all up. If you have kids younger than 9, watch the shows with them, avoid some of the scari-er ones (like the Halloween-themed episodes), and make your own call on the *Itchy & Scratchy* interludes. You may feel they're so extreme and cartoonish that they're okay; you may not. In each episode, you will come across plenty of inappropriate behaviour, with references to sex and alcohol, but remember, we are being invited to laugh at it. Bart may seem cool but he doesn't exactly benefit from his laissez-faire, "have-a-cow" attitude. And the show does touch on themes that will resonate with kids – as in the episode where Lisa reinvents herself in a desperate bid to appear cool to some new friends only to discover they would have liked her anyway.

The contemporary chronicling of *The Simpsons* shows means that watching the current series on TV is the obvious way to consume. But if you feel the need for a little history, **The Simpsons Christmas Special** (1989) and **The Simpsons Political Party** (1999) boxed sets are real standouts, while **The Simpsons Third Season** DVD contains some of the show's classic episodes - from the splendidly titled *Stark Raving Dad* to *Brother Can You Spare Me Two Dimes* in which Danny deVito reappears as Bart's brother.

▭ UK, US; ◉UK, US | PG (UK) NR (US)

Teenage Mutant Ninja Turtles 1987–96

Cowabunga! The pizza-scoffing, sewer-dwelling, criminal butt-smack-ing, mutant turtles – bizarrely named after artists from the Italian Renaissance – ran for half a dozen seasons from 1987 to 1996. They have their own Nintendo game, and get rerun on TV quite often, but if you want the core offering, then the **TMNT Classic Cartoons** DVD gathers together the first series and the last. They are quite a lot of fun, so long as you're happy with the level of violence – TMNTs do like to fight. The live-action movies are rather darker stuff, or at least the first one, the mega-hit **Teenage Mutant Ninja Turtles** (1990) is: this told the Turtles' "origin story", in which the four little reptiles are mutat-ed by radioactive goo into human-sized crime fighters, taught martial arts by super-rodent Splinter, and go out to dispense justice, order pizza, and rock out. The other two movies were watered down, to the disappointment of their following (boys from 7 to 15).

▭ UK, US; ◉UK, US | PG (UK) NR (US)

Tom And Jerry 1940–80

Itchy & Scratchy for the over-30s, *Tom And Jerry* was one of the most successful cartoons of all-time, beginning life in 1940 as the creation of Hanna-Barbera and still going strong on TV reruns. The perfect pairing of two natural enemies – cat and mouse – allowed the series to rely on fast action and pure sight gags. The first episode had Jerry mouse sparring with Jasper the cat, but after MGM held a naming competition, Tom cat was born. The classic cartoons were produced by Fred Quimby, regarded as a studio hack by many of his colleagues and a man not afraid to admit his own ignorance, and were scored by Scott Bradley. In the 1960s, rather disastrously, the characters were allowed to speak – although Chuck Jones's cartoons in of this era sometimes match the quality of the originals. The earlier episodes, with the black housekeeper, are rarely shown now out of political correctness but the best of the cartoons focus on the eternal contest between cat and mouse, a conflict smug Jerry always wins. Best supporting character was probably the dog Spike, useful in putting even more fear into Tom if the storyline required. Criticized for violence in the 1940s and 1950s, the series is, at its best, beautifully drawn – if Tom swallows a bowling ball, then the animators go the whole hog and give him a bowling ball-shaped head.

Classic episodes to watch out for include *Puss Gets The Boot*, *Bowling Cat Alley* and *Yankee Doodle Mouse* and *The Cat Concerto*, often described as the greatest cartoon of all time, in which Jerry tries to interrupt Tom's piano concert. These are available on the North American DVD **Tom and Jerry's Greatest Chases**, and in the UK on various **Classic Collection** DVDs. Any kids could (and do) enjoy *Tom And Jerry* – but as most of the violence involves easily accessible household implements (forks, hammers, doors) best not to try any of the stunts at home.

▄▄▄ UK, US ◉ UK, US | NR

Top Cat 1961–62

They just don't make cartoons like this any more. In fact, they didn't even make them like this for very long – just thirty episodes of *Top Cat* were created by Hanna-Barbera in 1961–62. The idea was essentially Sergeant Bilko in cartoon form with TC as the fast-talking conniver and Bilko regular Maurice Doberman providing the voice of Benny the Ball. Each episode saw TC and his cohorts do varying degrees of battle with the eternally frustrated Officer Dibble. In the UK, the show was renamed **Boss Cat**, so as not to clash with a brand of pet food. This didn't prevent this becoming a mainstay of British children's television programming. The closing credits, in which TC prepares for a good night's kip, made millions of kids wish they could have lived in a dustbin too.

📼 UK, US | U (UK) NR (US)

Totally Spies 2001–present

Totally Spies is, like an animated version of *Charlie's Angels* with a gentle seasoning of *Clueless*, as three high school Beverly Hills girls – Sam the logical, intelligent one, Clover the blonde drama queen and Alex the clumsy baby of the group – lead a double life as espionage agents. Wearing the latest skin-tight fashions, the girls are true James Bond-style agents, travelling the world as agents of WOOHP, fighting crime and outlandish villains in half-hour, action-packed episodes while dispensing 007-esque one-liners. Perfect for feisty young girls. Shown regularly on Cartoon Network, and available on American DVDs.

◎ US | NR

Wacky Races 1968

Based on the 1966 Blake Edwards movie *The Great Race*, Dick Dastardly and chums were the highlight of Hanna-Barbera's adventure period. Eleven very individual teams battle it out in motor races across America, each with their own sneaky tricks up their sleeve to outdo the other. With a fantastic theme, exhilarating animation and oddball characters (the Slag Brothers, Dastardly and Muttley and the Ant Hill Mob the best; Penelope Pitstop and Peter Perfect the most boring), this is a must for kids of 5 and above, offering more thrills and spills than Formula One manages these days.

📼 UK | U (UK) NR (US)

5

Christmas

Santa's big break

Now that the spirit of Christmas on TV seems to be about the ratings war, a household stock of the best Christmas movies seems more essential than ever – especially if you want to use the festive season to remind the offspring that December 25 is not entirely about Ninja Turtles and Barbie dolls. And there is a surprising store of good Yuletide stuff. Starring in a cracking Christmas film has been something of a rite of passage for movie stars, so you can find everyone from Michael Caine to Bill Murray playing Scrooge, and anyone from Whoopi Goldberg to Will Ferrell implicated in films designed to tug at our heartstrings. This is also a section where you should definitely try some of our grown-up recommendations – all the old perennials, such as *White Christmas*, which, albeit a bit slow-moving, should hook most kids on the song-and-dance routines.

Bush Christmas 1947

Five children pursue horse thieves, liberate the stolen horses and, for their pains, get hung up on meat-hooks before a timely rescue party arrives. Set in the Blue Mountains of New South Wales, this is a Christmas movie without tinsel, but the comfort and joy is to be found in the way the kids interact as equals. The narrator jars a bit today, but kids from 6 to 10 should enjoy this – once they accept that, as this is Christmas down under, there'll be no flying reindeer or snow.

▣▣▣ US │ U (UK) NR (US)

A Christmas Story 1983

The memoirs upon which this festive comedy is based – by US radio personality Jean Shepherd – were called *In God We Trust, All Others Pay Cash*. And it is the cynicism retained that makes this tale – of a greedy kid who wants Santa to bring him a rifle – stand out from traditional Hollywood festive fare. Still more remarkable is that it is directed by Bob Clark, best known for grosser fare such as *Porkys*. It is a film full of small but perfect moments, like the hero being triple-dog-dared to stick his tongue to a frozen lamppost.

▣▣▣ UK, US ◉UK, US │ PG (UK, US)

Elf 2003

Elf is as charming and as seductive as its catch line promises: "This holiday discover your inner elf." Will Ferrell is simply sublime as the boy who grows up to be an oversized elf and runs away from the North Pole after realising that he is human. You fear, after a few minutes, that the gag might run out of humour but thanks to Ferrell's ingenuous turn (and able support from James Caan, Mary Steenburgen, and Bob Newhart) it never does. There's a sweetness, a naivety about Ferrell that keeps the joke alive, and makes the audience want to suspend disbelief.

Quite a few critics went into "Bah humbug!" mode on this film's release, while a few suggested it was too adult for its target audience. That's a fair point – the movie does start slowly – but the film's self-confidence, its reluctance just to chuck gags in every few seconds, is part of its strength, and there's a heart to the story that most kids will appreciate. During the closing scene, when the whole cast gradually begins to sing an a cappella version of "Santa Claus Is Comin' To Town", many cinemas found that the kids joined in the singalong, and clapped at the end of the movie.

If you haven't watched this already, prepare to discover just how many laughs Ferrell can get simply by getting caught in a shop revolving door. And if you don't laugh... well, Ebenezer, prepare to meet some Christmas ghosts. An essential festive treat.

US ◉US | PG (UK, US)

Christmas films just don't come better than Elf

The Flight Of The Reindeer 2000

Only Ralph Thomas (John Boy from *The Waltons*) could carry this TV movie off, playing a scientist who sets out to prove that reindeer can fly and ends up a captive at the North Pole. Beau Bridges offers sterling support in a fable that any kid who still believes in Santa should adore.

📼 US | U (UK) G (US)

How The Grinch Stole Christmas 2000, 1966

Watch the big budget 2000 version of the Dr Seuss tale, with Jim Carrey as the bitter green grinch who steals all the Christmas presents, and you might feel someone has also stolen the humour from this story. For the most part, it's dark, even depressing stuff although there is a little girl who shows touching faith in the grinch and it all turns out well in the end. Not quite a barrel of laughs – the genuine laugh-out-loud moments could be fitted into a much smaller receptacle.

However, don't despair, for without much fanfare, there is a new DVD and video release of the original **1966 TV production**, directed by the great Chuck Jones and featuring the voice of Boris Karloff as the mean greenie. This keeps the original, classic story intact, and just adds a terrific soundtrack. And as if that wasn't enough, it comes in a smashing double bill with **Horton Hears A Who!**, one of Dr Seuss's most touching stories, about an elephant who discovers, inside a daisy, a tiny city called Whoville. It, too, was directed by Chuck Jones.

JIM CARREY VERSION 📼 UK, US ◉UK, US | PG (UK, US)
CHUCK JONES VERSION 📼 UK, US ◉UK, US | NR

Mickey's Christmas Carol 1983

With Mickey as Bob Cratchit, Goofy as a ghost and a Donald-esque Scrooge, this cartoon version of the Dickens tale could have turned out horrendous. But it isn't – and it wouldn't be going overboard to suggest this 25-minute short, a regular slot on American Yuletide TV schedules, is a minor masterpiece. Scrooge is maybe a bit too cute for comfort, and there's more sentiment than snow, but it stands up nicely to annual viewing.

📼 UK, US ◉UK, US | U (UK) G (US)

Miracle On 34th Street
1947, 1994

New York - Santa's kinda town

Director John Hughes maintains that this movie should be remade every twenty years so that a new generation can understand it. You may prefer the Oscar-winning **1947 original** in which Natalie Wood is the child who doesn't believe in you know who and Edmund Gwenn in Macy's department store is – as his name Kriss Kringle suggests – no part-time St Nick. Most kids, however, will be happier with Hughes's charming remake in which Richard Attenborough excels as Kringle, and Mara Wilson is endearing, not twee, as the girl.

📼 UK, US ◎ UK, US | U (UK) PG (US)

Mole's Christmas 1994

This animated take on an episode in Kenneth Grahame's *The Wind In The Willows* unites many of the voice talents which made its predecessor (*Adventures Of Mole* – see p.111) so fantastic. The tale is about Rat and Mole trying to elude weaselly pickpockets as they head home for Christmas. Made for UK TV, it was released on video, then withdrawn, so you'll need to scan cyberspace in search of a copy.

📼 UK but currently unavailable

The Muppet Christmas Carol 1992

Many of the Muppet movies (see p.126) were flawlessly scripted and performed, and this vehicle for Miss Piggy, Fozzie and the gang was possibly as good as they got, lifted as it is by a well-judged performance from Michael Caine as Scrooge, memorably heckling with Statler and Waldorf as the Marley brothers.

📼 UK, US ◉UK, US | U (UK) G (US)

The Nightmare Before Christmas 1993

 "Attacked by Christmas toys – that's strange. That's the second complaint we've had." Director Tim Burton's labour of love is one of the most remarkable movies ever inspired by Christmas – and Halloween. Using real old-fashioned stop-motion, three-dimensional animation, and with a fine, subtle score by Danny Elfman (who also sings Jack's songs beautifully), it may just be Burton's most perfect accomplishment – a real, entertainingly warped treat for kids aged 7 and over.

The story is splendidly weird. Halloweentown's Jack Skellington, (another of Burton's loveable misfits – like Beetlejuice or Edward Scissorhands) is feeling under-employed planning stunts for October 31, and so decides to bring his peculiar organisational genius to bear on Christmas. Somehow kids don't appreciate his Yuletide gifts of shrunken heads and a toy snake, delivered on a coffin-shaped sleigh and pulled by skeletal reindeer, and when he's shot down, he comes to his senses, and makes amends.

Burton claims that the source for his tale was a trip to the shops where he saw the Halloween shop display being replaced by Christmas decorations. The juxtaposition of ghouls and reindeer inspired the poem on which this film was based. The canny thing about the film is that, while offering a macabre twist on the festive movies which used to fill the Christmas TV schedules, it pays homage to them. It's one of those movies that is so visually rich it repays repeated viewing – you're always spotting new things tucked away in the corner of the screen.

The movie was adored from the get-go by critics, who reached for phrases like "fabulously inventive" with almost monotonous regularity. Credit for that must go not just to Burton's vision but to the patient craft of director Henry Selick. Filming took three years because although there were a hundred crew members, they could produce, on average, only some 60 seconds of film a week.

📼 UK, US ◉UK, US | PG (UK, US)

Prancer 1989

Eight-year-old farm girl Rebecca Harrell nurses a wounded reindeer she believes belongs to Santa while her dad, Sam Elliott, struggles with debt. Obvious, sometimes too winsome for its own good, and – at 102 minutes – overlong, this film is still surprisingly charming and will appeal to kids from 4 to 7.

▭ UK, US ◉UK, US | U (UK) G (US)

Robbie The Reindeer/Hooves Of Fire 1999

This claymation-style tale – released as **Robbie The Reindeer** in the UK and **Hooves of Fire** in the US – has a lot going for it. The story is a wry Christmassy yarn (an out-of-condition reindeer trying to get fit to pull the sleigh), there are no irritatingly gloopy songs that kids will sing around the house for days, the vocal cast is a dream (Robbie Williams narrates, other parts are voiced by Ardal O' Hanlon, Alistair McGowan and Steve Coogan, while in the US version the likes of Jim Belushi and Britney Spears chipped in), and there's enough eccentric wit and humour to amuse the grown-ups. The sequel – **Legend Of The Lost Tribe** – is almost as good.

▭ UK, US ◉UK, US | U (UK) NR (US)

Rudolph The Red-Nosed Reindeer 1998

This gentle (none too sophisticated) animation of the familiar tale of the oppressed reindeer again features a stellar vocal cast (John Goodman, Debbie Reynolds, Eric Idle, Bob Newhart and Whoopi Goldberg). There are a few extra twists in the tale and some slapstick humour which will appeal to younger kids.

▭ UK, US ◉UK, US | U (UK) G (US)

Santa Claus The Movie 1985

Diminutive Dudley Moore was perhaps the British actor least likely to carry a hit movie, but after the success of his loveable drunk in *Arthur*

(1981), Hollywood manufactured hit comedies for him for much of the 1980s. This is one of Moore's merrier efforts – even if the opening scenes at Santa's North Pole are far superior to the rather standard plot (greedy toy magnate and grumpy child) which follows. Still, the whole family should find a few laughs here.

📼 US ◉UK, US | U (UK) PG (US)

The Santa Clause 1994

Tim Allen's movie debut is better than the dopey premise – divorced dad fatally scares Santa off the roof and dons the red and white suit to finish St Nick's mission – would suggest. Allen does a nice comic turn but the real gem is the script, written by Steve Rudnick and Leo Benvenuti, which takes the premise into some intriguing scenarios. A comedy with heart – unlike its sequel **Santa Clause 2** which improves eventually but is dismal for the opening 40 minutes.

📼 UK, US ◉UK, US | U (UK) PG (US)

Santa Who? 2000

Leslie Nielsen's brand of avuncular absent-mindedness makes him perfect casting in this tale of an amnesiac St Nick. The doyen of deadpan makes more of this minor festive fare than it probably deserves, though the scene where he has to relearn Christmas carols is well done.

◉UK, US | U (UK)

Scrooge/A Christmas Carol 1951, 1970, 1984

For parents in their forties, Alastair Sim's appearance as Charles Dickens' misanthrope in **Scrooge** (released as **A Christmas Carol** in the US) cannot be beaten, reminding them of a childhood where it was almost as consistent a feature of the Christmas TV schedules as *The Sound Of Music*. Though in black and white (avoid the horrendous colourized edition), this is a genuine classic, with Sims backed by such stalwarts British thesps as Michael Hordern, Jack Warner and a young George Cole.

Britain's most charming man, Alistair Sim as Scrooge

If you've seen it enough times, then you could ring the changes with the 1970 musical version, **Scrooge**. The songs aren't marvellous but Albert Finney is good as Scrooge, and there are nice roles for Alec Guinness and Kenneth More. **A Christmas Carol** (1984), with George C. Scott as Scrooge, also has its fans, and is more faithful to the original story (and a tad scarier) than the Sim version.

1951 VERSION 📼UK, US ◉UK, US │ U (UK) NR (US)
1970 MUSICAL 📼UK, US ◉UK, US │ U (UK) G (US)
1984 VERSION 📼UK, US ◉UK, US │ PG (UK, US)

The Simpsons Christmas Special 1989

You know what to expect but the tag line convinces you this won't disappoint: "Twas the Week Before Christmas and Fate Played a Joke. No Tree and No Presents, Homer was Broke!" Somehow, Monty Burns's stinginess, Bart's tattoo, the family's lack of funds for presents, just makes the festive goodwill even more heartwarming when it finally arrives.

📼 UK, US ◎UK, US | NR

The Snowman 1982

You may find it hard to get past the over-familiar strains of the "Walking In The Air" theme but don't leave this one to the kids — it's too good. A wordless animated rendering of Raymond Briggs's picture book, *The Snowman* tells the story of a boy who is taken to meet Father Christmas by the snowman he's just built. It carries a real sense of magic, with economy and precious little sentimentality. The end is beautifully bittersweet. Good for 20 minutes of your family's time any Christmas.

📼 UK, US ◎UK, US

• •

MORE GROWN-UP CHRISTMAS MOVIES

Jack Frost 1998

Too dark, and in parts too darn miserable, to be a cuddly Christmas classic, this well-acted yarn is worth persevering with. Michael Keaton plays a neglectful drummer dad who is killed just before Christmas only to come back, a year later, as a snowman in the family front yard. The scenes where father and son (a fine performance by Mark Addy) are reunited in a seriously weird way will put a lump in your throat. Kids younger than 5 probably won't stay the pace.

📼UK, US ◎UK, US | PG (UK, US)

National Lampoon's Christmas Vacation 1989

This comedy of festive anguish is as funny and relevant as its predecessor (*National Lampoon European Vacation*) is lame and sexist. The Griswold family Christmas is threatened by familiar foes: distant relatives who don't stay distant enough, parents-in-law pettiness, financial uncertainty and the need of the dad (Chevy Chase) to make each Yuletide definitive. There's cursing of the "kiss my ass" and "shit" variety, innuendoes that may soar over your child's head, but kids from 7 upwards will love this hilarious reminder that every family Christmas trembles, as Chase puts it, "on the threshold of hell".

📼 UK, US ⊙UK, US | PG (UK, US) or PG-13 (uncut in US)

Scrooged 1988

Bill Murray is a venal TV exec whose bah humbug attitude to Christmas is summed up by the TV trailers for his festive spectacular – trailers so dark they literally frighten one old viewer to death. As the Christmas ghosts scare him to his senses, you see he has reason for hating Christmas – his dad's idea of a present being a lump of meat. Murray takes a movie to realise what every male watching realises from the start: that old girlfriend Karen Allen is just too gorgeous to be passed up. But there are plenty of laughs, quite scary ghosts and a schmaltzy yet invigorating ending which avoids being corny thanks to fine work by director Richard Donner. The

language, the ghosts, the occasional scene, make this best suited to kids of 7 and over.

📼 UK, US ⊙UK, US | PG (UK) PG-13 (US)

White Christmas 1954

There's more to this hardy festive perennial than Bing Crosby crooning his way through the bestselling Christmas song of all time. Notably Danny Kaye, as Crosby's army buddy and showbiz partner, who pops around the screen singing, "Chaps, who did taps, are doing choreography" amid his routines with Vera-Ellen, the love interest with toothpick-thin legs. It's hard to resist this movie, at any age: there's nifty dancing, plenty of Yuletide sentiment, romantic confusion, a few laughs and some of Irving Berlin's finest songs ("Sisters" and "Count My Blessings").

📼 UK, US ⊙UK, US | U (UK) NR (US)

6

Classics

once were books

As Ben Gunn says to brave young Jim Hawkins in *Treasure Island*, "Many's the long night I've dreamed of cheese – toasted, mostly." Classic novels by the likes of Robert Louis Stevenson, Frances Hodgson Burnett, and Sir Walter Scott were a rich part of childhood's cultural heritage, but today, thanks to phenomena such as the *Harry Potter* books, they are largely neglected in print. Though novelists like Stevenson had a fine eye for the kind of disturbingly specific detail (why just fifteen men on a dead man's chest?) which resounds in a child's imagination, their diction and their narrative

Classics by another name

We have reviewed several classics else-where in this book:

The *Greek myths* are featured in the **Action & Adventure** chapter. Hugh Lofting's *Dr Dolittle* appears in **Animals**. Kipling's *Jungle Book* comes in **Animation**. The *Roald Dahl* movies are to be found in **Fantasy**, as are Tolkien's *The Hobbit* and *The Lord Of The Rings*, C.S. Lewis's *The Lion, The Witch And The Wardrobe/Chronicles of Narnia*, and J.M. Barrie's *Peter Pan*. Dickens's *Christmas Carol* is in **Christmas**, and *Nicholas Nickleby* is in **Schools**. Jane Austen's *Emma* and other novels are in **Romance**, along with Truman Capote's *Breakfast at Tiffany's* and Shakespeare's *Romeo and Juliet*. And, lastly, H.G. Wells is to be found under **Sci-fi**.

techniques can make them a bit of a labour for today's children. But they have inspired some fine movies over the years and celluloid may be the easiest way to effect an introduction to the works of the masters.

The Adventures Of Huckleberry Finn 1960

Movie directors have returned to Mark Twain's classic novel at irregular intervals. The standout is probably this version, directed by Michael Curtiz (whose previous credits included *Casablanca* and *Yankee Doodle Dandy*), which manages to be suitably rambunctious, entertaining and, at times, quite moving, although he has toned down some of Twain's grimmer conceits. Imaginatively cast (with silent movie comic Buster Keaton as a lion tamer, Tony Randall excelling as a con man

Michael Curtiz's Huck still has the edge

and world light-heavyweight boxing champion Archie Moore as Jim) and well made; it's just a pity that Eddie Hodges as Huck doesn't quite convince.

The **1993 remake** (PG in US and UK), with Elijah Wood as Huck and Robbie Coltrane and Jason Robards supporting, is enjoyable.

▭ US ◉UK, US | G (US) U (UK)

Alice In Wonderland 1951

Even Disney couldn't straighten out the oddities in Lewis Carroll's books – which, at times, anticipate the chemically inspired psychedelia of the 1960s – and this animation is ultimately not quite a success. That said, some of the scenes are brilliantly done (notably the Mad Hatter's party, the Cheshire Cat and the "Off with her head" trial), but there are too many songs (fourteen) and the wackiness lacks the twisted logic of Carroll's original work. Such is the power of the author's imagination that kids up to 7 may get spooked by some of the scenes, or by the air of general unease which hovers over the proceedings.

▭ US ◉UK, US | U (UK) G (US)

Anne Of Green Gables 1985

"Mrs Hammond told me God made my hair red on purpose and I've never cared for him since." The beauty of Kevin Sullivan's movie of Lucy Maud Montgomery's novel is that, though elegantly and loving-ly made, it brings out the tartness in the source, giving the familiar tale of orphan Anne Shirley's life in a new town real power. The 199-minute running time may mean you have to take this in more than one sitting but even boys of the right age (6 or 7) will be hooked. Sullivan also filmed the book's sequels, **Anne Of Avonlea** (1987) and **Anne Of Green Gables, The Continuing Story** (1990), with the same cast, headed by Megan Follows as Anne.

Don't confuse these classic versions with the many other made-for-TV versions of the story, which was first filmed by Hollywood in 1934.

▭ UK, US ◉UK, US | NR

Arabian Nights 1942/2000, The Thief Of Baghdad 1940

John Rawlins's **Arabian Nights** was made to cash in on the success of Alexander Korda's *The Thief Of Baghdad*, but it turned out a triumph – and absolutely the best film ever in which a character (played by Billy Gilbert, the voice of Sneezy in *Snow White*) bangs his belly into other characters to the sound of timpani. A movie of quite beautiful colours, and trembling on the edge of send-up, this makes for a very enjoyable 86 minutes – if you can track down the video.

Rawlins' film is not to be confused with Pasolini's brilliant but distinctly adult *Arabian Nights* (1974), nor indeed with *Scooby-Doo And The Arabian Nights*. If you want a modern version of the story, try the US made-for-TV **Arabian Nights** (2000) scripted by Peter Barnes and starring Mili Avital as Scheherazade.

Alternatively, try Alexander Korda's **The Thief of Baghdad** (1940), which stands up surprisingly well. Six directors, escalating budgets and a pesky world war forced the shoot to relocate from North Africa to America, but the movie finally got made. Its plot (based on the silent classic of 1924 starring Douglas Fairbanks) is suitably action-packed: Prince Ahmad, conned by the evil magician Jaffar into abandoning his throne, is locked in jail, where a mysterious thief, Abu (Sabu), helps him escape and continues with him on his journey to save the love of his life from Jaffar's clutches. The action sequences, including Abu fighting a 300-foot-tall spider, guarantee thrills. Not one for arachnophobics, though.

1942 VERSION ▭ currently unavailable | NR
2000 TV VERSION ▭ US ◉ US | NR
THE THIEF OF BAGHDAD ▭ US ◉ US | U (UK) NR (US)

Beau Geste 1939

Gary Cooper stars, phlegmatically, in the 1939 definitive screen version of P.C. Wren's yarn about the foreign legion and the power of brotherly love. There is love, death, betrayal and action aplenty but younger kids may find the sadistic sergeant (an Oscar-nominated turn by Brian Donlevy) seriously scary. Talented as director William Wellman was, he filmed this as a virtual shot-for-shot remake of the **1926 silent version** with Ronald Colman in the title role. The heroism and the romanticism may seem a tad out of date but this will still appeal.

The **1966 remake** is worth watching only for Telly Savalas's turn as the sadistic serge – and for colour photography. Marty Feldman's **The Last Remake Of Beau Geste** (PG in US and UK) is scrappy but fun.

1939 VERSION ▭ US ◉ US | PG (UK) NR (US)

The Count Of Monte Cristo 2002

Purists may be dismayed by the liberties this rousing, visual feast of a swashbuckler takes with the Alexandre Dumas novel, but everyone else should enjoy this thoroughly – it's well played (especially by Jim Caviezel and Guy Pearce), has some nice one-liners ("I swear on my dead relatives and even the ones that aren't feeling so good") and bounces along. There's some sex, violence (the UK version had to hang a man in 6 seconds to avoid a 15 certificate) but children of 9 or over shouldn't be unduly disturbed.

▭ US ◉ UK, US | PG (UK) PG-13 (US)

Great Expectations 1946

David Lean's rendition of Charles Dickens's novel was arguably the finest moment of his career – a better film even than *Lawrence of Arabia* or *Dr Zhivago*, and arguably the best ever movie by a British director. It sets out its store in the opening sequence, where Pip is confronted by an escaped convict – the first of many menacing adult presences, which combine to create an eerie power. The movie succeeds, brilliantly, in showing you the world as imagined by the fearful Pip, and the cast is simply wondrous, uniting the talents of John Mills, Jean Simmons, Alec Guinness, Finlay Currie and Bernard Miles.

Somewhat astonishingly, when he decided to make his movie, Lean hadn't even bothered to read the Dickens novel. But perhaps it was this very arrogance that worked: you sense that Lean is more worried about making a great movie than filming every comma Dickens wrote. What he is faithful to in the book is the cast of picaresque minor characters, such as Pocket, Pip's boyhood friend and part-time tutor in pugilism.

Top hat, coach, dangling chicken – it must be Dickens

As there should be in Dickens, the film also has grisly details aplenty (a mass hanging slightly offstage, death masks on a lawyer's wall, Miss Havisham) but children from the age of 7 or 8 will find this compelling, just as they relish the scary bits in *Harry Potter*. In fact, Pip is in some ways a proto-Potter, a slightly colourless orphan hero who has to triumph over circumstance (albeit without any magical powers).

The **1997 remake** – starring Ethan Hawke – was, coincidentally, directed by Alfonso Cuarón, director of *Harry Potter And The Prisoner of Azkaban*. And like his Potter film, it is better than many of its reviews, paying homage to Lean's genius, suggested.

DAVID LEAN VERSION 📼 UK, US ◎ UK, US | PG (UK) NR (US)

CUARÓN VERSION 📼 UK, US ◎ UK, US | 15 (UK) R (US)

Gulliver's Travels 1996

Jonathan Swift's satire has out-foxed moviemakers since Dave and Max Fleischer created an inadequate animated version in 1939. So the idea of a TV mini-series made by Jim Henson and starring Ted Danson, aka Sam in *Cheers*, as Gulliver, didn't sound

Dickens on celluloid

Charles Dickens had a greater fund of stories than an entire guild of screenwriters. And he had the ability – more than any writer since Shakespeare – to create characters who became archetypes. So it's no great shock that more than 170 film or TV adaptations of his work have been made since a silent called *Death Of Nancy Sykes*, based on an episode from *Oliver Twist*, was made in 1897. By common consent, David Lean's **Great Expectations** is the finest adaptation of all but there are many others you might want to seek out to watch with your kids, notably:

A Tale Of Two Cities (1935) Ronald Colman is sublime as the self-sacrificing hero in this tale of intrigue at the time of the French Revolution. 📼 UK, US | U (UK) NR (US)

David Copperfield (1935) Billed as "MGM's greatest ever motion picture", the film doesn't quite live up to the hyperbole but W.C. Fields's Mr Micawber is reason enough to enjoy. 📼 UK, US | NR

Oliver Twist (1948) David Lean's second finest Dickensian work – easier to stomach, for many, than Lionel Bart's musical version. 📼 UK, US ◎ UK, US | U (UK) NR (US)

Elsewhere in this book, you will find reviews of:

Nicholas Nickleby (2002) A good modern version of the goings-on at Dotheboys Hall (see *Schools Stories – p.228*).

Oliver! (1968) Lionel Bart's immortal musical (see *Musicals – p.206*).

Scrooge (1951) Alastair Sim excels as the villainous title character (see *Christmas – p.87*).

Scrooge (1970) Musical starring Albert Finney (see *Christmas – p.88*).

A Christmas Carol (1984) George C. Scott in Alastair Sim's role (see *Christmas – p.88*).

too promising. But this production comes close to fulfilling Swift's idiosyncratic vision. Best watched in parts (it was aired in three hour-long episodes), the asylum scenes may spook younger kids, but this is an out-of-this-world adaptation of Swift's fantasy.

📼 UK, US ◉ UK, US | PG (UK, US)

Hans Christian Andersen 1952

Danny Kaye is about as fashionable as Wall Street raiders these days so this little gem, a completely invented biography of the Danish spinner of fairytales, often gets undeservedly overlooked. Kaye is slightly more subdued than usual but the gags, the songs and the pace seldom flag in this funny musical. Kids from 4 to 8 should enjoy.

📼 US ◉ UK, US | NR

Heidi 1965

Shirley Temple's turn as the Swiss miss in the 1937 movie has been known to make grown men feel faintly nauseous. This 1965 remake, dubbed into English from German, is livelier, and, thanks to the scenes with the frosty governess, tempers the sweetness of the story with a few sour notes. Eva Maria Singhammer shows that you don't have to be terminally cute to play Heidi. Suitable for kids from 4 or 5.

📼 US | NR

A High Wind In Jamaica 1965

This is slower than your average tale of pirates and kids but still rewarding. Anthony Quinn and James Coburn are never less than entertaining as pirate skipper and first mate, and grown-ups will enjoy spotting Martin Amis as one of the kids seized by pirates on their voyage home. Alexander Mackendrick directs from Richard Hughes's adaptation of his own novel and it's capably done – maybe just a few melodramatic minutes too long.

◎US | NR

The Hunchback Of Notre Dame 1996

Disney's version may not have the full gothic force of the 1939 Charles Laughton movie, but among the laughter and songs is darkness (and pathos) aplenty and the central message of the Victor Hugo novel – that there is room in the world for hunchbacks, gypsies, and people of all kinds, even those who regard themselves as normal – remains intact. Disney's sequel, however, is best left unmentioned.

If you're looking for a live-action alternative, the **1982 retelling**, with Anthony Hopkins as Quasimodo, is the best among a dozen or more choices.

DISNEY VERSION 📼 UK, US ◎UK, US | U (UK) G (US)
1982 VERSION 📼 UK, US | PG (UK) PG (US)

Jane Eyre 1944

Charlotte Brontë's romantic tale has been quite respectably treated by the denizens of the movie industry, and never more so than in Robert Stevenson's **1944 version**, in which Orson Welles plays Rochester so enigmatically that it's hard to imagine anyone – with the possible exception of Alan Rickman – bettering him. Some may find this version of the movie melodramatic, even campy, but then so is the story in which the governess falls for the romantic, ruined, hero. Mrs Rochester's madness may scare younger viewers but girls, especially, may be captivated.

The best of the other Janes (and they are many) are the **1970 version** (pairing George C. Scott and Susannah York as Rochester and Jane) and the **1996 version** (with William Hurt and Charlotte Gainsbourg), both worth watching.

1944 VERSION ▭ UK, US ◉ UK, US │ PG (UK) NR (US)

Kidnapped 1960

Aptly directed by Robert Stevenson, this adventure yarn from the Robert Louis Stevenson novel isn't dumbed down, smoothed out or lightened up. As the disinherited hero, James MacArthur is essentially a foil for Peter Finch's Jacobite adventurer (just as, in his most famous role, MacArthur's Dano was a foil for Jack Lord's Steve McGarrett in *Hawaii Five-O*). But Finch, supported by a fine cast (the young Peter O'Toole among them), and aided by the narrative drive of Stevenson's tale, makes this a very entertaining 90 minutes. **The 1971** remake, with Michael Caine in Finch's role, is halfway decent. Both can be enjoyed by kids of 5 and over.

▭ US │ U (UK) NR (US)

Knights Of The Round Table 1953

Loosely derived from Sir Thomas Malory's *Morte d'Arthur*, this retelling of the Arthurian legend is a cut above average for its time. Ava Gardner, as Queen Guinevere, at least makes you believe that nice Robert Taylor, as Sir Lancelot, would be sorely tempted, and the male leads – Taylor and Mel Ferrer as Arthur – excel in their parts. The story, with the obligatory meeting between Arthur and his rival Mordred at the sword in the stone, takes time to pick up speed but, by the time the last battle looms, it's galloping along at a cracking rate. There's also a minor treat in one of the battle scenes: an anachronistic truck is visible.

▭ Currently unavailable │ PG (UK)

Little Women 1994

The very suggestion might seem heretical but Gillian Armstrong's retelling of Louisa May Alcott's novel about four sisters may, in time,

Gillian Armstrong's sisterhood reach for the high notes

seem superior to the classic **1933 version** starring Katharine Hepburn. Like the Hepburn movie, Armstrong's film scrapes off the treacle which disfigured the 1944 MGM version. Susan Sarandon shines as the proto-feminist mother hen, Winona Ryder is wonderfully cast as the spirited Jo yet both almost have the movie stolen from them by Kirsten Dunst as little Amy. Claire Danes does especially well as Beth given that she had to play many scenes on her knees – she was too tall, otherwise, to convince as Ryder's little sister. Beth's death scene may upset younger viewers but in every other respect, this should be a treat for kids of 6 or 7 upwards.

UK, US ⊚UK, US | U (UK) PG (US)

Man In The Iron Mask 1977, 1998

There's a choice to be made here between the modern, action-packed but confusing **1998 movie** starring Leonardo DiCaprio, and Mike Newell's **1977 TV version** with Richard Chamberlain swashing his buckle (and supported by Patrick McGoohan, Jenny Agutter, Ralph Richardson and Ian Holm). Both of them are expensively and entertainingly made but for my money, the Chamberlain, clocking in at 26 minutes shorter than the DiCaprio effort, has a distinct edge.

1977 VERSION `[📼]` UK, US | PG (UK) NR (US)
1998 VERSION `[📼]` UK, US ⊚ UK, US | 12 (UK) PG-13 (US)

The Moomins

Finnish author Tove Jansson's classic *Moomin* books are quite unlike anything else in children's literature, featuring a family of Hippo-like trolls who have quirky, dreamlike but somehow true adventures in their Finnish valley home, sailing off to a lighthouse, discovering magic hats, awaking early from hibernation. For many of their fans (and they number the likes of Philip Pullman and Philip Ardagh), they are the greatest of all children's books – the kind of books that allow a child's imagination to spin off in entirely new ways.

The series has been animated twice: firstly in the 1980s by the Polish national film company, and then, in no fewer than 78 episodes, in a Japanese production. Both series have aired on TV in the UK. The Polish films seem to have disappeared into the ether, but the Japanese series has been issued in English on video (39 volumes!) and DVD, and a single video compilation of the first five episodes also appeared as *Moomin Mania*; they are all currently out of print but an eBay search might unearth them. The Japanese series is voiced sympathetically, and maintains surprisingly well the gentle pace and slightly melancholic air of the books. They are suitable for all ages, though under-5s may be frightened by a couple of episodes featuring the Groke – a sinister embodiment of Nordic darkness and gloom.

`[📼]` currently unavailable | NR

Mysterious Island 1961

Having read that Jules Verne's story *Mysterious Island* was America's most popular library book, producer Charles Schneer couldn't resist. For the sequel to *20,000 Leagues Under The Sea*, Verne had American Civil War POWs escape in a balloon only to wind up stranded on an island in the Pacific where, with two shipwrecked women, they encounter Captain Nemo's giant plants and animals. The gigantic animals were added by stop-motion master Ray Harryhausen to spice up the adventure. It's amazing how much fun you can have with giant crabs, chickens and bees. Perfect for younger children; older kids used to CGI effects may be less impressed.

📼 UK, US ◎ UK, US │ U (UK) NR (US)

The Phantom Tollbooth 1969

A real curio this. Chuck Jones, best known for creating Roadrunner and embellishing Daffy Duck and Bugs Bunny, leaves *Looney Tunes* behind to take on Norton Juster's children's classic about a bored young boy who drives through a magical tollbooth to enter a pun-infested world where characters have names like Officer Short Shrift. Some found Jones's part-animated fantasy too preachy, others found the songs icky, yet a few devotees loved it to bits. The difficulty is knowing which kids it would appeal to – it's too clever for many younger children yet equally it could irritate/infuriate kids of 9 and over.

📼 US │ U (UK) G (US)

Pinocchio 1940

 In an age when kids' animation is often long on sentiment and short on bite, Disney's 1940 adaptation of Carlo Collodi's story seems incredibly brave. For all its U/G classification, this tale of the puppet who wanted to be a real boy is dark, some-times cruel and quite scary – the scene where our hero's laugh turns into a donkey's bray is brilliantly, chillingly, realised. And there's real pathos and despair as Gepetto, trying to find his son, gets stuck in the stomach of Monstro the whale. It's just as well that we have cheery old Jiminy Cricket along as Pinocchio's conscience and our host to bring tears to our eyes – and win a couple of Oscars - with his rendition of "When You Wish Upon A Star".

For such a classic Disney production, there are a surprising number of continuity errors – like the horses changing colour on the merry-go-round. But this doesn't stop *Pinocchio* from being arguably the greatest animation produced when Walt Disney was running the studio; indeed, its only rival is *Snow White* (see p.165). But Collodi's classic tale of the boy who gets led astray has a universal quality that makes it all the more telling. This is the kind of story which, in its essentials – if not the details – any kid can imagine happening to them. And the boy suffers for his failings, being exploited as a freak and a virtual slave labourer, so that by the time he is joyously reconciled with his "father" Gepetto, you are almost as relieved and overjoyed as he is.

Pinocchio is brilliantly drawn, too – note how the very waves recoil in horror as the giant whale approaches. This is the kind of attention to detail which Disney lost in the 1970s and only rediscovered in the digital age. Fittingly, the film was lovingly restored in 1992 so it's well worth buying on DVD.

▭ UK, US ◉ UK, US | U (UK) G (US)

Pippi Longstocking 1997

"That's my Pippi," said author Astrid Lindgren, when she was shown this animated feature, "pretty funny but strong enough to lift a horse!"

And she was surely right: this may not be state-of-the-art Disney animation but the Swedish-Canadian collaboration has kept the spirit of her heroine, Miss Pippilotta Delicatessa Windowshade Mackrelmint Efraimsdottir Longstocking. If you're new to Pippi, these are stories about the world's strongest girl (well you would have to be with a moniker like that) who runs amok, in the nicest possible way, with her pet monkey, while her salty sea dog of a dad is living life on the ocean wave. The tales have a lot of charm and humour, enough interfering neighbours, bungling burglars and appealing animals to

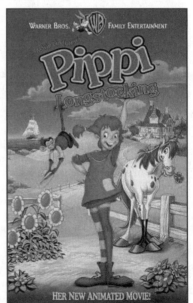

amuse kids from 3 to 9... and Scandinavians claim Pippi as a significant feminist model. The only point against the film is its songs – rather too many of them. There is quite a decent sequel, **Pippi's Adventures In The South Seas**, featuring lots of pirate action.

Some Pippi fans may recall the **1970 live-action** adventure, which was dubbed a bit strangely into English for TV, but which has its fans (and a recent DVD release). There is also a rather forgettable live-action film entitled **New Adventures Of Pippi Longstocking** (1988). Best plump for the animation.

📼 UK, US | U (UK) G (US)

Pollyanna 1960

Effervescent orphan transforms cheerless small town with her endless supply of gladness: it's hard to summarise the plot of Eleanor H. Porter's children's classic without making it seem simply insufferable. It is to the credit of director David Swift and Hayley Mills, who won a special Oscar in the title role, that the resulting Disney movie is, for the most part, charming and entertaining. At 134 minutes, it could have done with a gentle trim but Mills is exceptional. She froze for her first scene and father John took her to one side and told her: "You are like a great big white cabbage." This mysterious speech did the trick. The only danger to you or your kids is that you may, occasionally, overdose on saccharine.

📼 US ◉ UK, US | U (UK) G (US)

The Prince And The Pauper 1977

Mark Twain's novel of dual identity has never lit up the silver screen, despite well over a dozen screen adaptations. This is probably the most enjoyable – with Oliver Reed, George C. Scott and Raquel Welch hamming it up nicely. The real trouble, with this and the other adaptations, is the prince and the pauper – on film, they usually seem like plot devices, rather than fleshed out characters, a fault which might be traced back to Twain. Suitable for kids aged 6 and over.

📼 US ◉ UK, US | PG (UK, US)

Rikki Tikki Tavi 1975

Brought to you by an unusual blend of talents (Warner Bros animator extraordinaire Chuck Jones, from a story by Rudyard Kipling, and with narration by Orson Welles) this tale of a mongoose who protects his family from a couple of homicidal cobras is an uplifting 30 minutes. The story is well adapted and, as you would expect from Jones, brilliantly animated. As the narrator, Welles gives one of his most understated performances, not trying to steal the limelight from the characters.

US | NR

The Secret Garden 1993

Polish film-maker Agnieszka Holland's interpretation of the (often filmed) Frances Hodgson Burnett novel is one of those children's movies which are so good you completely forget they were made with children in mind.

Perhaps that wasn't so surprising, as Holland's previous films with children as heroes were both far from typical kids' movies: in *Europa Europa* she told the story of a young German Jew who joins the Hitler Youth to survive and in *Olivier, Olivier*, a French couple lose their son only to find him years later hustling on the streets of Paris.

The Secret Garden shares something of their tone. In the guise of a story about an orphaned girl (Kate Maberly) who exposes the secrets of a gloomy, forbidding manor, both the film and book make pertinent points about the

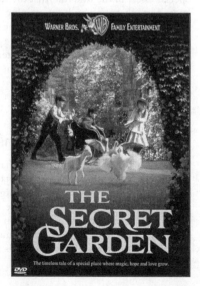
WARNER BROS. FAMILY ENTERTAINMENT

THE SECRET GARDEN

The timeless tale of a special place where magic, hope and love grow.

nature of life. The script by Caroline Thompson, who wrote *Edward Scissorhands*, helps retain the book's gothic ambience, although she soft-pedalled on some of the author's moralising. Maggie Smith judges it just right as the dastardly housekeeper and Maberly impresses as the kindly maid, forcing the viewer to take her seriously. But the honours really go to Holland who, as the *New York Times* reviewer noted, "homes in unerringly on the gulf between the worlds of children and adults, on the violence that abyss engenders and on emotions of jealousy and rage."

Kids aged 7 and over should be entertained, intrigued and moved.

▭ UK, US ◉UK, US | U (UK) G (US)

Swallows and Amazons 1974

This is a brave attempt to bring a popular series of children's novels by author Arthur Ransome to the silver screen. Holidaying in the Lake District with their mother (Virginia McKenna), the four Walker children sail to a nearby island in their boat, *The Swallow*, to set up camp, only to find the island inhabited by two girls who arrived in their own vessel, *The Amazon*. Rivalry ensues in a boating battle, but as a group together they uncover something far more serious. Quaintly nostalgic, almost a precursor of Enid Blyton's *Famous Five*, this is enjoyable, if minor, fare.

▭ UK, US | U (UK) NR (US)

The Swiss Family Robinson 1960

The real star of this (live-action) Disney film is the elaborate domicile which the stranded Robinsons make their desert island home. Disney jettisoned much of the novel, by Swiss pastor Johann David Wyss, keeping little more than the title and the premise of a family castaway and throwing in anything else they thought would give the story added zing. They also, probably unconsciously, imported what some viewers claim to be a peculiar number of phallic symbols. But that – and a spot of pirate crushing – is as edgy as this gets. Kids aged 5 and over should enjoy this, though the older they get, the tamer it may seem. They'll always love the tree house, though.

The **1998 remake** (with Jane Seymour) is amusingly bad – shame the jaguar, which bit two of the crew, wasn't given more screentime.

▭▭ UK, US ◉ UK, US | U (UK) NR (US)

Tales Of Beatrix Potter 1971

A cast including Wayne Sleep, Princess Diana's favourite ballet dancer, put on their dancing shoes – well, ballet slippers – to tell Beatrix Potter's wondrous stories shown in the appropriate Lake District setting. The best turn is by Frederick Ashton, the founding father of British ballet, as Mrs Tiggy-Winkle. The costumes take over before the end but this is, for the most part, charmingly, entertainingly, done.

Boys, unless they're Billy Elliot wannabes, may pass.

▭▭ US ◉ US | U (UK) G (US)

The Three Musketeers 1972

Director Richard Lester originally had this in mind as a vehicle for the Beatles. The clearest proof, perhaps, that he had his very own take on the Alexandre Dumas classic. Instead he got a dream cast (Oliver Reed, Christopher Lee, Charlton Heston, Richard Chamberlain and Michael York), along with Racquel Welch, who impressed once Lester had convinced her to stop over-acting. Originally, there was one very long script but the producers decided to cut the story in two so they had a sequel, **The Four Musketeers** (released in 1975), already made. Lester's double bill still seems fresh and funny today – as long as you don't worry about who did what to whom and with whom-else – although critic Pauline Kael rubbished them at the time as "an absurdist debauch". The sexual intrigue (it may fly over the kids' heads), brawling and the frequency with which opponents are run through make this most suitable for kids aged 6 and over.

The Lester version remains wholly superior to the **1993 remake** (PG) with Kiefer Sutherland and Charlie Sheen.

▭▭ UK, US ◉ UK, US | U (UK) PG (US)

All for one and one for all: Three (no, make that Four) Musketeers, 1972 style

20,000 Leagues Under The Sea 1954

In its day, this live-action Disney movie of Jules Verne's classic sci-fi novel, where the invention of the submarine was first mooted, was much admired for its lavish special effects. Art director John Meehan even won on an Oscar for the rivet-studded vehicle sailors initially mistake for a sea serpent – a craft that today looks about as realistic as *Thunderbirds*.

But that doesn't matter a fig since this is a film with big acting. James Mason turns in a terrific performance as Captain Nemo – insane, suave and sympathetic (he has a pet seal, after all). Kirk Douglas, as musclebound harpoonist Ned, is the everyman hero the kids can cheer on and even – when he turns his tonsils to "A Whale Of A Tale" – singalong to. And the duo are given sterling support by Paul Lukas, as the professor who Nemo assumes will be a kindred spirit, and by the great Peter Lorre, as Lukas's doubting assistant. Director Richard Fleischer makes a decent fist of it all and the tension never slackens too much over 127 minutes.

The battle scenes can be a bit scary – but nothing that most kids aged 6 and over can't handle – and they'll probably enjoy the idea of seamen dining on sea snake and smoking seaweed cigars. And if they get bored – which they almost certainly won't – you can whet their appetite by telling them there's a battle with a giant squid (one with tentacles 40 feet long that it took 28 men to operate and, for a reshoot, required 100 men to spring into action) on the way.

▭▭ UK, US ◉ UK, US │ U (UK) PG (US)

Tom Sawyer 1973

A musical *Tom Sawyer*? Sounds simply awful and, in this Reader's Digest adaptation of Mark Twain's most famous novel, the songs are very forgettable. But the performances (especially from Warren Oates as a drunkard, Johnnie Whitaker as Tom and Jodie Foster as Becky Thatcher), the staging of the key scenes and the photography make this a timeless entertainment. Kids aged 6 to 9 should enjoy. The **1938 version** with David Selznick and Norman Taurog is fine, too, but spoilt by the poor male leads.

▭▭ UK, US │ U (UK) G (US)

Tom Thumb 1958

Russ Tamblyn's finest 95 minutes. As the minuscule hero, he is at ease in a way he never looked when playing a character of average

Tom Thumb – he's in the money

height. And there's excellence all around here – from Terry-Thomas and Peter Sellers as the bumbling baddies, to the Peggy Lee-Soni Burke score and director George Pal's stop-motion Puppetoon animation of the talking and singing toys. Best of all, the movie signs off before its charm has worn off. This may endear itself to kids from 4 to 8.

📼 US ◉ UK, US | U (UK) G (US)

The Wind In The Willows: Adventures Of Mole 1995

Kenneth Grahame's *The Wind In The Willows* has tempted everyone from Walt Disney to Monty Python's Terry Jones, but few versions have captured the implied sadness of the tale as well as this animated British TV version, directed by Martin Gates. The voice casting is superb – Peter Davison is appropriately apprehensive as Mole, Hugh Laurie wonderfully ebullient as Toad – and the emotional depth of Grahame's story is captured impressively. Very young children may find the darkness of the wood a bit frightening. And adults may be driven a bit mad on eBay: this version was released on video but is currently unavailable (as is its festive follow-up, *Mole's Christmas* – see p.84).

If you can't locate *Adventures Of Mole*, then there is, confusingly, another **British TV version** – also from 1995, directed by Dave Unwin, gently animated with a narration by Vanessa Redgrave and the voices of Alan Bennett as Mole and Rick Mayall as Toad – that runs it a close second, though it too is currently out of print. And Monty Python fans might like to try **Terry Jones**'s rather manic 1995 film (released in the US as **Mr. Toad's Wild Ride**): Jones acts Toad himself, while Steve Coogan is Mole, and the songs are wild.

ADVENTURES OF MOLE 📼 currently unavailable | NR
UNWIN VERSION 📼 ◉ currently unavailable | NR
TERRY JONES'S VERSION 📼 UK, US ◉ UK, US | U (UK) PG (US)

7

Comedy

make 'em laugh

Kids love to laugh – and getting them do so is big business. The range of kids' comedy movies is enormous, from the goofy slapstick of Jim Carrey to the quickfire wit of the finest screwball comedies from the 1930s, and this selection is designed to offer as broad a sample as possible. One thing is doesn't include is **animation**: so for films such as *Shrek* or *Scooby-Doo* check our separate chapters on **Animation** (p.41) and **Cartoons** (p.63). And don't forget **Musicals** (p.197), either. As usual, we've also included a selection of more grown-up films, which kids might like just as much.

The Addams Family 1991

Altogether *ooky* if not as spookily original as the TV series (or the *New Yorker* cartoons it sprang from), this retread benefits hugely from the casting – especially Raul Julia and Anjelica Huston as husband and wife, Gomez and Morticia. A then-unknown Christina Ricci shines as

There was an ooky TV family long before the Osbornes ...

their daughter Wednesday. The plot is flimsy and doesn't quite spin out the 102 minutes, but that doesn't matter because there is much to smile at here. The tone is set early on when Morticia catches her daughter chasing her little brother with a knife, takes the knife away and gives her daughter an axe.

The sequel, **Addams Family Values**, is even better, and *ookier*, thanks to a fuller, sharper, script from Paul Rudnick.

Both films 🔲 UK, US ◉UK, US | PG (UK) PG-13 (US)

Bean: The Ultimate Disaster Movie 1997

One of the funniest moments in recent *Simpsons* history was when Homer went to London with a production team and met Tony Blair at 10 Downing Street. The team leave, awestruck by the encounter. "I can't believe we just met Mr Bean," muses Homer. Bean, however, is not to everyone's taste. Take Michael Palin, that most mild-mannered comedian: he bitterly dismissed this as "the Coca-Cola of comedy – I'd like to teach the world to laugh". And that was how many grown-ups received this movie – apart from the Japanese who loved it – in which Rowan Atkinson took his TV character and stretched him, pretty much literally, to movie size.

But that's grown-ups for you. Put this on the video (entitled simply **Bean: The Movie** in the US) and you will almost certainly notice three things. One, kids will laugh out loud quite a lot (notably when the hero smacks a sick bag over a passenger's head to amuse a kid, not realising the bag has vomit in it); two, as Roger Ebert said, it's really about 30 minutes too long ("At an hour, this would have been non-stop laughs; they've added 30 minutes of stops"); and three, the US PG-13 rating is a nonsense, presumably caused by someone on the classification board being unable to handle toilet humour. Not that any of these considerations are likely to bother most kids, for there's something about Atkinson's gauche, slightly malevolent, comic hero that they find compelling – just as they do his more recent – and rather funnier – **Johnny English** (see p.123). And even sourpuss adults might raise a smile as Bean, sent to oversee the installation of a painting in an LA art gallery because his employers in London can't abide him, has to give a speech about the painting of Whistler's mother.

Never (ever) trust this man with a sickbag

Bean fans will find no shortage of further **TV-based material** on a stack of video and DVD compilations. Best keep it quiet.

📼 UK, US ⊙ UK, US | PG (UK) PG-13 (US)

Big 1988

Josh Baskin is granted the one life-changing wish that every 13-year-old boy wants: not to be 13. He wakes up one morning in Tom Hanks's 30-year-old body, is chased out of his house by his knife-wielding mum, who assumes he's an intruder, moves into a hotel and, with his easy access to the adolescent mind, becomes a smash in the toy business and falls in love – which causes the inevitable complications. If you're going to watch one body-swap comedy from the 1980s, this is the one. You might not be comfortable with the sexual strand in the story but kids of 8 and over should enjoy.

📼 UK, US ⊙ UK, US | PG (UK, US)

Bill and Ted's Excellent Adventure 1988

This is the comedy where Julius Caesar is described as a "salad dressing dude" – which pretty much says it all about this 1980s teen apathy precursor of *Wayne's World* and *Beavis and Butthead*, and (let's get literary here), a seminal influence on the *Captain Underpants* books. The heroes (Keanu Reeves and Alex Winter), dim but impossible to dislike, just manage to pass their history class – thereby averting the end of the world – thanks to a time machine, meetings with figures like Beethoven and Napoleon, and a grasp of such adjectives

The most excellent Alex and Keanu

as "gnarly" and "triumphant" (along with a bit of swearing). The sequel **Bill & Ted's Bogus Journey** (1991) is almost as good.

📼 UK, US ◎UK, US | PG (UK, US)

The Borrowers 1997

"Fun, thrilling, smart and dumb in all the right places" is how movie cybergeek Harry Knowles sums up this film and he's spot-on. Derived from the Mary Norton stories, this tale of Lilliputian leprechaun-like creatures that live in people's houses and borrow stuff is well cast (with Jim Broadbent, John Goodman, Celia Imrie), well directed (by Peter Hewitt), and topped off with some fine special effects. Some fans of the books found the movie had too much mayhem but it is a funny, charming piece of children's entertainment.

📼 UK, US ◎UK, US | U (UK) PG (USA)

Candleshoe 1977

Candleshoe is a decently made, well acted, Disney family entertainment in which Jodie Foster (as an urchin) and David Niven (the butler with an amusing array of disguises) shine brightest. Foster is recruited by small-time crook Leo McKern to find the treasure hidden somewhere in the girls' school run by Helen Hayes but, ultimately, turns the table on him. Good for kids from 5 or 6 upwards.

UK, US ⌾ UK, US | U (UK) G (US)

Crocodile Dundee 1986

It's easy to forget that Paul Hogan was once genuinely entertaining. There's enough quirky detail in this tale of a figure famed for his croc-odile-wrestling skills for it to endure — one of Hollywood's more entertaining blockbusters from the 1980s. The scene where Hogan shows a knife the size of the Australian outback to a mugger is still a treat even now. Occasional violence, and some substance abuse, account for the rating which, especially in the UK, seems harsh.

UK, US ⌾ UK, US | 15 (UK) PG-13 (US)

One man and his croc

comedy

Dennis (The Menace) 1993

John Hughes's movies about Hank Ketchum's cartoon character (*not* the hero immortalised in the British comic the *Beano*, a confusion which led to the film being called **Dennis** in the UK) are terribly likeable and quite funny. The 7-year-old boy-menace gets into some fantastic (yet, from his point of view, perfectly understandable) scrapes: when he finds his long-suffering neighbour, Mr Wilson, in bed. Wilson is pretending to be asleep but, alarmed, Dennis decides the man has a headache, tries to give him an aspirin, and ultimately ends up firing the pill into Wilson's mouth with a sling-shot. The menacing figure of thief Switchblade Sam, is unnecessarily disturbing for younger kids. Otherwise, this film is easy to watch and like. The sequel, **Dennis The Menace Strikes Again** (1998), isn't as effective though any film in which Don Rickles and George Kennedy get it on to Wild Cherry's "Play That Funky Music" can't be entirely bad.

📼 UK, US ◎ UK, US | PG (UK, US)

Dr Dolittle 1998

Crude, vulgar, with a lot of gags about bodily functions, this Eddie Murphy movie doesn't have a lot in common with the original Hugh Lofting stories apart from the name and the fact that the doctor in question can talk to animals. Yet that doesn't stop this being an effective, funny comedy with Murphy, as the title character, playing it straight for once. Among the highlights are a nice opening scene where the Doctor discusses what dogs think about people with a canine voiced by Ellen DeGeneres. Vulgar but not objectionable, it is probably suited to kids of 7 or 8 and over. Its sequel, **Dr Dolittle 2**, adds little to the mix.

For more innocent Dolittle fun, see the original Rex Harrison **Dr Dolittle** (p.30).

📼 UK, US ◎ UK, US | PG (UK) PG-13 (US)

Flubber 1997

Flubber is a rubber-like substance which wreaks havoc wherever it goes and there are times when it seems to have blown a few holes in

John Hughes's script. But kids, especially from 5 to 8, won't mind; they'll hoot at the basketball players with springs in their heels and probably be helpless with mirth as flubber bounces around inside the bad guy's body. Robin Williams, as the absent-minded professor, makes this palatable even if a few girls – and mums – might find his habit of forgetting his wedding a tad patronising.

📼 UK, US ◉ UK, US | U (UK) PG (US)

Freaky Friday 2003

 This hugely successful comedy remake – the 1976 original starred Jodie Foster – isn't going to change the world, force anyone to face unpleasant but valid truths, or startle you with its originality. But the body-switch drama should ensure that grown-ups and kids alike have fun for 93 minutes, even when a tidal wave of sentimental guff threatens to sweep all away at the end. Jamie Lee Curtis and Lindsay Lohan, who has some of Foster's screen presence, are on top form as the mother and daughter who swap bodies thanks to a fortune cookie. You think you can see all possible permutations of humour but director Mark S. Waters adds some nice, new touches.

📼 US ◉ UK, US | PG (UK, US)

Friends 1994–2003

They were gorgeous, they were hilarious, and despite the theme song's line about "always getting stuck in second gear" they were obviously having the time of their lives. Was it any wonder that kids loved *Friends*? In the 1960s, the madcap Monkees were the teen idols younger kids loved to watch on TV – even if they didn't get all the jokes. In the 1990s, Joey, Ross, Chandler, Rachel, Monica and Phoebe were the characters millions of grown-ups laughed along with and who also appealed to kids of 5 and over.

There was no great mystery to their allure. The show offered eye candy and/or role models for boys and girls. The one-liners zinged back and forth so that even if they flew over children's heads (and a lot of the innuendos do) there was another gag not too far behind. And every so often, there was an inspired piece of physical comedy such as the episode where Ross contrived to get a turkey on his head. You might, of course, have to explain what a lesbian is but, apart from a few moments like that, this enduring sitcom is worth savouring together. All the series are available on DVD, if you need more of a fix than the repeats on TV can provide.

📼 UK, US ◎ UK, US | NR

George Of The Jungle 1997

"It was a strange experience watching *George Of The Jungle*. The movie would meander along, not going anywhere, and then – pow! – there'd be an enormous laugh." It's hard to disagree with Roger Ebert about this live-action film of Jay Ward's 1960s cartoon about George, the dopey, clumsy king of the jungle. But kids tend to latch on to the good things in movies, and there's plenty enough to amuse. Standout scene? Probably the entrance of Shep, the elephant, whom George has trained to behave like a dog. There's some mild violence and crude humour but nothing much to worry 5-year-olds and up.

📼 UK, US ◎ UK, US | U (UK) PG (US)

Ghostbusters 1984

 The 1980s generation marvelled at the state-of-the-art special effects in this multi-million dollar scare comedy, and even today the movie seems ahead of its kind. Bill Murray plays the flippant sleazeball at the head of a motley trio of scientists whose mission is to rid the Big Apple of its undead. Murray delivers a terrific performance, pursuing a possessed Sigourney Weaver, while Dan Aykroyd and Rick Moranis offer spook support. There's swearing and innuendo but kids from 7 upwards won't be bothered, and should find the movie a lot of fun – even if they're sometimes slightly scared by the effects.

The sequel, **Ghostbusters II** (1989) sees the scientists facing bankruptcy, before, inevitably, returning to heroic status. It has some of the charm of the original, but none of its novelty, or pace.

📼 UK, US ◎ UK, US | PG (UK, US)

Happy Days 1974–84

A long-running TV comedy with a heart, *Happy Days* featured a handsome family (the Cunninghams) and its very own cuddly rebel, the Fonz (Henry Winkler, in a part coveted by Mickey Dolenz and Mike Nesmith). In its sweet, sugary, innocent way it dealt with the kind of issues your kids might face (not being cool, being bullied, having crushes) and, in its early years, did so with a fresh humour. The series went on too long – the episode where Fonzie jumped over a shark inspiring *www.jumptheshark.com*, a website on which various programmes are analysed for the point at which they lost the plot. Winkler based his character on Sylvester Stallone, whom he had recently co-starred with.

◎US | G (US)

Harry And The Hendersons 1987

Also known as **Bigfoot And The Hendersons**, this comedy warning about the perils of adopting, and concealing, an abominable snowman in your home, was produced by Steven Spielberg's company but lacks the genius he brought to, say, *E.T.* Cute, heartwarming, not quite as funny as it could be, this is half-decent family entertainment for kids of most ages, with some strong language, which benefits from an unusual cast (including John Lithgow, Don Ameche, David Suchet).

▭▭▭ UK, US | PG (UK, US)

Home Alone 1990

The fact that this conventional comedy about an 8-year-old boy accidentally stranded alone at home for Christmas took $534 million at the box office is more astonishing than anything in the film itself. Director Chris Columbus and writer John Hughes tell this tale from the perspective of the disgruntled child and its comic success is due to their understanding of a child's mind and, hard as it might now be to believe, in Macaulay Culkin's charming performance. He's never cute and never exactly spiteful but you know the burglars who try to break in to his house don't stand a chance. There's a lot of cartoon violence as

Macaulay Culkin - home alone with a mirror

the burglars get their come uppance but most kids of 7 and up will enjoy seeing their own fantasies lived out on screen. The sequels – **Home Alone 2** and **3** – aren't as good, but no disgrace to the franchise.

📼 UK, US ◉UK, US | PG (UK, US)

Honey, I Shrunk The Kids 1989

Two unsung heroes of the American cinema take a bow here. Rick Moranis, best known as nerdy Seymour in *Little Shop Of Horrors*, is hilariously goofy as the scientist who shrinks his own kids by accident. And director Joe Johnston brings the sureness of touch which made *The Rocketeer* and *Jurassic Park III* such commercially satisfying movies. How the shrunken kids cope with water sprinklers and giant insects is the hook for a thrilling comedy which has bags of charm, a few chills and no pretensions. It probably didn't quite merit two **sequels**.

📼 UK, US ◉UK, US | U (UK) PG (US)

Hue And Cry 1947

Hue and Cry was the first classic Ealing comedy. Directed by Charles Crichton, this gem has Alastair Sim as the child-phobic writer of crime stories for a boys' comic who, together with a mob of East End urchins, prevents a gang of criminals from making some of these stories come true. There's a fantastic free-for-all between boys and villains at the end but there's no real malice – apart from the scene where a secretary is threatened with a white mouse by one of the boys. Like many comedies from this studio, it doesn't overstay its welcome, the caper coming to a close in 78 minutes flat. Best suited to kids from 5 to 10.

▭▭ UK ⦿ UK | U (UK) NR (US)

Johnny English 2003

You don't have to be a kid to enjoy Rowan Atkinson but it obviously helps. It would be tough to assemble a group of 6 to 12-year-olds and keep them from howling at this spoof Bond movie. Yet it can leave grown-ups distinctly cold, almost

as much as *Mr Bean* does. Admittedly the dialogue isn't the most sparkling (if you don't find a line such as "I think I'd rather have my bottom impaled on a giant cactus than exchange pleasantries with that jumped-up Frenchman' funny, then do not advance to Go), but this is so clearly a good idea, well executed, that it's a bit sourpuss to resist.

Oddly enough, the idea actually came from a British TV advert, in which Atkinson played a hopeless secret agent. In this film (and there will surely be sequels), he is accidentally signed up by MI6 with a mission to protect the crown jewels. His

ROWAN ATKINSON

JOHNNY ENGLISH

"FUN, FUN, FUN. A HILARIOUS COMEDY."
– Jim Ferguson, ABC-TV

123

potential nemesis is the evil Frenchman Pascal Sauvage (a splendidly hammy John Malkovich), who plans to steal the crown, and take over Britain. And his Bond girl is Interpol agent, Natalie Imbruglia. Slapstick ensues.

Not one for repeated viewings, perhaps, but a showing of *Johnny English* simply cannot fail.

📼 UK, US ◉UK, US | PG (UK, US)

The Little Rascals 1994

Desson Howe, reviewing this film for the *Washington Post*, was struck by the contrast between a father and a daughter watching the film. "As the movie progressed, the father sank lower into his chair... watching with mute, eye-rolling exasperation," while the 4-year-old daughter sat spellbound. Asked to choose her favourite part of the film, she said: "Everything." She didn't even mind that the boys belonged to something called the He-Man Woman Haters Club. That dichotomy will be rerun in a thousand living rooms – if anyone ever buys or rents this comedy about a group of boys who always win the local go-kart race. Girls older than 4 might possibly resent all this movie stands for.

📼 UK, US ◉UK, US | U (UK) PG (US)

The Love Bug 1969

Dean Jones is the racing driver who gets tangled up with Herbie, a Volkswagen Beetle with a mind of its own – a mind of his own being something that Dean himself badly lacks. Good-natured, implausible, with the odd sharp line, and some strange scenes (remember when Herbie gets drunk and contemplates suicide?), this is the best of an extended series. The stereotypical scenes of 1960s hippies somehow only add to the humour. Don't buy it on DVD unless you're a completist – there are just too many extras.

📼 UK, US ◉UK, US | U (UK) G (US)

Mork and Mindy 1978–82

Mork and Mindy was the kids' TV comedy which made a star of Robin Williams, playing a member of an alien race that had evolved from chickens. Williams improvised most of his routines, which must have been tough on co-star Pam Dawber (Mindy) but she usually manages to keep up as her alien lodger changes her life forever. The manic comic actor has occasionally failed to persuade viewers as a human in his movies, but he is genuinely funny as an Orcan.

US ◎US | NR

Mouse Hunt 1997

"He's Hitler with a tail. He's *The Omen* with whiskers. Even Nostradamus didn't see him coming!" That just about sums up the mouse who stops the Smuntz brothers (Nathan Lane and Lee Evans) from making the most of the antique mansion they have inherited. The slapstick stunts abound as the mouse, wittingly or unwittingly, gets vengeance on the brothers who try to exterminate it. If you don't like slapstick, you might have to grin and bear it, but kids will probably warm to this film which, as it details the destructive consequences of the brothers' animus, shows some of the gleefully cruel wit of a *Looney Tunes* cartoon.

UK, US ◎UK, US | PG (UK, US)

Mrs Doubtfire 1993

The plot, in which estranged dad Robin Williams disguises himself as a nanny so he can be close to his kids and wife, is really just an excuse for Williams to wear drag and give free rein to his genius for comic improvisation. You'll laugh, look furtively away (when director Chris Columbus really cranks up the schmaltz) and wince at the scene where Williams is compelled to be himself and the nanny from heaven at the same time. It's funny, mainly when Williams is on form, but it does feel like more of a warm-hearted TV sitcom than a movie. Some of his gags, especially when his ex (Sally Field) becomes roman-

Golden silents

Silent movie comedians, deprived of dialogue, often had to be unusually inventive. And some of their work may tickle children's funny bone. Here are five golden silents to try – all available on video or DVD.

1 **The General (1927)** Don't be put off by the tag line ("Love, Locomotives and Laughs") – this is Buster Keaton's finest work. A running time of 75 minutes without speech might tax the patience but there are plenty of great visual gags here and Keaton's deadpan delivery has worn better than the mugging of some of his rivals, notably Charlie Chaplin.

2 **The Strong Man (1927)** Harry Langdon was the baby-faced clown who was a comic genius – as long as he had Frank Capra directing him. In this charmer, he plays a Belgian war veteran who finds his blind American pen-pal girl-friend by the simple expedient of asking every girl he meets if she is Mary Brown.

3 **Steamboat Bill Jr (1928)** Classic Keaton comedy about an effete son and a cantankerous father.

4 **The Gold Rush (1925)** The picture Charlie Chaplin wanted to be remembered for – the Tramp goes to the Klondike in search of gold, ends up eating his boot and sees dancing dinner rolls.

5 **Slapstick Encyclopedia** If you're serious, this (pricey) five-disc set is a wonderful greatest hits of the silent comedy era.

tically involved with Pierce Brosnan, are a bit near the knuckle, hence the US rating.

📼 UK, US 💿 UK, US | PG (UK) PG-13 (US)

The Muppets 1992

Kermit, Miss Piggy, Fozzie have had more durable movie careers than many human TV stars who tried to make the jump from the small screen. Most of their movies have been efficiently made, and well targeted so that if you like Muppets you'll like the original **The Muppet Movie** (1979), their take on **Treasure Island** (1996), their New York odyssey (**The Muppets Take Manhattan**, 1984), **The Muppet Christmas Carol** (1993 – see p.84), even **Muppets from Space** (1999).

📼 UK, US 💿 UK, US | U (UK) G (US)

The Music Box 1932

Laurel and Hardy have one obvious asset as far as kids are concerned – they just look ridiculous. Pudgy Ollie, striving constantly for respectability, his uneasiness revealed by his constant fiddling with his hat and tie, and pale-faced, ghostly Stan, who can always be counted upon in a crisis to stroke his hair absently and, if that fails, burst into tears.

Off screen, their partnership was almost as mysterious. Laurel insisted on being paid more than (some say twice as much as) Hardy because he did all the work while Ollie just strolled in off the golf course when the gags, the camera angles, the stunts had all been worked out. Yet, when Hardy died in 1957, Laurel spent much of the remaining years of his life watching reruns of their old films and, as he told a visitor, he always watched his partner: "He fascinates me so much. He really was a funny fellow, wasn't he?"

The Music Box is their finest half an hour, probably more successful than some of their better known movies such as **Way Out West** and **Sons Of The Desert** although the latter may be their funniest ever full-length feature, helped considerably by the *Trail Of The Lonesome Pine* sequence. *The Music Box*'s premise is disarmingly simple: they have to deliver a piano to the home of Professor von Schwarzenhoffen. Out of that mission springs all kids of mayhem in which butts are kicked, policemen are enraged, staircases repeatedly mounted, and houses virtually destroyed. From the masterful comic timing and inventive physical comedy on display you would never guess that this was made partly because Laurel and Hardy had a contractual obligation to the Hal Roach studio to work off. That explains why, instead of devising a new movie, the boys decided to remake an old silent on the same theme which starred a washing machine, instead of the piano.

As Ollie often said to Stan: "There's a right way and a wrong way of doing things." Mercifully, Laurel and Hardy always chose the wrong way.

▭ UK, US ◉ UK, US

The Nutty Professor 1963, 1996

One fact everyone knows about **Jerry Lewis**: the French think he's a genius, an adoration as bizarre as their affection for the late Sacha Distel. But watch this comedy and you may think the French have a point. For once Lewis, the actor-writer-director, doesn't fatally unbalance the film which, with his dual role – as nerdish prof turned lounge lizard singer thanks to a chemical potion – would have been easy to do.

The **Eddie Murphy remake**, almost as good, earned a 12/PG-13 rating because of one odd scene where Murphy, as his grandma, discusses various sexual practices. Turn the sound down for that and – as long as you have a high threshold for flatulence jokes – you'll be fine. Lewis's comedy can be enjoyed by kids of most ages. And if you start believing he's a genius, there's any number of movies you can watch to set you straight.

ORIGINAL 📼 US ◉UK, US | PG (UK) NR (US)
EDDIE MURPHY REMAKE 📼 UK, US; ◉UK, US | PG (UK) PG-13 (US)

The Parent Trap 1998

The 1961 original had Hayley Mills as the matchmaking twins and it worked – but sagged, especially in the summer camp scenes. This 1998 remake, with Lindsay Lohan as the twins – and Dennis Quaid and Miranda Richardson as the ex-husband and wife who are reunited by childish wiles – is zappier, with neat special effects and a sentimental tone which should delight young girls.

📼 UK, US ◉UK, US | PG (UK, US)

The Real Howard Spitz 1998

Kelsey Grammer fits the role of a curmudgeonly writer who creates a bovine detective called Crafty Cow that kids love. Trouble is, Howard (Grammer) hates kids so much he hires someone to impersonate him in public. Meanwhile he dashes across LA trying to find the father of a girl who's been giving him advice. Grammer never quite surrenders his peevishness in an above-average comedy which pastiches film noir. There is some strong language but kids of 7 or 8 and over should warm to this.

📼 UK, US ◉UK, | PG (UK, US)

See Spot Run 2001

This is undoubtedly the finest movie ever made in which a spiky haired postman is locked out of his own flat by a canine FBI agent and slides, repeatedly, into dog poo. Oscar Wilde it ain't, but *See Spot Run* has an inventive energy which many better movies lack. The start is slow but the action and the laughs pick up as the postman (David Arquette) agrees to look after a child – mainly because he wants to make headway with the boy's mum – and, through a chain of events too complex to be narrated here, acquires an FBI dog wanted by the Mafia. You can see many of the gags coming – but when they arrive director John Whitesell often delivers them with a nice twist. And the dog poo scene will make every adult wince – and every child laugh out loud.

UK, US ⊚UK, US | PG (UK) NR (US)

A Shot In The Dark 1964

There's not much to choose between Blake Edwards's first two Inspector Clouseau movies. Peter Sellers steals the first, **The Pink Panther** (1963) from its "official" stars, David Niven and Capucine, and the Pink Panther cartoon is sublime. But **A Shot In The Dark** may be even funnier. These movies may seem over familiar – and the pace is a fair bit slower than we've seen in some decades – but to watch them again with kids is to realise how funny the jokes are. And the laughs never really let up in this one – right from the moment embattled police chief Herbert Lom says, "Give me ten men like Clouseau and I could destroy the world". And then there is the unforgettable sequence where Clouseau asks a man if his dog bites and, assured that it doesn't, is bitten. "But you said your dog doesn't bite," yelps Clouseau. "Yes," says the man, "but that is not my dog." True genius.

UK, US ⊚UK, US | PG (UK) NR (US)

A Simple Wish 1997

Martin Short is the bumbling fairy godmother whose attempt to grant a girl's wish – that her actor dad gets a part – goes badly wrong. But the real fun is the battle between two other fairy godmothers (Teri Garr and Ruby Dee) with struck-off fairy Kathleen Turner who goes so OTT you wonder there's any scenery left by the time the film ends. There's a nice pastiche of an Andrew Lloyd Webber musical, too, with songs co-written by director Michael Ritchie, so this really is fun for all the family.

UK, US ⊚UK, US | U (UK) PG (US)

Splash! 1984

This refreshing comedy about a man (Tom Hanks) who falls in love with a mermaid (Daryl Hannah) leaves all the best jokes to John Candy. Hannah is more persuasive as a mermaid than as a human being and the film is funny and charming, if slightly too long. There's some swearing and nudity but not enough to worry kids of 7 and over.

📼 UK, US ◉ UK, US | PG (UK, US)

Spy Kids 2001

 The original *Spy Kids* is a beguiling, inventive, adventure comedy which panders skilfully to childish fantasies while amusing the parents. Antonio Banderas and Carla Gugino are the experienced and, so they think, secret spies who get into trouble, thanks to the nefarious schemes of Floop (Alan Cumming) who has been kidnapping agents, giving them a serious makeover and trapping them in his children's TV programme. In the end, it is their kids, whose spycraft is a well-kept secret from their parents, who come to the rescue. There are plenty of gadgets (electro-shock bubblegum, a submarine that resembles a fish) and there's a quiet wit about the whole affair which keeps you smiling. **Spy Kids 2: Island Of Lost Dreams** works almost as well but as for **Spy Kids 3-D Game Over**, the last two words of the title say it all.

📼 UK, US ◉ UK, US | U (UK) PG (US)

Twins 1988

A real rarity: a one-note comedy that actually works. Danny DeVito and Arnold Schwarzenegger are on top form as the genetically engineered brothers who rediscover each other at the age of 35. There's some swearing but this is a good-natured romp which most kids of 6 or 7 should enjoy.

📼 UK, US ◉ UK, US | PG (UK, US)

MORE GROWN-UP COMEDY

Ace Ventura, Pet Detective 1994

The *Washington Post* reviewer called Jim Carrey's **Ace Ventura** "a mindless stretch of nonsense" – and he was a fan. Carrey plays Ace, the gumshoe who makes a living tracking down fugitive goldfish, as if he's paid for each joule of energy he expends. Which is just as well, because the plot stinks, the rest of the cast look like they're in another film, and there's a strain of homophobic jokes and sexual innuendoes which drag this film down. Watch for Jimbo's routines only, and if your kids get a taste for them, try **Dumb And Dumber** (1994), or **Bruce Almighty** (2003).

🎞️ UK, US ⊙ UK, US │ 12 (UK) PG-13 (US)

Airplane 1980

The first – and definitive – spoof of every Hollywood cliché by Jim Abrahams, David and Jerry Zucker. The gags come so fast and furious in this disaster flick send-up that kids will never be bored. There's plenty of innuendo (including one sight gag about oral sex which your kids won't get) and cartoon violence but for kids aged 8 and over this could be real treat. Pass on the sequel.

🎞️ UK, US ⊙ UK, US │ PG (UK, US)

Barefoot In The Park 1967

There's enough physical comedy, cracking one-liners ("A dog? That's a laugh – one look at those stairs and he'll go straight for her throat-?") and an exceptional cast (Robert Redford underplaying beautifully, Jane Fonda overplaying beautifully) to ensure this Neil Simon comedy never loses its sparkle.

🎞️ UK, US ⊙ UK, US │ PG (UK) G (US)

Bringing Up Baby 1938

The lead player is so devastatingly attractive – we're referring to the leopard – that for once Cary Grant and Katharine Hepburn are outshone. A box-office bomb in 1938, *Bringing Up Baby* got director Howard Hawks fired from his next film – but it's recognised as a classic now. With some of the niftiest banter on celluloid, this screwball comedy never loses momentum.

🎞️ UK, US ⊙ US │ U (UK) NR (US)

The Court Jester 1956

This swashbuckling spoof gave Danny Kaye his most successful screen role. He is simply hilarious in this underrated gem as a valet who saves a kingdom from bad old Basil Rathbone. Unconvinced? The scene between Kaye and Mildred Natwick in which the poison's in the vessel in the pestle, the chalice from the palace has the brew that's true, but the chalice from the palace was broken and replaced with a flagon with a dragon is worth the price of admission. Go on, treat yourself.

🎞️ US ⊙ UK, US │ U (UK) NR (US)

Duck Soup 1933

Watch the Marx Brothers' crazed antics in this film, often rated as one of the top

100 movies ever made, and you'll see why Eugene Ionescu, who gave us the demented satire *Rhinoceros*, cited the Marx brothers as his biggest influence. Kids may nor may not get the send-up of fascism and the barbs about war ("there isn't time to dig trenches, we'll have to buy them ready-made") but it doesn't matter – they'll probably love the hat-switching, and the dreadful puns.

📼 UK, US ⊙ US | U (UK) NR (US)

Harvey 1950

Not to every kid's taste – the humour may be too gentle and the story too slow-moving for some – but it's hard not to like a film in which James Stewart has an imaginary friend (a 6ft 3 1/2 inch palooka) and gets to say lines such as "I've wrestled with reality for 35 years and I'm happy, doctor. I finally won out over it."

📼 UK, US ⊙ UK, US | U (UK) NR (US)

Monty Python's Life of Brian/Monty Python and the Holy Grail 1979, 1975

Kids like the absurd as much as adults, and these two *Monty Python* features can still hit the mark for kids of 8 and up. **Life of Brian**, as well as being a very funny satire on Christ's depiction in the movies, is a romp, and kids are likely to howl with delight at the scene of an alien spaceship coming down to Jerusalem: an all-time great movie moment. The **Holy Grail** is a bit slower-paced, but even more silly, with the knights using coconuts to make horse noises, and the grail guarded by a killer

rabbit glove puppet. The films' adult classifications are perverse, to say the least.

BRIAN 📼 UK, US ⊙ UK, US | 15 (UK) R (US)

GRAIL 📼 UK, US ⊙ UK, US | 15 (UK) PG (US)

Road To Utopia 1946

The best of the *Road* movies: Bob Hope and Bing Crosby are two vaudevillians in Alaska at the turn of the 19th century hoping to strike gold – and to win Dorothy Lamour's affections – to a mocking narration by humorist Robert Benchley. If this goes down well, try **Road To Morocco** and **Road To Rio**.

📼 UK, US ⊙ US | U (UK) NR (US)

Some Like It Hot 1959

The best comedy ever? Tony Curtis and Jack Lemmon witness a mob massacre, disguise themselves as female musicians and fall in love with Marilyn Monroe. Lemmon, getting the fuzzy end of the lollipop, ends up with Joe E. Brown who, in the final scene, is unfazed by his partner's sudden change of sex. It's that kind of film – switching from broad to subtle comedy in an instant, full of parodies, and full of laughs. Monroe's sex appeal is sometimes blatant – especially when she sings "I Want To Be Loved By You" – but this is ideal for kids of 7 or older.

📼 UK, US ⊙ UK, US | U (UK) NR (US)

What's Up, Doc? 1972

Peter Bogdanovich's homage to screwball comedy in general – and to *Bringing Up*

Baby in particular – is as funny a comedy as Hollywood has produced in the last forty years. This time, the absent-minded male is a musicologist (Ryan O' Neal) who becomes hopelessly ensnared in the schemes of eccentric college drop-out – Barbra Streisand. Bogdanovich throws in mistaken luggage, a jewel theft, government spies, and a fabulous slapstick car chase across San Francisco.

UK, US UK, US | U (UK) G (US)

8

Dinosaurs

they're not extinct – really

D
inosaurs, with or without a bikini-clad Raquel Welch in close proximity, have fascinated moviemakers for three-quarters of a century. But they only really captured the box office with Steven Spielberg's electrifying, scarifying *Jurassic Park*, where the beasts came truly alive and menacing. Since then, these glamorous prehistoric pets have seldom been off our cinema and TV screens. Although the law of diminishing returns may have begun to apply, with *Jurassic Park IV* pencilled in for a 2005 release, this species of movie doesn't look destined for extinction anytime soon.

Dinosaur 2000

Disney's digitally animated dinosaur tale wasn't the triumph the studio intended, possibly because the storyline – and the voices – are straight out of cuddlier fare such as *The Land Before Time* (see p.136), while the animation strives for realism. It's not bad but older kids might enjoy *Jurassic Park* more and younger kids may have more fun with *The Land Before Time* series.

UK, US ◉ UK, US | PG (UK,US)

Dinotopia 2002

Lilliput with dinosaurs. That's the high concept here. Can Carl and David make the ostrich-like citizens confront the perils that endanger their very existence before it's too late? Of course they can – but it's a close-run thing. The effects hold up better than the plot – or the acting – but kids from 5 to 8 won't especially mind.

UK, US ◉ UK, US | NR

Jurassic Park 1993

Richard Attenborough is the affably crazed scientist whose theme park goes badly awry, endangering his guests' lives and earning over $400 million at the box office. Steven Spielberg's classic is still electrifying even after repeated viewing. Probably because screenwriter David Koepp, in adapting Michael Crichton's novel, operated on the credo: "Whenever the characters started talking about their personal lives, you couldn't care less. You want them to shut up and go stand on a hill where you can see the dinosaurs." For *Seinfeld* fans, there's the added joy of seeing Wayne Knight (Newman, the sinister postman) getting his comeuppance. The film is genuinely scary so the tricky part is deciding at what age kids could/should enjoy it. One reviewer has suggested no kids below 10 should watch this, which seems a tad high – kids aged 5, with nerves of steel, could have a great time.

That's more than can be said for the flaccid sequel **The Lost World**. However, *Jurassic Park III*, directed by Joe Johnston, is satisfyingly vicious – a "nice little thrill machine" in the words of Roger Ebert.

UK, US ◉ UK, US | PG (UK) PG-13 (US)

Dinosaur Jnr - one of the leaf-eating varieties

The Land Before Time 1988

A displaced brontosaurus called Littlefoot and his friends embark on some hair-raising adventures as they try to find their families and sing a few songs to keep their spirits up. The formula, cuddly dinosaurs for kids – aged 6 and under – who might find *Jurassic Park* a bit scary, was so effective there have been nine sequels.

UK, US UK, US | U (UK) G (US)

The Land That Time Forgot 1975

And a film sci-fi legend Michael Moorcock is still trying to forget. He co-scripted this feeble effort in which Doug McClure (Trampas from *The Virginian*) heroically takes his submarine through uncharted havens and encounters monsters even less convincing than his acting. That said, this is not a bad film for under-5 dino-fans to while away a wet Sunday afternoon if it's on TV.

US | PG (UK) NR (US)

One Million Years BC 1966

"This is the way it was," said the tag line, neatly glossing over the fact that man and tyrannosaurus never went head to head and that there is little scientific evidence to suggest that all Neanderthal women were as beautiful – and as well shaved – as this film would suggest. The paucity of dialogue means that, for all of Ray Harryhausen's effects and the sight of a scantily clad Raquel Welch, the tension does slacken – although a giant, homicidal, turtle is a minor treat. At 91 minutes, this is probably a film to watch while you and your kids are doing something else. Good for kids aged 5 to 8.

📼 UK, US ◉UK, US | PG (UK) NR (US)

Valley Of Gwangi 1969

Failed touring circus enters forbidden valley, recruits massive allosaurus as star attraction, only for the beast to escape and terrorize all and sundry. You can tell most of the money went on Ray Harryhausen's special effects – and even now they make this movie very watchable. For kids up to the age of 8 – any older and they'll laugh at the special effects.

📼 UK, US ◉UK, US | U (UK) G (US)

Walking With Dinosaurs 1999

There were some sneers about the scientific credibility of this BBC TV series – re-creating in nature-documentary style the life of dinosaurs – when it was first released. But such concerns do not, finally, detract from the fact that this is a towering achievement, judged purely on its ability to make you feel as if you were sitting behind a bush watching these creatures endure their nasty, brutish and short lives. The episode where the terrifying beasts get their comeuppance – thanks in part to a stray meteor – even makes you feel sorry for them. Well worth buying on DVD for the extras, if you can. Kids of 5 or 6 may find some of the scenes quite scary, so treat yourself and watch together.

If kids enjoy this, they will almost certainly be up for the genuinely documentary **Walking With Beasts** (see p.143).

📼 UK, US ◉UK, US | NR

When Dinosaurs Ruled The Earth 1969

Loosely adapted from a J.G. Ballard story, with only 27 words of dialogue, this epic from the Hammer stable is very educational. Your kids will learn that the bikini wasn't a 20th-century invention at all – they were worn by the predecessors of *Playboy* playmate Victoria Vetri in prehistoric times. And, if you were nice to dinosaurs, they sometimes saved your life – good to know if some mad scientist ever does do daft things with their DNA and resurrect them. Also suited to kids up to the age of 8 – for the same reasons as *Valley Of Gwangi*.

US | PG (UK) G (US)

9

Documentaries

facts of life

F acts can, as Ronald Reagan so famously observed, be stupid things. But served up in the right way they can enthral children whose thirst for knowledge – be it for mathematical equations or more obviously riveting stuff (the fact that a cockroach can live for several days after its head has been chopped off) – has not yet been quenched by intellectual fatigue.

Alas, good children's documentaries are as rare as perfect summers, which is a big shame because – as Bodil Cold-Ravnkilde, of the Danish Film Institute put it – "Once you have seen children – burning with curiosity about their surroundings – become wiser, captivated, informed and even more assured citizens after seeing a proper documentary that touched their hearts, you'll know how meaningful a documentary can be for children and how important it is for us to supply inspiring documentaries to our kids."

The Blue Planet 2001

It's easy, especially in Britain, to take David Attenborough for granted. In our imagination, he seems perpetually to be bur-bling on, in those hushed, enthused tones of his, while standing in an exotic pile of animal droppings. All his work is terrific, and compulsively watchable, but this series on the ocean really makes you sit up and gawp. Ecosystems never filmed before, marlin zipping around at 60mph (or so it seems), insights into the delicate web of relationships which makes the ecological balance work (most of the time), this eight-part BBC TV series has it all. Treat yourself and buy the two-DVD pack. Kids of absolutely any age will be enthralled.

📼 UK, US ⊚ UK,US | NR

Children Of Theatre Street 1977

This fascinating, Oscar-nominated documentary about the Kirov Ballet, adroitly narrated by Princess Grace of Monaco, may make young girls beg you to move to St Petersburg. It's not quite fly-on-the-wall – some of the scenes seem staged – but still a real insight into the ballet company's life and work.

US | PG (US)

The Endurance 2000

Ernest Shackleton's 1914 Antarctic expedition was captured on film by an Australian cameraman, Frank Hurley, and it is Hurley's extraordinary images which fascinate, in this blindly admiring account of an expedition of derring-do. Even in 1914, the expedition – as became apparent when the survivors returned to be greeted, not as heroes but as malingerers – seemed somewhat old-fashioned. But this is an impressive account of a brave, almost foolish, adventure.

US ⊚UK, US | PG (UK) G (US)

For All Mankind 1989

For those kids who still dream of being an astronaut – and find *Apollo 13* (the movie, that is) a bit slow – there is nothing better than this lyrical love song to the Apollo space programme. Director Al Reinert wisely eschews talking heads, heavy voiceovers and statistics as dry as the Sea of Tranquillity to focus on the essential question kids – of all ages – want to answer: what's it like to fly in space? Almost perfect.

US ⊚UK,US | NR

Ghetto Princess 2000

Not to be confused with the sexploitation movie of the same name, this award-winning film from Cathrine Asmussen is a nicely observed

41-minute documentary about two girls – one Danish, one Turkish – who realize that their cultures are about to pull their friendship apart. The days of school discos and trips to the local swimming pool may soon be over as Yagmur will soon not be allowed to wear a swimsuit in public and will have to spend her weekends studying the Koran. This is still doing the film festival circuit – the dialogue is in Danish, with English subtitles – but it's just the kind of documentary that deserves a broader audience.

🎞 not currently available | NR

Into The Arms Of Strangers 2000

This documentary exploration of how 10,000 Jewish children were saved from the Holocaust by finding foster homes in Britain is not for every child. But for kids of 11 and over, it is compelling, if at times harrowing, viewing. Director Mark Jonathan Harris occasionally bullies viewers into the appropriate emotional response but the stories retold here (and the story of the 1.5 million who weren't saved) are so powerful that they make their own case. Like *Schindler's List*, this is a story about, as *The Onion* put it so well, "small redemptive pockets of courage and humanity" in the midst of genocide. At 117 minutes, it's not short – and it is emotionally gruelling – but this is a very good film about a very difficult subject.

🎞 UK, US ◉UK,US | PG (UK,US)

The Living Desert 1953

Cute Disney documentary about life in the sands, especially suited to younger kids.

🎞 US | NR

Savage Skies 1996

Early – and one of the best – examples of the so-called weather porn documentary, which most kids will enjoy – unless they're nervous or live on the top floor and have their room buffeted by high winds every night. Tornadoes, hurricanes, monsoons, and some lightly worn learning about our climate and our planet: this film has got it all.

▭ UK, US | NR

That's Entertainment 1974

Cleverly constructed corporate propaganda for MGM which astounds both with the quality of its hosts (Frank Sinatra, Bing Crosby, Gene Kelly and Liza Minnelli) and the power of the classic performances excavated from the vaults. The sequel, **That's Entertainment II**, is almost as good. Any kid could enjoy this, though they may make you fast forward the links.

▭ US ◎US | U (UK) G (US)

Walking With Beasts 2001

Emmy award-winning sequel to *Walking With Dinosaurs* (see p.137). In some ways, this BBC–Discovery Channel collaboration is even more of a voyage of discovery than its illustrious predecessor – as it shines a spotlight on creatures that many of us never suspected existed. More than one viewer has reported that the series fascinated their cats.

▭ UK,US ◎UK, US | NR

10

Drama

the play's the thing

D rama can provide a welcome change of pace from the stunt-infested, wisecracking action and adventure movies which the film business seems to churn out on a daily basis. At its best, drama can raise real issues that you and your children might be confronting, or simply offer a story so compelling that kids are engrossed in a tale that takes them to a different world. And it's good, sometimes, to find films which suggest there's more to human relationships than the banter of villain and hero or the wisecracking repartee of potential lovers. Here are some of the best dramas aimed at an audience that is either primarily, or encompassing, kids. Once again, you'll find a "more grown-up" section at the end, and see also our **Classics** (p.91) and **Fantasy** (p.170) chapters.

Alaska 1996

Brother and sister go searching for missing dad but find a cuddly polar bear and a ruthless hunter (Charlton Heston) in pursuit. Chuck, directed by his son Fraser, is so wonderfully evil you almost forget the magnificent scenery. The kids – Thora Birch and Vincent Kartheiser – aren't bad either. But the bear out-acts everyone.

📼 UK, US ◉UK, US | PG (UK, US)

BMX Bandits 1983

Australian exploitation movie capitalizing on the popularity of BMX bikes and the beauty of the young Nicole Kidman. Chiefly famous, today, for dodgy dialogue and a scene where Nicole's stunts are visibly being performed by a male double, this is nonetheless an entertaining yarn about pesky meddling kids who foil the crooks thanks to their BMX bikes.

📼 Currently unavailable | PG (UK) NR (US)

The Boy From Mercury 1996

Intriguing tale about an 8-year-old boy in Dublin who blames his unhappiness on the fact that he's from the planet Mercury. Martin Duffy's first film as writer/director blends sci-fi and kitchen-sink drama to great effect. James Hickey is magnificent as the boy and there's top support from Rita Tushingham, Tom Courtenay and Sean O'Flanagain.

📼 UK | PG (UK) NR (US)

Children Of Heaven 1997

"Very nearly a perfect film for children," said critic Roger Ebert of this award-winning Iranian movie, adding, "to see this is to be reminded of a time when the children in movies were children and not miniature stand-up comics". Mohammad Amir Naji and Mir Farrokh Hashemian impress as poor siblings who try to mask the loss of a pair of shoes by sharing a pair to school. It does have subtitles but none that will tax an 8 or 9-year-old. They might just be intrigued by this glimpse of a different culture, the simple premise of the story, and enchanted by the gentle comedy. If this goes down well, other Iranian movies for children worth considering are **The White Balloon** (1995), **The Runner** (1984) and **The Apple** (1998).

▭▭ US ◎US | NR (UK) PG (US)

Danny The Champion Of The World 1989

This TV adaptation of a Roald Dahl favourite features real-life father and son Samuel and Jeremy Irons as Danny and his dad. The story is set in rural England, some time in the 1950s. Danny lives with his widowed father in a caravan next to their motor garage – a quiet, almost idyllic life until Robbie Coltrane, an evil landowner, tries to take their land. Danny, his father and a hotch-potch of quirky villagers, including Jimmy Nail as a gamekeeper, set up all manner of schemes to foil his plans – and steal his pheasants. It is innocent storytelling, perfect for fans of Enid Blyton-style adventures, but with a bit more bite and humour (albeit not quite as much as in the book).

This is one of the Dahl movies not currently available on video or DVD; surely an oversight as even the crotchety author noted, "they have captured the atmosphere of the time and place splendidly."

▭▭ UK currently unavailable | U (UK)

Diamond's Edge 1988

Adapted from his own book, *The Falcon's Malteser*, by Anthony Horowitz, this starts with an appealing premise: dim private eye Tim and his smart younger brother Nick are given Maltesers to guard. That's the springboard for a kids' film noir, set in London rather than LA, and paying affectionate tribute to the genius of Dashiell (*Maltese Falcon*) Hammett. Sadly, Hammett's estate wouldn't let the film be called *The Falcon's Malteser* so the name had to change – it was called *Just Ask For Diamond* on its cinema release. Tight budgets meant that some of the cooler scenes from the book didn't make it into the movie but this still works. Colin Dale got the role of Nick partly because he was one of the few (out of 350 boys) who had heard of Humphrey Bogart. Patricia Hodge is sublime as charlady turned seductive Brenda von Falkenberg. Pity it's not more widely available.

📼 US │ U (UK) PG (US)

The Elephant Man 1980

The Elephant Man is the only David Lynch movie which could get a "Must See!" icon for a children's audience. But then Lynch directs this tale with unusual restraint, astutely sensing that the story of a catastrophically deformed man (John Hurt) who ekes out a living as the star of a freak show doesn't really need any of his trademark flourishes. Hurt's make-up (which Lynch, amazingly, tried to apply) is a triumph, and the crew tracked down casts of the head, arm and foot belonging to the real elephant man, John Merrick, at a London hospital. But the performances – by Hurt and Anthony Hopkins in particular – are even better. The tale is bleak at times, especially when depicting the persecution of Merrick and his final accidental death by asphyxiation, but the movie is a powerful statement about human dignity. Clearly, it isn't for younger kids but depending on the child, 8- or 9-year-olds might enjoy this.

The other Lynch movie which might appeal to kids is **The Straight Story** (1999) which won Richard Farnsworth an Oscar as a man who travels for hundreds of miles on a lawn mower to see his sick brother.

📼 UK, US ◉ UK, US │ PG (UK, US)

Grey Owl 1999

Pierce Brosnan leaves the 007 tux at home and dons a Native American headdress to play Archibald "Grey Owl" Belaney, a grammar school boy from Hastings who pretended to be a Mohawk guide in Canada and lectured and worked to protect the environment. For some reviewers, Richard Attenborough's liberal-conscience biopic is flawed by the fact that Brosnan's character is a fraud, but others found much to admire in the star's performance. It is an intriguing, unusual tale for older kids – not entirely successful but, like most Attenborough movies, a quality affair, if slightly longer than it needs to be.

📼 UK, US ◎ UK, US | PG (UK) PG-13 (US)

Harriet The Spy 1996

This isn't quite as vibrant as the Louise Fitzhugh novel it's based on but it's still entertaining. Michelle Trachtenberg is the girl who spies on her schoolfriends and neighbours and, to sharpen up her writing skills, scribbles her caustic thoughts down in a notebook. Inevitably, the notebook gets stolen. Director Bronwen Hughes doesn't make the most of the material, and some scenes look amateurish, but Trachtenberg is an appealing heroine and Rosie O'Donnell wonderfully warm as the nanny. Kids of 8 and over should go for it.

📼 UK, US ◎ UK, US | U (UK) PG (US)

Holes 2003

 A lot of kids in the 8 to 10 age range rate Louis Sachar's book *Holes* as one of their absolute favourites – so this Disney live-action movie needed to stay faithful to the story. Which it did, pretty much, give or take a cameo from Whoopi Goldberg, and a soundtrack that rocks. But as the lead review on Amazon.com put it – "What's not to like?"

The story is a winner. Stanley Yelnats (Shia LaBeouf), a poor New York kid, is wrongly accused of stealing a pair of sneakers and is sent to Camp Green Lake, a juvenile prison camp in the bed of a dried-up lake, somewhere nasty in Texas. There, along with an engaging cast of delinquent detainees, he is forced to dig endless holes in the desert earth, under the eye of cruel warden Sigourney Weaver. The warden hopes that the kids will unearth a secret treasure, buried by a Wild West era female outlaw (depicted in flashbacks by a nicely feisty Patricia Arquette). And if you've not read the book, you don't want to know more than that. Just sit back and enjoy, and then log on to iTunes to download the catchy and unirritating title rap. The PG, by the way, is a bit of a mystery. Anyone from 6 up should enjoy this.

▭ UK, US ◉UK, US | PG (UK, US)

The Journey Of Natty Gann 1985

A very different kind of Disney movie. Meredith Salenger is a revelation as the 14-year-old girl who travels 2000 miles on the open road to find her father, accompanied for some of the way by John Cusack's drifter. Set in the Great Depression, this is a dark, realistic movie in which the heroine falls in with the wrong sort and spends some time in a juvenile institution, so it's not for all kids. Indeed, even Disney seems a bit nonplussed by its creation, if the shoddy DVD re-release is anything to go by. But this is a movie which will raise real issues for you and your kids to discuss.

▭ US ◉UK, US | PG (UK, US)

Little House On The Prairie 1974

The only real question in each episode of this heartwarming American TV series (derived from the books by Laura Ingalls Wilder) was: when was the dad (Michael Landon) going to cry? He sometimes wept in an open field, so it could have been something to do with the pollen count or perhaps just the strain of looking after a little house, a wife and three little daughters on the banks of Plum Creek in the 1800s. This was the kind of show in which a daughter could marry a blind tutor who regained his sight – in other words, it made *The Waltons* look like a masterpiece of kitchen-sink realism.

▭ UK, US ◉UK, US | NR

Loch Ness 1996

Kids expecting to see *Jurassic Park*-style spills and thrills with the Scottish monster will be disappointed. Ted Danson plays a scientist, burned out after an unsuccessful search for Bigfoot, sent to prove a negative – that Nessie doesn't exist. But the emphasis, in this enjoyable

Ted Danson out for a nice quiet spot of fishing on Loch Ness

fantasy, is on his romance with single mum Joely Richardson, whose daughter knows a thing or two about "water kelpies". Richardson, and Ian Holm as the local laird who guards Nessie's secrets, are the best things in the film. Nessie, of course, is stunning when she appears but she's more of a guest star.

📼 US ◎ US | PG (UK, US)

The Mighty 1998

Director Peter Chelsom takes plenty of risks with this tale of two misfits – and most of them come off. Lumbering outcast Max (a sensational performance from Elden Henson) teams up with another misfit (Kieran Culkin), a hunchback dubbed "Freak" by his classmates. For kids who suspect they stand out like sore thumbs (and what kid doesn't?), this movie, based on the children's book by Rodman Philbrick, will have some resonance. It's an intriguing mix of the extraordinary and ordinary with a spot of implausible derring-do (and a cool toboggan ride). But at the movie's heart is the way the misfits discover the power of imagination, trying to live by the chivalrous code they have learned from reading tales of King Arthur and his knights. The film is shot through with nicely observed humour ("Sometimes seems like the whole world has just seen me on 'America's Most Wanted'," Max complains) and has some quietly effective scenes. Sharon Stone is a revelation as Kevin's mother, and Harry Dean Stanton and Gena Rowlands offer great support as Max's grandparents, and the impeccable acting is rounded out by a scene-stealing cameo from Gillian Anderson as a barfly. For some critics, the parts of the movie don't quite gel – but they still add up to a very different kind of film which older kids, maybe of 9 and over, should respond to.

▭▭ UK, US ◉ UK, US | PG (UK) PG-13 (US)

The Railway Children 1970

 The tales of E. Nesbit (as with J.K. Rowling, the initial helped conceal the fact that the author was a woman) seem a natural for the cinema, and *The Railway Children*, directed by Lionel Jeffries, remains (despite a British TV remake) their definitive moment on film. The story revolves around the Waterbury family, who are reasonably content with life until their father is taken away in the night by two strangers and they are forced to move to Yorkshire without him. The two sisters (Jenny Agutter and Sally Thomsett) and brother (Gary F. Warren) become enchanted by the railway close by their new home, and which sparks their adventures. The story is not always compelling, though there are memorable episodes, often involving Jenny Agutter, as the older sister who relishes the adventure yet begins to realize the responsibilities she has to face. It would be easy to dismiss the appeal of this movie – on its release, or today – as sentimental nostalgia. Easy but wrong. The user comments on the Internet Movie Database show that there are generations of railway children – parents who remember it the first time, children who have just fallen for its charms. There was even a British pop group called the Railway Children in the early 1980s.

▭▭ UK ◉ UK, US | U (UK) G (US)

Run Wild, Run Free 1969

This gentle movie centres on a timid boy (Mark Lester, fresh from singing his heart out in *Oliver!*) who is brought out of his shell by his love for a horse. John Mills gives a nicely judged performance as the retired colonel who supplies the affection the boy's parents don't give, but both Mills and Lester are almost outshone by the Dartmoor scenery. A forgotten film that deserves to endure.

UK | U (UK) NR (US)

The Secret Of Roan Inish 1993

Producer Maggi Renzi and director John Sayles made this film with one ambition in mind: "To give every kid and parent we know one guaranteed good hour and a half." Fiona (Jeni Courtney) is the girl who believes she and her family are half descended from the selkies (seals). She knows this is possible because she has seen a child carried out to sea in a cradle by seals on Roan Inish. With this conceit – and this being Ireland – Sayles could have easily opted for blarney and whimsy but he keeps this tale grounded, taking the girl's story at face value. It's a good film to look at, thanks to some fine cinematography from Haskell Wexler, and good to watch, despite (or perhaps because of) its slow pacing.

UK, US ◉UK, US | PG (UK, US)

He's not heavy, he's my brother - Fiona and selky friend

Simon Birch 1998

This unashamedly sentimental tear-jerker – in which an illegitimate boy Joe (Joseph Mazzello) becomes friends with a cocky dwarf (Ian Michael Smith) – was inspired by John Irving's novel *A Prayer For Owen Meany*, and is narrated in flashback by the grown-up Joe (Jim Carrey). It is well acted and well written, though the dwarf gets most the best lines: teasing his friend, whose mother won't reveal the identity of his father, he says, "I don't understand why she doesn't just tell you. You're already a bastard, might as well be an enlightened one." A strangely engaging movie, especially for older kids dealing with those same fears about being a misfit.

UK, US ◎UK, US | PG (UK, US)

Stuart Little 1999

 Maybe it's the source – this movie springs from E.B. White's classic tale published in the 1940s. Or maybe it's just the charm in Michael J. Fox's voice but, for 84 minutes, this film about an adopted mouse trembles on the edge of being annoyingly, icky and cute – but never puts that last foot wrong. Some critics just flat out couldn't accept the fact of the mouse's lack of stature, but your kids won't have that problem and should enjoy this quiet, gentle, family movie in which the animals are as loquacious as the humans (Hugh Laurie and Geena Davies). The plot, in case you missed out, is daft but effective: an only child's parents adopt a mouse in place of a kid, and after an initial sulk, the unlikely siblings bond inseparably.

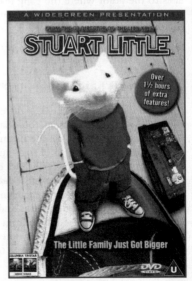

A WIDESCREEN PRESENTATION

FROM THE CO-DIRECTOR OF THE LION KING

STUART LITTLE

Over 1½ hours of extra features!

The Little Family Just Got Bigger

DVD

U

Rather against expectations, the sequel, **Stuart Little 2** (tag line: "A little goes a long way!") doesn't feel too much like a cash-in. The Little family cat, Snowball (Nathan Lane), gets a starring role, there's a fine chase sequence, and even a hint of cross-species romance between Stuart and a yellow bird called Margalo (voiced by Melanie Griffith).

📼 UK, US ◉ UK, US | U (UK) PG (US)

War Of The Buttons 1993

The French version of this novel was rated X in 1962 because the combatants' habits of cutting the buttons off their rivals' clothes led, inevitably, to a scene of a naked fight among lots of boys. David Puttnam toned things down slightly after finally persuading novelist Louis Pergaud to let him make the movie. The author objected, initially, that "childhood no longer exists" but they worked that one out. The film is set in County Cork in the 1970s where the boys of Carrickdowse and Ballydowse are always at war – a war that escalates to the point where the gang leaders, Fergus and Geronimo, are sent to reform school. Think *Lord Of The Flies* but, this time, with an uplifting ending.

📼 UK, US | PG (UK) NR (US)

When the Whales Came 1989

It's surprising that this is the only novel by Michael Morpurgo to make it onto film – and surprising, too, that it is not better known. For this is a terrific story, centred on the Birdman (Paul Scofield), a strange old loner who – with the help of two children – takes it upon himself to protect Bryher, one of the Scilly Isles off the coast of Cornwall, from a curse caused by the slaughter of stranded whales. The tale is set during World War I and gets across the harshness of those times on the islands, as well as the natural beauty of the land and seascapes. Scofield is excellent and there is strong support from both of the children, as well as Helen Mirren, David Suchet and other British actors. It is quietly stirring stuff, good for anyone from age 6 and up.

📼 US | U (UK) PG (US)

Whistle Down The Wind 1961

Well-crafted, entertaining, slightly old-fashioned tale in which Hayley Mills and her siblings discover a stranger (Alan Bates) in the barn and ask him who he is – only for him to exclaim "Jesus Christ!" in exasperation. He is, it turns out, a convicted murderer on the run. Director Bryan Forbes wisely avoids any forays into laboured symbolism and lets the cast do the work which they do magnificently, Bates is an endearing fugitive and 6-year-old Alan Barnes turns in a stunning performance as little brother Charles. The film was later converted into an Andrew Lloyd Webber musical, but don't let that put you off.

▭ UK, US ◉ UK, US | U (UK) NR (US)

The World Of Henry Orient 1964

It's not often you see a movie stolen from Peter Sellers but Merrie Spaeth and Tippy Walker do just that as the adolescent boarding schoolgirls who pursue Sellers, an egotistical, yet gifted, concert pianist. But Sellers only has eyes for his new mistress Paula Prentiss and she assumes that the girls, following them around, are spying for her husband. A touching, funny movie about the agony of adolescent infatuation. Director George Roy Hill returned to the theme of young love in his 1979 film **A Little Romance**, which is also worth seeing.

▭ UK, US ◉ UK, US | U (UK) NR (US)

• •

MORE GROWN-UP DRAMA

A Man For All Seasons 1966

Paul Scofield is sublime as Sir Thomas More, the man who keeps his virtue but loses his head in King Henry VIII's England. Scofield makes More's virtue – and his vanity – wonderfully clear while Robert Shaw rescues the king

from buffoonery and makes him charismatic and formidable.

▭ UK, US ◉ UK, US | U (UK) G (US)

The Bicycle Thieves 1948

In Italian director Vittorio de Sica's masterpiece, father and son try to recover the stolen bicycle dad needs to earn some money and keep the family off the breadline. The plot's very simplicity, the naturalness of the setting and the acting, its relative brevity (93 minutes) and some delightful touches – such as father and son stopping for a pizza they can ill-afford – mean this is a seriously affecting movie which, despite the subtitles, could appeal to kids aged 6 and upwards.

📼 UK, US 📀 UK, US | U (UK) NR (US)

Captains Courageous 1937

Freddie Bartholomew is the spoilt brat who is forced to learn some lessons about life by Spencer Tracy and his fellow fishermen – Tracy won an Oscar for this.

📼 UK, US 📀 UK, US | NR

To Kill A Mockingbird 1962

Gregory Peck picked up an Oscar in this adaptation of Harper Lee's novel as lawyer Atticus Finch fighting prejudice in a small town in the southern states. His performance, to be fair, is matched by the rest of the cast, especially the child actors. Charming, subtly told (by director Robert Mulligan) and with some unsettling scenes (the attempted lynching, the kids returning in fancy-dress costume, accompanied by a phantom pursuer), this should appeal to kids on the verge of their teens.

📼 UK, US 📀 UK, US | PG (UK) NR (US)

Little Man Tate 1991

Jodie Foster's directorial debut moves slowly at times, has cloying moments, yet is made compelling by Adam Hann-

Byrd as Fred, the troubled, gifted 6-year-old son Foster fights to get the best for. Dianne West as a child psychologist and Harry Connick Jr offer sympathetic support. Kids will be fascinated by Fred, a prodigy whose tale is well told by Foster, something of a prodigy herself – she starred in *Taxi Driver* when she was just 14.

📼 UK, US 📀 UK, US | PG (UK, US)

The Long Walk Home 1990

You could regard this as a kind of more challenging companion film to *Driving Miss Daisy*. In this case, a white woman (Sissy Spacek) is brought to a greater understanding of racial discrimination in America by her maid (Whoopi Goldberg, powerfully understated for once). This understanding is acquired in 1950s America, in Montgomery, Alabama, to be precise, where a black woman Rosa Parks has refused to stand at the back of the bus, a decision which would lead the black community (led by the young Martin Luther King) to boycott the buses. The film takes care not to make Spacek or Goldberg mere symbols – their understanding is at the heart of the film. Eventually, Spacek is drawn into the boycott, leading to conflict with her racist husband. The acting, the script and the gospel music give this movie, which isn't perfect, real power.

📼 UK, US 📀 UK, US | PG (UK, US)

Paper Moon 1973

Ryan O'Neal is the Bible-toting con man who takes for partner a brattish kid (his real-life daughter Tatum O' Neal) who gradually becomes almost his surrogate mother. There's lots of snappy patter in this episodic charmer, the last completely successful movie to be directed by Peter Bogdanovich.

🎞UK, US ⊙UK, US | PG (US)

The Winslow Boy 1999

Fourteen-year-old naval cadet is expelled for stealing five shillings. He denies it – and his father (Nigel Hawthorne) almost bankrupts the family trying to prove the son's innocence and to prove that his own word must be accepted. David Mamet's reworking of Terence Rattigan's play is a minor masterpiece, well-cast and well-played, but probably best suited to older children – maybe 10 and over.

🎞UK, US ⊙UK, US | U (UK)

11

Fairytales

ogres, frogs and princesses

Jacob Ludwig and Wilhelm Carl Grimm were born too soon. Today, they would be multi-millionaires, lording it in Hollywood as their story ideas inspired an endless procession of scary yet heartwarming kids' movies. Without their fairytales, the movie business would be a lot poorer, culturally as well as commercially. Good as *Toy Story* and *Finding Nemo* are, there's nothing like a classic fairytale to intrigue, enchant, scare and deliver a quick moral lesson on the way, and as *Shrek* (reviewed in **Animation** – p.43) has shown, ogres, frogs and princesses aren't quite redundant yet awhile.

Special mention should be made of the **Faerie Tale Theater series** – classic live-action fairytales made in the 1980s for the HBO network. These are far from big-budget movies, but they are authentically medieval-looking, nicely cast (everyone from Mick Jagger to Christopher Reeve to Jennifer Beals pops up), and reasonably faithful to the stories, including their less sugary and often eerie dimensions. Most have been reissued on DVD.

Barbie As Rapunzel 2002

World-famous doll meets classic fairytale: how could it fail? And indeed, this entertaining combo hit the mark nicely for girls of 4 to 7, with Anjelica Huston's vocal talents as unbalanced witch Gothel and the obvious care and craft which have gone into the animation, raising it a bit beyond the fluff level. It is probably best to bite the bullet and plump for the **Barbie Fantasy Tales Collection** (which will also get you **Barbie Swan Lake** and **Barbie In The Nutcracker**), but it's available on its own, if one Barbie movie feels more than enough.

▭▭ UK, US ◉UK, US │ U (UK) G (US)

Beauty And The Beast 1991

Perhaps the greatest compliment you can pay this animated version of the romantic tale of outer and inner beauty is that it stands comparison with *Snow White* and *Pinocchio* – in other words, it's up there with the best films Disney has produced. Disney had planned to film *Beauty* in the 1930s and again in the 1950s but the studio paused until the 1990s. It was worth the wait – this was the first animated feature to be nominated for the best picture Oscar.

The animation is indeed excellent. But *Beauty And The Beast*'s enchanting appeal is the studio's rediscovery of Walt's magic formula. The 600-year-old story is one of the best fairytales, with a simple premise – a young prince deformed unless he can find someone wise enough to love him. And Disney has grafted upon the plot a strong cast of supporting, chattering, gossipy players – a clock, a candlestick and a teapot – a device that the studio, at its best, does brilliantly. The songs, notably "Be Our Guest" and the title track (Angela Lansbury on top

Cinderella, Cinderfella...

Cinderella is the most filmed of all the fairytales, from the days of silent film to the demands of Christmas cable TV networks. Here are some alternative options to the classic Disney animation (reviewed below).

Cinderella 1922 Walt Disney's first attempt to bring Cinderella to the screen was as a seven-minute animated short.

Zolushka 1947 Such a classic, even the sub-titles shouldn't get in the way of kids appreciating this fantastic Russian musical. ⊙US | NR

Cinderfella 1960 Jerry Lewis plays Cinderfella in this farce, destined to be put upon by his step-mother and brothers until a spirit helps him win Princess Charmant. ▭UK, US | U (UK) NR (US)

Cinderella 1984 Jennifer Beals was Cinderalla in this Faerie Tale Theater production – a favourite for many. ▭ US | NR

Rodgers & Hammerstein's Cinderella 1964 Julie Andrews was the original stage star in this fine musical, though she lost out on the film version to a very young Leslie Ann Warren. Top songs, as you'd expect, and a great cameo from Ginger Rogers. ▭UK, US ⊙UK, US | U (UK) NR (US)

The Slipper And The Rose 1976 Bryan Forbes's musical takes the story from Prince Charming's side. It's overlong at two and a half hours, but the sets are great and the songs (by the Sherman brothers) are good, too. ▭UK, US ⊙UK, US | U (UK) NR (US)

Ever After 1998 probably the best Cinders "remake", to date: the film's premise is that this tale, set in the 16th century, is the "real" *Cinderella* fairy-tale. Drew Barrymore is Danielle who despite being tormented by her stepmother and sisters grows up to be a strong-willed young lady, good at swordfighting, and happens across a troubled Prince Henry. Clever old Leonardo da Vinci is on hand for a spot of match-making. ▭UK, US ⊙UK, US | PG (UK, US)

form) are simple and catchy, too – perfect for younger children and for the story, because they advance plot and character. One reason they may be so strong, as composer Alan Menken reveals on the DVD release, is that the score was recorded live in the studio. And the movie feels real: the Beast's gothic castle and wolves are convincing.

Oddly, Disney ended up making this on the quick, flushed with confidence after the success of *The Little Mermaid* in 1989. They had a finished script before they started making it, another first for Disney; they dropped in some neat touches – note the way that Beauty and the Beast, as two misfits, are the only characters who wear blue – and some witty gags ("I always say if it ain't baroque don't fix it").

▭ UK, US ⊙UK, US | U (UK) G (US)

Cinderella 1950

The Disney animation of *Cinderella* remains most kids' introduction to the story of the young girl finding her Prince Charming. And it's hard to argue with that. As a fairytale for children aged 3 and up, it's a classic, replete with cheery songs ("Bibbidi Bobbidi Boo"), wicked but not scary step sisters, and comical, cutesy animal friends.

For alternative versions of the story, see p.160. The one you absolutely don't want in your house is Disney's own **Cinderella II – Dreams Come True** (2002), a straight-to-video sequel so redundant, and so poor (rotten songs, dumb stories about mice), that even the studio seems embarassed, and is discontinuing it.

▣ UK, US ◉UK, US | U (UK) G (US)

The Emperor's New Clothes 1987

From the ever excellent Faerie Tale Theater stable, this Hans Christian Andersen tale is an adaptation rather than a remake of the fairytale – which isn't such a bad thing in this case. Originally quite a satirical fairytale, this child-friendly version focuses more on the romance between Nicholas and Princess Gilda than how stupid the emperor and his court are. Played for laughs, with slapstick and some dodgy songs, this should appeal to children under the age of 10.

▣ US | G (US)

Fairytale: A True Story 1997

This absorbing film is based on the true story of cousins Elsie and Frances, who conned the world into believing they had real pictures of fairies, at their home in Cottingham. They were championed by Arthur Conan Doyle and Harry Houdini, who are among the characters here, but it is the fairies who hog the limelight.

▣ UK, US ◉UK, US | U (UK) PG (US)

Fun And Fancy Free (Mickey And the Beanstalk) 1947

One of Disney's final "package films" – and the last featuring Walt himself (as the voice of Mickey) – Fun And Fancy Free is divided into the tales of Bongo The Bear and Mickey & The Beanstalk. Bongo is a circus bear who dreams of a life in the wild, but when his wish finally comes true, he struggles to cope with the real world – it's not bad for a story inspired by a piece in *Reader's Digest*. However, the DVD is worth the price for Mickey's exploits alone. The gang is all there with Goofy and Donald along for the ride to face Willy the Giant at the top of the beanstalk and take back the magic singing harp. Just over an hour long, this should keep younger kids occupied, particularly if you can get them to play the accompanying trivia game.

📼 UK, US ◎ UK, US | U (UK) G (US)

Hansel And Gretel 1988

There are many versions of this Brothers Grimm tale around, but this Faerie Tale Theater production is the only decent one we've seen. It was made, with an eye to the budget, in parallel with *Sleeping Beauty*, though the simplicity of the sets won't bother kids under 8. The acting is at times enjoyably OTT (particularly Joan Collins as the witch), but the stunning forest and candy-covered witch's house are vibrant, and the songs are catchy.

📼 US | PG (UK) NR (US)

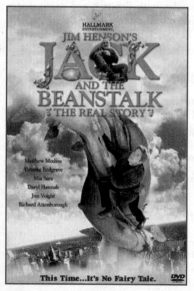

Jack & The Beanstalk: The Real Story 2001

Don't be put off by its made-for-TV status, this is a quality Jim Henson movie, and an imaginative update on the old tale. Matthew Modine plays Jack Robinson, a company CEO troubled by his family curse, no Robinson ever having lived past 40. When his aunt (Vanessa Redgrave) arrives and reveals the tale of his ancestor, a giant, Jack, follows her to a new world to right wrongs and end the curse. Although quite dark in tone, the Henson magic, here in the form of CGI wizardry rather than puppets, shouldn't trouble kids even as young as 5. However, at three hours long, and with a stellar cast (which also includes Richard Attenborough, Daryl Hannah, Jon Voight, and Honor Blackman), it has enough twists and turns to hold an older audience.

📼 US ◉ UK, US | PG (UK) NR (US)

The Little Mermaid 1989

Ariel the mermaid has proven to be a favourite of more mature men, narrowly losing out to Jessica Rabbit in the sexiest animated character stakes. That said, you don't need to worry, *The Little Mermaid* is an old-fashioned romance, loosely based on a Hans Christian Andersen story, in which Ariel falls in love with a human prince. Love-struck she strikes a deal with the evil Ursula – human legs in exchange for her voice unless the prince kisses her. Marking the beginning of the Disney renaissance following a ten-year slump after the failure of *The Black Hole*, the studio re-emerged with an involving plot, a stout, fully rounded female lead, a peerless villainess Ursula (based on Divine) and the most detailed animation since *Fantasia*, one two-minute sequence taking ten animators a year to complete. Top marks for those who spot cameo appearances by Mickey, Donald and Goofy.

📼 UK, US ◉ UK, US | U (UK) G (US)

The Pied Piper 1980

There are two versions of *The Pied Piper* worth your attention. The first is a stop-motion **puppet animation** (1980), with an outstanding narration by Robert Hardy of Browning's original poem. It was made by Cosgrove Hall Films, the people who gave us *Count Duckula* (see p.65), and is arguably an even better film than any of the studio's more traditional animations. The second is an excellent live-action **Faerie Tale Theater** production (1982), a good-looking movie, featuring Eric Idle – an inspired choice – as the piper. Both films are proper fairytales – a bit eerie, and probably not suited for kids much under 5.

COSGROVE HALL 📼 UK ◉ UK | U (UK)
FAERIE TALE THEATER 📼 US | NR (US)

The Princess And The Goblin 1992

This is a Hungarian adaptation of a nineteenth-century English novel: a tale of a flame-haired child-princess who is saved from a pack of menacing goblins by a miner's son. He hears of the goblins' plans to take over the kingdom and the Goblin Prince's plan to marry Irini. Guided by the princess's great-grandmother, the two young children defeat the goblins and save the day. The animation isn't hugely sophisticated, but it's a well-paced romp, with menacing yet humorous goblins (Rick Mayall voicing their king), that young kids should enjoy.

▭▭▭ US | U (UK) G (US)

Red Riding Hood 1988, 1991

The **Faerie Tale Theater** production of *Red Riding Hood* is one of their best – albeit a pretty spooky episode. You won't want to leave a 4-year-old alone to watch Amelia Shankley (Red Riding Hood) set off through the forest. But fairytales are meant to be scary, and this is not exactly unremitting, with some neat song-and-dance sequences, and, incidentally, a nice performance from Isabella Rosselini.

A gentler alternative is the 1991 animation, **Red Riding Hood And Goldilocks**, narrated enthusiastically by the ever chipper Meg Ryan. The story gets a liberal rewrite, with Goldilocks acquiring a Southern molasses accent ("big bowl of porridge, the sorta big bowl, and the notbigatall bowl"). Its one horror factor is the wolf's graphically described fate.

FAERIE TALE THEATER ◉US | NR
MEG RYAN ▭▭▭ US | NR

The Singing, Ringing Tree 1957

Once seen, rarely forgotten, this East German take on the Beauty and the Beast tale – a haughty princess has to learn humility – was "dubbed" into English (the German sound was turned down and an English narration added on top) for the BBC's series of folk and fairy tales, aired in the 1960s. But the dubbing – retained on the recent DVD release – only reinforces the weirdness of this film, with its hyper-real

colour, bulbous-eyed fish, nasty gnomes and a princess with the hots for a grizzly bear. Enigmatic, surreal, but magical, this is worth watching – though kids under 5 may find the fish a tad spooky.

◎UK | NR

Sleeping Beauty 1959

It's hard to believe that Disney's 1959 animation was a flop on its initial release, nearly bankrupting the studio, for this has all a young child could wish for. A lush, widescreen production made it a real spectacle – then (and now on the restored DVD) – with a fantastic castle backdrop for the struggle between good Prince Philip and the deliciously malevolent Maleficent (one of the great Disney baddies). The film has a wonderful animated dragon fight as its climax, but in true Disney fashion, it is the bit-part creations – the castle's villainous warthogs and imps, and a trio of good but bungling fairies – who steal the movie. The songs, particularly "Once Upon A Dream," are by now almost as legendary as the story, while the movie's music is, of course, classic by definition, taking some of the best tunes from Tchaikovsky.

▣ UK, US ◎UK, US | U (UK) NR (US)

Snow White And The Seven Dwarfs 1937

Branded "Disney's Folly" by Hollywood executives before its release in 1937, Snow White was the first of a string of full-length animated features which made Walt Disney's name – and filled the studio's coffers. Kids these days may be used to computer-generated graphics from hits such as *Toy Story*, but Disney's pre-war hand-drawn characters stand the test of time, and the film retains its appeal simply because it's so well done.

The balance of the story is finely judged, with just enough humour to leaven the darkness. Snow White's romance with the prince is all very well, but the true pull for children – particularly younger kids yet to learn the word romance – are the wicked queen, memorably sinister (but not, as in the original story, hoping to feast on her victim's heart), and the dwarfs. Walt grasped the importance of the "little people" as they were referred to in the studio, if not in the movie title. He initially conceived of a cast of fifty – including Blabby, Gabby, Shifty and Nifty – but the seven who remained – Bashful, Doc, Dopey, Grumpy, Happy, Sleepy and Sneezy – are memorable enough. They were anonymous in the original Grimms' tale but Walt gave them cuddly names in his drive to make the story appeal to kids.

The genius of the animation lies in the detail and the hard work. Disney and his animators realised that the cels they used to draw their short cartoons weren't big enough for this film and used larger ones. This may sound technical and abstruse but you can see the reward when Snow White runs through the forest – the trees couldn't have stretched out their branches to grasp if this decision hadn't been taken. Disney also used a "multiplane camera" which, by placing several layers of drawing under each other and moving them separately, creates a three-dimensional effect.

Still more enduring was the structure Disney brought to this animated fairytale. The use of satellite and sidekick characters remains an essential part of the Disney formula today, as does the insistence on continuous novelty. Scenes dominated by one character or a single speech are rare and there's invariably a song or a dance number on the way. The musical interludes in more recent Disney animations haven't always been spaced as successfully as in the master's heyday but this film is virtually Disney's sacred text.

Snow White is dark, and the wicked queen is genuinely scary, but watch it with your kids – buy the two-disc DVD version if you can – and you'll see why the great Russian director Sergei Eisenstein hailed this as the greatest movie ever made.

▭▭ UK, US ◉UK, US │ U (UK) NR (US)

Jim Henson HOME ENTERTAINMENT

The Storyteller 1987

MUST SEE! This is quite a starry production pairing: Jim Henson (*Muppets, Labyrinth*) and Anthony Minghella (*The English Patient*). The two got together in the mid-1980s to film a series of Greek myth (see p.15) and fairytale stories for HBO. This DVD collection features nine of the fairytales, with John Hurt as the storyteller, introducing live-action shorts (22 minutes each) directed by Minghella and with lashings of magical Henson creatures. The stories include *Hans My Hedgehog*, about a young cripple who helps a lost king in the woods; *Death And The Soldier*, in which a poor soldier (Bob Peck) is given a magical sack in which he captures gremlins; and *Sapsorrow* – a twist on the Cinderella legend. There is also a second volume of stories on DVD, and earlier videos are still around with two or three episodes on each tape.

US ⊚US | G (US)

The Swan Princess 1994

The Swan Princess is an animated take on the ballet, *Swan Lake*: the story of Prince Derek and Princess Odette, who are brought up together as children only to fall in love. Evil sorcerer Rothbart throws a spanner in the works, snatching Odette and turning her into a swan. Directed by former Disney animator Richard Rich, this could be mistaken for a Disney production, with impressive animation and a succinct story. It is suitable for all ages.

If there are ballet fans in your house, then **Schwanensee** (1967) is a piece of history, with dance legends Rudolf Nureyev and Margot Fonteyn taking the leads.

Both titles: 📼 UK, US; ◉UK, US | U (UK)

The Three Billy Goats Gruff & Three Little Pigs 1989

An unexpected, yet successful, blend of jazz and kids' animation (from the Rabbit Ears studio) makes these two timeless tales work. Art Lande's jazz arrangement and Holly Hunter's narration beautifully accompany a pair of stories of brains triumphing over brawn. One for younger kids, from 3 or 4.

📼 UK, US | U (UK) NR (US)

Thumbelina 1994

Girl the size of a thumb meets – and falls for – a boy the size of a slightly larger thumb, and stays true despite marriage proposals from a toad, a beetle and a mole. Director Don Bluth obviously decided that what Hans Christian Andersen's tale of vertically challenged romance needed most was some Barry Manilow songs. Not great but not bad – again for younger kids.

📼 UK, US ◉UK, US | U (UK) G (US)

The Wacky World Of Mother Goose 1966

Although the animation hasn't stood the test of time too well, Margaret Rutherford's portrayal of the title character makes this an amusing film to watch. Led by Rutherford's characteristic jutting chin, a bevy of fairytale characters leave their homeland, allowing the evil Count Warptwist to take over the kingdom from Old King Cole. Jack Sprat however, goes in search of Mother Goose so she can save the day. Once again, a film for younger viewers.

🔲 UK, US ◉UK, US | U (UK) NR (US)

Walt Disney Fables 2003

There are four volumes of these fables, each containing vintage Disney shorts, reworking classic fairy stories through Mickey Mouse, Goofy, Donald Duck and the crew. The animation has retained its rich palette and is thus perfect for younger kids, whilst the stories are cute and easy to digest. Of the four, Volume One stands out thanks to the dulcet tones of Bing Crosby on *The Legend of Sleepy Hollow*.

🔲 UK ◉UK | U (UK)

Fantasy

another world...

Every child has an active fantasy life – imaginary kingdoms they hold sway over, imaginary friends, and (best of all) imaginary parents – either completely imaginary or borrowed from a friend whose mum and dad seem far more glamorous and exciting than their own. The definitive childhood fantasy – and one we never quite lose – is to transform oneself, to be bolder, more beautiful, wittier, taller, thinner, endowed with better eyesight, more money, etc – something that a good fantasy movie can make very real. Other fantasy movies are rooted in the harsh yet sentimental stories that lie at the heart of so many fairy tales (see previous chapter). Or they may invent entirely imaginary worlds, and even languages, as in Tolkien's novel (and now classic fantasy movie) *The Lord of the Rings*.

We have included in this chapter several animations as well as "live-action" movies. But you may also want to check our chapters on **Animation** (for Miyazaki's classic *My Neighbour Totoro* and *Kiki's Delivery Service*, as well as *Shrek*), **Cartoons**, **Drama** and **Sci-fi**, many of which cross over with the films reviewed here.

The Amazing Mr Blunden 1972

Lionel Jeffries directed this period ghost story from Antonia Barber's novel, with Diana Dors in fine form as warty Mrs Wickens, the house-keeper whose hobbies include killing young children. Laurence Naismith is almost as effective as the amazing Mr Blunden, amazing because he's a guilt-ridden ghost. Not as dark as it sounds – as you can judge from the ratings, this can be enjoyed by all the family. A well-imagined, if sometimes slightly muddled, tale.

📼 UK, US ◉UK | U (UK) G (US)

Back To The Future 1985

 "Charm, brains and a lot of laughter," is how Roger Ebert sums up this enduring slice of futuristic comedy. Michael J. Fox is Marty, who travels back in time thanks to his eccentric inventor friend Dr Brown (Christopher Lloyd) and gets to do what every teenager has always wanted to do – find out what his parents were like when they were teens. Director Robert Zemeckis brings a sure comic touch to this, plus a little shot of Capraesque whimsy. One of the many things that makes this film such a feel-good experience is its innocent optimism. The effects are reasonably well done but they don't overshadow the human comedy. The scene where Mart realizes his mum has the hots for him could have been icky but it's handled tactfully – it was one of the ideas that led many studios to turn this

Back To The Future – a natural for sequels

down. Steven Spielberg eventually produced, which was just as well because he was able to fend off some of the dafter suggestions – such as the insistence, from a Universal executive, that the film be called *Space Man from Pluto*. There is one violent scene – where Doc is gunned down by terrorists – as well as the brief Oedipal twist in the plot. But all kids should find this good fun. It's been re-released on DVD, as have the sequels, of which **Back To the Future III** is easily the best.

📼 UK, US ⊙US, UK | PG (UK, US)

Beetle Juice 1988

No plot, juvenile humour, slow to get started, at times bland – all these criticisms have been levelled at Tim Burton's supernatural comedy. And they're all true. But as critic Leonard Maltin observed, regard this as a "live-action cartoon" and it works beautifully. The film's central conceit is that the afterlife might well be just as mundane as life itself – you could be plagued by bureaucracy, and have trouble making your mark as a spirit. This masterstroke propels the film, helped by Michael Keaton's astonishing performance as the maniacal exorcist Betelgeuse (pronounced Beetlejuice). In this film, Keaton has all the fizz and screen presence which he lacked in Burton's next epic, *Batman*. It is, as pun-loving critics have said, dead funny. But younger kids (say below

10) could be disturbed by some of the goings-on. There are various sexual references and a fair bit of swearing, but even so, the UK 15 certificate seems, in retrospect, a tad harsh.

📼 UK, US ◎UK, US | 15 (UK) PG (US)

The BFG 1989

"You must not show children anything grisly unless it is also funny. If it is both funny and grisly they will love it!" That was Roald Dahl's advice, words which more moviemakers should follow if the results are to be as delightful as this animated classic. The film begins with a little orphan girl, Sophie (named after Dahl's niece, now a grown-up model and actress), being carried off by a stalking giant, so she assumes, to become his next meal. But the Big Friendly Giant (BFG) is a vegetarian, unlike his fellow giants Fleshlumpeater and Gizzardgulper, who dine, nightly, on "human beans". Sophie and the BFG devise a plan to stop this feast, enlisting the queen of England and her armed forces to help.

Voiced by an illustrious cast of British sitcom stars (David Jason, Mollie Sugden, Frank Thornton

Roald Dahl

There has never been a better children's writer than Roald Dahl. His every book is a masterpiece, gripping kids from first to last, whether he is writing for young kids (*The BFG* and *James and the Giant Peach* are good for 4-year-olds), or his core audience of 5- to 10-year-olds (a dozen or so classics from *Matilda* to *The Witches*). The movies of his books, in truth, don't match the reading experience, but, with Dahl's stories and creation of fantasies that every kid can relate to, they are still pretty good.

Dahl was born in Wales in 1916 to Norwegian parents and with a fearsome Norwegian grandmother whom he immortalised as Helga, the grandmother of Luke in his book *The Witches*. His principal desire, before he became a writer, seemed to be to see the world – it was his major motivation for joining Shell rather than going to university. As a fighter pilot in the Royal Air Force, he saw a lot of the world, from the skies, in World War II before crash-landing in Libya and fracturing his skull. "You do get bits of magic from enormous bumps on the head," he said later and it was while he was recovering, that he began writing stories derived from his strange dreams.

His first children's novel, *James and the Giant Peach*, was published in the US in 1961. Like his subsequent works, it was darker than much children's literature, influenced by Dahl's memory of his miserable schooldays where "masters and senior boys were allowed to wound other boys, sometimes quite severely". School authority figures are often dealt with unkindly in his books, notably in *Matilda*, and miscreants and tormentors tend to get a nasty and vengeful comeuppance. Critics often point to this "cruelty" in his books, and Dahl in life was not the easiest or nicest of writers, weathering charges of anti-feminism and anti-Semitism (which he refuted). But, as he claimed, "I never get complaints from children – just giggles and squirms of delight."

continued overleaf

173

continued...

Dahl's film and TV career began in the 1960s. He was, for a time, as famous for his long-running TV series *Roald Dahl's Tales Of The Unexpected* as for his books. He also wrote the screenplay for the films of two of his friend Ian Fleming's works: *You Only Live Twice* and **Chitty Chitty Bang Bang** and scripted a little-known British horror flick, *The Night Digger* (1971). But his biggest gift to the movie industry was his own children's stories. Many are yet to be filmed – and there is a remake of **Charlie And The Chocolate Factory** (previously filmed as the musical, **Willy Wonka**) in progress – but there are half a dozen available, all worth a viewing. Be warned, however, that **The Witches** (filmed by Nicolas Roeg) is a seriously scary movie, not advised for kids below 9 or 10.

For reviews, see: **The BFG** (*Fantasy, p.173*), **Danny The Champion of the World** (*Drama, p.146*), **James And The Giant Peach** (*Animation, p.181*), **Matilda** (*Fantasy, p.186*), **Willy Wonka And The Chocolate Factory** (*Fantasy, p.193*), and **The Witches** (*Fantasy, p.194*).

and Michael Knowles), this movie was destined for cinema release but, after a late switch, made its debut on Christmas television in the UK, ensuring that the film has never quite had the recognition it deserved – especially in the US. It is terrific entertainment for kids aged 4 and up.

US ©UK, US | U (UK) NR (US)

Darby O'Gill And The Little People 1959

Walt Disney loved *Darby O'Gill And the Little People* – and the chances are, if you can find it, you will too. Darby is an ageing caretaker of an estate who spends more time telling tall stories in the pub than looking after the grounds. When a younger man (Sean Connery) is sent in to replace him, Darby worries – but he is saved by capturing the king of the leprechauns. The movie isn't as cloying or cute as it sounds, partly because Albert Sharpe is so effective in the title role. Fans claim this is the best live-action film Disney ever made, which is over the top, but it is certainly a minor masterpiece, and, after years of neglect, is finally finding an audience. Disney would be chuffed – he spent 19 years preparing this movie.

US ©US | U (US)

The Dark Crystal 1982

Jim Henson wanted to show that "puppetry can do a lot more than people have seen so far" with this movie. He proved his point but *Dark Crystal* was so demanding to make he never contemplated a sequel. Which was a pity because this futuristic fantasy, in which a boy is raised to save the world from decay by restoring the life-giving power of the crystal of the title, is one of Henson's top works. Some critics have found it ponderous, wishing the Muppeteer had given writer David Odell more licence, and there are obvious echoes of *The Lord Of The Rings* and *Star Wars*. However, *Dark Crystal* is genuinely creepy (it's perhaps best for 7-year-olds and up), and fires the imagination. If you enjoy it, you may also want to try Henson's **Labyrinth** (see p.181).

UK, US ◉UK, US | PG (UK, US)

Dragonheart 1996

Revolting peasants! Wicked kings! Poetic monks! All this and the voice of Sean Connery. Connery's character is Draco, a 10th century dragon who teams up with Dennis Quaid's itinerant knight to take on a nasty monarch (David Thewlis), as if he's auditioning for a part in a British pantomime. Actually, it is all sublimely silly, with expensive computer-animated special effects, a monk (Pete Postlethwaite) who says things like "Pride goeth before a fall", and a script which really includes lines such as "The peasants are revolting! The peasants are rebelling!" If you're under 12, or can think that way, you'll enjoy it. Connery's absence is the main reason why the sequel, **Dragonheart: A New Beginning** (1999), isn't as effective.

UK, US ◉UK, US | PG (UK, US)

Sir Dennis Quaid (right) and Sir Sean Connery

Dragonslayer 1981

"In the Dark Ages, magic was a weapon, love was a mystery, adventure was everywhere... and dragons were real." So boasted the studio tag line. Dragons may have been real in the Dark Ages but in 1980s Hollywood, their fire had to be faked with a military flame-thrower. If the same device had been used on the script, it might have saved the makers a lot of money: it cost $18 million and made just $6 million. This wasn't entirely a matter of quality – critic Leonard Maltin found it an "enjoyable fantasy adventure" while others felt the computerized dragon alone made the movie worthwhile. But, in the early 1980s, Hollywood hadn't found the knack for making fantasies like this that could appeal to adults and children, and it's just too violent and gory for younger kids. Still, Ralph Richardson excels as the Merlin-esque wizard, and the film convincingly creates a far-off, mythic land.

📼 US ◎ UK, US | PG (UK, US)

Edward Scissorhands 1990

Edward Scissorhands started life as a doodle by the teenage Tim Burton, when he was living in suburbia in Burbank, California. The image stuck with him and inspired this sophisticated, visually stunning, modern fairytale.

Edward (Johnny Depp) is the boy with the unusual appendages who lives in an imposing, hilltop castle which Avon lady Peg (Dianne West) assumes is deserted. But she discovers a shy, strange teenager with a scarred face, so white he looks as if he's auditioning for a part in a Japanese kabuki drama, and with blades for fingers. The blades were supposed to be fingers but Edward's inventor (Vincent Price) died before he could give his Frankenstein a pair of human hands. Peg becomes a kind of fairy godmother to Edward with predictably unfortunate consequences. He falls foul of a gaggle of suburban women who dictate the community's mores, a gaggle based on Burton's old neighbours in Burbank, where people never came out of their houses or communicated unless it was to savour a slice of neighbourly misfortune. Edward challenges the blandness, cutting hedges and hair (canine and human) into odd shapes and, in one memorable scene, making ice sculptures.

Kids will identify with the hero's loneliness, partly because it springs from the director's own teenage angst: "It's in the inability to communicate, the inability to touch, being at odds with yourself; how you are perceived as to what you are." Depp, one of the few modern movie stars who can be as eloquent without words as the stars of the silent era, captures his torment and delight. And, for once, the studio (Fox) didn't insist on a happy ending; instead, there's a brief but violent knife fight which leads to the tragic denouement – and helped earn the movie a PG-13 certificate in the US. That and a bit of profanity aside, it seems suitable for most kids of seven and over.

▦ UK, US ◉ UK, US | PG (UK) PG-13 (US)

Escape To Witch Mountain 1975

Watch this fascinating movie and you almost feel you're seeing a prequel to the *Harry Potter* tales – albeit one in which the special-effects budget ran out after spinning a coat rack and hiring a crane to suspend children in mid-air. Adapted from the Alexander Key novel, the story tells of two orphans, Tia and Tony, who find an evil capitalist plotting to use magic powers for his own ends. They flee to Witch Mountain with the help of a crusty but likeable camper, a pet cat and a magic harmonica. Disney hasn't quite got the pacing right but this is a likeable, well-acted film, with veteran Ray Milland effective as the sinister millionaire, and Donald Pleasence adding capable support.

The 1978 sequel **Return To Witch Mountain** is no disgrace either, thanks, in part, to the presence of Bette Davis and Christopher Lee.

▦ US ◉ UK, US | U (UK) G (US)

Harry Potter and ... 2001–2004

It's worth recalling that the *Harry Potter* phenomenon didn't begin with branded toys, or a multi-billion dollar advertising campaign. It was a grassroots phenomenon – driven by the appeal of a book, and by the wondrous escapism of its tales of witches and wizards – tales in which evil is defeated at the last, but only after we have been suitably scared, amused and intrigued.

Plenty of critics – and readers – had arrows ready to fire at the first movie, **Harry Potter And The Philosopher's Stone** (**Sorcerer's Stone**, in the US; 2001), but most set them down, on sight of the meticulously realized world of Hogwarts and its denizens. Indeed, seeing the movie when it first came out was quite a moving experience, as audiences hung on every frame, eager to see just how their own imagined characters would look, how the wizards would find their magic Platform 9$\frac{3}{4}$, what the Sorting Hat would look like. Even the minor figures would receive gasps of recognition ("There's Ginnie Weasley!"). And most of them, it must be said, looked just about right, with Alan Rickman (Snape), Maggie Smith (Professor McGonagall), Richard Harris (Dumbledore) and Robbie Coltrane (Hagrid) stamping their parts with absolute conviction, and underlining J.K. Rowling's determination to have British actors in this very British creation. The kids, too, turned out good, with Daniel Radcliffe defining Harry Potter's image, and his cohorts, Rupert Grint (Ron) and Emma Watson (Hermione) looking almost born to their roles.

There was at times, perhaps, something of the Christmas bag of tricks about the film, a British celebration of character acting. But there were genuine thrills – especially the closing chess scene – that, had there been any kids in the audience who didn't already know the story, might have been seriously scary. And, throughout, you had to take your hat off to the attention to detail in Chris Columbus's direction, the quality of the effects, and the score, marvellously provided by John Williams. All contributed greatly to the magic of keeping a very long film – 152 minutes – from sagging.

Harry Potter And The Chamber Of Secrets (2002) – the second film in a planned sequence of seven – had a lot to live up to, with, to be honest, a rather weaker and less engaging book plot. It was perhaps inevitably a little disappointing, both for the drama, and for lacking the freshness of seeing everything for the first time. But there was nothing to complain of. All the previous cast were back, just a little older, aided and abetted by Kenneth Branagh's delightful turn as the vain, handsome Gilderoy Lockhart, bestselling author, and the special-effects department had to pull a rabbit out of the hat in its creation of Dobby, the house elf. Most kids found him enchanting, even if, for critics, he was overly reminiscent of Jar Jar Binks in *Star Wars*, and not quite up to Gollum standards.

The film world collectively raised its eyebrows when Alfonso Cuarón was chosen to direct the third film, **Harry Potter And The**

Prisoner Of Azkaban (2004). Cuarón's previous movie had been *Y Tu Mamá También*, a much acclaimed but very adult film, with a lot of close-up sex. In the event, the film was something of a triumph – with the wizard trio coming of age in a film whose style was far more character-driven, far more in your face, far more dramatic. Grint and Watson, in particular, looked like real actors, no longer child stars, while Cuarón managed to conjure a real sense of magical worlds in operation, with a coherency that made you recall the earlier films more critically than you had felt at the time. He and the effects department managed humour nicely, too, with a splendid outing for the wizards' bus, driven along by a shrunken head voiced by Lenny Henry. Michael Gambon, meanwhile, cruised into the part of Dumbledore vacated by Richard Harris's death.

And so the cast (with all key players signed up) move on to *The Goblet of Fire*, under the direction of Mike Newell – best known for *Four Weddings And A Funeral*, but also a stalwart of the *Indiana Jones* TV series (and *Into the West* – see p.180). The book is almost as good a tale as that in *Azkaban*, but a great deal longer, which has prompted rumours that this will be at least three hours, maybe four, with that most fantastic yet almost obsolete movie convention, the Intermission. All will be revealed in time for Christmas 2005.

[📼] UK, US ⊙ UK, US | PG (UK, US)

The Hobbit 1977

The appeal of J.R.R. Tolkien's charming tale just about survives a brutal cut in this Tolkien-lite cartoon adaptation, co-directed by Jules Bass, who had spent most of his time, previously, making Christmas movies for kids. John Huston, Otto Preminger and Don Messick (the voice of Scooby-Doo) lend their larynxes, and the animation itself isn't bad. However, to try and encapsulate such an epic story in 77 minutes required not the surgical skills of a rewrite man but the mathematical efficiency of data compression. That said, they made the distinctly wobbly decision to keep the songs, which are really pretty dreadful. All of which said, this is currently the only film version of the book, so Tolkien fans may well feel an urge to check it out.

[📼] US ⊙ UK, US | PG (US)

Hocus Pocus 1993

Bette Midler explained why she wanted to make *Hocus Pocus*, which she hoped would be a bewitching comedy:"There's usually nothing for my 6-year-old to see. This has no four-letter words, the violence is minimal, it's broad and silly and I don't have to worry what I look like." Critic Roger Ebert, in contrast, said, "Watching this movie is like attending a party you weren't invited to, and where you don't know anyone and they're all in on the joke and won't explain it to you." Roger wasn't too impressed by the witches (Midler, Sarah Jessica Parker and Kathy Najimy) who try to drain the life force out of two teenagers and their little sisters so they can live for ever, saying the harridans didn't have personalities, only decibel levels. But what do critics know? *Hocus Pocus* has achieved quite a cult following on video, and is a minor treat for kids who can handle a fair amount of dialogue about death, a zombie which keeps losing his head while all around people are keeping theirs, and plenty of slapstick violence. Not a film, then, for kids much under 7.

📼 UK, US ◉ UK, US | PG (UK)

The Indian In The Cupboard 1995

Lynne Reid Banks's trilogy of novels about a magic cupboard in which a plastic model of an Indian comes to life is one of the great modern fantasy classics in children's fiction, and the plot is an absolute gift for a movie. Which makes this wooden film all the more disappointing. Perhaps, just perhaps, if you've not read the books, you might warm to it, and kids can be very tolerant. But Melissa Mathison (who scripted *E.T.*) mucks about with the screenplay when she could have adopted it straight, and Frank Oz, who directed *Little Shop Of Horrors* with such verve, seems to lack commitment here. The PG rating is barely necessary, as the (modest) violence is entirely bland.

📼 US ◉ US | PG (UK, US)

Into the West 1992

A film about two boys and their magic white horse. Put like that it sounds like standard Disney fare. Yet written by Jim Sheridan (*In The*

Name Of The Father), and directed by Mike Newell, this Irish western is refreshingly different. The movie starts grimly. Gabriel Byrne is the dad who used to lead a tribe of travellers, lives in a flat and grieves for his wife who has died in childbirth. His sons endure a miserable existence until their grandfather brings them a white horse which they keep in the flat until the police take it away. The boys kidnap the horse and run away with it – with Byrne in pursuit, reconnecting with his old life and meeting Ellen Barkin. Kids will enjoy the wonder and adventure, you might enjoy the relationships (especially between real husband and wife Byrne and Larkin) and appreciate how the hunt for the horse and the boys redeems the father. There's some cursing and minor violence but this will be a treat for kids aged 7 and over if they persevere.

▭ UK, US ◉ UK, US | PG (UK, US)

James And The Giant Peach 1996

Like all of Roald Dahl's stories, *James and the Giant Peach* presented the moviemakers with some challenges. In the book, James's parents "suddenly got eaten up (in full daylight and on a crowded bus) by an enormous angry rhinoceros" leaving James to be plunged into a living hell with two cruel aunts. In Dahl's fictional world, this kind of thing can happen to any parent, or orphan; however, for the movie, director Henry Selick felt obliged to tack on a moral – the kind of thing Dahl would never have approved of. That aside, the movie is a rather ingenious combination of animation and live action, the transition coming after James crawls into the giant peach and begins his adventures. As cruel at times as life itself, this is probably best for kids of 5 and over.

▭ UK, US ◉ UK, US | U (UK) PG (US)

Labyrinth 1986

Jim Henson was so fed up with the comparative financial failure of *Dark Crystal* (see p.174), he decided to make a film combining puppets with real actors. "Nasty and funny puppets work well," he decided, "but straightforward heroes and heroines don't." So in this film, Sarah is given thirteen hours by Jareth (David Bowie), king of the goblins, to negotiate a giant labyrinth and win back her grizzling brother. Kids will be amused by the goblins, the clumsy dwarf and by the sugar plum fairies – grown-ups, as the *Radio Times* noted, might get more fun out of David Bowie's Tina Turner wig. Ten minutes too long, and with a narrative that doesn't quite match the special effects, this isn't quite the *tour de force* it could have been. Maybe they should have kept a few more ideas from Terry Jones's original script.

📼 UK, US ◉UK, US | U (UK) PG (US)

The Last Unicorn 1982

Christopher Lee must spend most of his spare time reading fantasy novels. He was the acknowledged Tolkien expert among the cast of the *Lord Of The Rings* trilogy, and when he arrived to do his voiceover for this animation, he apparently had a copy of the Peter Beagle novel

Starring the voices of
Jeff Bridges Mia Farrow Angela Lansbury Christopher Lee

THE LAST
UNICORN

The Magical Fantasy Adventure Based on the Bestselling Book

with passages underlined that he thought must not be omitted. Beagle was himself a Tolkien scholar and his story of *The Last Unicorn* shows the considerable influence of the *Rings*. The ultimate unicorn (voiced by Mia Farrow) is turned into a human but has to decide whether to save her species by becoming a unicorn again or stay as she is so she can love Prince Lir (Jeff Bridges). There are some fine lines ("No cat anywhere ever gave anyone a straight answer"), some uneven animation and a few songs (courtesy of Jimmy Webb, creator of such greats as "By The Time I Get To Phoenix"). But it's the strength of Beagle's original fantasy which carries this.

The Last Unicorn is being remade for a Christmas 2005 release but this version is more than adequate.

📼 US ◉US | U (UK) G (US)

The Lion, The Witch And The Wardrobe 1988, 1979

Walt Disney recently announced plans to film all of C.S. Lewis's **Chronicles of Narnia** novels – which may be a blessing for fans. They haven't been very well served to date, with a **BBC TV adaptation** in the 1980s – an era before the current sophistication of computer special effects – coming across a bit too amateurish (in a *Dr Who* kind of way), and further let down by some rather wooden acting. It has its fans, however, and the stories are strong enough to keep your interest. The BBC has recently reissued them as a four-disc DVD, including all their filmed episodes: **The Lion, The Witch And The Wardrobe**; **Prince Caspian**; **The Voyage Of The Dawn Treader** and **The Silver Chair**.

An alternative is the 1979 animated verions of **The Lion, The Witch And The Wardrobe**, directed by Bill Melendez. The animation is a bit patchy and this was clearly not a Disney-budget production, but the story is reasonably well told and coherent.

BBC CHRONICLES OF NARNIA 📼 UK, US ◉UK, US | U (UK) NR (US)
ANIMATION 📼 US | NR

The Little Vampire 2000

Too often in kids' movies, it's the kids' acting that lets everyone – them, moviemakers, us – down. Not so in *The Little Vampire*, which is blessed with two strong turns from Jonathan Lipnicki as the lonely boy Tony and from Rollo Weeks as his lonely vampire pal. Richard E. Grant camps things up as the patriarch of a family of vampires desperate to become human again, while Jim Carter is the vampire hunter, as you can tell from his neon crucifix. It's arresting, with a couple of genuinely inspired moments and a few laughs. However, the reversal of the usual plot – making the vampires the heroes – doesn't come off quite as well

Jonathan Lipnicki faces up to lonely vamp Richard E Grant

as in the original (German) novels by Angela Sommer-Bodenburg. The best review may come from Anna Popplewell, who plays the vampire Anna, Tony's love interest. On user comments posted on the Internet Movie Database, she said, "My brother and sister, 5 and 9, both loved it and so did an audience full of children at the test screening. Children above 12 may find it a little babyish."

UK, US ◉UK, US | U (UK)

The Lord Of The Rings 2001–03

J.R.R. Tolkien's meisterwork was notoriously unfilmable – a view Ralph Bakshi's 1978 **animated cartoon** version only seemed to confirm. But in 2001, director **Peter Jackson**, like the heroes of Tolkien's epic saga, did the impossible – and did it, for the most part, wonderfully well. All three parts of his trilogy – **The Fellowship Of The Ring**, **The Two Towers**, **The Return Of The King** – stand up separately as movies and cohere as a whole. Which is, of course, what they deserve. For all the erudition, songs, geography and vast cast Tolkien built into his epic, he was smart enough to give it a very simple premise: a group of nine heroes have to destroy a ring in a certain place in order to triumph over evil. And it is this classic quest, which Jackson never quite loses sight of over a trilogy that represents his epic cinematic achievement.

Jackson's casting was inspired. Sir Ian McKellen is a perfect Gandalf, Elijah Wood carries off the difficult part of Frodo, Christopher Lee is effectively evil as Saruman the White and Viggo Mortensen is tight-lipped, like a Gary Cooper hero, as the warrior Aragorn. But the triumph is really down to the director and his team. Using computer generated images, Jackson turns his homeland New Zealand into the magical landscape of Middle Earth. Even the Hobbits' Shire, which could have easily ended up looking like Noddy's Toyland, is vividly, convincingly drawn. Jackson has created some fantstic set pieces, notably the epic struggle at Helms Deep in *The Two Towers*, a marvellously thought through and staged battle scene which John Ford would have envied. This is matched by the contest between Sam Gamgee and Shelob, the giant spider, which is scarier than the whole of *Arachnophobia*.

Such is the acclaim – and the trilogy's assembly of awards – that it seems heretical to find flaws. Yet for this reviewer, Jackson, praised for the ruthlessness with which he condensed Tolkien, could have been tougher still. The indecisive walking-talking trees and the Gollum-Frodo-Sam conflict both test the patience in *The Two Towers*, a movie which at times feels like one long battle scene. And the film-makers' delight in creating a computer-graphic Gollum perhaps led them to dwell on the character and his interminable internal conflict, to the point where he is in danger of becoming as irritating as – let's pick a name at random – Jar Jar Binks. The attempt to give the female characters more prominence also seems half-hearted and ineffectual.

But these are quibbles in what is a stunning visual drama, which could stake a claim, almost unique among classic adaptations, of being actually better than the book.

The films all have parental warning ratings – and *The Return Of The King* was given 12A and PG-13 designations, in the UK and US, due to the violence depicted. It's hard to say if the classifiers have got this right. There is a lot of battling going on, and the violence, especially in *The Two Towers*, is powerfully realized; and the visions which plague Frodo as he carries the ring in the opening movie are pretty scary too. Most kids of 8 or 9 should be OK with all these films in a cinema;

younger than that and you may find watching at home on video is a usefully muted experience. One thing, though: if you've not read the books, you'll need to watch with a very patient kid who has, if you want to understand quite what's going on.

If you are buying the video or **DVD**, opt for the latter if you can. There are some terrific special features (including a fascinating movie on the filming of the trilogy), and true fans will be pleased to find that they are actually a fair bit longer than the cinema films, with several extended and extra scenes.

▭ UK, US ◉UK, US │ Fellowship Of The Ring (PG, UK; PG-13, US); The Two Towers (12-A, UK; PG-13, US); The Return Of The King (12-A, UK, PG-13, US)

Lost Horizon 1937

Hollywood's finest dream fulfilment movie? It's hard to think of one better. Ronald Colman guarantees the film's success with the conviction and dignity he brings to his role as the traveller who accidentally discovers a heaven on earth in the mythical eastern kingdom of Shangri-la. One of director Frank Capra's finest. (Make sure you get the Capra film and not the dreadful 1973 musical remake.)

▭ UK, US ◉UK, US │ U (UK) NR (US)

Matilda 1996

Danny DeVito had to convince Roald Dahl's widow Felicity that he was a fan before she sold him the movie rights to *Matilda* – one of the author's darkest fantasies. DeVito clearly had the conviction. He directs, stars as Matilda's hideous dad, and cast his other half Rhea Perlman as the heartless, terminally selfish mum. His real triumph, though, was in the casting of Matilda (Mara Wilson) – a top performance that centres the movie – and in shooting it from a child's-eye view, putting the hypocrisies and evasions of the grown-ups into sharper relief. You are absolutely with Matilda – a child with the power to move things just by concentrating on them – right from the outset, and it's hard to resist a cheer as she wins out over her parents and the Trunchbull, the horrendous headmistress (marvellously played by Pam Ferris) who wants to make child-throwing an Olympic sport.

Younger kids, 5 and under, may be so scared by the Trunchbull that they forget to laugh, but everyone else will enjoy it. And it has to be said that the violence is mostly at the expense of the evil headmistress, whose line in insults (calling pupils "squirming worms of vomit") helped earn the movie a PG rating.

[cassette icon] UK, US ⊚UK, US | PG (UK, US)

The Neverending Story 1988

If you or your kids love the Michael Ende novels this movie was based on, you might find this a travesty. Ende certainly did, taking his name off the credits. But approach it without advance knowledge and you might find it agreeable enough, albeit a bit slow to start. The story is about an overweight German boy who picks up a book and becomes embroiled in the battle to save the magic world of Fantasia from evil forces; the fattie becomes, in this screen adaptation, a cheery American boy. Still, director Wolfgang Petersen handles the fantasy with assurance, even if the tale, in truncated form, seems rather simplistic and the acting a bit iffy. Kids up to the age of 8 will probably be dazzled by the effects and enjoy the story.

There is nothing good, though, to be said of **The Neverending Story II: The Next Chapter**, which is every bit as dull as its title.

[cassette icon] UK, US ⊚UK, US | U (UK) US (PG)

Peter Pan 1953, 2003

Disney's animated take on J.M. Barrie's classic novel is hard to beat, even if it takes serious liberties with the source. The sadness which underpinned Barrie's tale – perpetual childhood can be confining as well as rewarding – is largely gone here. But its absence isn't likely to be missed by kids, who will laugh at Captain Hook's running battle with the crocodile, enjoy the songs (especially Sammy Cahn and Sammy Fain's "You Can Fly") and generally have a seriously good time.

The **2003 live-action version**, by Australian director P.J. Hogan (whose adult credits include *Muriel's Wedding* and *My Best Friend's Wedding*), divided critics and viewers, some suggesting the story had got its soul back, others sensing that this is not quite a kids' movie. It

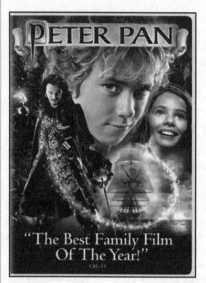

certainly throws away the jokiness of Disney, ramping up the pre-adolescent relationship between Wendy and Peter Pan, and adding some real villainy to Neverland (Jason Isaacs – Lucius Malfoy in *Harry Potter* – neatly doubles up as Mr Darling and Captain Hook). Best for kids of 7 and up, perhaps. And buy it on DVD so you can see the alternative ending, where Peter, poor love, returns to find Wendy married.

Steven Spielberg's salute to the legend, **Hook** (1991), which stars Robin Williams as a grown-up Peter Pan, now a bsuinessman, returning to battle Hook (Dustin Hoffman) for his children's love, is lacking in charm or heart but carried, just, by the actors – especially Williams and Bob Hoskins as Smee.

1953 VERSION 📼 UK, US ⊚ UK, US | U (UK) G (US)

2003 VERSION 📼 UK, US ⊚ UK, US | PG (UK) PG (US)

HOOK 📼 UK, US ⊚ UK, US | U (UK) PG (US)

Pete's Dragon 1977

A decade earlier, this Disney mix of animation and live action might have been magical. But Disney had lost its way in the mid-1970s and this charming tale, in which lonely boy Sean Marshall becomes best friends with a dragon called Elliott, doesn't quite work – despite a cast which includes Mickey Rooney, Jim Dale and Helen Reddy. The dragon gets all the best scenes but, at 123 minutes, it's at least 20 minutes too long.

📼 UK, US ⊚ UK, US | U (UK) G (US)

The Princess Bride 1987

When writer William Goldman first touted the script of *The Princess Bride* around Hollywood, the then unknown Arnold Schwarzenegger was keen to play the giant, Fezzik. However, it took until the mid-1980s for Goldman to garner serious interest in his unusual fairytale, by which time Arnie had moved on to heavier weaponry. Which was perhaps no bad thing, for Billy Crystal stepped into the breach as the giant, Miracle Max; director Rob Reiner recalls having to leave his own set whenever Crystal featured as he laughed so much he would become nauseous.

The story is about a girl called Buttercup (Robin Wright, now Mrs Sean Penn), who is kidnapped by the evil Prince Humperdinck (Chris Sarandon). Her childhood love Westley (Cary Elwes) sets off to rescue her and, whilst searching, meets a giant swordsman – Miracle Max. The action starts out in classic fashion with a grandfather (Peter Falk) read-

ing the tale out of a book to a less-than-thrilled kid ... but there's something in his voice that suggests we're not in for an ordinary fairytale, and indeed we're not as the story comes alive in the darned strangest ways. This is a hugely entertaining film, with intelligent humour, enthralling fight sequences (Cary Elwes giving Errol Flynn, whom his character was based on, a run for his money), and delicious cameos by Mel Smith, Peter Cook and Carol Kane. It's far funnier and more successful, for my money, than *Monty Python And The Holy Grail* or most Mel Brooks movies. You

chuckle, kids gasp. The only downside is that you may have some explaining to do when junior goes back to school and announces: "My name is Inigo Montoya. You killed my father. Prepare to die…"

📼 UK, US ◉UK, US | PG (UK, US)

The Red Balloon 1956

Le Ballon Rouge picked up awards at Cannes on its release, and half a century on it can be classed pretty categorically as a classic. It is a short film – just 30 minutes – about a young Parisian boy befriended by a red balloon with a will of its own. You can read various allegories into this enchanting tale, but you don't need to in order to enjoy it. It is only a pity that director-writer Albert Lamorisse, so fertile in his imagination here, never managed to entrance audiences to the same degree with the full-length feature films he made in the 1960s. A pity, too, that more care wasn't taken with the film's transfer to DVD.

📼 US ◉US | NR

Sabrina The Teenage Witch 1996

Sixteen is a confusing time – especially if, like Sabrina, you discover that you're a witch. Unlike some teen sitcoms, this is genuinely funny, witness the heroine's description of her day in one episode: "boredom followed by dullness with a dash of echh!" One online enthusiast claims this show combines "the wit of *The X Files*, the spectacle of *The Love Boat* and the soap-opera plots of Beverly Hills 90210" which may be putting it a bit strong but this is still quite a lot of fun. A half-decent cartoon series was spun off it, too.

📼 US ◉UK, US | U (UK) PG (US)

Spirited Away 2001

You may be noticing that pretty much every film made by Japanese animator Hayao Miyazaki gets a "Must See!" in this book. There's no conspiracy about it. Miyazaki is simply the most imaginative film-maker alive – a superb storyteller and a genius animator. Once hooked, kids and adults alike really will want to see every one of his films, which, thankfully, are now finding their way into mainstream DVD release – in quality English dubs – in both the US and UK.

Given that he has been Japan's most popular film-maker for the past 25 years, it's amazing that *Spirited Away* was the first Miyazaki movie to get any kind of general cinema release in the US or UK. It is not the first Miyazaki film kids should see: that should be *My Neighbour Totoro* (see p.51) or *Kiki's Delivery Service* (p.48), which are pitched firmly at children, or the gentler *Castle In The Sky* (p.233) or knockabout action of *Castle Of Cagliostro* (p.4). By contrast, *Spirited Away* is distinctly more grown-up fare, whose bizarre creations would disturb younger children. However, once kids are accustomed to the Miyazaki universe, there's no reason why anyone aged 8 or up shouldn't enjoy this strange tale of a sulky girl who finds herself lost in a spirit world, populated by weird Japanese spirits, gods and witches, and, like Dorothy in Oz or Lewis Carroll's Alice, has to find a way back to reality. Her adventures, aided at times by a spirit boy, and by a river god, are fantastic, exciting, and, at times, very Japanese and alien. But the girl's journey, and her personal growth, are ultimately moving, even if you can't quite work out what has been going on before you.

Kids who enjoy *Spirited Away* will want to take in **Princess Mononoke**, Miyazaki's previous film (1997). This, too, is a grown-up anime: a tale, set in a medieval-looking Japan, of battles between the animal gods of the forest, led by a girl warrior (Mononoke), and iron miners who are polluting and destroying their universe. It's not an easy narrative – indeed, one of its qualities is that you are never quite sure who is good or evil – and it has some quite violent scenes. But again, while not for young kids, it is essential viewing for fans.

SPIRITED AWAY ▣▭▭ US ◉ UK, US | PG (UK, US)
PRINCESS MONONOKE ▣▭▭ US ◉ UK, US | PG (UK) PG-13 (US)

The Sword In The Stone 1963

Originally released in Disney's heyday, *The Sword In The Stone* hasn't fared as well as *Snow White* or *Cinderella*, but it still stands up as a stand-alone feat of storytelling and animation. Accompanied by the humorous owl

Archimedes, Merlin the magician chances upon Wart. A Cinderella figure, Wart works hard every day whilst his lazy brother trains to be a knight. Merlin sets out to help Wart prepare for his later role of King Arthur by teaching him the ways of the world. Wart's adventures are perfect for children under 8, with no violence and plenty of magical buffoonery.

▭ UK, US ◉ UK, US | U (UK) G (US)

The Tenth Kingdom 2000

This epic 10-hour mini-series – a little like a modern version of *Narnia* – never delivered the audience on television but, on DVD, it can be properly appreciated. It's the story of a New York girl, Virginia, who with her school janitor dad who are led by a bewitched prince into a kind of parallel fairytale zone – a fragmented kingdom ruled by queens Snow White, Cinderella and Little Red Riding Hood, and threatened by trolls and goblins. The movie gets stranger and more involving as it develops – and, for all the fairytale backdrop, it is at times violent and genuinely scary (a lot more Grimm than Disney). The film also has some sexual content, and it was given a 15 rating in the UK. While that may be extreme, if kids are watching on a video at home, it is still not a film for anyone under 9 or so.

▭ UK, US ◉ UK, US | 15 (UK) NR (US)

Time Bandits 1981

Young Kevin (Craig Warnock) decides sleep is less fun than travelling through time with a band of outlaw dwarves. And, on the evidence of Terry Gilliam's enjoyable fantasy, he's right. Gilliam, one of contemporary cinema's great magicians, is helped by Sean Connery, Ralph Richardson (playing God, he wears his own suit in the movie), Shelley Duvall and assorted Pythons. And this is a fabulously odd epic adventure, with the dwarves seemingly clueless as to why Gilliam has set them off to confront Napoleon, Robin Hood and Agamemnon (Sean Connery, of course). There's some violence and swearing – and the ending where Kevin's parents are killed off can be a shock – but, like a lot of Gilliam's work, this is not only weird, but genuinely funny.

▭ UK, US ◉ UK, US | PG (UK, US)

Willy Wonka & The Chocolate Factory 1971

Urban myth has it that Roald Dahl was so angry with this movie of his book *Charlie and the Chocolate Factory* that he refused to let the sequel, *Charlie and the Great Glass Elevator*, be filmed. Dahl initially adapted his own book for the screen but it was then rewritten by Dave Selzer – which might explain Dahl's angst. But whether Dahl liked it or not, kids almost certainly will. This is one film where that old cliché – "This is one film I could watch over and over again" – really is true.

Dahl's storyline is a superb invention. The Willy Wonka chocolate factory produce a special lottery edition of chocolate bars, in five of which are hidden a golden ticket, which entitles the winner to a tour of the chocolate factory and the chance of the ultimate prize – a life-time's supply of chocolate. There are some nice scenes in which the world is gripped by a mania to find the winning bars, counterpointed by the hopes and disappointments of Charlie and his poor family, but the film really gets going when the five winning children – four brats, and the achingly good Charlie – arrive at the Wonka's factory. There,

they discover the heavy price they can pay for mis-demeanours which, though they seem trivial, reveal their inner selfishness. The names are a bit of a give-away – a girl called Veruca Salt is never going to last long in Dahl's world. Dahl's books were never snug and comforting, and director Mel Stuart captures this malevolence well, aided by a superb turn by Gene Wilder, who manages to be sweet and sour as Wonka, musing, "Well, well, well! Two naughty, nasty little children, three good, sweet little children left!" All, of course, turns out well in the end, Dahl restricting his cruelty (as usual) to the nasty kids.

The movie is, technically, a musical, but it is reviewed here as the songs seem almost incidental to the proceedings. Not that they're unmemorable. Indeed, there are few stranger or *more* memorable song-and-dance sequences on film than that of the Oompa-Loompas. There are some neat touches for adults too (the photo of the finder of the last ticket flashed up on a Paraguayan newscast is Martin Bormann) along with allusions to Ogden Nash, Shakespeare, Wilde and Keats. A movie to treasure, for kids of all ages – right up to 70.

A remake, under Dahl's original title, **Charlie And The Chocolate Factory**, is scheduled for release in 2005, directed by Tim Burton, and with Johnny Depp as Wonka.

▣ UK, US ◉ UK, US | U (UK) G (US)

The Witches 1990

This book has resisted the idea of including horror films – popular though they are among Tweenies. But *The Witches* merits a mention, since – as one of the best Roald Dahl books – you might expect it to be a regular kids' movie. Which it ain't. Filmed by Nicolas Roeg (director of the creepy *Don't Look Now*), using a lot of sudden "in your face" shots, this is a seriously scary movie, even if you have read the book. Kids who get nightmares from films can depend upon this to set them off, and one of the postings on the Internet Movie Database (imdb.com), which is worth browsing on this issue, suggests it is a more frightening film than *Silence Of The Lambs*. You have been warned!

▣ UK, US ◉ UK, US | NR (UK) PG (US)

The Wizard Of Oz 1939

The Wizard of Oz is rather more than a kids' musical. In fact, it's arguably the most famous film of all time. Novelist Salman Rushdie was moved to write a book about it, Judy Garland's whole life was dominated by it, and if you delve into cyber-space you will find such debates as whether you can see acts of midget

Dorothy wipes the Cowardly Lion's tears away!

suicide being performed in the background, or analysis of the work's Freudian, Marxist and feminist perspectives.

For those of you who don't know the story, the obvious question is why not? But, if you have just returned from Middle Earth, and have missed the film's annual visit to the TV networks, the plot is this. Dorothy (Judy Garland) lives in miserable black and white Kansas, where neighbour Mrs Gulch threatens to have her dog Toto done in, then she and Toto are displaced by a tornado into the magical, multi-coloured, world of Oz. But is Dorothy happy? Not a bit of it – she wants to go home and can only get there by going to the Emerald City to see the wizard who rules Oz (although he turns out to be a bit of an impostor). Along the way, she picks up a dysfunctional family of allies who are all lacking one thing (courage, a heart, a brain) they need to get on in life.

Garland, possibly because she didn't have much of a childhood her-self, brought just the right note of wistful vulnerability to her per-formance. Her yearning is expressed most beautifully in "Over The Rainbow", a massive song, recorded hundreds of times subsequently, yet which was almost cut before the film's release. For Rushdie, the film's "driving force is the inadequacy of adults, even good adults, and how the weakness of grown-ups forces children to take control of their own destinies". Roger Ebert says the film "feels real and important in a way most movies don't – it fills a void that exists in many children. For kids of a certain age, home is everything. But over the rainbow, dimly guessed at, is the wide earth, fascinating and terrifying". Ultimately, the search for meaning may be counter-productive. After all, the film had three and a half directors (Richard Thorpe, Victor Fleming, George Cukor, and King Vidor) and ten scriptwriters.

Some younger kids find the Wicked Witch of the West sequence too much to watch – and the tornado scenes are quite scary – but most kids will enjoy Oz, even if they need to sit on your lap the first time the Wicked Witch cackles. And, by the way, despite extensive analysis, the suggestion that you can see depressed munchkins ending it all in the background remains unproven.

📼 UK, US ◉ UK, US | U (UK) G (US)

13

Musicals

supercalifragilistic

There ain't nothing like a song to grab a child's attention. It is no coincidence that, for example, *Joseph And The Amazing Technicolor Dreamcoat* started life as an idea for an end-of-term school play. It isn't just the songs, it's the whimsy and warmth musicals offer that kids enjoy so much. For that reason, the "more grown-up musicals", reviewed in brief at the end of the chapter, are almost as likely to touch a chord with kids as those intended for their consumption.

As well as those reviewed in the pages following, you will find a few other musicals dotted around other chapters of this book. *The Wizard Of Oz* and *Willy Wonka And The Chocolate Factory*, for instance, are reviewed under **Fantasy**, while *Dr Dolittle* is in **Animals**, as these films all seem more about story than songs. And, of course, many Disney movies – notably *Lady And The Tramp* and *The Lion King* (**Animation**), and *Alice in Wonderland* (**Classics**) – have a significant musical base. So if you don't find a movie here, check our index.

Annie 1982

The world's richest man has his heart melted by the world's sweetest girl and agrees to help her find her parents. Carol Burnett, as the alcoholic orphanage boss, has the best lines ("Why any kid would want to be an orphan is beyond me"). But Aileen Quinn shines in what could have been an insufferable title role, derived from the *Little Orphan Annie* strip, one of the most popular comic characters in 1930s America. The standout song is "Tomorrow". Not great. But not bad either.

▭ UK, US ◉UK, US | U (UK) PG (US)

Bugsy Malone 1976

Alan Parker made this movie after his kids complained about not being allowed to see *The Godfather*, so Bugsy Malone is, almost literally, *The Godfather* for kids – with youngsters playing American gangsters. Only there's gunk in the guns, not bullets, which makes for the film's most celebrated scene – a custard pie fight that's to die for. As a musical for kids, starring kids, *Bugsy* could have been terminally cute but Parker, in a career-making movie, lets the performances take centre stage. Scott Baio (Chachi in *Happy Days*) and Jodie Foster impress most, but the whole thing has a splendid madness, in its affectionate pastiche of vintage Hollywood. It's let down only by a lack of memorable songs.

▭ UK, US ◉UK, US | U (UK) G (US)

Is there a better fight scene? Custard pies fly in Bugsy Malone

Chitty Chitty Bang Bang 1968

Chitty Chitty Bang Bang is a scrumptious musical comedy. Truly. Dick Van Dyke dropped his cod Cockney accent from *Mary Poppins* to become mad inventor Caractacus Potts, the creator of the flying car in the movie's title, who comes into conflict and falls in love with sweet heiress Sally Ann Howes (in a role obviously devised for Julie Andrews). You'll believe a car can fly!

It's hard to imagine that such a delicious confection could scare anyone. But, when the flying/swimming car is stolen by a foreign government and the Potts family chase the thieves to the kingdom of Vulgaria, where children are banned/imprisoned, Robert Helpmann is so sinister as the child catcher, that even older kids have found this a bit scary. Some hand-holding may be necessary for younger kids when he turns up in the town square with his sweets and his cage. But like all baddies, he gets his comeuppance, in a riotous finale as the kids escape from their slave labour.

Scripted by Roald Dahl, from an Ian Fleming story, this is an utterly charming musical/comedy/adventure which makes light work of its two-and-a-half hours' screen time. It's customary to lament the fact that Howes, not Andrews, is playing opposite Van Dyke but she holds her own, and brings a great range, power and tenderness to the songs, which are pretty splendid – especially the title track ("Ohh chitty,

The car's the star - **Chitty Chitty Bang Bang**

chitty..."), "Lovely Lonely Man" and "Me Ol' Bamboo" (where Dick Van Dyke *does* come over a bit Bert).

UK, US UK, US | PG (UK) G (US)

The Five Thousand Fingers Of Dr T 1953

MUST SEE!

Only Dr Seuss (see p.65) could have dreamed up a story like this. A boy falls asleep at the piano after a particularly tiring lesson and dreams of Dr T, such an obsessed piano teacher that he has 500 boys playing the instrument 24 hours a day, seven days a week. If the boys try to escape, their path is blocked by an electric fence. To topple the evil empire – and free his mother (who's been virtually hypnotised by Dr T) – the boy links up with a sympathetic plumber who becomes a reluctant surrogate father.

Seuss wrote the script, the songs and even supervised the design of the sets. And the dialogue is shot through with his peculiar genius. At one point, the teacher asks a pupil: "Is it atomic?" and the boy snaps back: "Yes, sir, very atomic!" But the masterstroke is the image of the massive winding double-decker piano keyboard with 500 seats, one for each student; 500 boys, 5000 fingers.

You can see why *The Onion* decided that "kids' movies don't come any more Freudian or perverse". Seuss has created a movie which brilliantly combines childlike wonder and primal terror. Lewis Carroll crossed with Frank Kafka. The tag line, when this was first made, was "the wonder musical of the future!" Fifty years later, the boast still feels true. Seuss's barking genius has created a wonderful alternative to the traditional Hollywood musical.

📼 UK, US ◉ UK, US | U (UK) G (US)

Grease 1978

Olivia Newton-John in trousers so tight she had to be sewn into them, John Travolta in a role that Henry Winkler (Fonz in *Happy Days*) turned down, some seriously good songs ("Summer Nights", "You're The One That I Want", "Beauty School Dropout"), and a 1950s feel-good ambience… this movie could hardly miss. Some of the lyrics might raise a few questions in child's minds (such as the reference to a hooker in "Beauty School Dropout"), and if you have daughters, you might be uncomfortable with the implied message that they have to dress like tarts, set aside their principles and smoke like a small industrial town's worth of chimneys to achieve their dreams. But this is such a fun movie, with almost undiluted song-and-dance routines to enjoy – and its main effect is likely to be that kids will be singing these songs around the house for days.

The same, alas, cannot be said for **Grease 2**, which has just one great song from the Four Tops and a young Michelle Pfeiffer in a short skirt to recommend it.

📼 UK, US ◉ UK, US | PG (UK, US)

A Hard Day's Night 1964

Man on train: "Don't take that tone with me, young man, I fought the war for your sort." Ringo: "I bet you're sorry you won." As great, rebellious, movie lines go, it's an exchange up there (well, maybe just below) Marlon Brando's "Whaddya got?" when he's asked, in *The Wild One*, what he's rebelling against. Which was just one of the surprises for critics who went to see this first Beatles' film, sharpening their sneers, only to find a smart, irreverent work that refused to take itself – or anything else – too seriously. *A Hard Day's Night* made almost all of the rock and roll musicals which came before – and has made many of those made since – look dated, contrived and distinctly unhip.

Much of the credit has to go to the Beatles themselves. They may look like clones of each other in this movie but their individuality shines through the dialogue, much of which was added to exploit their natural comic timing. And then there are the songs – it's hard to think of another movie soundtrack blessed with such an abundance of quality ("A Hard Day's Night", "She Loves You", "Can't Buy Me Love", "And I Love Her", "All My Loving"). However, director Richard Lester does a fantastic job, too, creating a semi-documentary style that made a virtue of the limited budget ($500,000 – after all, nobody was sure if the Beatles weren't just another fad). He also subtly recast the Fabs – George was the mean one, McCartney the cute one, Lennon the cynic, and Ringo the odd Beatle out. Harrison, he says, was easiest to direct, hitting the right note straightaway.

At the time, *A Hard Day's Night* was a film for anyone under about 25. Forty years on, it can still thrill its original audience, but the Beatles have some kind of magic that captures kids of any era. So put this on the video, and prepare for a singalong.

▭▭ UK, US ◉ UK, US | U (UK) G (US)

Help! 1965

Though not as authentic as *A Hard Day's Night*, this Beatles movie is still enjoyable. The plot – in which an eastern cult tries to grab a ring off Ringo's finger – is as slight as any Elvis film of the same era. However, Richard Lester never lets the pace slacken and the classic songs – the title track, "Ticket To Ride", "You've Got To Hide Your Love Away" – make this a treat.

▭▭ UK, US ◉ UK, US | U (UK) G (US)

Joseph And The Amazing Technicolor Dreamcoat 1999

The Andrew Lloyd Webber factory has produced so many musicals in the last thirty years that the sheer ubiquitousness of his output is starting to work against him. His early work – with Oscar-winning lyricist Tim Rice – still stands up best. *Evita* is the more satisfying collaboration but was curiously filmed by Alan Parker with Madonna in the lead role. This biblical tale, devised for a school production, and still rolled out for that purpose, is in part an excuse to romp through different musical styles – the Pharaoh's Elvis impersonation is spot-on. The movie version stars Donny Osmond as Joseph, with support from old hands such as Joan Collins and Richard Attenborough. It's hammy, hummy, extravagant and compelling.

[▭▭] UK, US ◎ UK, US │ NR

Lili 1953

There's a lot to like about *Lili*: Leslie Caron as a waif who joins a carnival, Mel Ferrer as a self-pitying puppeteer, a wonderful fantasy ballet sequence and some fine magic tricks, courtesy of Jean-Pierre Aumont and Zsa Zsa Gabor. Caron's scenes with the puppets are sublime and the script (by Helen Deutsch from the Paul Gallico story) has some great lines. Asked about Lili's qualities as an actress, Ferrer says: "She's like a little bell that gives off a pure sound no matter how you strike it, because she is in herself so good and true and pure." Wonderful stuff.

[▭▭] UK, US │ U (UK) G (US)

Little Shop Of Horrors 1986

Little Shop of Horrors ran off-Broadway for years – a kind of junior cousin to *The Rocky Horror Show*. It is the story of an über-nerd called Seymour Krelborn who is hopelessly in love with a flower-girl, Audrey. Hopelessly, that is, until he buys a plant during a solar eclipse, and finds it drinks blood, bullies him, and is – as the song so rightly puts it – "A Mean Green Mother From Outer Space".

The musical was based on a 1960 film, which starred a young Jack Nicholson, and there are folk who prefer that version. But you have to have a real aversion to musicals not to fall for this movie, with Rick Moranis worryingly (for him) convincing as Seymour, Ellen Greene as Audrey, Steve Martin as a sadistic dentist (worth the price of admission in itself), and Levi Stubbs Jr of the Four Tops as the voice of the plant. On top of which, there is a very funny score by Howard Ashman and Alan Menken, who were promptly signed up by Disney to write for *The Little Mermaid* and *Beauty And The Beast*.

Great for kids, 6 and up, so long as they're not due for a dental visit any time soon.

UK, US UK, US | PG (UK) PG-13 (US)

Mary Poppins 1964

What can you say about Julie Andrews and *Mary Poppins*? The two were made for each other, and Andrews, with her amazing, elastic, perfectly pitched voice, was just made for musicals. Despite making the parts her own on stage, she had missed out on the films of both *My Fair Lady* and *The King and I* when Disney signed her up to be Mary Poppins. Legend has it that they then had to wait nearly two years, as she was pregnant at the time, but what a wise delay. It's impossible to imagine anyone else in the role of singing nanny.

Gliding across the skies, and sliding up bannisters with panache, Andrews is well supported by Dick Van Dyke, despite his odd Cockney accent, by David Tomlinson as the stuffy pedantic father who hires her to look after his kids against his better judgement, and Glynis Johns as the suffragette mother. Disney did a wonderful job with the sets too – London looks plausible yet fantastically unreal. And the story, from a novel by P.L. Travers, is simply an enchanting one for children. Who can resist the idea of a nanny and her chimney-sweep chum who can whisk you off into the dream worlds of a pavement chalk drawing?

Of course, the songs and dance routines are, as Mary would say, practically perfect in every way. "Supercalifragilistic" is almost a rite of childhood, "Step In Time" (performed by a dozen sweeps on the London roofline) almost defines exuberance. "A Spoonful Of Sugar", "Chim-chim-cherree" … these are real, living classics, every one. Full credit to Richard M. and Robert B. Sherman – the largely unsung brother-songwriting team, who worked with Disney for four decades (where their greatest moment came with *Jungle Book*).

Perhaps what is most remarkable of all about *Mary Poppins*, though, is that it weighs in at 2 hours and 20 minutes – far too long for a kids' movie – yet miraculously, not a bit of it. In fact, the only sour note one could sound (and Julie Andrews, of course, does not do sour notes) is that there is almost a cruelly in Mary Poppins leaving the kids at the end, flying off because the wind is changing.

UK, US UK, US | U (UK) G (US)

The Monkees late 1960s

The Monkees was a TV series, rather than a musical, or even a movie (we'll pass over for now their psychedelic cult film, *Headz*). But Davy, Micky, Pete and Mike have to be in this book: for a time in the 1960s they looked like being bigger than the Beatles, and they were the first band that went huge with kids. The secret of the TV shows was zany, knockabout fun, and terrific, pure pop music (penned by the likes of Neil Diamond and Mann and Weill), propelled by the irresistible TV theme tune ("Hey Hey, We're The Monkees"). Recent reruns on Disney's TV channels have given the show a new lease of life. The shows are clearly very dated and can drag a bit for kids today, but they can still seem both smart and funny. In one episode, Davy refuses to water someone's horse saying, "I'm not a stable boy!" only to receive the crushing rejoinder: "I don't care about your mental condition; water my horse!"

UK, US UK, US | NR

The Music Man 1962

Good, clean viewing for kids of any age – although older ones might want to head for the hills during some of the songs. Robert Preston drives the film forward with his silver-tongued oratory, energy and charm, amid a fine clutch of songs ("Ya Got Trouble", "Till There Was You"), and a rousing production number at the end with 76 trombones. Still one of a half a dozen truly essential musicals.

UK, US UK, US | U (UK) G (US)

Newsies/The News Boys 1992

It's nice to see a musical based on real events of some import – a strike by paper boys in 19th-century New York against their exploitation by publisher Joseph Pulitzer. *Variety* probably best summed up the end result when it called the production a "strange cross between *Oliver!* and Samuel Fuller's *Park Row*." Christopher Bale is effective as the hero newsboy, while Robert Duvall isn't as the tyrannous press baron. However, director Kevin Ortega doesn't quite seem to know what to make of his own story.

▭ UK, US ◉UK, US | PG (UK, US)

Oliver! 1968

MUST SEE!

How did Lionel Bart get away with it? Dickens' *Oliver Twist* is a dark story – about an orphaned boy, a cruel workhouse, about London thieves and low-life, exploited boys, prostitution and murder. And yet *Oliver!* (don't forget that exclamation mark!) is a really jolly film, brimful of cheerful energy and absurdly catchy songs ("Food Glorious Food", "Consider Yourself") that kids absolutely adore. Perhaps the key to it all is that – in addition to a couple of absolutely top

parts for boys – Mark Lester as Oliver, Jack Wild as the Artful Dodger – there are a further 82 boys in the cast. It is a film which genuinely belongs to its audience.

That said, there's some decent support from the grown-ups, notably Ron Moody as Fagin and Oliver Reed as Bill Sikes. And the London locations are terrific, too. The film belongs to those days when there were intermissions to change the reels, and is an impressive 2 hours and 26 minutes long. But you wouldn't cut a minute of it.

▭ UK, US ◉UK, US | U (UK) G (US)

The Pirates Of Penzance 1983

This is a beautifully faithful movie of the Gilbert and Sullivan operetta, with an unlikely – but effective - trio of leads (Kevin Kline, Linda Ronstadt and Angela Lansbury). Director Wilford Leach decided to insert "My Eyes Are Fully Open" – from *Ruddigore* – into the score, one of the fastest numbers in the entire Gilbert and Sullivan repertoire, presumably just to give the cast an even bigger challenge.

▭▭ UK, US ◉US | U (UK) G (US)

Robin And The Seven Hoods 1964

Like many Rat Pack movies, this updating of the Robin Hood legend (Robbo is a gangster, played by Sinatra; Dino is his buddy Little John and Sammy is Will) feels as if it was made as much for the cast's pleasure as ours. Bing Crosby underplays nicely as the bookkeeper Alan A. Dale. A minor musical, with a slightly pointless plot, but with enough wry humour, decently staged musical numbers and laid-back cool to appeal to kids of 5 and over, as much as Sinatra fans.

▭▭ UK, US ◉UK, US

Song Of The South 1946

Song Of The South pioneered mixing animation and live action, and gave the first ever lead role in a Disney movie to a black actor, James Baskett. Its story is based on old slave tales, compiled by Joel Harris Chandler, and in some opinions is flawed – fatally – by what the National Association for the Advancement of Colored People called "the impression it gives of the idyllic master/slave relationship" – an opinion with which Disney seems almost to have agreed, when at one point the studio announced the film would be "retired" – before later changing its mind. The shame is that, the core reservation aside, this is a movie with big heart, lots of cheer, some great songs (notably "Zip-a-Dee Doo Dah") and, as the NAACP said, "remarkable artistic merit".

▭▭ UK ◉US | U (UK) G (US)

The Sound Of Music 1965

It's amazing to think that Julie Andrews made *The Sound Of Music* virtually back-to-back with *Mary Poppins*. And that Rodgers and Hammerstein rose to the challenge and created a soundtrack even more memorable. Which they did, with songs so original and so catchy that they became overnight classics, part of the English-speaking world's musical vocabulary. You don't even have to have seen this movie (though it's hard to know how you've avoided doing so) to know, off by heart, "Do-Re-Mi", "Maria" or "My Favourite Things" – a tune so sublime that it can work equally for Julie Andrews as a singing nun as for John Coltrane.

Much has been said about the quality of Julie Andrews's voice, which tragically was destroyed by surgery in her later life. But watch *The Sound Of Music* and you cannot fail to be amazed, as she launches into "Do-Re-Mi" and effortlessly rolls through four octaves. So it was wonderfully apt that music is at the very centre of this story, of a singing nun, Maria, who is enlisted as nanny for a motherless clan of Austrian children, and not only brings them to life through song, but helps them escape from the Nazis by dint of an award-winning performance of "traditional" songs.

But so much for the music. *The Sound Of Music* matches it with an exciting story, that will genuinely engage kids seeing it for the first time, and the other actors (for this is Julie Andrews's film) provide top support. Christopher Plummer (who dubbed it "the sound of mucus") does the stiff Austrian captain to a T, Eleanor Parker is splendidly dry as the baroness ("I must remember to bring my mouth organ..."), and – as generations of cross-dressing men attending *Sound of Music* singalongs will attest – the nuns are a treat.

All of which said, this is a long movie, and one that – with its Nazi backdrop – will not be easily understood by kids under 6 or so. Pick your moment, and enjoy it again, together.

📼 UK, US ⊚UK, US | U (UK) G (US)

MORE GROWN-UP MUSICALS

High Society 1956

A musical remake of *The Philadelphia Story* with nine flawless Cole Porter songs and a cast which includes Frank Sinatra, Bing Crosby, Grace Kelly and Louis Armstrong — it's very hard to go wrong. And this doesn't. One highlight, among many, is Crosby and Sinatra's duet of "Did You Evah?"

UK, US ⊙UK, US | U (UK) NR (US)

The King And I 1956

Yul Brynner deservedly won an Oscar as the monarch involved in a platonic romance with Deborah Kerr's governess. *The King and I* has enough quality, spectacle and music to enchant most kids under the age of 10. The 1999 Disney animated remake is adequate, and good for younger kids.

UK, US ⊙UK, US | U (UK) G (US)

Fiddler On The Roof 1971

A musical that works as a drama, too. The songs (particularly "If I Were A Rich Man"and "Sunrise, Sunset") are superb, and are tied to a strong emotional story about the breaking down of tradition in a Jewish family, the art of surviving — spiritually and physically — on as little as possible, and religious oppression. At 181 minutes, you may have to take this in stages, and there are some shockingly violent scenes, but this tale of Topol and his daughters, scattered across America, Russia and Siberia, is accessible enough for kids of 8 or 9.

UK, US ⊙UK, US | U (UK) G (US)

My Fair Lady 1964

There really is no more genteel, sumptuously staged musical than *My Fair Lady*, in which Rex Harrison's Professor Higgins moulds Cockney sparrow Audrey Hepburn and falls in love with her. The songs range from good to great (with "On The Street Where You Live", "I Could Have Danced All Night" and "I've Grown Accustomed To Her Face" in the latter category). Harrison almost didn't get the part: director Jack Warner wanted Cary Grant but the suave idol told the studio head: "Not only will I not play Henry Higgins, if you don't cast Rex Harrison in the role, I won't even go to see the picture."

UK, US ⊙UK, US | PG (UK) G (US)

Singin' In The Rain 1952

Singin, In The Rain has virtually trademarked the tag "the best musical of all time", and its absurd plot and slapstick are hugely appealing for kids — especially the title track, of course, famously performed by Gene Kelly with a 103 degree fever, and Donald O'Connor's fabulous slapstick tap sequence on "Make 'Em Laugh". Treat yourself to the DVD, which comes with bags of extras.

UK, US ⊙UK, US | U (UK) NR (US)

Strictly Ballroom 1992

Baz Luhrmann had the idea, wrote the script and directed this movie about competitive ballroom dancing in Australia, combining all these roles with the aplomb of an accomplished dancer. Only real life could be this weird – or this compelling. Best of all, Luhrmann keeps it tight – after 94 minutes, the story has run its course and the movie is over.

📼UK, US ⊙UK, US | PG (UK, US)

Viva Las Vegas 1964

Easily the best of the King's 1960s musicals – but then it had a decent director (MGM veteran George Sidney), a charismatic love interest (Ann-Margret with whom Elvis had a brief, intense, affair), and real songwriters (Pomus and Shuman who wrote the stunning title track). There's not a lot of hip shaking but the songs – and the gags – keep flowing as Elvis tries to win the race and the girl.

📼UK, US ⊙UK, US | U (UK) G (US)

14

Romance

it must be love

What are rules for, except to be broken? With this chapter, we've thrown away the kids/grown-up film distinctions, and simply included reviews of good romantic movies that children are likely to enjoy. After all, there's nothing like a good love story to tug at heartstrings – enchanting girls and forcing boys slyly to wipe their eyes at the denouement. Many of those included have a splash of comedy, too. And they are, for the most part, suitable for any drama-loving kids of 7 and up.

Anastasia 1997

Anastasia saw 20th Century Fox taking on the mighty Disney, with this unusual animated tale of a former Russian princess, who with the aid of a servant boy searches for her family, lost during the Russian Revolution. Meg Ryan, the voice of Anastasia, needed some persuasion to take the part: Fox had to make an animated short of Anastasia reading Ryan's lines from *Sleepless In Seattle* to convince her. As this is kids' entertainment and not a history lesson, the Russian Revolution has been sidelined; the emphasis here is on mad monks, goblins and romance. It's not ideal for kids under 4 who may not appreciate the romance and may find the villain a tad too scary.

For an equally enjoyable film, with rather more accurate history, try the 1956 **Ingrid Bergman version**.

▭▭▭ UK, US ◉UK, US | U (UK) G (US)

Breakfast At Tiffany's 1961

This is a charming hymn to high style and high living with Audrey Hepburn excelling as Holly Golightly. The censorship of the day meant that Hepburn's elegant heroine is a socialite, not a call girl as in Truman Capote's original story. One of those films that just becomes easier to watch as the years roll on – there's a great deal more to it than Audrey singing "Moon River".

▭▭▭ UK, US ◉UK, US | PG (UK) NR (US)

Casablanca 1942

Casablanca is the seventh greatest film of all time, according to voters on the Internet Movie Database – a low-ish rating, really, for such a classic, possibly because even adults disagree as to whether Bergman *[plot spoiler alert: don't read on if you've been hiding under a hill of beans]* was right to leave Bogie.

Bergman's beautiful, Bogie is cynical, Claude Rains is suavely villainous, yet ultimately sympathetic, Paul Henreid is consistently virtuous yet ultimately unsympathetic and Dooley Wilson is on piano: what's not to like? Watched with kids, the movie may surprise you with some amusing follies – such as Ingrid's attempt to walk around the dark streets of Casablanca incognito in a white cardigan, and a Bulgarian woman who throws herself on Rick's mercy but has an English accent so upper class you wonder if she's a minor royal. Somehow this only adds to the fun.

UK, US ⊚UK, US | U (UK) PG (US)

Clueless 1995

Clueless is a treat, a mad but inspired idea: take the plot of Jane Austen's *Emma*, use it very, very loosely, and relocate the action to a Beverly Hills school. Zipcode 90210. Directed by Amy Heckerling (*Fast Times At Ridgemont High*), and with Alicia Silverstone totally charming in the lead, it works like a dream.

The plot is genuinely funny and cute. Cher (Silverstone) and Dionne (Stacey Dash) are two good-natured, popular high school girls ("named after great singers of the past that now do infomercials") who set out to give new girl Tai (Brittany Murphy) a makeover and match-make for their teacher (Wallace Shawn as a splendid geek) in the hope of better grades. As the title suggests, you may think you're watching two Beverly Hills airheads, but *Clueless* is peppered with smart, satirical observations and a wonderful line in vernacular (as if!), and, alongside the romance, it offers a string of real laugh-out-loud moments.

Despite its 12/13 ratings, there is little to offend here, a little swearing and drugs aside, though the movie will probably be appreciated more by those soon to become teenagers. And for anyone who enjoys it, there is all of the original Austen to try (see below).

UK, US ⊚UK, US | 12 (UK) PG-13 (US)

Emma 1996

Today's children may not be quite as interested in the finer nuances of friendship and love, but the charm of Jane Austen's novels will be lost on few – and (see box on p.214) there is no shortage of movies to lure them in. This is one of the best versions of – arguably – the most satisfyingly filmic of all Austen's narratives.

Austen in the movies

Jane Austen wrote six of the great romantic novels of all time: *Northanger Abbey*, *Sense and Sensibility*, *Pride and Prejudice*, *Mansfield Park*, *Emma* and *Persuasion* (the first three were written before 1800, the others between the publication of *Sense* in 1811 and Austen's death in 1817). They have all been filmed by the BBC in recent years, as mini-series, typically lasting five to six hours in all, and the stories have appeared as movies since 1940, when Laurence Olivier stepped out as Mr Darcy. Here are the better versions:

Northanger Abbey (1986). Austen's gothic satire is a lot of fun, and this BBC drama keeps the spirit nicely, with Peter Firth (Henry Tilney) staking his claim as Austen hero. 📺UK, US ⊙UK, US | NR

Sense And Sensibility (1995). Emma Thompson scripted and Ang Lee directed this accessible Austen tale: younger children shouldn't have any difficulty understanding Elinor loves Edward and Marianne (a spirited Kate Winslet) thinks she loves Willoughby but really loves Colonel Brandon. 📺UK, US ⊙UK, US | U (UK) PG (US)

Pride And Prejudice (1940, 1995). Laurence Olivier and Greer Garson shine as Darcy and Elizabeth in the 1940 movie – and you get the story in two hours. But for many, the role of Darcy has been mugged for all time by Colin Firth in the 1995 BBC adaptation.

1940 📺UK, US ⊙UK, US | NR * BBC 📺UK, US ⊙UK, US | NR

Mansfield Park (1990, 1983). Patricia Rozema incurred the wrath of Austenites in rewriting Mansfield Park for her 1999 movie, starring Frances O'Connor as Fanny Price. It has a coherence, and it works as a film, but if you want Austen's version, then the BBC's 1983 mini-series, with Sylvestra LeTouzel, plays it straight. ROZEMA 📺UK, US ⊙UK, US | U (UK) PG-13 (US) * BBC 📺UK, US ⊙UK, US | NR

Emma (1996). See review on p.213 of the Gwyneth Paltrow movie – the best of a multitude of versions.

Persuasion (1995). Amanda Root is Anne Elliot and Corin Redgrave superb as her father in this nicely crafted movie version. Ciarán Hinds is the love interest, Captain Wentworth. The PG is for (very) mild language. 📺UK, US ⊙US, UK | U (UK) PG (US)

Eager to shake off the shackles of being Brad Pitt's other half, Gwyneth Paltrow took on the role of Emma as a means of displaying both her acting talent and her knack for the English accent. Emma likes to match-make for her friends, yet fails to look after her own heart. Old-fashioned but delightful, it is good for girls (or sophisticated boys) from 10 and up, and a terrific follow-up for anyone who enjoyed the *Emma*-inspired plot of *Clueless* (see p.213).

UK, US ◎UK, US | U (UK) PG (US)

Gregory's Girl 1981

Alongside *Local Hero*, this is Bill Forsyth's finest film – and it had the freshness of being his first proper feature, made with a Scottish cast whose accents were thick enough to need dubbing for US release. A wry, touching, tale of a love triangle between school team goalkeeper John Gordon Sinclair (then known as Gordon John), lethal goalscorer Dorothy (Dee Hepburn) and her pal, played by Claire Grogan, the film both rings true and amuses. It's not quite a classic but it does prove that John Hughes isn't the only movie director who can turn teen uncertainty into commercial – and artistic - gold. Watch out for Chic Murray as a piano-tinkling headmaster with a penchant for pastries. An enduring film that is good for boys as well as girls, of 8 and over.

UK, US; ◎UK, US | PG (UK, US)

Class striker - Dorothy heads for the penalty spot

Groundhog Day 1993

MUST SEE!

Groundhog Day was set to star Tom Hanks until director Harold Ramis came to his senses and realised he was far too nice to play sarcastic weatherman Phil Connors. Instead the role went to Ramis's *Ghostbusters* cohort Bill Murray, who is perfect as the disaffected weatherman doomed to relive the same day (and punch the same irritating old school friend) for eternity, unless he can mend his ways. The first half is all about comedy, with Murray and his sardonic wit and his Punxsutawney chums, who all miraculously possess the loveable quirks and eccentricities you always find in Hollywood's imaginary small-town America. The second half of the movie is pure romance, as almost-too-sweet Rita (Andie MacDowell), more of a romantic vision than a character, comes to see a new side to Phil. A brilliantly original romantic comedy, with some sexy moments. The moral? Perhaps, as Roger Ebert put it: "just because we're born SOBs doesn't mean we have to stay that way."

UK, US ◉UK, US | PG (UK, US)

I'll just read that again – Bill Murray in Groundhog Day

Houseboat 1958

With Cary Grant his usual charismatic self, and Sophia Loren stunningly beautiful in a shimmering, skin-clinging dress in the climactic scene, this is certainly one you can watch along with. Grant plays Tom, a lawyer with custody of his three children after their mother's death, who hires Cinzia (Loren) as a nanny. The five are forced to move onto a tiny houseboat when their new family home is delayed and the usual series of unexpected events unfold before Tom eventually realises he loves Cinzia. Off screen, Grant fell for his co-star much faster, eventually proposing. Not the most original movie in the world but smartly played, bright and with a heart – there are some exceptionally sensitive scenes where Grant explores the father-son relationship with his difficult son David.

📼 UK, US ◉UK, US | U (UK) NR (US)

It Happened One Night 1934

If it hadn't been for Clark Gable's raucous off-screen behaviour, which led to the star being loaned from MGM to Columbia as punishment, the world might never have had this movie – one of the greatest romantic comedies of all time. Claudette Colbert, who hated the film, is wealthy heiress Ellie on the run from her father who won't let her marry. On the road she meets Peter (Gable), a newspaper hack always on the lookout for a good story. Despite countless reworkings of the "girl hates guy but eventually they fall in love" theme, kids should still appreciate what a classic this is. And if not, you can always tell them elements of *Bugs Bunny* were based on Gable's performance.

📼 UK, US ◉UK, US | U (UK) NR (US)

Ladyhawke 1985

Move beyond the dated soundtrack, by prog rock artist Alan Parsons, and *Ladyhawke* is an underrated gem. A wholesome-looking Matthew Broderick is Philippe, a thief but not a very good one. On the run from the bishop of Aquila, he becomes the equerry of Captain Navarre. Navarre's story gradually unfolds: he and his love, Isabeau, have been cursed by the bishop to be together in human form only at sunrise and sunset, Navarre a wolf by night and Isabeau a hawk by day. A classic tale of good combating evil and love winning in the end, *Ladyhawke* rises above its contemporaries with thrilling action and bright comedy. Perfect for children 7 and above.

📼 UK, US ⊙ UK, US | PG (UK) PG-13 (US)

Local Hero 1983

 Following the unexpected success of *Gregory's Girl*, Bill Forsyth made this warm, funny, endearingly eccentric, slightly meandering comedy in which the ruthless capitalism of Houston oil's business is defeated, or to be more accurate, deflected, by the fey locals in the Scottish Highlands. Peter Capaldi, Denis Lawson, Fulton Mackay, Jenny Seagrove and Burt Lancaster all give strong performances but Christopher Rozycki, as the Russian captain who is a hearthrob to the old ladies who sit at the back at the dance, almost steals the show. As do the Northern Lights that Lancaster travels to Scotland to see.

📼 UK, US ⊙ UK, US | PG (UK, US)

A Matter Of Life And Death/Stairway To Heaven 1946

Emeric Pressburger-Michael Powell's *Stairway To Heaven* (as it was called in the US) is one of the films Martin Scorsese cites as inspiring him to become a director. The opening scene, in which an RAF pilot (David Niven – who else?) leaps from his plane without a parachute but doesn't die is one of the most famous in movie history. The film has obviously dated (the debate over the value of England seems, at half a century's remove, a bit provincial) but Niven is in fine form as the pilot whose love for June (Kim Hunter) leads, eventually, to a trial in heaven as to whether he be allowed to live. It's brilliantly realised – thanks in part to production designer Alfred Junge – while excessive profundity is always avoided by comic relief. As you would expect from Pressburger and Powell, the movie offers a most original projection of heaven: the angels carry their wings under their arms in dry cleaner bags. Touches like that lift this movie from the realms of the very good to the truly great. Suitable for older kids – maybe 8 and over.

📼 UK, US ⊙ UK, US | U (UK) PG (US)

Much Ado About Nothing 1993

Although Kenneth Branagh sticks pretty closely to the text, children as young as 7 should have no problem understanding who loves who and who the villain is. The stellar cast (Emma Thompson, Kate Beckinsale, Denzel Washington) supported ably by the likes of Richard Briers and Imelda Staunton, make this seem effortless but then, as the closing scene of the whole cast singing "hey nonny nonny" was done in one take – and none of the singing was redubbed – maybe it was. The cast are pretty good to look at and so is Chianti, which doubles for Messina, and the high spirits and fizzing energy of the director and his cast are infectious. Michael Keaton, as Dogbery, looks as if he wishes he was still in Beetlejuice, otherwise there's nothing much wrong with this classic slice of light Shakespeare.

▇▇▇ UK, US ◉ UK, US | PG (UK) PG-13 (US)

My Girl 1991

On its release children flocked to see *My Girl* to cry over Macaulay Culkin's character's death, whilst parents were happy to watch the brat croak. For those not around during the heyday of the 1990s male answer to Shirley Temple, *My Girl* is a surprisingly cute movie about pre-adolescent love and friendship, with a few lessons about death thrown in. Suitable for children of 8 and above, although the bee-sting scene may scare.

▇▇▇ UK, US ◉ UK, US | PG (UK, US)

Pillow Talk 1959

You may need to explain why strangers can listen in on Doris Day's telephone conversations, but this is the only puzzling aspect of this, the first of three movies starring Day, Rock Hudson and Tony Randall. In the classic love-hate plot, Hudson is playboy Brad Allen, who takes a dislike to his disapproving neighbour Jan (Day), and she to him, until he meets her face to face. Here on in, he tries to woo her by pretending not to be the neighbour she hates. In its day this was considered risqué, with a feet-touching scene too hot for some censors, but you shouldn't feel any concern allowing children as young as 5 to watch.

▭ UK, US ◉ UK, US | U (UK) NR (US)

The Red Shoes 1948

The ninth best British movie ever made – and that's official, from a survey by the British Film Institute. It isn't hard to see why The Red Shoes, boasting humour, romance and music, is held in such esteem. You certainly don't have to be a dance fan, or even a young girl, to enjoy this romantic fable of a ballerina, Victoria (Moira Shearer), who must choose between her first love, ballet, and her second, a young composer (played by Marius Goring).

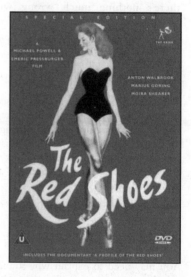

Shearer was a Sadler's Wells ballerina who proved to be a talented actress. Originally producer Alexander Korda had the exact opposite in mind, casting his wife Merle Oberon and hiring a double to do her dancing. But Michael Powell and Emeric Pressburger took control of the project and created this genuinely haunting movie. Part of the charm is that Powell stayed true to his own sense of the story. The exterior of the Mercury Theatre is shown in the rain because that's how he remembered it. Breathtakingly colourful, a fifteen-minute recital of Hans Christian Andersen's "The Red Shoes" is the film's ultimate triumph, and the sequence showing a young girl at first obsessed by, and then possessed by, her red ballet shoes, will have kids on the edge of their seats.

▭ UK, US ◉ UK, US | U (UK)

Roman Holiday 1953

Director William Wyler nearly cancelled production of *Roman Holiday*, originally a Jean Simmons vehicle, when the actress proved unavailable. Fortunately, Audrey Hepburn was on hand to take a legendary screen test, in which the cameraman kept shooting after her scene ended. This candid footage won her the role as a princess enjoying 24 hours of fun in Rome in the company of a crusty news reporter (Gregory Peck). It's easy to understand how anyone could fall in love with Hepburn's character, the human incarnation of Bambi. Both Peck and Wyler were happy to help her with her art. The missing hand scene was ad-libbed by Peck from a Red Skelton routine, garnering genuine surprise from Hepburn, while Wyler was forced to make her cry when she couldn't fake it. A beautiful love story for all ages.

UK, US ⊚UK, US | U (UK) NR (US)

Romeo And Juliet 1968, 1996

Of the many movies of this immortal tale of teenagers in love, Franco **Zeffirelli**'s retelling has stood out for forty years – the most obvious reason being his decision to cast two actors (Leonard Whiting and Olivia Hussey) who were roughly the age of Shakespeare's star-crossed lovers. This being Zeffirelli, he also chucked half of the text – deeming it surplus to requirements. The end result largely proves him right, in casting and cutting.

But there was room for another Romeo – and **Baz Luhrmann** staked a claim to the definitive modern version with his brilliantly conceived reinvention starring Leonardo DiCaprio and Claire Danes. Luhrmann introduces the tale as a news report about star-crossed lovers and proceeds with a movie that is part MTV video, part Hong Kong action-picture, part *The Sopranos*, while staying the course with Shakespeare's script and language. Oh – and the soundtrack is cool, too, featuring the likes of Stina Nordenstram.

ZEFIRELLI VERSION UK, US ⊚UK, US | U (UK) G (US)
LUHRMANN VERSION UK, US ⊚UK, US | PG (UK) PG-13 (US)

Roxanne 1987

Watching this movie makes you remember how funny Steve Martin can be – real, laugh-out-loud funny. He rejigs this whimsical tale, creating a wonderful role as the big-nosed, small-town fireman who gets the impossible girl (Daryl Hannah), who, in the idyllic world of movies such as this, sees beyond the nose to discern his inner quality.

Anyone who has ever felt awkward and out of place will appreciate this movie – and it's pitched nicely for pre-pubescent kids. You also get 25 nose jokes, courtesy of Martin's hero, in what must surely be the greatest movie challenge since cool hand Luke munched his way through a few eggs.

▭ UK, US ◎ UK, US | PG (UK, US)

Titanic 1997

If studio heads had cast Matthew McConaughey, or Macaulay Culkin had auditioned better, James Cameron's epic wouldn't have been so epic, the box office take might have been a few hundred million lighter and we wouldn't be doomed to seeing Celine Dion's "My Heart Will Go On" rerun on music channels for an eternity. Leonardo DiCaprio is the main attraction (though Kate Winslet does well in a difficult role) in this love story of Jack and Rose, which dwarfs the actual sinking of a ship. It is a soppy film, and at times too scarily realistic for young children, but love-struck older children, especially girls who can adore Leo and pretend they are Rose, will probably love it.

▭ UK, US ◎ UK, US | 12 (UK) PG-13 (US)

Topper 1937

For its day, *Topper* boasted ground-breaking FX technology, but this isn't the way to sell this to your children. Instead, tell them the plot: two crazy party-animals must, upon their death, do one good deed for a living person (thereby effectively haunting them), so they can finally get to heaven. *Topper* has ghosts, special effects and wild characters kids will fall in love with, and who fall back in love with one another to give us a good, old-fashioned romantic happy ending. The only down-side: Cary Grant just isn't in it enough.

📼 UK, US ◎ UK, US | U (UK) NR (US)

Tuck Everlasting 2002

This romantic fantasy comes with a moral ("Do not fear death – fear the unlived life") and a bucketload of sentimentality. Rebellious mop-pet Alexis Bledel goes for a walk in the woods, always liable to lead to unforeseen complications in Hollywoodland, and is taken to meet the Tuck family who have discovered a spring which offers eternal life. Director Jay Russell doesn't quite bring the same aplomb to this adap-tation of a classic slice of children's fiction as he did to *My Dog Skip* and you may feel, at times, that the film itself threatens to last for an eternity. But it's well acted, well shot and finally worth the effort.

📼 UK, US ◎ UK, US | PG (UK, US)

Schools

top of the class

School stories are back in fashion, it seems. Would *Harry Potter* have been quite so big without Hogwarts Academy? Probably not. But then it's a very long traditon. Schools have been part of the movie experience since the dawn of Hollywood. The main change being that the movies have got lighter: the black and white classics tended to echo back to childhoods spent in institutions of torture. Modern school movies have more fun. As well as those reviewed here, you'll find a few schools in other departments, such as **Cartoons** (*Recess*), **Fantasy** (*Harry Potter*, *Matilda*) and **Romance** (*Gregory's Girl*). Browse around...

Bedknobs And Broomsticks 1971

Often compared to *Mary Poppins* (kooky guardian takes children on a series of crazy adventures), *Bedknobs* is more Sweetex to *Poppins* sugar. Angela Lansbury, in a role Julie Andrews turned down, is Miss Price, an apprentice witch in the guardianship of three children. With the help of her magic bedknob she flies them to her defunct witchcraft school to find a spell book and repel the Nazis. Good as Lansbury is, this can be quite a slog in parts, even if you're watching the truncated 98-minute version. The songs (some restored in the 133-minute version now available on DVD) and animation are the highlights, the football match scene worth the price alone.

▭▭ UK, US ◉UK, US | U (UK) G (US)

The Belles Of St Trinian's 1954

There's nothing children like better – chocolate excepted – than a film where kids run the show. The first and best adventure of the Trinian's girls involves stealing a racehorse, undercover cops and the dodgy dealings of Flash Harry (George Cole in a role that anticipated Arthur Daley in the British TV series *Minder*). The comedy is anarchic and slapstick, with the sublime Alastair Sim (in drag as headmistress Fritton) and Joyce Grenfell excelling. The belles are splendid, too, as they boss things around.

▭▭ UK, US | U (UK) NR (US)

Billy Madison 1995

Preposterous, good-natured fun, *Billy Madison* is the creation of Adam Sandler, the low-brow genius whose comic, at times crude, infantilism strikes a chord with kids. Billy is the 27-year-old only child of a multi-millionaire who must return to school and graduate if he is to inherit his father's company. The inevitable mishaps occur, one involving a former wrestler, Revolting Blob. Not all the jokes succeed, but enough do to keep things moving. Should appeal to kids of 9 and above.

▭▭ UK, US ◉UK, US | PG (UK) PG-13 (US)

Boys Will Be Boys 1935

In his first schoolmaster role, for which he was to become famous, Will Hays is blustering, dishonest, amusing and occasionally mean as the mortarboard-clad headmaster. Although the plot features the theft of a necklace, the best moments surround day-to-day life in the school. A former prison teacher, Hays is Alec Smart (later Smart Alec) who forges a letter of recommendation to get a post at Narkover, a public school for crooks, whose pupils are more adept at bombings and theft than the Classics. Good, old-fashioned fun.

UK ◉UK | U (UK) NR (US)

Goodbye Mr Chips 1939

Forget the dismal 1969 musical remake, Robert Donat is the quintessential Mr Chips in this 1939 version, and beat off stiff competition from Clark Gable (*Gone With The Wind*) to win the year's best actor Oscar. The stiff upper lip boarding school on display may seem a world away from 21st-century schooling, but this is a hard film to dislike. From the book by James Hilton, who based Chips on his own Classics master at Cambridge (W. H. Balgarnie), we see Chips as naïve, eager young master and doddering old hand. One of Chips's pupils is played by a very young John Mills.

UK, US ◉UK, US | U (UK) NR (US)

A Little Princess 1995

Based on a novel by Frances Hodgson Burnett, who also wrote *The Secret Garden* (see p.106), this is a movie about a girl who loses her father and then finds him. Sara (Liesel Matthews) moves from India to a private New York school when her father goes to fight in World War I. Her wealth means she is initially treated well by the headmistress, Miss Minchin (Eleanor Bron), and favoured by her peers thanks to her fantastical tales from India. Miss Minchin doesn't appreciate such creativity, though, and when Sara's father is reported dead, and apparently broke, she banishes her to the attic with Becky, a young black servant.

A bit of a classic from Harry Potter director, Alfonso Cuarón

The film was originally made in 1917 with Mary Pickford and again in 1939 starring Shirley Temple, but Mexican director Alfonso Cuarón (who took the helm of the *Harry Potter* series for the third movie), has made the fable appealing to modern kids and adults. He told *The New York Times*: "After twenty pages of the script, I knew I had found a film I wanted to do. The pages were vibrating in my hands." Cuarón eschews the kind of elaborate sets and OTT performances often found in children's movies to hold attention, instead trusting the story, creating a wonderfully atmospheric movie. *Variety* called it "A classic from the moment it hits the screen" – and they weren't wrong. This is perfect for any little girl who wants to be a princess and any child who has been separated from their parents for a long time will understand what is going on here.

Incidentally, the star, Liesel Matthews, who was chosen from 1000 children, was a member of the family which owns the Hyatt hotel chain. Seven years after the film was made, in one of those life-imitating-art stories which form such a large part of movie lore, she sued her father for allegedly draining $1 billion from her trust fund.

▭▭ UK, US ◉ UK, US │ U (UK) G (US)

Madeline 1998

There was always a danger that a screen adaptation of Ludwig Bemelmans's rhyming tales of Madeline the orphan and her eleven friends at Covington school would lose its simple charm. But Bemelmans's illustrations of the school and girls are very much brought to life here. Madeline (nicely played by Hatty Jones) may be the smallest of her cohorts, but she is also the bravest, equally capable of getting herself into – and out of – tricky situations. The crux of the film is the tried and tested tale of Madeline's efforts to save her beloved school. Frances McDormand is just right as Miss Clavel, who runs the orphanage and dispenses wisdom, while Nigel Hawthorne offers strong support. Ideal for girls from 5 to 9.

▭▭ UK, US ◉UK, US | U (UK) PG (US)

Never Been Kissed 1999

All the clichés are present – heartless glamour girls, nerds and randy sports stars, yet *Never Been Kissed* is a charming film. Josie (Drew Barrymore) is an undercover reporter researching a scandal at a high school. Having been a nerd first time around, she hopes to become popular, but with a wardrobe that makes Christina Aguilera look the epitome of subtle good taste, her plan goes awry until her brother (David Arquette) turns up to help. There's romance (in the form a handsome English teacher) and everyone wins in the end. It may not be the most original film, but Barrymore and Arquette make this an enjoyable way to spend 107 minutes.

▭▭ UK, US ◉UK, US | 12 (UK) PG-13 (US)

Nicholas Nickleby 2002

 Charles Dickens's third novel, *Nicholas Nickleby* was so powerful in its portrayal of sadistic Wackford Squeers, the head of Dotheboys Hall, that new laws were passed to reform private education. Adults seeking a thorough adaptation of the novel may find this modern version on the slight side, but for children, at 132 minutes, this is ample time to be immersed in Dickensian England. The performances all guard against caricature. The usually affable Jim Broadbent excels as Squeers, Christopher Plummer is suitably appalling as the hero's evil uncle, Tom Courtenay shines as the uncle's alcoholic servant and Charlie Hunnam is handsome enough in the title role. All in all, an excellent introduction to Dickens (for more on whom, see p.97) for children of 8 and above.

▭ UK, US ◉UK, US | PG (UK, US)

The Prime Of Miss Jean Brodie 1969

If all teachers were as liberated as Miss Brodie, viewing lessons in life and love more valuable than English and Maths, schools might boast better attendance records – although who knows what would happen to the grades? The film was originally set to star Vanessa Redgrave, but Maggie Smith made this role of Brodie her own, nabbing an Oscar in this adaptation of the Muriel Spark novel. Brodie looks prim and proper, but ignores her curriculum, much to the annoyance of her headmistress (Celia Johnson, whose sterling performance is often overlooked), and fluctuates between her married lover and her suitor. Brief nudity earned it a PG rating, and might give your children unrealistic ideas about the exciting lives their teachers might lead.

▭ UK, US ◉US | PG (UK, US)

Saved By The Bell 1989–92

Saved By The Bell was a kind of early-1990s *Recess* – a comedy tale of Bayside High School kids and their early teenage scrapes. It's still shown on TV in the US, and maybe not quite worthy of watching on DVD. See too many episodes on the trot and you begin to muse... is there really no limit to the number of times that loveable dweeb Screech can get smacked in the face?

▭ US ◉US | NR

School Of Rock 2003

 Parents aware of the previous works of actor Jack Black (*Orange County*), writer Mike White (*The Good Girl*) and director Richard Linklater (*Dazed And Confused*) may fear this isn't suitable for their offspring. But the three have created a

film for and about kids, largely free of sentimental guff – and with the funniest closing credits in years.

Black overplays beautifully as Dewey, a metalhead sacked from his band, due to his limelight-stealing habit of playing too many long guitar solos and then diving into the crowd, whether the audience is ready to catch him or not. Broke, he impersonates his friend to get a job as a supply teacher in fourth grade at a private school, pay the rent and get his friend's poisonous girlfriend off his back. Black's class, inevitably, enter the local Battle of the Bands contest – and his plans begin to unravel when his flatmate's girl calls the police.

This may sound like a cutesy, convoluted plot, but Black remains an impudent loudmouth throughout, sharing his hangover, his views on the establishment, and a lovingly detailed history of rock and roll and heavy metal, with his astonished charges. His manic performance is matched by the control of Joan Cusack, as the stiff, secretly scared, headmistress who comes alive only when she has a few beers too many and someone puts a Stevie Nicks record on the jukebox.

A bit like *Dead Poets Society* revisited – with heavy metal instead of poetry, and where nobody dies – this is a movie so well made that it compels you to feel good. But it's really for kids, of 8 and up (despite the US ratings).

◎UK, US | PG (UK) PG-13 (US)

To Sir, With Love 1967

Sidney Poitier is Mark, an engineer by trade who takes a teaching job in an East London school to make ends meet before he gets a "proper" job, but quickly realizes he has an aptitude for it. The plot may sound clichéd now, but this was the original "teacher in a rough school" film, around long before Michelle Pfeiffer and her class of rappers in *Dangerous Minds*. Pfeiffer's (distinctly grown-up) film is actually blander and less believable than this forty-year-old British movie. Poitier carries the credibility, but the largely British cast – including Lulu, who sings the title track, and Judy Geeson, who develops a crush on her teacher – all give strong performances.

📼 UK, US ⊚ UK, US | PG (UK) NR (US)

Tom Brown's Schooldays 1940

Director Robert Stevenson sticks close to the original narrative of Thomas Hughes's famous novel in this **1940 version**, and thus loses none of the story's drama. Freddie Bartholomew, who was second only to Shirley Temple in the child star stakes when this was made, gives one of his finest performances as East, friend and room-mate of Tom Brown (Jimmy Lydon – who took the role of bullied Tom Brown to support his alcoholic father and family of nine siblings). The **1951 remake** isn't as effective, though it has a memorably horrific roasting scene (don't ask), and John Forrest's Flashman is a monument to vicious snobbery.

📼 US | U (UK) NR (US)

The Worst Witch 1986

Originally made for TV, the adventures of Mildred and her witch academy chums had big-screen potential on its release. If you don't know them, the *Worst Witch* books, written by Jill Murphy, are best described as a version of Enid Blyton's *Mallory Towers* boarding school stories but with added witchcraft. All this was, of course, years before a certain scarred boy wizard. The movie has the added bonus of Tim Curry hamming it up as the Grand Wizard. Two TV series followed.

📼 UK, US ⊚ US | NR (UK) G (US)

Sci-fi

another planet

cience fiction can be a more effective mind-broadening device than travel. As a genre, it's full of big themes (Are we alone? Are we destroying our planet? Is reality really real?) and even bigger spectacles (think Kong batting a biplane away). And since the success of *Star Wars*, the sci-fi movie has gone mainstream, as important to the movie business as westerns were in the 1940s and 1950s. This hasn't always been for good but it does mean there's no shortage of movies which can stretch or boggle kids' minds.

As in the previous chapter, we've made no distinction here between **kids' and grown-up films** – though we've pointed up the scariness quota. And, once more, you will find some films that could be accounted sci-fi elsewhere in the book. Check the index if you can't find your movie.

Atlantis: The Last Empire 2001

Atlantis marked Walt Disney's first foray into territory normally associated with anime, the Japanese school of animation, as they gave Mike Mignola, the comic-book artist who created the underground comic character *Hellboy*, the reins to influence the visual style. Mignola brings a comic-book energy, as well as the wide-eyed, anime-style characters, to the film. Set in 1914, a crew of adventurers led by nerdy linguist Milo Thatch set off to find the legendary lost continent. This motley crew are voiced by a stellar vocal cast: John Mahoney is the billionaire assembling a team to find the lost continent, Michael J. Fox is the voice of his linguist, and the diving team is led by a rough and ready character whose dialogue is delivered by James Garner. And Atlantis is ruled by a king, whose lines are all the more effective for being rendered by Leonard Nimoy. It is, as critic Roger Ebert says, "rousing in an old pulp science-fiction kind of way" but it's let down by poor plotting.

The sequel, **Atlantis: Milo's Return** (2003) is strictly last-movie-left-in-the-video-store territory.

📼 UK, US ◉UK, US | U (UK) PG (US)

Castle In The Sky 1986

 The floating island-city of Laputa, mentioned in Jonathan Swift's *Gulliver's Travels*, is the magical inspiration at the centre of this frequently astounding movie by Hayao Miyazaki, a modern sci-fi fable with an ecological message which also manages to be genuinely enthralling. It has superficial similarities with *Atlantis* (above) — at least in the sense that you feel the Disney-*Atlantis* crew had seen *Castle in the Sky*, were in awe of it, and not at all clear how they could do something similar.

The story begins as a boy, Pazu, watches a young girl called Sheeta fall out of the sky — and is saved from a very messy end by the magic pendant she's wearing. The pendant is the key to finding the floating island-city of Laputa, and a clue to Sheeta's real identity, so boy and girl are soon pursued by ruthless bureaucrats, and by apparently villainous, but essentially good-hearted, air-pirates.

The pirates are wonderfully observed, especially their chuckling old woman leader, and the adventure never loses its grip – this is on a par with *Indiana Jones* as a rollercoaster ride. There are passages, too, notably when Sheeta and Pazu finally land on the island-city to find an eerie, ruined paradise, and be confronted by a mysterious robot, that are as imaginatively outstanding as anything Miyazaki has ever filmed. The director works his trademark obsessions, both obvious (a fascination with flight) and less obtrusive (a penchant for having pigs in his movies), into this enchanting tale which, at times, leaves the viewer with an almost childish sense of wonder.

Most of *Castle in the Sky* is suitable for kids of any age but be aware that in the last half an hour, hundreds of soldiers literally fall to their deaths, as the villain runs amok.

▣ UK, US ◉ UK, US | PG (UK) NR (US)

The Black Hole 1979

The Black Hole doesn't quite live up to the simple genius of its tag line: "A journey that begins where everything ends." But this Disney film isn't bad – the special effects work and Maximilian Schell does well as the scientist who really is going to do what Captain Kirk promised and boldly go where none has gone before – into a black hole. It's a great idea, decently made, but lacks the kind of street smarts Disney has brought to recent hits.

▣ UK, US ◉ US, UK | PG (UK, US)

Close Encounters Of The Third Kind 1977

At 132 minutes – and with a slow, almost frustrating, start – Steven Spielberg's haunting sci-fi movie may tax your kids' patience. But it's worth persevering. Richard Dreyfuss, never far from mania as an actor, smashes up the house and scares his own kids as his character's obsession with the spacecraft he saw – and is given a dose of sunburn by – deepens. You may decide this is only for kids of 8 and over, but it is a truly haunting, imaginative experience.

Kids may also have fun looking out for references to other blockbuster movies like *Star Wars* (especially three R2D2 sightings) and *Jaws*. The movie has a similar power to the great sci-fi classics of the 1950s, such as *The Day The Earth Stood Still*. Spielberg, who was interested in UFOs as a phenomenon, treats the subject with serious devotion, not playing it for kitsch laughs. And the result is genuinely powerful – an intelligent alternative to the swashbuckling sci-fi flicks which Hollywood began to churn out by the bucket-load in the mid-1970s.

📼 UK, US ◉UK, US | PG (UK, US)

The Creature From The Black Lagoon 1954

Beauty and the beast with gills – yep, this time the beast is half-man, half-fish and he's hiding in the Amazon jungle, worrying about his appearance and his unsatisfactory social skills. Still, it isn't long before the fish is fondling Julie Adams's feet underwater... but then the silly girl had gone for a dip in the notorious Black Lagoon, from which no human had returned alive, in her bathing suit. Fifty years on, the film remains intriguing and, at 80 minutes, it doesn't hang around long enough to bore.

📼 UK, US ◉US, UK | PG (UK) G (US)

The Day The Earth Stood Still 1951

Made by Robert Wise, who later directed *The Sound Of Music*, this 1951 sci-fi classic is a carefully paced, thoughtful, largely gore-free parable about an alien who comes to earth to tell humanity to stop warring. In spirit, this anticipates *Close Encounters* – even though it was made 25 years before Spielberg's epic.

📼 UK, US ◉UK, US | U (UK) G (US)

Dr Who And The Daleks 1965

Serious aficionados of this long-running British sci-fi TV series will want to buy the programmes on video/DVD but Peter Cushing isn't bad in this movie venture as the time lord constantly at war with what the *Radio Times* described as "mobile nobbly tin cans forever shrieking 'Exterminate!'" The attempt to inject some humour doesn't really work but, taken on its own merits, this is a reasonably enjoyable film.

📼 UK, US ◉ US, UK | U (UK) NR (US)

E.T. – The Extra Terrestrial 1982

MUST SEE! With a face compiled from poet Carl Sandburg, a pug dog and Albert Einstein, and a voice supplied by Steven Spielberg, Pat Welsh and Debra Winger, E.T. was destined to be extraordinary. He is also rumoured in conspiracy circles to be one of the many disguised Christ characters in modern movies (well his mum is called Mary). Talk of the Christ motif may be, in part, a tribute to the movie's emotional depth. A film in which a cute alien botanist becomes friends with a 10-year-old boy and then breaks his heart by having to leave for his own planet could have turned out as mushy and as corny as that summary makes it sound. But it doesn't. Spielberg's decision to shoot the story in the order it unfolds probably helped the child actors – and the emotions on display in the final scene are all too real. This is an emotionally uplifting movie which is full of pain: the pain of the boy Elliot at the separation of his parents and of E.T.'s own very real pain.

E.T., in some ways, spins off another great resonant children's movie, *The Wizard Of Oz*. Instead of Dorothy being accidentally stranded in the alien weirdness of Oz, we have an alien accidentally stranded in a part of America every bit as humdrum as Dorothy's Kansas. And it, in turn, has had huge influence on the popular movies of the past twenty years. Peter Bradshaw, in *The Guardian*, made the case eloquently that "without *E.T.* there would be no *Toy Stories*, without *E.T.* there would be no *X Files*, without *E.T.* there would be no *Harry Potter*. In the strange and beautiful love story of *E.T.* lies the genesis of Douglas Coupland's vision of *Generation X*: people in the West growing up in a secular, affectless society, yearning to feel rapture, and looking for love in the ruins of faith."

For many critics, *E.T.* is simply the greatest children's movie of all time and children of all ages can get something out of this.

📼 UK, US ◉ US, UK | U (UK) PG (US)

E.T. - he really, really, had to go home

Forbidden Planet 1956

"Another one of them new worlds. No beer, no women, no pool par-
lours. Nothin' to do but throw rocks at tin cans, and we gotta bring our
own tin cans." An unusually jaundiced view of space exploration –
from Cookie, a character in this sci-fi movie loosely inspired by
Shakespeare's *The Tempest* – given that this was made in the 1950s. But
then *Forbidden Planet* is an unusual film, both for its time and even
when you watch it today.

Walter Pidgeon is Dr Morbius, trying to protect his discoveries and
his daughter from the world, and especially from the starship crew
investigating the planet (led, amusingly in hindsight, by Leslie Nielsen,
aka Frank Drebin). Pidgeon and Nielsen – playing straight – don't
quite have the star power to ignite this, so it feels like a very fine B-
movie. In fact, the real stars are Robbie the Robot, who grabs most of

the comic one-liners, and the weird, electronically generated score. The fact that the monster is called Id is final proof that we're in very strange territory here. Younger kids will love the robot; but then most kids will enjoy this genuinely cultish movie.

📼 UK, US ◎ US, UK | U (UK) G (US)

Godzilla 1998

"We need bigger guns", "To him you're just a pair of breasts that talk", and "If he's the first of his kind, how can he be pregnant?" Lines that tell you all you need to know about Roland Emmerich's *Godzilla*. You might be compelled to watch it – pester power and all that – but you'll find a peculiarly charmless affair; *Jurassic Park* with one dinosaur and no characters you feel anything but indifference towards. Then again, you might love it. This was, after all, created as a blockbuster movie, to watch with a bucket of popcorn and go "Wow!" every time the giant radio-active lizard steps up for a bit of rampage in New York.

And if somehow a giant radioactive lizard on the rampage rings your bell, then you may well want to explore the original **Godzilla, King of the Monsters** (1954), a Japanese movie, re-cut for the US, in which the beast sets about trashing Tokyo. If you get hooked, there are many, many sequels.

1998 VERSION 📼 UK, US ◎ US, UK | PG (UK) PG-13 (US)
1954 ORIGINAL 📼 US ◎ US | NR

The Incredible Shrinking Man 1957

Grant Williams gets lost in mist, finds some glitter on his chest, suddenly starts losing height and weight. Not surprisingly, he becomes embittered and runs away, finding brief solace with a sideshow midget, Clarice, before returning to live in a doll's house – which he has to flee after an attack by a cat. Meanwhile his wife and brother assume he is dead. There aren't too many laughs in this doomy sci-fi movie, made when paranoia about radiation was at its height, but it's compelling and short (81 minutes) and should entertain kids of 7 and over.

📼 UK, US ◎ US | PG (UK) NR (US)

Invaders From Mars 1953

Jimmy Hunt is a boy who hears noises in the night. He sees a space-ship land, watches his dad (Leif Erickson) go out to investigate and soon notices that his parents have radios in the back of the necks. With the aid of a psychologist, an astronomer and an army colonel, he fore-stalls a Martian invasion. He wakes up... obviously it's all been a dream. But then he hears the same noise he heard at the very start of the movie. This is an unusual, atmospheric film which owes part of its unique look to the fact that the sets were made for a 3D movie – but the studio couldn't find a camera. A minor classic which should suit kids of 7 and over.

📼 UK, US ◉ US, UK | PG (UK) NR (US)

Invasion Of The Body Snatchers 1955

Kevin McCarthy is the small-town doctor whose patients keep telling him their loved ones are behaving strangely. It turns out they are repli-cants, created by clever pods from outer space. This is a quiet chiller, not too gory, but not, given its very plausibility, to be watched by kids who worry about things going bump in the night – 8s and over should be OK.

📼 UK, US ◉ US, UK | PG (UK) NR (US)

The Iron Giant 1999

Taken from the poet Ted Hughes's story, this animated fea-ture works on many levels at once. It's a tale about a boy trying to hide an alien from his mum (not easy as the alien in question is a tall iron giant). It's a Cold War parable – the boy tells the giant he doesn't have to be a weapon: "You are what you choose to be." It's a fantasy about a paranoid powerful govern-ment which seeks to destroy the alien, of a kind *The X-Files* creator Chris Carter might have been proud of. And it's a gentle, affection-ate tribute to many of the greats of the animation business. The newspaper headline "Disaster Seen As Catastrophe Looms" scanned by one character is the same as that read by Jim Dear in *Lady And*

The Tramp and by Jiminy Cricket in *Fun And Fancy Free*. The two train men, Frank and Ollie, interviewed by the government agent, are caricatures of the great Disney animators Frank Thomas and Ollie Johnston.

But for all the in-jokes, and the stuff for grown-ups to spot – such as the cartoon version of the US government commercial from the 1950s advising kids to shelter from H-bombs by hiding under their desks – *The Iron Giant* is also a tense, involving and extremely well-animated story. Any child of 5 and over will enjoy this, initially as a great romp and, later, picking up on the questions the movie raises.

📼 UK, US ⊚ US, UK | U (UK) PG (US)

Journey To the Center Of the Earth 1959

Recently knighted professor James Mason is given a small piece of rock which leads him to a long-lost route to the earth's core. But instead of adding it to the rockery in his garden, like any ordinary mortal, he decides to trace the route, accompanied by bland pop idol (Pat Boone) and the widow of a rival named – by the scriptwriter (not Jules Verne) – after the city of Gothenburg. They confront giant lizards, encounter giant mushrooms and discover an underground ocean, but director Henry Levin keeps this light-hearted, and not too scary. Still, it's a reasonably faithful Verne adaptation and whiles away a couple of pleasurable hours.

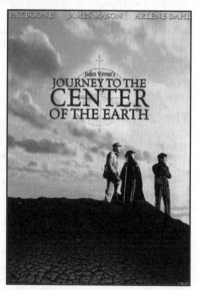

📼 UK, US ⊚ US, UK | U (UK) G (US)

King Kong 1933

 You could argue that this monster movie has been more influential in the development of the modern movie business than more intellectually celebrated masterpieces like *Citizen Kane*. It certainly pointed the way to movies defined by special effects, cataclysmic destruction and the kind of non-stop shocks you normally have to go on a rollercoaster to guarantee. And not all those movies are so bad. This original *King Kong* was the film playing in Steven Spielberg's memory when he shot *Jurassic Park*.

King Kong, however, has a simple aim – to scare. Directors Merian C. Cooper and Ernest B. Shoedsack may have done other things – as the surfeit of theories about the real Marxist/political/Freudian/religious meaning of the movie shows. But Cooper was clear: "I want Kong to be the fiercest, most brutal, monstrous damned thing that has ever been seen." Kong, to give the monster his due, doesn't start like that – he's reasonably content on his tropical island (apart from a few fights with some other beasts, including a T. Rex) until a showman lures him with a beautiful blonde and drags him to "civilisation" where he becomes a freak turn on Broadway. Breaking free, he derails subway cars, climbs the Empire State building, swats a biplane with his hand and cares for Fay Wray. He does remove a few of her clothes but only out of curiosity – a scene of him tickling her and sniffing his fingers was cut, as was a scene where some of his victims fell to their deaths in the mouths of giant spiders.

The movie was, *Variety* concluded, "a long screaming session for Wray, too much for any audience". They were wrong: it raked in $90,000 in its first weekend, the biggest ever opening, and in a recession. Today, some of the effects have dated and the native sacrifice scene at the start is a bit risible. But kids of 9 and over should enjoy.

UK, US ◎ US, UK | PG (UK) NR (US)

Lilo & Stitch 2002

Lilo & Stitch is a groovy, fast-moving, animated tale in which the broken home of Lilo and her big nagging sister Nani gets even more broken up when an alien called Stitch, invented to attack and destroy, drops in unexpectedly. Alas, he is being chased by the aliens who created him and their efforts further complicate Nani's attempts to placate scary social worker Cobra Bubbles who is threatening to put Lilo in a home. All turns out well in the end, even for Stitch who turns out to be a lonely, confused kid in alien form.

There are plenty of laugh-out-loud moments, some neat songs (Lilo is an Elvis fan) and the kind of warm glow that you get from Disney classics like *Dumbo* but not from *Treasure Planet*. It is sci-fi of a kind, and seems to appeal to kids from 4 upwards.

📼 UK, US ⊚ US, UK | U (UK) PG (US)

Mars Attacks! 1996

This is a demented slapstick movie from Tim Burton in which ruthless Martians cause havoc only to be repulsed by the yodelling of Slim Whitman. Plenty of starry cameos, some cartoon violence (notably when Jack Nicholson's president comes to grief), and a nice tribute to Ray Harryhausen, the special effects genius.

📼 UK, US ⊚ UK, US | 12 (UK) PG-13 (US)

Mars Attacks! It really is that kind of a movie

Men In Black 1997

The *Men In Black* parts were originally offered to David Schwimmer (Ross from *Friends*) and Clint Eastwood. Luckily, both turned it down, and Will Smith and Tommy Lee Jones stepped into their perfect roles, as hip, wisecracking, black-suited agents employed to defend earth from aliens. There are great special effects, some unusual aliens, some truly unpleasant stunts and director Barry Sonnenfeld paces the laughs and the thrills brilliantly. It doesn't repay repeated viewing, though, and the sequel **Men In Black II** is only for diehards. Kids of 6 and over should enjoy this.

📼 UK, US ◎ US, UK | PG (UK) PG-13 (US)

Planet Of The Apes 1968

Apparently, during breaks in the filming of this sci-fi epic, the "apes" almost always socialised with "apes" wearing the same species of suit. Even on film sets, gorillas and orang-utans aren't bosom buddies. Nothing quite that surprising happens in the movie of Pierre Boulle's novel but this film still stands up, even after several sequels, a long-running TV series and a questionable Tim Burton remake. Charlton Heston is the space traveller who, with his crew, ends up crash-landing into a planet ruled by apes. He is tortured and tried (to see if he should be castrated or lobotomised – the film never confronts the question of which one's worse) before escaping with his newly acquired, beautiful, silent girlfriend.

The movie works as an entertainment, thanks to the eccentric score by Jerry Goldsmith (allegedly written while Jerry was wearing a goril-la suit), a strong story and nicely contrasting performances from chest-beating Heston and subtle simians Kim Hunter and Roddy McDowall. *Planet Of The Apes* also works as an allegory of whatever you want to believe it's an allegory for – race, class, power, or even animal rights. There is some violence but this film should be fun for kids of 7 and up.

📼 UK, US ◎ US, UK | PG (UK) G (US)

Robinson Crusoe On Mars 1964

The title says it all really. Paul Mantee is stranded on the red planet, has to fend for himself and bond with an alien he rescues from a slave ship.

An intelligent pulp sci-fi movie, more about relationships, with added special effects, which didn't do well enough at the box office to green light the pre-planned sequel, *Robinson Crusoe In the Invisible Galaxy*.

📼 UK | NR (UK, US)

Short Circuit 1986

Roger Ebert felt that the robot, Number 5, managed to rise above his material in this sci-fi-spoof about a government robot that goes AWOL, is adopted by pet-loving Ally Sheedy, but must be reclaimed by his creator Steve Guttenberg who, inevitably, falls in love with Sheedy even though she does make her living driving an ice-cream truck. There's some swearing (hence the PGs) but director John Badham keeps this bubbling along nicely.

📼 UK, US ◉ US | PG (UK, US)

Star Kid 1998

Bullied, ignored, Joseph Mazzello isn't having much luck with girls until he finds a cyborg's intelligent suit. His struggles to control the suit provide some fine comedy, and his new powers lead to the kind of retributive justice many kids in Joe's position would dearly love to dish out. There's some violence, and strong language, but this is essentially an appealing movie about a boy who lives his life in the comic books.

📼 UK, US ◉ US, UK | PG (UK, US)

Star Trek: The Wrath Of Khan 1982

Everyone has their own *Star Trek* favourite, often determined by how old they are. But this movie has some of the strengths of the original seminal TV series without which there would have been no *Next Generation*, *Deep Space Nine* or *Voyager*. The adventures of the *USS Enterprise* and crew had got off to an iffy big screen start with *Star Trek: The Motion Picture*, so unsatisfactory it was dubbed *Star Trek: The Slow Motion Picture*. To ensure this feature worked, the producers drafted in one of the TV series' strongest villains, Khan (Ricardo Montalban), who chases Kirk across the galaxies. With a subplot about Kirk facing his own immortality – and a screenplay which draws on *Moby Dick*, *Paradise Lost* and *King Lear* – this is one *Star Trek* movie which should appeal to any sci-fi buff. It's quite long – 113 minutes – but director Nicholas Meyer keeps it flowing so kids of 8 and over shouldn't lose patience.

▭ UK, US ◉US, UK | PG (UK, US)

Star Wars 1977–2005

 A long long time ago in a galaxy far away… Life before *Star Wars* seems so distant it could have been another time or another universe. For good and ill, *Star Wars* changed movies, and ushered in an age where special effects-driven blockbusters were the movies the film industry counted on.

Watched again, the first film in the series, **Star Wars** (1977), which perversely was actually **Episode IV: A New Hope**, seems too modest to have started a revolution. It is essentially a goodies and baddies western in space, or Lucas's take on Kurosawa's samurai movies, trimmed out nicely with some mythology and filled out with the kind of ensemble cast of virtuous main heroes and comic supporting characters you used to find in classic Walt Disney movies. The effects in the first film hold up, partly because they're as much about the past as the future. Harrison Ford's turret had a gun on it just about suited for shooting World War II planes, but far too slow to be effective at the kind of speeds he would travel through space. Yet there are some fine scenes – the alien drunks – and some nice touches, such as a chess game played with living creatures, long before *Harry Potter*. Lucas makes this work and performs similar feats on the next two movies, the slick **Episode V: The Empire Strikes Back** (1980), where the sinister Darth Vader seems ominously well poised, and **Episode VI: Return Of The Jedi** (1983).

The fourth movie – **Episode I: The Phantom Menace** (1999) – matched the first three, boasting sumptuous digital special effects, and brought in more star power with Liam Neeson and Ewan McGregor. The downside was Jar Jar Binks, a computer-generated character who spoke a barely comprehensible patois and was obviously supposed to be cute. This was followed by **Episode II: Attack Of The Clones** (2002), whose final gladiator-style scenes almost rescued the movie, after an interminable and meaningless romance between Padmé and Anakin.

Which brings us to the present, or, rather, takes us back to **Episode III** – the missing chapter in *Star Wars*' peculiar emergence, due to screen in 2005, and in which, hear ye, all who listen, Anakin at last becomes Darth Vader.

Some films in the series have been unavailable in recent years, but it looks like they will all be back, at least on DVD, by 2005.

[▭▭] UK, US ⊚UK, US | PG (UK, US)

The Time Machine 1960

Special effects maestro George Pal strips down H.G.Wells's novel to the basics with Rod Taylor as Wells, travelling into the year 802,701, where he finds damsel in distress Yvette Mimieux being victimized by dudes in shaggy blond manes who turn out to be Worlocks. Enjoyably easy entertainment in a movie whose budget necessitated Pal to use oatmeal to represent volcanic lava.

[▭▭] UK, US ⊚UK, US | PG (UK) G (US)

Titan A.E. 2000

This slam-bam animated space opera from Don Bluth may just be a better movie than *The Phantom Menace* and is certainly more thrilling than *Attack Of The Clones*. There are awe-inspiring moments here – and awe is inspired, not by effects, but by the realization of a vivid imagination. Matt Damon voices the space bum who has to find a spacecraft to save humanity. Some of the dialogue jars (one especially irritating sequence being: "I'm out!"; "Let's do this!"; "It's been fun!"; and "Who's your daddy?") but, overall, as another famous galaxy-trotting captain might say, mission accomplished.

[▭▭] UK, US ⊚UK, US | PG (UK, US)

The War Of The Worlds 1953

Orson Welles's notorious 1938 radio version of H.G.Wells's novel created real panic in America. In this movie, the panic is in the eyes of the extras as civilization collapses around them. Director Byron Haskin keeps a tight grip for 81 minutes – although there are some unintentionally comic moments. Best suited to kids of 7 and over.

[cassette] UK, US ◎ UK, US │ PG (UK) G (US)

Sport

a league of their own

There's nothing like a well-made sports movie to fuel a child's fantasy life. But not every sport, it seems, makes for great movies. Baseball has an honourable tradition, perhaps because it is easy to look authentic. American football and (real) football are virtually absent from dispatches, though the latter is possibly on the rise, with the success of *Bend It Like Beckham*. Basketball, too, is on the up. But whatever the sport, the right movie – be it *Space Jam* or *National Velvet* – can deliver an hour and a half of unpretentious fun.

Air Bud 1997

He sits. He stays. He shoots. He scores. Even the flint-hearted editors of *Halliwell's Film Guide* call this Disney production "an enjoyable piece of whimsy that should appeal to the young". After his dad dies, Josh and his mother move to a new town where the boy's attempts to fit in are hampered by his lack of basketball savvy. Enter Buddy, a dog who has (according to his owner) shot and scored with a regulation-sized basketball 22,000 times. You can pretty much guess the rest. There's some strong language but hopefully that won't put you off this Lassie for the 1990s. The **sequels** – four of them, in which Bud tires of basketball and turns to American football, football and baseball – are lame variations on the same theme. The PG tags are due to (pretty damn mild) language.

📼 UK, US ⊚ UK, US | PG (UK, US)

The Bad News Bears 1976

Director Michael Ritchie took two of movieland's oldest clichés – a baseball team of misfits trying to make the grade and a boozy cynical veteran coach (played by Walter Matthau) – and made a marvel out of them. Tatum O'Neal, as the pitcher who's waiting for her bra almost as anxiously as Matthau is anticipating his next beer, is easier to watch than her dad Ryan ever was. Genuinely funny, appealing to kids aged 6 and over (though there is a fair bit of cursing and some racial slurs), this deserves to be better known. Just shun the **sequels**.

📼 US ⊚ UK, US | PG (UK, US)

Bend It Like Beckham 2002

Who would have expected a British Asian comedy about football (the soccer kind) to have crossed over to international success in the US? But maybe that just shows how international a language sport can be, at least when it's presented as a comedy, can-do movie. And the story is perhaps more American than British: Jess (Parminder Nagra), an Indian girl born in the UK,

"A Winner! Hugely Enjoyable!"
— Leah Rozen, PEOPLE

wants to emulate David Beckham and become a football star. Although forbidden by her traditional family, she secretly joins a girls' team, helped by her football-mad British friend, Jules (Keira Knightley), is coached up, and... well, you don't want to spoil the end. The performances are perfectly pitched, even on the field of play, under the direction of Gurinder Chadha (*Bhaji on the Beach*, *What's Cooking?*), and the movie deals lightly with serious issues of nationality, feminism and aspiration. The 12/PG-13 ratings are presumably down to talk of sexual issues ("Jess is not Lebanese...").

US UK, US | 12 (UK) PG-13 (US)

Breaking Away 1979

This was a real sleeper: a low-budget movie made with what seemed a less than stellar cast and by a director, Peter Yates, who had fallen out of fashion after the success of *Bullitt*. The plot has four unemployed teenagers channel their resentments by entering a 500-mile bike race against the preppy, snobbish, college students. Dennis Quaid is the most effective of the four as Dave, who admires all things Italian, especially the food and the cycling. His relationship with his dad (Paul Dooley) as it moves from incomprehension to respect is one of the movie's real pleasures. The sport is incidental, and a bit clichéd even by the genre's standards: this is really just a good movie about growing up. There's talk about sex, but none onscreen, some swearing, and a boy appears to lock himself in a fridge underwater, but there's nothing here that should prevent kids from 8 or 9 watching – and enjoying.

📼 US ◉UK, US | PG (UK, US)

Cool Runnings 1993

Don't be fooled: this may be a film about that unlikeliest of sporting topics, a Jamaican bobsleigh team, but it is essentially a stereotypical feel-good sports movie. And it is very well done – thanks in part to the writing of Michael Ritchie (who helmed skiing movie *Downhill Racer* and *The Bad News Bears*). A sweet, well-made comedy with John Candy excelling as the coach with a point to prove. There's some swearing but nothing very offensive, and the premise is unusual enough to grab the attention of kids aged 7 and over.

📼 UK, US ◉UK, US | PG (UK, US)

The Cup 1999

The first commercial movie made in Bhutan, this is a well-told, true-life tale of Tibetan monks' obsession with football in general – and the 1998 World Cup final in particular. Twelve-year-old student monk Orgyen wants to watch the World Cup final because it's between France and Brazil "and France supports the cause of Tibet". From this simple premise, writer-director-lama Khyentse Norbu has fashioned a satisfying film which offers real insight into the lives of the young monks and meets western audiences' expectations of timing and character development. Some critics felt the comedy was too cute but kids, of 6 and over, won't mind.

📼 UK, US | PG (UK) G (US)

Cup Fever 1965

British supporting actor Norman Rossington may only play the driver in this Saturday morning matinee movie but that makes him the only actor to have co-starred with the Beatles, Elvis and Sir Matt Busby, the Manchester United boss. Sir Matt is on hand here to help the kids of Barton United – and they need help, coached, as they are, by Bernard

Cribbins, who was to British children's TV in the 1960s and 1970s what Bob Dylan was to folk music in the 1960s. Susan George makes her screen debut in a career which eventually propelled her onto the arm of Prince Charles. Good, clean, innocent fun for kids from 4 upwards.

◉ UK | NR

Escape To Victory (aka Victory) 1981

Made in the twilight of John Huston's career, this film has all the usual absurdities of a standard prisoner-of-war movie – and all the kind of clichés and incongruities we have come to expect when Hollywood does soccer. It is a bit of a hoot, though: a wartime tale of English POWs (with Pele and Sly Stallone guesting) defying the Nazis. Footie fans will enjoy pointing out to kids the great Pele and Bobby Moore – and chuckling over Stallone's goalkeeping.

▱ UK, US ◉ UK, US | PG (UK, US)

Evel Knievel 1971

The possessor of America's most heroic tan, George Hamilton, plays the ultimate American hero, a man who was paid millions to jump over 19 buses on his motorbike. Obviously, public transportation was in a much better state in the 1970s. The odd bit of nurse-groping apart, there's not much to object to here. Any kid old enough to go wow at the sight of Knievel in full flight should find this amusing.

▱ US ◉ UK, US | NR (UK) PG (US)

Grand Prix 1966

Although John Frankenheimer (who helmed *The Manchurian Candidate*) is directing, this suffers from the same flaw as almost every other motor-racing movie: when it's not on the track, cast and crew seem to lose track of what they're doing. The race sequences stand the test of time and nothing that's come along since has surpassed this. But at 175 minutes, it's probably one for the older kids.

▱ US ◉ US | PG (UK) NR (US)

Tom Hanks and Geena Davis take Madonna out to the ball game

A League Of Their Own 1992

Alcoholic baseball coach (Tom Hanks) is hired to help a women's base-ball team: a nice premise, but this is not brilliantly made (by director Penny Marshall) and at 122 minutes, overlong. That said, the movie is saved by the performances – Hanks (who provides most of the laughs), Geena Davis, Rosie O'Donnell and Madonna – and by its charm. Madonna's presence may be enough to hook kids aged 6 and over.

📼 UK, US ◎ UK, US | PG (UK, US)

National Velvet 1944

This was probably the last movie starring Liz Taylor in which the director – Clarence Brown – fretted that the star's breasts weren't big enough. Odd really, given that Taylor was 12 when she starred as Velvet, the girl who races her horse in the Grand National. Brown, who also made *The Yearling*, another touching film about the bond between child and animal, keeps this in soft focus,

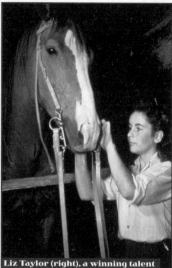

Liz Taylor (right), a winning talent

allowing Taylor and her co-star Mickey Rooney to charm the audience into submission. Even grown-ups have found themselves strangely moved by the manipulative, yet compelling, finale. Suitable for "kids of all ages", although boys nearing the age of 10 might like to pass.

A kind of sequel, **International Velvet** (1976), starring Tatum O' Neal, directed by Bryan Forbes chokes on its own syrup.

📼 US ◉ UK, US | U (UK) G (US)

The Natural 1984

Robert Redford won a baseball scholarship as a teenager ("it's just a terribly tiresome round of practice and steaks") and, though he flunked, that experience may account for his wonderfully wistful performance as Roy Hobbs, the slugger trying to break into the game at an age when most players retire. Corny, predictable, adorned with the trappings of Arthurian legend by director Barry Levinson, this still packs a powerful emotional punch – one that kids aged 7 and over, and not unduly troubled by holes in the plot, will appreciate. It's not for fans of the original novel by Bernard Malamud, which had a dark, deflating ending. Here, the good guys finally win out.

📼 UK, US ◉ UK, US | PG (UK, US)

The Rookie 2002

Dennis Quaid carries this movie which, as Roger Ebert has pointed out, relies on two of the oldest formulas in sports movies: the little team that makes it and the old-timer who realises his youthful dream. This is based on a true story about a high school baseball coach who gets a second chance to play in the big leagues, but even the true story seems to be based on old Hollywood movies about the romance of baseball. You could almost see this as a companion movie to *The Natural*. It is so skilfully crafted that, as Ebert says, you want to hug it. Rachel Griffiths, from the seminal TV series *Six Feet Under*, does well in the clichéd role of Quaid's supportive wife and Quaid himself turns in a poignant performance. But at 122 minutes, it's just a bit too long.

📼 UK, US ◎UK, US | U (UK) G (US)

Searching For Bobby Fischer 1993

 Probably the finest, most thoughtful, movie ever made about chess. Films about budding geniuses aren't always works of genius themselves. But this insightful study, of a prodigy called Josh who wants to be the next Bobby Fischer, is absorbing, and raises some nice issues about the problems such a prodigy faces coping with such an unusual talent. For once, the "based on a true story" rings true: sportswriter Fred Waitzkin wrote the book about his son Josh's life as a chess prodigy that this film sprang from, and Josh later became America's junior chess champion.

With its boy hero (Max Pomeranc who plays Josh was a decent chess player), and the sensitivity with which the story is told. this is probably accessible to kids of 9 and over and even to kids, and grown-ups, who know nothing about chess. *Rolling Stone* was especially impressed with Pomeranc's performance – "a finely tuned performance without child-actor hamming" – but director Steve Zaillian deserves much of the credit for taking the right risks to tell this story.

📼 US ◎UK, US | PG (UK, US)

Space Jam 1996

The premise for this movie sounds like one of those spoof synopses at the start of Robert Altman's *The Player*: take Michael Jordan, America's biggest sporting legend since Ali, throw him into a movie with Warner's looniest tunes and make sure the gags and the action never lag. But it works: this is fast, painless, quite amusing, and even kids who aren't old enough to thrill to footage of Jordan in action will happily while away 87 minutes.

The unbilled guest appearance by Bill Murray is almost worth the price of admission. Kids from 4 to 9 will probably love it.

▭▬ UK, US ◉UK, US | U (UK) PG (US)

• •

MORE GROWN-UP SPORTS MOVIES

Chariots Of Fire 1981

A Jew and a Scotsman run for Britain in the 1924 Olympics. Boiled down to basics, this movie doesn't sound like much. But it tugs at the heartstrings so subtly and is so well made, it's easy to forget and forgive even the Vangelis theme. The cast (Nigel Havers, Nigel Davenport, John Gielgud, Ruby Wax) and craft (direction by Hugh Hudson) make this feel like a superior BBC serial. Kids under 7 or 8, though, may not stay the distance (two full hours).

▭▬UK, US ◉UK, US | U (UK) PG (US)

Field Of Dreams 1989

Your kids might not follow every nuance of the plot but they may still get hooked on Kevin Costner's quest. There's something about his character's quixotic dream of building a baseball pitch in his backyard which strikes a chord with children. The reviewer on the Internet Movie Database sums it up succinctly: "It's American. It's corny (pun intended, I'm sorry). It's laughable... but naively beautiful."

▭▬UK, US ◉UK, US | PG (UK, US)

Hoop Dreams 1994

There are two obvious problems with this documentary: one, it's long (170 minutes), and two, it does swear a bit. But this stirring tale of two teenagers trying to escape the slums by playing basketball is worth the effort – and could be an uplifting experience for older boys.

▭▬UK, US ◉US | 15 (UK) PG-13 (US)

Hoosiers 1986

Gene Hackman as an ageing coach – and a drunk – transforms a high school basketball team. Transcends the clichés by all-round excellence.

▭▬UK, US ◉UK, US |

Rocky 1976

Uplifting rags-to-riches boxing tale with Sylvester Stallone as the boxer/actor who had one unlikely shot at stardom. Sly also wrote the Oscar-nominated script in which he challenges mouthy almighty world champion Apollo Creed (Carl Weathers). The movie's against-all-odds story won an against-the-odds best picture Oscar in 1976, the year of *Taxi Driver*. There's some violence, as you might expect, swearing (often mumbled) and some sexual references. The **Rocky sequels** should have been thrown out of the ring.

▭▬UK, US ◉UK, US | PG (UK, US)

18

Superheroes

beyond good and evil

Superhero comics first flourished in the 1930s when the world was faced with Hitler and Mussolini: supervillains demand superheroes. So the curent craze for superhero movies – **Spider-Man**, **X-Men**, even a spoof superhero movie such as **The Incredibles** – may be as much a reflection of the uncertainty of our times as Hollywood milking a profitable formula. Mind you, with **X-Men 2** selling over $400 million in cinema tickets, and *Spider-Man* ranking 11th top box-office movie of all time, profit might have something to do with it.

It took a while for Hollywood to work out the effects to make a really convincing superhero movie, but once Richard

Donner showed it could be done, with **Superman** (1978), there was no holding back. The world was ready to be saved and the big event movie was upon us.

So, too, were DVDs. More than any other kind of movie, superhero films are worth buying on **DVD** – which often come with very cool extras.

The Adventures Of Buckaroo Banzai Across The Eighth Dimension 1984

Nobody plays a neurosurgeon rockstar samurai warrior superhero like Peter Weller. As *The Onion* noted, "He retains his cool and sincerity whether he's driving a jet car through a mountain, playing a trumpet or wooing a suicidal spitfire who turns out to be the long-lost twin sister of his dead wife." That sentence captures the quirkiness of this sci-fi comedy in which our hero accidentally opens a hole in time and has to close it. It also explains why, after flopping at the cinemas, *Buckaroo Banzai* has acquired a cult following on video and DVD. Kids of 7 and over might well sign up for membership, so long as they don't worry too much about coherent stories.

📼 US ◉UK, US | PG (UK, US)

Batman 1989, Batman Returns 1992, Batman Forever 1995, Batman & Robin 1997

Batman (1989) – the first real big-money appearance for the caped crusader – was a pioneering film from Tim Burton, a brilliantly realized film noir take, inspired by artist Bob Kane. Its only real controversy was over Michael Keaton's performance in the title role. For some, notably the *Washington Post*, he was the brooding presence at the heart of the movie. For Roger Ebert – and many viewers – he is so low-key you forget to care about him. Certainly, for all of the haunting gloominess Burton brings to his Gotham City, the movie loses something whenever Jack Nicholson's Joker is off-screen. But it is a triumph, whatever you think of Keaton – dark, psychological and scary, and almost meriting its 15/PG-13 ratings. It certainly isn't pitched as a kids' movie – Burton was looking

Michael Keaton *is* the Caped Crusader

More of the Caped Crusader

Batman and Robin have inspired more blockbusters than any superhero. Their first adventures – serials shot for Columbia in the 1940s – were entertaining, at times racist, and introduced concepts from the Batcave to Batlore. But subsequent movies – live-action or animated – differ wildly in quality, approach and rating. Here's a guide to the most influential movies.

Batman 1966 Adam West and Burt Ward star in this spin-off of the spoofy, ratings-grabbing, 1960s TV series. Notable for Lorenzo Semple Jr's apparently endless supply of throwaway gags, the sincerely tongue-in-cheek performances of hero and sidekick, and for Stafford Repp, as Chief O'Hara, the police chief who never solves a crime, an outstanding example of quiet, consistent, measured stupidity. Oh, and Commissioner Gordon, for once, has a standout line: 'Penguin, Joker, Riddler... and CATWOMAN, too! The sum of the angles of that rectangle is too monstrous to contemplate!"

📼 UK, US ◉ US | U (UK) G (US)

Batman Beyond 1999 Half-decent animated movie, spun off from the acclaimed TV series, with George Takei (Sulu from *Star Trek*) among the cast of voices. Bruce Wayne has retired but a boy dons the batsuit to avenge his father's murder. Opinions vary on how effective and likeable the Batboy character, Terry McGinnis, is. Some prefer another feature-length spin-off from the same series, **Batman Beyond The Return Of the Joker**, though at 132 minutes it is a tad long. The **Batman/Superman** movie, out of the same stable, is a neat way to pass a wet Saturday morning, if not quite as intriguing as the combination of superheroes might have promised.

📼 UK, US ◉ US | NR

Batman: Mask Of the Phantasm 1993 Stylish, at times very violent, animated feature with Mark Hamill voicing the Joker. The Phantasm is a vigilante who wipes out crime bosses, his killings blamed – by cops and crims – on the caped crusader. The story, told in flashback, might confuse younger kids but has the same dark feel as the Burton films and animated TV series. A sequel, **Batman & Mr Freeze: Subzero**, was launched, direct to video, in 1998.

📼 UK, US ◉ US | PG (UK, US)

more at teenagers and college kids – though kids of 10 and over should enjoy it. The same caveats apply to Burton's **Batman Returns**, where the villains – Danny deVito's Penguin and Michelle Pfeiffer's Catwoman – have the best lines, and indeed costumes, outshining Keaton's batsuit.

With **Batman Forever**, Joel Schumacher took over from Burton and Val Kilmer from Keaton, in a lighter, funnier movie. The enemies this time are the Riddler (Jim Carrey) and Two-Face (Tommy Lee Jones). But Batman is not alone. Step forward Robin (Chris O'Donnell). It's pure bubblegum, right from the opening rubbery scene. As, to an even greater degree, is the fourth movie in the series, **Batman & Robin**, in which George Clooney gets the bat-suit – and a new Batmobile – and with O'Donnell and Alicia Silverstone (Batgirl) takes on Arnold Schwarzenegger (Mr Freeze) and Uma Thurman (Poison Ivy).

BATMAN 📼 UK, US ◉ UK, US | 15 (UK) PG-13 (US)

BATMAN RETURNS 📼 UK, US ◉ UK, US | 12 (UK) PG-13 (US)

[]

BATMAN FOREVER ▭ UK, US ◉ UK, US │ PG (UK) PG-13 (US)
BATMAN & ROBIN ▭ UK, US ◉ UK, US │ PG (UK) PG-13 (US)

Doc Savage: The Man Of Bronze 1975

"Peace will come to all who find/Doc Savage! Doc Savage!/He's a friend to all mankind, pure of heart and mind!" The rest of the film doesn't quite live up to the theme song, and fans of the original pulp-fiction hero were disappointed by this tame affair. The story, in which Doc (Ron Ely) sets out to find his dad's killer and ends up in a valley overflowing with gold, might have worked. Might just pass a wet Sunday afternoon if there's nothing else on television – but older kids will find this a bit lame.

▭ US │ PG (UK) G (US)

Flash Gordon 1980

There's some debate about whether Flash Gordon is or isn't a super-hero – he may be super (saviour of everyone!) but he can't fly, can't fire webs or turn green or burst his shirts. Maybe it's best not be overly pedantic, for this campy, outrageous retelling of the Flash Gordon story has most of the other ingredients you would expect from a superhero flick: a world in peril, a fight between good and evil, a virtuous, beauti-ful and deadly dull heroine. In truth, the spoofy script (with extra gags from Lorenzo Semple Jr, the genius who camped up the *Batman* TV series) and Queen's over-the-top theme tune are the highpoints here. The lowpoints – and there many – include Sam Jones and Melody Anderson as

hero and heroine and a football-inspired fight in Emperor Ming's throne room. But the cast is marvellously rounded out – with Max von Sydow as Flash's nemesis the Emperor Ming and Topol (as Doctor Hans Zarkov), assisted by Peter Wyngarde, Brian Blessed, Timothy Dalton and the lovely Ornella Muti – and the film doesn't take itself too seriously. There's nothing too scary, and older kids might enjoy watching the sets wobble. If this goes down well, it might be worth finding the **Buster Crabbe original** made in 1936 – it's just been reissued on DVD.

UK,US UK, US | PG (UK,US)

Hulk 2003

Ang Lee's retelling of the Marvel superhero's story divided the critics. For some, notably Roger Ebert, the movie's thoughtful, talkative tone was a welcome relief: "It is not so much about a green monster as about two wounded adult children of egomaniacs." Banner (Eric Bana) has hulkish moments because of his dad's genetic experiment and a lab accident. His friend Betty Ross (Jennifer Connelly) has a cold, military dad who is determined to destroy the Hulk. For most kids, this scene-setting – which takes up 45 minutes of the movie – is a side issue, the real question is how credible/scary is the Hulk? Even Ebert admitted, "He's convincing in close up but jerky in long shot – just like his spiritual cousin King Kong." Philip French, in *The Observer*, summed it up when he said, "Ang Lee fails to turn a comic strip into a cosmic trip." Even your kids might be puzzled that, as his body explodes, his purple jockey shorts grow with him, and aren't ripped apart like the rest of his clothes. There are some impressive action scenes but the real problem with this film isn't violence, it's boredom – grown-ups might find it more satisfying than kids will. And younger kids might well be better served by the innocuous **1970s TV series** starring Bill Bixby which has now been reissued on DVD.

UK,US UK, US | 12-A (UK), PG-13 (US)

The League Of Extraordinary Gentlemen 2003

"A disastrous debacle", "a very over-egged pudding low on thrills", and "incomprehensible action, idiotic dialogue, inexplicable motivations, causes without effects, effects without causes, and general lunacy". And those were some of the kinder reviews. Adventurer Allan Quartermain (Sean Connery) and a cast of extraordinary allies (invisible men, vampiresses, Dorian Gray, an agent called Tom Sawyer, a Captain Nemo, a chap called Jekyll with an alter ego called... you can guess the rest) try to stop a plot to trigger a new world war. The highlight? The idea of Nemo steering his submarine through the canals of Venice is hard to beat. One heap of $100 million hokum which you and your kids might enjoy poking holes in.

▭ UK,US ◉UK, US | 12 (UK) PG-13 (US)

Mighty Morphin Power Rangers 1995

"It's morphin time!" Oh not it's not, said millions of parents and quite a few broadcasters worried by the levels of violence in this children's TV show. But the kids won out, of course, and in 1995 the Power Rangers got their own blockbuster movie.

The Rangers – four athletic youngsters and a boffin – are not quite superheroes. They can't fly, they don't take potions that turn them into human-bats. But they transform, they do cool stuff like skydiving, and they get to protect the Earth from a super-villain – Ivan Ooze in this movie. To defeat Ooze, the Rangers have first to travel to a distant planet to restore their supernatural powers, lost when trying to save their leader, Zordon. And do they make it? Well, let's just say they have a fight on their hands (the stiff old Canadian broadcasting commission complained that a quarter to a third of each Rangers' episode is taken up by fighting). So this probably isn't best suited to kids under 5.

▭ UK, US ◉UK, US | NR

The Rocketeer 1991

Based on the graphic novels of Dave Stevens, this is *Indiana Jones* meets *Flash Gordon*. Bill Campbell, who won the title role over Johnny Depp, is perfect as the awkward pilot and his superhero alter-ego. Our hero is not much of a pilot at first (too preoccupied by his girlfriend who he fears is about to leave him to make it in the movies) but on discovering a rocket pack he becomes a confident go-getter called the

Rocketeer. Lucky, really, as he finds himself fighting gangsters, Nazis and a movie star (Timothy Dalton) trying to steal his girl and the pack. The good and bad guys are clearly defined, particularly the sneering Dalton, and the special-effect-laden action sequences make this worth watching. Harmless good fun.

📼 UK, US ⦿ UK, US | PG (UK, US)

Spider-Man 2002 and Spider-Man 2 2004

 After a dozen years of bitter legal battles, Peter Parker and his arachnoid alter ego finally made it to the big screen in the capable hands of director Sam Raimi. Unusually for a super-hero movie (especially one helmed by a man famous for launching the *Evil Dead* franchise), this doesn't work through gim-micks or thrills. The performances – from Tobey Maguire in the dual role, Kirsten Dunst as love interest, James Franco as Parker's friend and romantic rival, and Cliff Robertson as Parker's uncle – and the emo-tional heart of the story make this film connect. Maguire is never quite as convincing when he dons the suit, and the action sequences are OK, but not great. But, the story is so convincing that neither you, nor your kids, will probably mind. The only real minus is Willem Dafoe's one-dimensional turn as the villainous scientist/Green Goblin. And despite the ratings, prompted by some of the violent action, kids as young as 5 can enjoy these movies.

A sequel was inevitable, if only to explain why Parker reckons he can never be more than a friend to the girl he loves. But against the usual expectations, **Spider-Man 2** turned out better than the original – in fact, turned out to be the greatest modern superhero movie, bar none. Director Sam Raimi created a special effects extravaganza with a real story, soul and a fine comic sense. The idea that being a super-hero is as much a burden as a gift had been inherent in Stan Lee's hero since the very start and Raimi has Peter Parker put away his spi-der suit in a Tony Soprano-style panic attack until the super-villain-ous Dr Octopus (Alfred Molina) with his sinister mechanical arms forces him to reconsider. The first half is a little talky and kids may find Parker's soul-searching a little wearing but there are thrills aplen-ty later. Tobey Maguire is again credible in the title role, while Molina makes sure his villainy doesn't seem mechanical; but both are topped by J. K. Simmons, simply inspirational as Parker's self-serving motormouth boss.

SPIDER-MAN 📼 UK,US ◎UK, US | 12 PG (UK) PG-13 (US)

SPIDER-MAN 2 📼 ◎Forthcoming | PG (UK) PG-13 (US)

Superman 1978

A triumph. From the most convoluted screenwriting credit in recent movie history (screenplay by Mario Puzo, David Newman, Leslie Newman, Robert Benton, from the story by Mario Puzo, from the comic strip by Jerry Siegel, and Joe Shuster) emerged a film that packed cinemas across the globe and launched a movie franchise that it took two seriously bad sequels – **Superman III** and **Superman IV: The Quest For Peace** – to kill. But let's forget that bit of inglorious history. The first Superman, directed by Richard Donner and starring Christopher Reeve as the Man of Steel/Clark Kent, really did persuade you that, yes, a man can fly. Reeve, who based his characterization on the young Cary Grant and put on 30lbs to play the role, carries it off well, especially since it was only his second movie.

Kent is, of course, from the planet Krypton, saved by his mum (Susannah York) and dad (Marlon Brando, who plays his scenes as if mentally calculating his fee) from their dying world. Realizing that he's an exceptional boy he reacts to the death of his adopted father by retreating, like Jesus in the wilderness, to the Arctic to regroup. Here, he learns all about Krypton and Earth and develops into the hero who will fill the blue Spandex suit. As his alter ego, Clark Kent, he is hired by the *Daily Planet* in Metropolis where he falls for colleague Lois Lane who, sadly, only

Animated Supermen

If the first two *Superman* movies leave you – or your kids – wanting more, you could check out the **1941 animated collection** produced by Max and Dave Fleischer, recently reissued on DVD. The plots are simple, formulaic to the letter, but the 17-episode series is a triumph of imagination and design, with stunning backdrops. Its only mnus point is that some editions of the DVD also include the uncut 138-minute superflop **Supergirl** (1984) in which Faye Dunaway chews the scenery as a witch and Helen Slater is a super ordinary heroine.

The Man of Steel will return to our big screens in 2006, with Christian Bale slated to take on the hero.

has eyes for Superman... meantime, the Man of Steel has to prevent Lex Luthor (Gene Hackman) from detonating a nuclear warhead in the San Andreas Fault. (The worst thing Hollywood folk can imagine happening to the world is for their own home state to be destroyed.)

Puzo had genuine reverence for the Superman character, which is why this, more than perhaps any other movie, has a credible, intriguing, sympathetic superhero at its centre. In fact, Puzo was so besotted that his script ran to two movies, which is why **Superman II** (1980) wasn't just a cashing-in exercise but a proper companion to the original. Both films (the latter directed by Richard Lester) are fine family entertainment, suitable for kids aged 5 and over. The next two in the series are, as noted, for completists only.

ALL FOUR MOVIES ▭ UK,US ◉ UK, US | PG (UK,US)

X-Men 2000 and X2 2002

Proposals for mutants to be registered so they can't use their powers against mankind prompt Nazi concentration camp survivor Magneto (Sir Ian McKellen) to declare war on humanity. Can wheelchair-bound prof (Patrick Stewart) and his champion mutants – played by James Marsden, Halle Berry, Hugh Jackman, Famke Janssen and Anna Paquin – save the world? Director Bryan Singer's first **X-Men** movie is a qualified success. There's plenty of derring-do but the film at times feels a bit like a marketing exercise, designed to launch as many toy figures as possible in 104 minutes.

The sequel, **X2**, delivers on the promise of the *X-Men* premise. The thrills don't let up, from the opening assault on the White House, as they take on Brian Cox's evil military scientist. Alan Cumming is a welcome, campy, addition to the cast and the script is sharper, both funnier and, at times, more melancholy. You might just be exhausted by the time it ends, after 133 full-on minutes, but you won't be bored. The ratings for both films are mainly due to violence (sometimes quite brutal, expecially in X2), brief foul language and some sex.

X-MEN ▭ UK, US ◉ UK, US | PG (UK0 PG-13 (US)
X2 ▭ UK, US ◉ UK, US | 12-A (UK) PG-13 (US)

19

Under-5s

play it again, dad

Finding something to entertain under-5s can be a real struggle for a parent. For a start, as the author of the "Movie Mom" reviews on Yahoo, puts it: "Pre-school children can think very concretely and even the most rudimentary of stories may appear to be a series of unconnected scenes to them. They love repetition, and just as they become attached to a toy or a blanket, they will want to see the same favourite video over and over." What may seem repetitious to us, may just be them piecing the stories together.

Psychologists (mostly) suggest that children under 6 don't distinguish clearly between **fantasy and reality**, so that even if you tell them that something – the alien in *E.T.* for example – is

Preschooler movie buffs start here...

Here are 20 top movies, reviewed elsewhere in the book, which under-5s should enjoy, just as much as older kids. And which you may just find yourself watching time after time after time ...

The BFG One of Roald Dahl's most endearing tales. After watching this, kids will want their very own big friendly giant. *Fantasy, p.173*

The Blue Planet This BBC documentary series on the ocean is almost as entertaining as *Finding Nemo*. *Documentaries, p.140*

Cinderella No child should reach the age of 5 without seeing Disney's take on the fairytale romance. *Fairytales, p.160*

Finding Nemo This fishy tale has so many gags it doesn't matter if the very young get only one in five of them. *Animals, p.30*

Jungle Book Simply one of the bare necessities of life for young kids. *Animation, p.46*

The Land Before Time The charming, light, funny adventures of Littlefoot and his fellow dinosaurs. *Dinosaurs, p.136*

Lilo & Stitch Two misfits (an alien and a little girl) click in a funny animated yarn, helped by regal music from the King. *Sci-Fi, p.241*

The Lion King Disney's glorious epic is a stirring tale, well told, with laughter, sadness and hummable songs. *Animals, p.34*

Looney Tunes Bugs, Daffy and co – a wacky bunch of toon heroes that kids will take years to tire of. *Cartoons, p.70*

Mary Poppins Magical musical comedy which is supercalifragilisticexpialidocious. *Musicals, p.204*

The Moomins These shy, plump, magical creatures have been known to mesmerize the very young. *Classics, p.102*

The Muppets Kermit, Fozzie, Miss Piggy and the gang can usually be counted on to raise a laugh. *Comedy, p.126*

My Neighbour Totoro Fantastic, gentle Miyazaki animation about a forest sprite that will entrance the very young. *Fantasy, p.51*

Pippi Longstocking A high-spirited heroine whose antics should entertain both boys and girls. *Classics, p.104*

The Road To El Dorado Brisk, animated adventure in which two loveable rogues become gods in South America and help invent basketball. *Action & Adventure, p.13*

Rugrats They whine, they argue, they ought to get on your nerves, but in the TV series they're seriously captivating. *Cartoons, p.73*

The Snowman Haunting, perfectly-told festive tale which makes even the over-familiar "Walking In The Air" acceptable. *Christmas, p.89*

Stuart Little Beguiling whimsy about an adopted mouse, in which the rodent steals the acting honours – and hearts. *Drama, p.113*

Three Billy Goats Gruff Classic tale of three goats, brilliantly narrated by Holly Hunter. *Fairytales, p.168*

Tom And Jerry Relentless, funny, cartoon-violent... the eternal contest between cat and mouse never loses its appeal. *Cartoons, p.77* not real, they may not believe you. There's also the question of how long pre-schoolers should watch movies and TV programmes for. The guidance is continually changing but in the summer of 2002, the American Academy of Pediatrics recommended little or no TV for kids under 5.

Presumably some of those pediatricians had forgotten what it's like to have a child that age. True, too many parents use TV – or movies on TV – as a sedative but by the time children get to 3 and 4, many of them will only calm down, and get some necessary physical relaxation, if they can watch something they like. And, from 3 to 5, the first visit to the cinema is a real rite of passage – for child and parent. On top of which, the standard of pre-schoolers' entertainment has improved tremendously over the last decade or so, with the success of children's channels such as Nickelodeon.

The reviews below focus on movies, or TV movies, that will appeal very largely to pre-schoolers. But kids in this age group will also enjoy a lot of films reviewed elsewhere in this book. So don't be put off browsing other chapters – pointers to which are included in the **Top Twenty** box, opposite.

The Adventures Of Elmo In Grouchland 1999

When Elmo's blanket is thrown away, he jumps in the trash can after it and finds himself in Grouchland, a world where stems are treasured and flowers cut off. The rest of *Sesame Street* follow in pursuit – sufficient excuse for the usual supply of puns, inspired silliness, and all-round good cheer that we have come to expect from the inhabitants of this street. Vanessa Williams has a nice role as the trash queen.

📼 UK, US ◎UK, US | U (UK) G (US)

Alvin & The Chipmunks 1961–2000

Chipmunks have been good to the Bagdasarian family. It all began when singer-songwriter Ross Bagdasarian heeded the advice of his children and released "The Chipmunk Song" – an annoying ditty apparently sung by a trio of the squeaky animals. It became a massive novelty hit in the US and the chipmunks (who probably couldn't even play their own instruments) soon earned their own animated series, *The Alvin Show*, which made its debut in 1961. Its stars were named after three Liberty Records executives: Simon (the smart one), Theodore (the loveable fool) and Alvin (the star of the show). The series was revived in the 1980s, with Ross Bagdasarian Jr voicing the chipmunks, alongside Nancy Cartwright (Bart Simpson), and guest appearances from the likes of Dolly Parton. In 1987, they even had their own full-length feature, **The Chipmunk Adventure** and then thirteen years later they met **Frankenstein** in an unlikely sequel.

Chipmunks is probably the opposite of an acquired taste – a series that young kids love, but thankfully not for ever.

BOTH FILMS 📼 US | U (UK) G (US)

Are You My Mother? 1991

P.D. Eastman's funny story about a baby bird hatched while its mother is absent and its quest to find her is the source for a wonderful animation. On the video, you also get two extras: *Go Dogs Go!* (canines of all stripes in all kinds of motion in all kinds of vehicles) and *The Best Nest* (a cautionary grass-is-greener tale starring Mr and Mrs Bird).

📼 US | NR

Babar 1999

After his mother dies, the young elephant Babar moves to the big city, learns about the ways of humankind, and returns to the jungle to act as a peacemaker, become king and build a new elephant city: the French model of colonization. This recent animated movie, adapted from the books by Jean and Laurent de Brunhoff, feels oddly out of time in other ways, too: no in-jokes for grown-ups, no comic side-kicks, just a strong, simple storyline, and a few laughs for younger kids

– at whom this is squarely aimed. The loss of Babar's mum is no *Bambi*-style tragedy, though, so any toddler can enjoy this.

📼 UK, US ◎ UK, US | U (UK) G (US)

Banana Splits 1969

 "Drooper, who invented spaghetti?" "Spaghetti was invented by a guy who used his noodle." Flipping like a pancake, popping like a cork, this furry foursome were one of the strangest ensembles ever to have their own hit TV show. Anarchic, nonsensical, with a mailbox that refused to dish out the mail, a bin that wouldn't take the trash and a pair of odious Sour Grape girls whose appearance would inevitably trigger hysteria from Bingo, Drooper, Snorky and Fleegle. Originally designed to sell breakfast cereal, this Hanna-Barbera show continues to have a loyal following in cyberspace, with many adults still pining for one of those buggies the Splits used to drive around theme parks while singing their drippy songs. The video release doesn't, alas, include all of the cartoons and live-action adventure (**Danger Island**, on which *Lethal Weapon* director Richard Donner got his start) shows which were part of the programme's original line-up. But they're still great fun for the 7 and under set.

📼 UK, US | NR

Barney's Great Adventure 1998

Watch Barney on television and you wonder if the director has ever heard of the term "retake". But the missed cues and fluffed lines are largely absent in this tale in which Barney, the thunder-thighed purple dinosaur, and three children discover an egg from out of space. Less stomach-churning than the series.

📼 UK, US ◎ UK, US | U (UK) G (US)

The Bear 1999

Raymond Briggs's haunting, magical tale of the friendship between a girl and a polar bear who gets accidentally separated from his family is both sad and enchanting. There's no dialogue but, in its 26 minutes, you don't miss the words. For younger kids, of 3 to 5, you may find that this becomes frequent viewing and leads to requests to go to the zoo and see a real polar bear.

📼 UK, US | NR

Bear In the Big Blue House 1997

Bear is seriously groovy (he makes the *Sesame Street* gang look square) and has enjoyably repetitive adventures on his TV series, trying to find his friend Shadow, and mulling things over – and singing to – Luna. When your kids grow out of this, you'll be quietly sorry.

📼 UK, US ◎ UK, US | NR

Blue's Clues – Blue's Big Musical Movies 2000

Young kids like this so much you suspect there's some subliminal brainwashing going on. Blue's a cute pup with a friend, Steve, who is eternally enthusiastic and, more worryingly, invariably surprised when he gets one of the clues which will solve the episode's riddle. This is their first appearance on the big screen and is, unlike many similar ventures, as charming as the series it sprang from.

📼 US ◎ US | NR

Bod 1975

If a cartoon means a spot of a "R&R" for you, don't play your children *Bod*. A barrage of questions is set to follow, not least "why is that bald boy wearing a dress?" Or maybe it's a bald girl! With every *Bod* episode (and there are only 13) you get a *Bod* adventure with the follically-challenged one meeting Aunt Flo, PC Copper and Farmer Barleymow somewhere along the way, followed by a story about Alberto Frog and his band, a song and a game of Bod Snap. Aimed at pre-schoolers, you could live to be 100 and still never quite "get" *Bod*, or even why such simple stories are so entertaining. If you can't wait for the repeats, **Bumper Bod** contains all 13 episodes, sadly minus Alberto.

📼 UK | U (UK)

The Brave Little Toaster 1987

This movie of the charming novella by Thomas M. Disch is a classic quest film with a twist – the difference being that the heroes of this odyssey are five domestic appliances: a toaster, a radio, a bedside lamp, an electric blanket and a vacuum cleaner. The appliances have to find the young master they're supposed to serve to save their cottage from being sold. Disney originally bought this, planning to make it into a 3D movie, but that deal fell through. This is, said the *Washington Post*, "a kids' film made without condescension, a celebration of gizmos and gutsiness...You're likely to leave with a warm, toasty feeling." The straight-to-video sequels – **Brave...Goes To Mars** and **Brave...To The Rescue** – aren't bad but didn't have the budget to match this.

▣ UK, US ◉UK, US | U (UK) NR (US)

Bugs Bunny's Third Movie (1001 Rabbit) 1982

Despite the name, this is actually a collection of Bugs Bunny and Daffy Duck's finer celluloid moments. Bugs and Daffy are rival book salesmen. While burrowing to Pismo Beach, Bugs takes a wrong turn ending up in the land of Sultan Yosemite Sam. There, to cheat death and to allude to a classic fairytale, he must read to the Sultan's son. The gang's all there – Porky Pig, Sylvester and Tweety – with the best bits from each of their cartoons seamlessly spiced together to create 75 minutes of cartoon heaven voiced by the master, Mel Blanc.

▣ UK, US | U (UK), G (US)

Clifford The Big Red Dog 2000

American animated TV series of the classic books in which the cuddly red dog tries his best when confronting such issues as sleepovers, trouble at the park, and homesickness.

▣ UK, US ◉UK, US | NR

Dumbo 1941

Dumbo was Walt Disney's personal favourite of all his movies, perhaps in part because this tale of an elephant who learns to fly was overlooked and underrated at the time of its release, close on the heels of *Fantasia*. Yet, as *The Onion* has argued persuasively, it is a film that is highly ambitious emotionally, taking its protagonist pretty close to the heart of darkness. There's real feeling in the way Dumbo's mother cradles him through the cage in her trunk but then the whole film "evokes more sympathy for an outcast cartoon elephant than would seem possible or even bearable".

The story is universal: how to cope with growing up and having to deal with [insert whatever it was you disliked about yourself as a kid]. The bizarre "Pink Elephants On Parade" sequence jars a bit but it is as bold as anything in *Fantasia*. One enthusiast in cyberspace calls Dumbo "elegant, vivid, and occasionally grotesque in the manner of vintage *New Yorker* cover art". Sounds highfalutin to say that about an animated movie about an elephant with big ears but he's got a point.

▨ UK, US ◉ UK, US | U (UK) NR (US)

The First Snow Of Winter 1998

Sean is a baby duck who, through his own negligence, gets left behind when his family fly off for winter. But he is consoled by a generous, and rather generously proportioned, vole (voiced by Father Ted, Dermot Morgan), some haunting flute music and a bit of jigging that would shame Michael Flatley's *Riverdance*. Just half an hour long, this animation is heartwarming, stuff, suitable for kids aged 3 and over.

▨ UK, US | U (UK) G (US)

Fraggle Rock 1983

For some heretics, this – not *The Muppets* – is Jim Henson's finest work for kids. The wacky underground creatures have a lot of fun, sing some decent songs, and have episodes with neat titles such as "The Great

Radish Caper". Inventive programming like this shows up the deficiencies of stuff such as *Barney*. Such was the show's appeal that it has inspired a host of fan sites on the Internet.

[cassette] US [disc] UK, US | NR

Franklin 1997

This was a TV series springing from the children's books by the wonderfully named Paulette Bourgeois about a turtle called Franklin. The purists insist that it began to "jump the shark" (see p.121) when the bear began wearing a blue vest but that won't worry your kids. The spin-off movie, **Franklin And The Green Knight** (2000) isn't bad – and is available in more formats.

[cassette] US [disc] US | NR

Homeward Bound: The Incredible Journey 1993

Two dogs and a cat left on a ranch set off across the mountains to find the family they live with. A brave venture by Disney – the animals speak without *Babe*-style lip-synching, which can take a while to get used to – which has enough humour, striking wildernesses and charm to keep kids intrigued for 84 minutes.

[cassette] UK, US [disc] UK, US | U (UK) G (US)

Huckleberry Hound And Friends 1989

In the first animated show to win an Emmy, Huckleberry Hound was a versatile canine. A blue-haired dog, never happier than when whining his way through "My Darling Clementine", Huckleberry could be a Scotland Yard detective, a foreign legionnaire or a scientist trying to neutralize an intelligent potato. Huckleberry's other great service was to introduce a little-known bear called Yogi (see p.282) to the world. The hound's adventures are perfect for younger kids; after a certain age, they may find this lacking a certain oomph.

[cassette] UK, US | G (US)

Little Bear 2001

Maurice Sendak's character stars in his first feature-length movie, an animated tale of loveable Little Bear and an adventurous camping trip with Father Bear and his friends Duck, Cat, Owl and Hen. The adventures – and relationships – are well-handled. Hard to dislike.

📼 UK, US ◉ UK, US | NR

The Magic Pudding 2000

Young koala bear Bunyip Bluegum thinks he's an orphan but, on coming of age, discovers he has parents called Tom and Meg. Where are they? And why did they call him Bunyip? The rest of this frenetic Aussie animation, based on the novel by Norman Lindsay, is an attempt to answer these questions. The curious koala meets up with some mates who have an eternally regenerating magic steak and kidney pudding (voiced, to great tyrannical effect, by John Cleese). The writers have taken a few liberties with Lindsay's original story and, at times, the result can feel as indigestible as the magic pud. But pre-schoolers will probably enjoy this for its unflagging energy, bizarre plot and for its intriguingly bad-tempered steak and kidney pudding.

📼 UK, US | U (UK) NR (US)

The Magic Roundabout: Dougal And The Blue Cat 1971

This movie treatment of British puppet TV show *The Magic Roundabout* survived both a jump to the big screen and a switch to a longer story – it runs for 82 minutes, whereas the series it sprang from consisted of five-minute episodes. It's a weird, oddly psychedelic tale, with a rather scary premise (bad goings-on at the top of the hill, draining the world of colour). But, oddly, none of that seems to bother most small kids, who perhaps know all along that Dougal, the sugar-craving, canine egomaniac, will triumph over – and ultimately befriend – Buxton the blue cat. Fenella Fielding's vocal talents suit the Blue Cat marvellously and Eric Thompson (Emma's dad) is on hand to voice Dougal and make sure this stays true to the spirit of the series, which was imported from French TV, and which he re-scripted.

The original TV series and a perfectly good, much later series (**The New Magic Roundabout**, 1997) are also available on VHS.

📼 UK | U (UK) NR (US)

The Many Adventures Of Winnie The Pooh

Pooh never gets the critical plaudits of Disney features like *Pinocchio* or *Snow White* – but you'll find a lot of parents (and pre-schoolers) who firmly believe this is Disney's best ever movie, bar none. And the reason? It lies principally in the wit of A.A. Milne's creation, which, even with a pretty loose brief from Disney, survives in trumps, and is worthy of the kind of repetition that young kids crave. It's partly the songs ("I'm Just A Little Black Raincloud..."), which are fun and, as Pooh would have wanted them, hummable. And, well, this is such a very good movie – brilliantly animated and sensationally well voiced. Tigger's bounding entry, the scene where Pooh eats too much honey and gets stuck in the entrance to Piglet's house, Pooh's balloon-powered ascent up the honeytree – there are so many pleasures, big and small.

Although it all hangs together very nicely, this wasn't actually made as a movie but as three independent Winnie the Pooh stories: "The Honey Tree", "The Blustery Day" and "Tigger Too!" Sterling Holloway (as Pooh) and Paul Winchell (as Tigger) usually get most of the praise but credit must also be due to Ralph Wright who makes Eeyore, the pessimistic donkey, mournful and delightful.

The "sequel" features – **The Tigger Movie** and **Piglet's Big Movie** – have almost no relation to the Milne stories, and are witless twaddle. Which is not to say that small kids won't like them, of course.

📼 UK, US ◉UK, US | U (UK) NR (US)

Mr Benn 1970

Despite suggestions of his religious, political and even Freudian significance, Mr Benn remains an enjoyable cartoon character. Amazingly only thirteen episodes were produced, though in Britain they have hardly been off the BBC ever since they were made. Mr Benn is an ordinary, suited businessman who each morning leaves

No. 52 Festive Road and pays a visit to a fancy-dress shop owned by a mysterious fez-wearing man. There he chooses a costume, anything from a clown to a hunter, goes into the changing room and emerges in a different world where problems are to be solved before he can return to suburbia. Beautifully animated and written by David McKee, this has been cited as an influence on everything from *Taxi Driver* to *Buffy The Vampire Slayer*.

📼 UK | U (UK) NR (US)

Panda! Go, Panda! 1972

This Japanese animation – an early work by Miyazaki (see *My Neighbour Totoro*, p.51) – is a kind of *Pippi Longstocking* with pandas. An orphan, Mimiko, lives at home with her grandmother, who leaves her alone and goes off to the city. But of course, she's not alone for long, as a pair of cute, mischievous and talking pandas move in, and join her in a series of adventures. The DVD consists of two separate half-hour films (originally made for Japanese TV), with almost identical plots. They are entirely delightful, and perfect for very young kids, with all of the charm but none of the complexities of Miyazaki's more mature films. Good for multiple repeat viewings – but even on a single showing, you won't be able to get the theme tune out of your head for weeks.

◎ US | NR

Pingu 1986

Is there any pre-schooler who, once shown a *Pingu* video, hasn't fallen for its charms? The little animated-clay penguin lives on the ice-cap with his mother, his postman father and his baby sister Pinga. And he has a mate called Robbie the seal. Pingu's adventures are pure slapstick, taking simple scenarios (hide and seek, looking after an egg, getting jealous, a snowball fight, riding a bike) that any toddler can relate to, and playing them for all they're worth. There is no actual dialogue, unless you count the *wak-wak* Pingu-talk as language. And perhaps it is: it is certainly expressive, and young kids will instinctively concentrate on the speech and understand

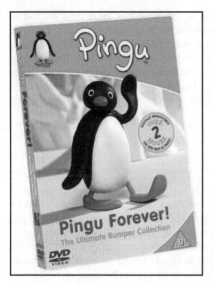

its intent. The character was created by Silvio Mazzola, in Switzerland, although as his creator says "he does not seem very Swiss at all."

Pingu is available on a range of UK (and a few US) videos, as well as a recent highlights DVD. It doesn't really matter which episodes you buy. They will all get played repeatedly.

UK, US ◎ UK, US | NR

Popeye 1929–present

"Short, balding, ornery and downright ugly" – and that's how his official website describes Popeye, the most famous sailor since Sinbad. It's enough to have the man himself flipping his lid, crying "Tha's all I can stands, and I can't stands, no more" and throwing a few punches. Popeye first appeared in 1929 with a walk-on part in a comic strip by Elzie Segar that was supposed to revolve around Olive Oyl and her family. But Popeye muscled in and made it his own, exploring his unlikely but enduring love for Olive, and getting into countless scrapes and contests with Brutus, a hairy heavy with a glass jaw. He has since starred in 600 cartoons, and one awful live-action comedy (with Robin Williams on spinach-eating duty). For such an enduring hero, Popeye can be something of an acquired taste – boring as many kids as he fascinates.

UK, US ◎ UK, US | U (UK) NR (US)

The Road Runner Show 1966-1973

Created by Chuck Jones, the simple premise behind Road Runner – a mute bird unable to fly being constantly chased down an American highway in the desert by the hapless Wile E. Coyote and his bag of ACME wonders – is a tad repetitive for some. Originally Jones saw the characters as a comic parable of modern technology against the forces of nature, but children don't need to worry about this. First seen in 1949, by 1962 the beep, beep bird had his own series. Chuck's earlier episodes are some of the best. But if the inevitability of Wile's failure fails to excite, try Road Runner's adventures opposite Bugs Bunny, a far worthier foe.

📼 UK, US | G (US)

Roobarb 1974, 2000

 Despite an annoyingly catchy theme tune and simple jelly-wobbly animation any child with a felt-tip pen should be capable of emulating (the creators themselves used felt tips), *Roobarb*, named after writer Grange Calveley's Welsh terrier, was one of the best-loved British cartoons of the 1970s. An excitable green dog, Roobarb is always trying to liven up his humdrum life in the back garden much to the amusement of his cynical rival, the pink cat Custard and the twittering Greek chorus of birds. Richard Briers's enthusiastic voices made the most of lines such as "Suddenly Roobarb decided the whole idea of being a loaf of bread had gone a bit stale". Performing all 24 voices over 30 episodes, Briers based characters on people he knew – a witty crow's voice is his impression of Noel Coward. For all the wince-inducing puns, there's an underlying message here about hubris and folly too. There is a later series – **Roobarb And Custard Too** (2000) – but the original is the best.

📼 UK, US ◉ UK | U (UK) NR (US)

Sesame Street Presents: Follow That Bird 1985

This is a smartly crafted, quest movie in which Big Bird, after being persuaded to join a family of birds, decides he misses his friends so much he has to walk back to them. Chevy Chase, John Candy, Sandra Bernhard and Waylon Jennings all lend a hand.

📼 UK, US ◉ UK, US | U (UK) G (US)

Snoopy Come Home
1972

In *Snoopy Come Home*, the second *Peanuts* feature movie, and the only one not to focus on Charlie Brown, the infamous beagle receives a letter from his previous owner, Lila, who is sick and missing him. Already tiring of seeing "No Dogs Allowed" signs in the neighbourhood, Snoopy decides to leave, much to Charlie Brown and co's distress. Full of songs, buddy moments between Snoopy and Woodstock, and with all the gang in on the action (even little-seen character 5 95472) this is a must for *Peanuts* fans – and ideal for ages 3 to 8.

The same applies to **Bon Voyage Charlie Brown** (1980), in which Charlie Brown and his friends go to Europe as exchange students. Made to celebrate the 30th anniversary of Charles Schultz's character, it breaks one *Peanuts* rule: the adults talk. Dissenters violently disagree but many *Peanuts* fans think is the best movie from the comic strip.

BOTH FILMS 📼 UK, US | U (UK) G (US)

Play's the thing: educational videos

Sesame Street is one of the few educational TV shows that scores highly on both sides of the Atlantic. Here are others, from the UK and US, that are worth exploring for a spot of home pre-schooling.

Baby Einstein... 2004
Using real objects – and music from the likes of Schubert and Schumann specially reorchestrated to appeal to toddlers, this series aims both to entertain and to introduce them to the wider world. 📼UK, US ⊚UK, US | NR

Dora The Explorer's Rhymes And Riddles 2003
Plucky Dora the Explorer and her pal Boots step inside a huge book of nursery rhymes and have to solve the biggest riddle of all. 📼US ⊚US | NR

Fun Song Factory 2003
"Oh, the wheels on the bus go round and round..." It's part of the unique charm of this British series that the troupers hosting this perform such child-friendly classics with the same intensity that Mick Jagger used to bring to "Brown Sugar". 📼UK | NR

Good Morning Maisy 2004
Lucy Cousins's *maisy* (and *nursery rhyme*) books are terrific for young kids and these simple videos have good segments on the ABC, counting, colours, shapes, and the farm. 📼UK, US ⊚UK, US | NR

Richard Scarry's Best .... Ever 1990s
Richard Scarry is to educational videos for 2 to 4-year olds what Elvis Presley is to rock'n'roll. He bestrides the genre like a colossus, with an astonishing collection of learning material which will help kids count, singalong, learn the alphabet and generally have fun. 📼US, UK ⊚US | NR

Sesame Street 123 Count With Me 1997
Join Ernie at the Furry Arms Hotel for a musical lesson in how useful counting can be. It's an invitation your kids won't be able to resist. Bert and Ernie's *Worldplay*, in the same series, is another useful buy. 📼US ⊚US | NR

Spongebob Squarepants 1999

It's amazing how many laughs you can generate starting from the simple premise that your hero is a sponge living under the sea. The weird highlights of this show's first season include: Spongebob and a few jellyfish taking to the dance floor to celebrate 1980s synthesizer madness, Spongebob failing an assertiveness training course, and Spongebob talking to his tongue. Compelling, strange and very funny.

▭▭ UK ◉ UK, US| NR

Thomas The Tank Engine 1980s

The Reverend W. Awdry's books about the talking steam trains show no signs of waning, more than fifty years on from publication – and in the UK at least, they have **Ringo Starr** to thank for that. The loveable Beatle narrated the first couple of series of these gently realized TV programmes. If you look online, you will find a bewildering array of **Thomas videos and DVDs**, but it is the Ringo ones that have the charm. Later episodes were voiced in the UK by Michael Angelis, while the American ones featured Alec Baldwin and George Carlin. Later shows also introduced "modern" Bob the Builder characters.

Whatever else you do, avoid the little red engine's mistaken outing on the big screen, **Thomas and the Magic Railroad**, which goes off the rails pretty quickly, with a plot so complex that the combined genius of Alfred Hitchcock and Billy Wilder couldn't fathom it (all aboard for a parallel world called Shining Time where a mopey Peter Fonda frets about his inability to make a train work?).

▭▭ UK, US ◉ UK, US | NR

Yogi Bear 1950s–70s

This smarter than your average bear made his debut on Huckleberry Hound's show, but within a year he was more popular than many of Hanna-Barbera's more established cartoon characters. Named after baseball star Yogi Berra (whose most famous quote, "It's déjà vu all over again!", sounds like a line from this cartoon), the bear has a voice based on Art Carney's character in the TV hit *The Honeymooners*. Early cartoons saw him as a space racer, an airship captain, and a pirate, but eventually a pattern for his show was established: the sarcastic, rule-breaking bear always out to cause Ranger Smith misery, particularly if it meant a picnic basket at the end. So successful was Yogi he even has a rock on Mars named after him.

The original Yogi is mysteriously available only on UK video at present, though he features on various American cartoon compilation DVDs. **The Hair Bear Bunch** (1971) is just Yogi with Afro hair, safari jackets, jive-talking but fewer laughs.

▭ UK, US ⊚US (on compilation) | G (US) U (UK)

20

Westerns

quick on the draw

Westerns can be a great, if slightly problematic, source of kids' viewing pleasure. They usually have a simple narrative drive (revenge, a clash between good and evil, a quest, a journey), offer plenty of action and, with a few obvious exceptions such as *Dances With Wolves*, clock in at around 90 minutes – just the right length. That said, the most obvious feature of any western is a gunfight, and deciding when, or whether, and/or which of these violent rituals is acceptable for your kids to watch is going to be a very personal decision. But not all westerns are as violent as those made by, say, Sergio Leone. And in many films, especially the older ones (pre-1966/67), violence is not often glamorised or used to excess. There is also the matter of tone. John Wayne's *McLintock*, his western remake of *The Taming Of The Shrew*, is full of violence but it is done in such a rollicking fashion that even kids will find it hard to take seriously.

Our reviews focus on good westerns which don't feature excessive or gratuitous violence. As general guidance, most of them are suitable for most kids **aged** 7 or 8 and over – unless an older age range is specifically suggested. A few (*Heller In Pink Tights*, *Sheriff Of Fractured Jaw*, *Support Your Local Sheriff*) could also be enjoyed by younger kids.

Blazing Saddles 1974

We don't want to encourage you to break the law but the ratings given to this film, in the light of other ratings given since, don't really make sense. Sure there's some swearing, a wagon full of innuendo, and some jokes about bodily functions, but does all that really add up to a film which can't be seen by 14-year-olds? There's something about Mel Brooks's daft humour, with all its cartoon slapstick feel, which kids find terribly appealing. The scene where Cleavon Little, the black railway worker, is asked to sing a song to entertain the cowboys and breaks into "I Get No Kick From Champagne" is a particular highlight. Madeline Kahn sends up Marlene Dietrich wonderfully and Harvey Korman is insanely effective – and effectively insane – as deputy governor Hedley Lamarr. The legendary beans scene is usually especially popular with older pre-adolescents.

📼 UK, US ⊚ UK, US | 15 (UK) R (US)

Butch Cassidy And The Sundance Kid 1969

Paul Newman (Butch) and Robert Redford (Sundance) light up the screen as wisecracking, safe-cracking outlaws in George Roy Hill's 1969 stylish comedy western. Light humour, light violence (Butch ends a rebellion by the Hole in the Wall gang by kneeing the leader, not shooting him), a simple plot, and three charming principals (don't forget Katharine Ross), make for a very pleasurable journey.

Given some suggested castings – Newman and Brando, Newman and McQueen, Newman and Beatty, Newman and Elvis – this could have ended up very differently. Redford got the part that made him because, he says, "they ran out of actors". That it worked so well is, partly, a tribute to Newman's sanity – he told studio execs and well-meaning friends, who complained that the then unknown Redford was getting too many close-ups, to back off. William Goldman's script sparkles, often in unexpected places, giving the buddy stars ample ammunition to fire at each other. There are some scenes set in what grown-ups realize (though kids may not) is a bordello, but there is enough action, humour and drama to entertain kids aged 7 and over.

▭ UK, US ◉ UK, US | PG (UK, US)

Cat Ballou 1965

"It's that way-out whopper of a western… a she-bang to end all she-bangs!" Don't be put off by the studio tag line, this is a funny comedy western in which Jane Fonda, Lee Marvin and Nat King Cole are all pressed into service. Cat (Fonda), defending her dad's spread against the evil railroad barons, hires drunken gunslinger Marvin with predictable, yet entertaining (indeed Oscar-winning), results. For all the drunken horseplay – and the occasional chaste bed scene – this is actually uplift-ing, with the perseverance, grit and idealism of Fonda's heroine shin-ing through.

▭ US ◉ UK, US | PG (UK) NR (US)

Destry Rides Again 1939

James Stewart is the slow-drawling – and slow to draw – Tom Destry who cleans up the town of Bottle Neck, making villainous Brian Donlevy's scowl deepen and provoking a fantastic cat fight between Marlene Dietrich and Una Merkel. Lanky and loveable as Stewart is, Dietrich, cast against type, steals the movie performing such numbers as "See What the Boys In The Back Room Will Have". You wonder how some of the songs slipped past the censor. In "You've Got That Look", bemoaning the romantic monotony of her existence – too

Jimmy Stewart gets the girl (Marlene Dietrich) – and the guns

much romance, not too little – she complains: "I should be brave and say, let's have no more of this/But oh what's the use when you know I love it?" This was Stewart's first western and it's just possible that he never quite topped this.

UK, US ⊚ UK, US | PG (UK)

El Dorado 1966

El Dorado was Howard Hawks's warm, amusing, tribute to the Old West – and to old hands John Wayne and Robert Mitchum. Ed (Lou Grant) Asner doesn't really convince as the baddie in a range war but that is just a sideshow. Mitchum steals the movie as the drunken sheriff and James Caan, as knife-throwing, Edgar Allan Poe-spouting, "Mississippi", is incompetent, fresh and charming. When Mitchum was asked to star, he asked the director what the movie was about. Hawks said, "It doesn't matter, it's got some great characters." He was right.

There's some broad comic violence – and a politically incorrect impersonation of a Chinaman – but kids aged 6 and over could be amused by this classic. If they like it, you really ought to try them on Hawks's masterpiece, **Red River** (see p.291).

▭ UK, US ◉ UK, US | PG (UK) NR (US)

Flaming Star 1960

Don Siegel, who would direct the first *Dirty Harry* movie, made this brooding western – and, for the time, it was surprisingly violent. Even more surprising was that Elvis Presley played the key part, of the half-breed Pacer, destroyed by divided loyalties as war erupts across the range. Presley's part was originally meant for Brando and Siegel threw a hissy fit when he first heard who the studio had in mind to replace mumbling Marlon. But the end result is a fine, adult western which, despite familiar absurdities, makes some cogent points about peace among men. Presley, given a chance to act and an able cast (Dolores del Rio, John McIntire, Steve Forrest), makes the most of this. It's worth watching and, although there's quite a lot of bloodshed, a few deaths, and one unpleasant scene where some ranchers try to force Dolores del Rio to kiss them, there's nothing here to scare any kid of 8 or under.

▭ UK, US ◉ UK, US | PG (UK) NR (US)

Heller In Pink Tights 1960

This colourful tale of a theatrical troupe in the Old West was much misunderstood on release. Director George Cukor was typecast as a women's director and was blamed for spending too much time pointing his camera at the gorgeous Sophia Loren, while Steve Forrest and Anthony Quinn vie for her affections. But the troupe, led by la Loren, is the real point of difference here and Cukor was right to focus on it. Western novelist Louis L'Amour rated this as the second-best screen version of any of his books and it's a very easy way to while away 100 minutes.

▭ US | NR

High Noon 1952

 Often called the first "psychological western" by critics who have forgotten that Henry King directed Gregory Peck in *The Gunfighter* two years before, *High Noon* is a tautly made classic – just 84 minutes of tension, drama and pictures of clocks ticking away to the moment of reckoning for Marshal Will Kane (Gary Cooper). Kids of 10 and over should be hooked – although, if they've watched any *Indiana Jones* movies, they may get a tad impatient with Coop's endless attempts to muster support, feeling that Harrison Ford would have come up with a fiendish plan which would have put paid to the Frank Miller and his gunmen. This is almost an anti-western – the good guy wins but with no thanks to his deputy or the townsfolk. And the clear message, as he throws his tin star in the dust at the end, is that these people are not worth serving. This may be because scriptwriter Carl Foreman was blacklisted in the McCarthy witch hunts. The waffling, cowardly, townsfolk may represent the people in Hollywood who left Foreman and his fellow victims to fight for themselves. Whatever the symbolism, it's still a great movie. As Coop said: "I like westerns because the good ones are real."

▣ UK, US ◉ UK, US | U (UK) NR (US)

Johnny Guitar 1953

Nicholas Ray's baroque, incredibly stylized western is one of a handful of great films made by the budget studio, Republic. Sterling Hayden uses his stiff screen presence to good effect in the title role. Johnny is a gunslinger called in by his ex, Vienna (Joan Crawford), to protect her saloon from enraged locals. Hysteria, melodrama and jealousy abound – and that's just on the set where Crawford once scattered actress Mercedes McCambridge's costumes over the highway. The same ingredients make the film compelling – McCambridge's love, Dancin' Kid, is obsessed with Crawford's character and McCambridge feels compelled to kill him. Hayden protects Crawford but has no illusions about her. "How many men have you forgotten?" Johnny asks Vienna. "As many women as you have remembered," she snaps back. This is, as François Truffaut said, "a hallucinatory western" and, as in *High Noon*,

the angry mob is inspired, not by the Old West, but by the McCarthy witch hunt which had swept through Hollywood in the late 1940s andearly 1950s.

📼 UK, US ◉ US | PG (UK) NR (US)

The Magnificent Seven 1960

"We had no script, a Japanese story that doesn't necessarily appeal to Americans, a Mongolian guy playing a cowboy…" Robert Vaughn was not overly optimistic about the prospects for this John Sturges movie. Initially, his pessimism seemed well-founded as the movie did slow business in America; but it became a favourite in Europe Universal persevered in America and The *Magnificent Seven* became such a hit that it generated three sequels and a TV series, made stars of Steve McQueen and James Coburn, and reinvented Yul Brynner (who was in danger of reigning forever as King of Siam). It also, singlehandedly, carved out a new genre in music – Great Western Movie Themes: the score by Elmer Bernstein is almost as famous as the movie.

The film itself – a western retelling of Japanese director Akira Kurosawa's *The Seven Samurai* – is today as often spoofed (as in the *Three Amigos*) as it is seen. Which is a pity, because this is a well-made western by a greatly underrated director (Sturges's other classics include *Gunfight At The OK Coral* and, best of all, *Bad Day At Black Rock*), and the plot is a good one. The magnificent seven are reluctant moralists, offered money to defend the inhabitants of a terrorized Mexican village – and when things aren't going well, they consider quitting. But they stay with it, and when the shooting is over, Yul Brynner touchingly points out that being a gunfighter doesn't have many rewards – they have no wives, kids or prospects.

There are quite a few deaths here, but none of them very graphic – and the story's moral core outweighs the violence. Even today, the action scenes look well-staged and it's fun, too, watching McQueen trying to upstage Brynner. He didn't get far – Brynner insisted that if he was really under threat, he'd retaliate by taking his black hat off.

📼 UK, US ◉ UK, US | PG (UK) PG-13 (US)

Don't try this at home: Henry Fonda in My Darling Clementine

My Darling Clementine 1946

Westerns wouldn't be westerns without John Ford – even if he did owe a lot more than he let on to pioneers such as Raoul Walsh – and this, if not the definitive Ford western, may be the most accessible to kids. They might, perhaps, be disappointed by the lack of gunplay: as critic Roger Ebert points out, "*My Darling Clementine* is more about everyday things – haircuts, romance, friendship, poker and illness." Henry Fonda and Victor Mature are simply immense as Wyatt Earp and Doc Holliday. The scene where Mature helps a drunken actor complete a speech about death from *Hamlet* may be his finest moment on screen. But, as the title suggests, the most important thing to happen to Earp in this movie isn't the gunfight but the arrival of Clementine, the Doc's old beau, whom the marshal falls in love with.

UK, US ⊚UK, US │ U (UK)

Red River 1948

This is a definitive cattle-driving western in which director Howard Hawks made the unlikely pairing of western screen giant John

Wayne and Montgomery Clift, the homosexual method actor, click. Wayne, for once, gets to play the conflicted character in a father-and-son tale which Hawks gives the scale of classical tragedy, Best watched on the biggest screen you can find. Dimitri Tiomkin's music, and Russell Harlan's photography, are as excellent as the acting and direction.

📼 UK, US ◉ UK, US | U (UK) NR (US)

Shane 1953

Brandon de Wilde, as the boy Joey who idealizes the golden hero Shane (Alan Ladd), gives kids a useful entry point to this classic but decidedly grown-up western. Complex, and at times dark (especially in the ruthless gunning down of the hapless Torrey), Shane is also thrilling, full of amazing touches, such as the juxtaposition of the kid's teeth cracking into his sweet and the crack of swapped punches in the fistfight in the local store. It is an adult western that works for kids, and one with a raft of moral issues – might versus right – at its heart; issues that may strike a chord in their own lives. The violence is never cheaply glamorized (and the shootings are very tame by today's standards).

Ladd is, as Raymond Chandler famously said, every small boy's idea of a tough guy – and he is simply resplendent as the ghostly buckskinned stranger who rides into town to save the homesteaders from the evil cattle barons, falls in love with Joey's mum (Jean Arthur) but doesn't do anything about it and then, after he's forced to draw his gun, rides off again, to the despair of Joey. Ladd perfectly personifies how Jack Schaefer, who wrote the original novel, saw his hero, a man who could be relaxed, yet lethal, with "the easiness of a trap set". Van Heflin offers fine support in the more difficult role of good but dull Joe Starrett, the man who holds the homesteaders together in their contest with evil until Shane has to ride to the rescue. Kids, especially the boys, will probably be shouting for Shane to come back too.

Director George Stevens was a perfectionist. One scene of the homesteaders departing in a wagon took 119 takes. For Torrey's funeral, he spent days making sure the clouds were correctly positioned in the sky. Nobody is sure quite what they meant, but that perfectionism worked brilliantly here – over all 118 minutes.

📼 UK, US ◎ UK, US | PG (UK, US)

The Sheriff Of Fractured Jaw 1958

Even though stiff upper lip Englishmen such as Kenneth More's character in this comedy western are an endangered species now, this piece of fluff, in which the terribly well-mannered More tries to turn Fractured Jaw into the kind of place Miss Marple could retire to – and not have to solve any murders – is odd enough to be genuinely funny. But then it is directed by Raoul Walsh, an even older hand at westerns than John Ford, and has Jayne Mansfield as the love interest. At one point, she lip syncs to Connie Francis's voice singing "In The Valley Of Love". Robert Farnon's witty soundtrack completes this minor treat. This was the first western shot in Spain – the set was later used, for more violent ends, by Sergio Leone. Catch it on TV because, alas, it's not on DVD and hard to find on video.

📼 UNAVAILABLE | NR

Support Your Local Sheriff 1969

Director Burt Kennedy had earned his spurs on the long-running TV series *The Virginian* and star James Garner had made his name as a riverboat gambler in the TV series *Maverick*... so, when they came to make a comedy western, they knew just what they were spoofing. Although it is not as well known as *Blazing Saddles*, there are those who insist that is the more successful film. Garner is charming and droll as the traveller on his way to Australia who agrees to become sheriff of a lawless town. He does so even though the jail isn't finished (no bars in the windows) and there's a bullying clan of ranchers (led by Walter Brennan, reprising his *My Darling Clementine* role for laughs). Maybe he's attracted to the mayor's beautiful but accident prone daughter (Joan Hackett). *Support Your Local Sherrif* – and its slightly less successful sequel *Support Your Local Gunfighter* (1971) – are genuinely entertaining satires of the genre. They don't fizz with Brooks's manic energy but they aren't quite as hit or miss either.

US ◉UK, US | U (UK) G (US)

True Grit 1969

 "Fill your hand with lead, you son of a bitch." It's at this point that one left-wing critic, who disapproved of anything Wayne stood for politically, felt obliged to get up out of his cinema seat and cheer at the press screening. Directed by Henry Hathaway, from Charles Portis's novel, *True Grit* is just that kind of movie. Wayne is both intriguing and hilarious as Rooster Cogburn, the "one-eyed fat man", who is paid by a recently orphaned girl (Kim Darby) to track down the man who shot her father. A Texas Ranger, mysteriously called La Bouef (and even more mysteriously played by Glen Campbell), joins them to get killed, along with the bad guy who shot Darby's dad. Wayne saves her in the nick of time from a rattlesnake pit – a nice twist because for the rest of the time she's been looking after him (well, trying to). At 128 minutes, this is a movie that meanders a little in the middle – but the last half an hour is rousing stuff. Kids aged 7 and over should enjoy it. The violence is not gratuitous nor lingered on.

UK, US ◉UK, US | U (UK) G (US)

Illustration Acknowledgements and Credits

COVER CREDITS

Front cover © Getty

Back cover A Close Shave © Aardman/Wallace & Gromit Ltd 1995

ILLUSTRATIONS

(2) Michael Todd Company Warner Home Video (4) Toho Tokyo Movie Shinsa Co. Lt Manga Entertainment Ltd (13) Morgan Creek Productions/Warner Bros Warner Home Video (36) Alcon Entertainment/MDS Productions LLC Warner Home Video (51) Studio Ghibli/Tokuma Group 50th Street Films/Toho Company Ltd Twentieth Century Fox Home Video (98) Channel 4 Television Corporation/ Jim Henson Productions/RHI Entertainment Inc Hallmark Home Entertainment (104) Svenska Filmindustri/ Columbia Pictures Corporation/Adham/Moshay/ Mohlman Turner Home Video (106) Warner Bros/ American Zoetrope Warner Home Video (123) Universal Studios/Rogue Male Films Ltd/Working Title Films Universal Pictures Video (140) British Broadcasting Corporation BBC Video (141) Apollo Associates/FAM Productions Criterion Collection (153) Columbia Pictures Corporation/Franklin Waterman Productions/Global Medien KG Columbia TriStar Home Video (162) Hallmark Entertainment/Jim Henson Productions Artisan (Fox) Video (165) DEFA Progress Film-Verleih GmbH Hen's Tooth Video (167) Henson Associates/TVS Television Columbia TriStar Home Entertainment (182) Incorporated Television Company Rankin-Bass Productions Carlton Visual Entertainment Ltd Communications New Line Cinema (188) Columbia Pictures Industries, Inc. and Universal Studios and Revolution Studios Distribution Company, LLC Red Wagon Productions/Allied Stars Ltd (189) The Princess Bride Ltd/Buttercup Films Ltd/Act III Productions MGM/UA Studios (193) Wolper Productions/Quaker Oats Company Warner Home Video (206) Romulus Films Ltd/Warwick Film Productions Ltd/ Columbia (220) Independent Producers/J. Arthur Rank Films/Archers Film Productions Carlton Visual Entertainment Ltd (230) MFP Munich Film Partners New Century GmbH & Co. SOR Productions KG Paramount/Scott Rudin Productions Paramount Home Video (240) 20th Century Fox/Cooga Mooga/Joseph L. Schenck Enterprises Inc. Fox Home Entertainment (250) Kintop Pictures/Bend It Films/Road Movies/RocMedia/ BskyB/British Screen Productions/Film Council/ Filmförderung Hamburg/Helkon Media AG/Works and Future Film Financing Fox Searchlight Pictures Twentieth Century Fox Home Video (261) 20th Century Fox/De Laurentiis Entertainment Group/Starling Productions /Famous Film Productions Image Entertainment (269) Children's Television Workshop/Jim Henson Productions Columbia Tristar Home Video (279) HIT Entertainment PLC Moviestore Collection: (8)Lucasfilm Ltd/Paramount Pictures Corporation (17) Helena Productions Ltd Warner Bros/Radiant Productions/Plan B Films (25) Kennedy Miller Production/Universal Pictures (27) Omni Zoetrope/United Artists (32) Columbia Pictures Corporation/Sandollar Productions (33)Warner Bros Productions/Donner Shuler/Donner Productions/Studio Canal Plus/Regency Enterprises Productions/Alcor Films (47) DNA Productions Inc/Nickleodeon Movies/O Entertainment/Paramount (54) Aurora Productions/Mrs Brisby Ltd/MGM/United Artists (75) Warner Bros Atlas Entertainment/Hanna-Barbara Productions/Mosaic Media Group Warner Home Video (82) Munich Carlyle Productions GmbH & Co. KG Shawn Danielle Productions/Gold/Miller Productions Guy Walks into a Bar Productions Mosaic Media Group/New Line Cinema (84) 20th Century Fox/Hughes Entertainment (88) Renown Pictures Ltd/George Minter Productions Scrooge (92) Formosa Productions Inc/Loew's Inc/Metro-Goldwyn-Mayer (96) Cineguild/Independent Producers/ The Rank Organisation Film Productions Ltd Universal Picture Company Inc (101) Novi Pictures/Columbia Pictures Corporation (109) 20th Century Fox/Alexander Salkind/Film Trust (110) Galaxy Pictures Limited/Metro-Goldwyn-Mayer (113) Orion Pictures Corporation/ Paramount Pictures (115) PolyGram Filmed Entertainment/Tiger Aspect Productions/Working Title Films Universal (116) Nelson Films Inc/MGM/Interscope Entertainment/De Laurentis Entertainment Group (117) Rimfire Films Paramount Pictures (122) 20th Century Fox Film Corporation/Hughes Entertainment (136) Universal City Studios/U-Drive Productions Inc/Sullivan Bluth Studios/Amblin Entertainment/Lucasfilm Ltd/Universal Pictures (150) Working Title Films/Polygram Filmed Entertainment MGM/United Artists (152) Skerry Movies Corporation/Jones Entertainment Group/Peter Newman Productions (172) Amblin Entertainment/Universal Pictures Universal City Studios (175) Universal Pictures Universal City Studios Inc (184) Avrora Media/Comet Film Produktion GmbH/Cometstone Productions/ Propaganda Films/Stonewood (195) Loew's Incorporated Metro-Goldwyn-Mayer (199) National Film Trustee Company/Bugsy Malone Productions/National Film Finance Corporation/Goodtimes Enterprises Paramount Pictures (200) Metro-Goldwyn-Mayer Studios Inc Dramatic Features/Warfield Productions (215) LakeFilm Productions/NFFC/Scottish TV (216) Columbia Pictures (227) Baltimore Pictures/Warner Bros (237) Amblin /Universal Pictures (242) Warner Bros (253) Columbia Pictures Corporation/Parkway Productions/Longbow Group Productions (254) Loew's Incorporated Metro-Goldwyn Mayer (259 Warner Bros/Polygram Filmed Entertainment (287) Universal Pictures Company Inc (291) 20th Century Fox

Index

C

D

Rough Guides travel...

Rough Guides are available from good bookstores worldwide. New titles are published every month. Check www.roughguides.com for the latest news.

...music & reference

Also! More than 120 Rough Guide music CDs are available from all good book and record stores.
Listen in at www.worldmusic.net